Line Change

Book 0 in The Playmakers Series®

BY G.K. BRADY

Trefoil Publishing

ISBN 979-8-9853283-2-5

Cover design by Getcovers
Edited by Jenny Quinlan, Historical Editorial
Proofread by Word Servings

Contents

Dedication

For the countless volunteers who so generously give their time and energy to coach children's sports.

Part 1

Chapter 1
The Bet

November 1997, Boston College campus

Marty LeBrun stepped back and took a pull on his nearly empty pint glass, his eyes riveted on his best friend hovering over the pool table. "You'll never make that shot," he mocked.

"Shut. Up," Zach Pruitt growled.

They were facing off across the pool table in a heated battle for the next round of beer. Just a regular postgame, Saturday-night victory celebration at their favorite campus hangout, the Pint Pot Pub. The place was packed, the music was loud, and the drinks were flowing. And while Marty and Zach hadn't flipped the switch from twenty to twenty-one yet, the bartenders had never raised eyebrows at their fake IDs and apparently didn't follow BC's hockey team closely enough to put players and their ages together.

The current scene was the usual one that played out after a weekend home game. Marty would beat Zach at pool, darts, air hockey, or arm wrestling. Sometimes all of the above. He couldn't best his friend on the ice, and while Marty's bar talents weren't *that* superior to Zach's, he was better at keeping his eye on the prize, whereas Zach's definition of "the prize" typically shifted from victory to which girl he would sweet-talk into bed later that night. Zach's single-mindedness at hooking up was a talent like no other Marty had witnessed before.

They might have competed like brothers, but Marty never entered that particular arena against Zach. First of all, there was that hard line best friends didn't cross. Ever. Second, what was the point when Zach would simply hand Marty his ass? Unlike his buddy, Marty wasn't particularly funny, good-looking, or gifted with a silver tongue, making him an excellent wingman instead. A role Marty was content to fill. Besides, without a constant parade of girls to distract him, he had time and energy to pursue more pressing goals, like breaking into the NHL, which, for a guy with more grit than skill, was like a climb up Everest. Without an oxygen tank.

What Marty lacked in natural ability, though, he strove to replace with passion and hard work. So far, those traits hadn't proved enough to entice a pro team to draft him, but he kept hope alive that someday he would make it into the bigs. Zach had beat him at that too, having his rights picked up by the St. Louis Titans when he had entered the draft. While St. Louis patiently waited, Zach would finish college and join his new club after graduation. His future was set.

Marty eyed his friend, who was still lining up his shot. There was always a chance Marty could follow Zach to his future team; stranger things had happened.

"I'm getting thirsty," he remarked dryly. In the midst of Zach suggesting what Marty could do with his cue stick, Marty lifted his eyes toward a small group that had just blown in with an icy wind. His heart stuttered to a stop. While he registered the cluster of beings, he had no clue how many there were or if they were human, animal, or extraterrestrial. All his attention was captured by the girl who stood in their center, shrugging off her puffy coat. Dressed in boots, ripped jeans, and a white off-the-shoulder sweater, she seemed to be encased in sunbeams, lighting up her smooth skin and her short, wavy golden hair.

Practical Marty did not believe in insta-love; he wasn't even sure real romantic love existed since he hadn't experienced it himself. That was the stuff of romance books, better left to writers with fanciful imaginations who could transform simple human biology—

aka the innate desire to reproduce—into something worthy of soulful ballads.

But logic and his beliefs were jettisoned in one go as he took in this ethereal creature. He was dumbfounded, bowled over, a cheesy cliché. His mouth must have swung open, and drool was probably leaking from it because when she raised her bright eyes to his, she quickly cast them away ... which made her allure even more powerful, if that was possible.

Yeah, Marty's NHL aspirations took top billing in his life, but he *liked* girls—a lot. He'd simply never laid eyes on one that stirred him quite the way this one did. In that moment, he would have turned over all his worldly possessions—meager though they were—if she had asked. And wingman status aside, it wasn't as if he was desperate for female companionship. An abundance of interested females always seemed to be hanging around. Okay, so they were there for Zach, but even in the large shadow Zach cast, Marty garnered more unearned attention than say, one of his botany classmates. Certainly more than he knew what to do with. He exercised discrimination—and caution—in the rare instance he contemplated letting his libido run loose. In other words, he was no manwhore. Unlike his best bud.

A poke to his ribs brought him momentarily back to Zach's cocky grin, one he was sporting in extra-large, before his gaze flew back to the blond. He barely registered Zach talking. "Did you see that? I came *this* close ... Hey! Earth to LeBrun." Zach waved his hand in front of Marty's face, snapping Marty out of his daydream, where he and the blond sat side by side on a porch swing, holding hands, staring into each other's eyes.

Where the hell did that *come from?* "Sorry, man. Brain fart. What were you saying?"

Zach pinched his thumb and forefinger together, lasering in on his own minuscule movement. "I was *saying* you were this close to buying the next round. But I decided to be generous and give you one more shot before it becomes reality." Zach downed the contents of his glass and chortled. "Can't wait. I'm pretty thirsty myself."

The blond and her friends—a guy with glasses and two other girls—jostled their way through the crowd toward the bar. The guy was in the lead, holding one girl's hand as he tried to carve out a path for the foursome. He wasn't big, so his progress was more a series of small maneuvers, like a fish fighting against a swift current. In the meantime, the blond and the other girl fell in behind, pressing in close.

"Holy shit! Who is *that*?" Zach absently whacked Marty's shoulder, his tone shot through with a reverence Marty hadn't heard out of him before.

Marty peeled his eyes away long enough to realize his buddy's gaze was fixed on the foursome. "Which one? The brunette?" *Please say the brunette.*

"Forget about the brunette. I'm talking about the blond." Zach's wide eyes were riveted on Marty's dream girl, and Marty's gut knotted.

Zach, who seemed as rattled as Marty, tipped his glass to his lips, realizing too late he'd already finished off its contents. After calling himself a dumbass, he looked at Marty. "She's the one you're checking out too, isn't she?" When Marty didn't answer, Zach leaned into him. "Tell you what. Instead of the next round, how about we raise the stakes? The winner gets first crack at her instead." Zach lowered his pool stick and pointed it in the blond's direction.

Could Marty break character and compete with his best friend for a chance to win over a girl who might already be attached? Might not like the look of him? Might not like guys at all?

Hell yes. For this girl, Marty was ready to chuck his entire rule book.

Her gaze swung toward them, and she gave them a half-smile before moving clumsily in the duckling line that had nearly reached the bar.

Zach slapped a hand over his heart dramatically. "Oh my fucking God! Did you see that, LB? She smiled at me."

"At us," Marty snapped.

Zach swiveled his head. "Wow, dude. You really like her, don't you? Let's call off the competition, then." He made a sweeping motion with his hand. "Take your best shot, with my blessing."

As big an ass as Zach could be, he wore his loyalty on his sleeve. He always had his friends' backs. That streak, along with his larger-than-life persona and love of hockey, was what Marty liked best about his bro.

"Hey! Are you assholes gonna play or what?"

In unison, Zach and Marty turned toward the guy complaining at the edge of the pool table. He threw out his hands in a what-the-fuck gesture, then jabbed his thumb over his shoulder. "You've got a line of people waiting here."

"Sorry, man," Marty apologized and took up position before Zach had a chance to tell *that* guy where to stick his cue. Out of habit, Marty found himself automatically slipping into the peacemaker role, which was ironic, considering Marty's on-ice fights in his juniors days tripled Zach's. Marty played with a sharper edge than his friend ever had. *You have to know your role.* Marty understood his really, really well.

He drew back his stick and tapped the cue ball, giving it the right amount of English to send the last striped ball into the corner—except it nicked an edge and rolled impotently to the side. Marty hung his head and handed Zach the cue.

Zach lined up, took a calculated shot, and remained stooped over the table, stock-still. Marty held his breath and watched helplessly as Zach's target landed in the pocket and clacked soundly against the other balls.

Zach burst upward with a "Fuck yeah!"

Tonight of all nights, how could Marty have let Zach beat him? He let out an exasperated sigh. "You've got the touch tonight, my man."

"Every night, you mean." Zach grinned as he handed off his cue stick to the guy who'd groused at them.

Though he hadn't meant for it to, Marty's disappointment must have shown all over his face because Zach quickly followed up with, "Hey, how about a redo? The pool table's going to be tied up for a while, but the dart board's open. I'll grab the beers, you grab the darts, and we'll throw for her instead. You down with that?" One corner of Zach's mouth quirked. He hadn't beat Marty in weeks, so his offer was practically a gimme.

Marty tamped down his excitement. "Sure, I'll take that bet."

He stood at one end of the bar, waiting for the bartender to pass him the darts, observing Zach at the opposite end. Surrounded by a gaggle of girls, his buddy laughed and joked as he waited for their brews. What was it about the guy that drew women to him like wasps to a summer picnic? Girls fawned all over Zach, telling him how cute he was or how impressive his hockey moves were—like they were probably doing right now. They also went to great lengths to tell him how hot his ripped bod was. But all the guys on the team were ripped. No choice there, what with the hours of practice and training they went through. As for looks? Marty was ill-equipped to figure out that side of the equation, though he suspected the dimples Zach flaunted had something to do with his appeal.

Marty had little time to dwell on the puzzle because the bartender finally handed him the darts just as Zach pointed him out to his new friends. Among them stood the blond and her buddies, and Marty's heart sank. It sank farther when Zach rounded the bar with two pints and the foursome in tow.

"We've got some folks interested in our little competition," Zach announced as he approached, a shit-eating grin splitting his face. He nodded toward the group and began introductions, but Marty didn't register anything until Zach reached the blond. "And this is Claudia."

She was beautiful from a distance, but up close? She stole the breath from Marty's lungs. An oval face with skin that reminded him of marble held a pair of brown eyes as glossy and rich as melted chocolate. Full pink lips were curved upward in a shy smile that revealed straight white teeth. The rest of her was equally appealing—he knew because he'd taken in every detail—but he didn't let his gaze wander from her face, locking in on those eyes that did funny things to his gut.

Mouth suddenly parched, he barely croaked out a "Hey," which he punctuated with an overly zealous nod.

He was in the midst of giving himself a mental slap when her smile widened. It was dazzling. "It's nice to meet you, Marty." *She* was dazzling.

"Yeah, same."

In the minutes that followed, his verbal skills left him completely ... as did his dart-throwing abilities. With Claudia in the small audience, Marty couldn't concentrate on anything but her. Whether it was the shine of her hair or her flowery perfume wafting up his nose, his brain continually vacillated between mostly frozen to permanently frozen. Consequently, Zach won, though to his credit, he didn't rub the victory in Marty's face. Instead, he offered to buy the entire crew plates of wings and more beer. That was Zach, spending the extra cash his folks sent him on his friends. Marty enjoyed no such luxury.

But the differences in their socio-economic statuses didn't matter right now. Marty had more urgent matters on his fevered mind.

Chapter 2

Crossed Signals

The six of them grabbed a table together. The couple cozied up on one side, and opposite them sat the two girls. To Marty's surprise, Zach plunked down at the end closest to the brunette—Megan—leaving only one seat open: the one perpendicular to Claudia. He jerked his head toward Claudia, mouthing, "Go for it."

Startled, Marty mouthed back, "You sure?"

Zach nodded, and Marty suddenly found himself both eager for and terrified of his Zach-less chance to talk to Claudia.

Marty slid into the seat and promptly picked up the menu, using it like a shield between himself and the girl who was making his pulse race uncomfortably. He scanned the sheet without reading a damn thing. Graceful fingers snaked over the top and eased the menu down, and there she was, smiling full-out at him.

"I think your friend is ordering wings for the whole table. Are you planning to get something different? Or maybe you have a wing allergy?" Her eyes danced with amusement.

He glanced around and realized he was the only one at their table holding a menu. He also realized Claudia was teasing him. At the opposite end, Zach smirked at him and rolled his eyes. Yeah, Marty was acting like a total dumbass.

"No, wings are fine. I just ... forgot." *Because you scramble my brain.* He took a big gulp of beer and spilled some down the front of his shirt.

Well, shit!

When he looked up, the amusement in Claudia's eyes was on full display in her wide smile. "Just learning to drink?"

"A comedienne, huh?" he countered.

"Mama always says laugh as often and as long as you can. She's constantly throwing out advice when it comes to living my life, but she rarely drops a real pearl of wisdom. That particular one, I have found, is a keeper." Her smile turned downright impish. God, she was adorable.

He let loose a laugh, relieving some of the tension coursing through him. "Sounds like a smart woman. And yeah, I just finished my third drinking lesson yesterday. What do you think of my progress so far? I think I might still have some ground to cover."

She giggled, and the happy sound made bubbles fizz in his bloodstream. *I made her smile. I made her laugh.* Not much could top that.

When they were done chuckling several beats later, she peered at him. "You have a nice laugh."

He froze, unsure what to say. "Uh, thanks?"

At the other end of the table, Megan was bent in conversation with Zach. He was probably only listening with half a brain because he lifted his chin at Marty and gave him a thumbs-up. Jesus, thank God his buddy couldn't hear what an idiot Marty was making of himself or he would never let Marty forget it. As it was, Zach already had a vault full of bumbles he could torture Marty with.

Claudia's brown eyes fastened on his as she took a sip of her beer. Absently, Marty wondered if she was old enough to drink or if the bartenders were so dazzled by her smile that they forgot to check her ID. "Hockey must take up all your time, huh?"

Her words jarred him out of his trance. "Most of it, yeah. Hockey and school don't leave much time for joining the drama club or the glee club." Panic suddenly welled inside him. "Oh shit. Are you in the drama club? Glee club? Wait. Does BC *have* a glee club?"

"I don't know." Her pretty mouth quirked. "When I started here last year, I wanted to join every club on campus, though I didn't make it through the entire list because Meg—thank God—talked some sense into me." He cocked an eyebrow at her, and she continued. "I grew up sort of ... stifled. Coming to BC was like strapping on a pair of wings, and I promised myself I'd experience everything campus life had to offer." She sat back with a wistful smile. "Megan accused me of not knowing my limits and reined me in before I overcommitted."

He snatched at the chance to get to know this beauty better. "So if you hadn't come to your senses, what kinds of groups would you have joined?"

She darted her bright eyes to the ceiling and chewed on her lower lip. "Oh, stuff like a jogging group, choir, the gardening club—"

"There's a gardening club?" The incredulity in his tone rang in his ears.

Her eyes twinkled as they landed back on his. "You don't have anything against gardening club, do you? They're mostly harmless, nerdy types." Her brows scrunched in a cute frown. "At least I think they are. I never joined, so ..." She flicked her hand toward Megan. "Meg would probably say I'm a gardening nerd. She complains about the plants she says are overflowing our apartment and choking her with chlorophyll."

Marty chuckled. "She does realize you can't choke on chlorophyll, right?"

"Yeah, but she loves drama." Claudia rolled those big brown eyes. "If there's none around, she creates it. It's one of the reasons we get along so well, I think. I avoid drama, but I can live vicariously through her, and being around my boring evenness balances her life out a bit. Yin and yang. Come to think of it, though, I think *she* should be in drama club. Maybe I'll suggest it." Another giggle from her, and he found himself grinning like an idiot. She waved her hand between them. "So are we okay here? I mean, with the gardening club and all ..."

We're more than okay. "I've got nothing against the gardening club. In fact, if I had any spare time, I'd probably join myself."

Those vivid eyes popped wide. "You're kidding! You like gardening? Or are you pulling my leg?"

"I'm fascinated by plants. I'm a biology major with an emphasis in botany." His lips twitched at the surprised expression on her face. "Not what you expected, huh? I might be here on a hockey scholarship—which I was lucky to get—but I have to maintain a decent GPA. And I'm a realist. My chances of breaking into the NHL are slim at best, so I decided to get an actual education while I'm here so that maybe one day I don't have to work summer jobs for restoration companies."

"Hmm, that's smart of you. And I totally get it—I'm here on a merit scholarship. What do you plan to do with a biology degree, assuming you don't become a professional hockey player?" Her gaze fastened on him as she tipped her glass to her lips.

"Haven't figured that out yet. Track plankton and whale migrations?"

"Bet you know a thing or two about mold after doing restoration work, huh?"

"Way too much." A fresh giggle effervesced from her, and he found himself longing to hear more. "Maybe I'll open a plant store or run an inner-city botanical garden. Or teach. For now, I live and breathe hockey." *And God, does that sound boring as hell!*

She sat forward and leaned her chin in her palm, seeming to appraise him. *Probably wondering how she can get away.*

He squirmed under her scrutiny, flustered and a little frustrated that he'd flunked the Zach Pruitt School of Charm. Everything tumbling from his mouth sounded incredibly inane, and he winced inside at his own absurdity. If only he could come up with the right words—*intelligent*, confident-sounding words—he might be able to sweep her off her feet and carry her away somewhere private, where they could talk without the steady thrum of music and conversation pulsing around them. As it was, they had to practically shout at one another to be heard. And those witty words eluded him.

His gaze took a quick tour around the table as he grappled with what to say. The couple, Rex and Alice, kept their heads together, though Marty wasn't sure if they were talking or making out. Either way, they were in their own world. At the other end of the table, Zach and Megan appeared highly animated, almost as if they were caught up in a heated debate, but the place was too damn loud to pick out a single word they exchanged.

Deciding to breach the awkwardness that stretched between Claudia and himself, Marty blurted out, "Where are you from?"

"I grew up in Salem. Not so far away, but far enough to keep my mom and aunt from *dropping in* every day. How about you?"

"Michigan."

"Is your family still there? Are you close?"

"Yeah, they're still there, and we're close. My dad died when I was fourteen, so it's just my mom and two younger sisters. They're super supportive ... not financially, but definitely big in the encouragement department." And if he could break into the NHL someday, he'd take care of them so they never had to worry about money again. Marty's dad had left his mother in decent financial shape upon his death, which allowed her to support his two sisters with a part-time job. But an interloper, who professed to be in love with his mom, was gunning for that modest nest egg.

He shook off the dark thought. "How about your family? You said your mom and aunt ..."

"My dad died too, when I was six, in a fluky job accident. My aunt moved in with us, and she and my mom watched me like hawks as I grew up. They were terrified every time I jumped rope or climbed on my bike. I guess they thought I'd launch myself into oncoming traffic or something. I had to sneak out if I wanted to pick flowers or play with bugs."

"You played with bugs?"

"Doesn't every kid?"

He chuckled. "So is this your sophomore year, and what are you studying?" *Yay! When your mind blanks, act like a journalism major.*

"Yes, I'm a sophomore, and I'm studying to be a teacher. So besides plants and dads, you and I might have that in common too."

"A biology teacher?" He fought a grin.

Another brilliant smile curved her lips, and she tapped her forefinger lightly on her chin. *Maybe I'm not coming across as big a dumbass as I think.* "No, an elementary school teacher. And if that doesn't work out, maybe I'll become a nurse."

"Kind of a big difference, isn't it?"

She shrugged. "Maybe, although they both entail taking care of people. I chose teaching because my mom's a teacher, and I like kids.

They're smaller and easier to catch if you have to chase them. Also easier to wrestle to the ground," she deadpanned.

Amusement percolated in his chest, masking some of his nervousness. "Is that all?"

"No," she snickered. "I think the overarching reason was that the coursework seemed a little easier."

"Giving you time to experience *everything* BC has to offer?"

She bobbed her head. "Yep, gotta get it out of the way while I'm young."

"And how's that going? Experiencing everything?"

"Oh, I have some work to do in that department." Her sly grin made him eager to find out what more she had to do in "that department."

"Tell me about you and Megan. Did you know each other before you came to BC?"

"Since we were five. We met on the first day of kindergarten, and we were instant best friends and still are." She crossed her middle finger over her forefinger. "How about you and Zach?" She side-eyed Zach for several extended beats, and Marty's heart fell. When she turned her attention back to Marty, her hair sifted around her face, a few glossy strands falling across one eye. He bit back the urge to sweep it behind her ear and cleared his throat.

"First I want to hear more about you and your best friend."

"Wait. Are you conducting an interview for the school paper? I hate to disappoint you, but that's going to be short article. Where's your mic?" She grasped the table's edge and peeked beneath before returning to an upright position. The gleam in her eyes told him she was joking.

"You're funny." *And gorgeous and sexy and smart.*

"Funny-looking, you mean? Looks aren't everything, you know."

Definitely not *funny-looking*. "Okay. So back to my question—"

She let out a gust of air, blowing the hair from her face. "We grew up together in Salem, along with Rex, though he didn't join our Scooby Squad until high school." She jerked her chin toward the male half of the couple Marty had completely forgotten about. "He's a history major. You might have seen him at MCAS."

MCAS, or Morrissey College of Arts and Sciences, was where Marty's course curriculum lived. Rex's would too. Marty darted another look at the guy, who still had a lock on his girlfriend, and shook his head when he didn't recognize him.

"The three of us have an apartment together," Claudia continued. "Although as much as Alice is around, I think there should be four of us on the lease." Her tone was light, devoid of even a trace of annoyance. "But everyone gets along. It works well. So when is it my turn to ask *you* twenty questions?"

"I've asked less than six, and I get the sense that you're evading."

"I think it's closer to fifteen, not that I've been keeping track." And there came that playful grin again that made his heart stutter in his chest.

"Feel free to fire away at any time. I have nothing to hide." He downed the remnants of his beer to coat his parched throat. "Besides," he added, "you're under no obligation to answer."

"I know, but what fun would that be?"

A server deposited fresh pints, and Claudia chugged the remnants of her first beer and took a long sip from the fresh one.

I think I love you.

Her fingers dabbed daintily at her lips. "My turn now. Tell me about you and Zach."

Shit. He much preferred hearing her talk, especially because he could delude himself that she wasn't even aware Zach was at the same table. "Um, yeah. Zach and I met four years ago when we wound up billeting with the same family. We were sixteen and homesick as hell, and we hit it off." They'd formed a tight bond, feeding off each other really well, on and off the ice.

"So you played together?"

"Yep. We were both wingers on the same line for most of that season. When it was time to pick a college, I was already set, so Zach decided on BC too." *And here we are, playing on the same team again.* With a hell of a lot of luck, that trend would continue.

"Sounds like you two are joined at the hip."

"Nah, but we're tight." He mimicked her move, crossing his own fingers. "People who know us say we're brothers from different mothers."

"Huh. Yet you guys seem really different." Her gaze slid to Zach once more, who was no longer engaged in conversation with Megan. In fact, she was tapping her fingers on the table, looking bored, while

Zach leaned back in his chair and exchanged eye flirts with various girls at the bar.

"We're really different? How so?"

"Let me get back to you on that one. I'm not sure I can put a finger on it yet."

"Is it because he's the captain of the hockey team?" Marty prodded.

"No, because before meeting you guys tonight, I didn't know a thing about the hockey team. Guess I'll need to attend a game. Are you a captain too?"

The thought of her sitting in the stands, watching them play, created a warm burble in his chest. "I'm an alternate, yeah. There are a few of us, but Zach is the top dog."

"Why him?"

Marty shrugged. "Zach is ... take charge. A natural leader. He's also the guy with the most points on our team, which gives him extra cred." Marty realized too late that he was advocating for Zach.

Just then, Zach raised his gaze, bouncing it between Marty and Claudia. He beamed a dimple-popping smile before turning back to Megan.

Claudia shifted in her seat. "Soooo ... captain of the hockey team, and he's really hot. I bet your friend gets a lot of girls, huh?"

Where is she going with this?

He had his answer in a heartbeat when she followed up with, "Does he have a girlfriend?"

And just like that, the happy bubble Marty had been building around himself popped. *Another one bites the dust.* Claudia had obviously fallen under the Zach Pruitt spell.

I have a nice laugh, but Zach is hot. Think I'd rather be hot. Damn dimples.

Marty quelled the pang of disappointment and let out an extended sigh. "No, he's not seeing anyone." *Yet.*

Sometime after they'd polished off the wings and a few more rounds of beer, they were back at the pool table, paired off in teams: Zach and Claudia against Marty and Megan. Marty wasn't sure how he got stuck with Megan, though playing with her wasn't terrible because she had a wickedly accurate shot. Besides that, she was easy on the eyes. With her dark hair, green eyes, and bright smile, she was a real looker. Marty liked smart girls, and she ticked that box too. She was also a flagrant flirt, brushing against him at every opportunity, and the later it got, the easier he found it to flirt back—especially when the girl he really wanted seemed to be mesmerized by Zach. In fact, Claudia had barely looked at Marty throughout the match, unlike Zach, whose eyes continually strayed his way as if asking for permission.

Marty reminded himself Zach had won the bet. Besides, it didn't matter; Claudia had obviously made her choice. While he had no designs on Megan, Marty reasoned it never hurt to get on the best friend's side on the off chance you had a shot at impressing a girl ... like an insurance policy.

When the game was over, he couldn't even say who had won. Megan bumped her hip against his. "What do you want to do now, hockey player?"

He glanced over his shoulder at a row of guys crowding the table. Another game of pool was obviously out of the question. "Maybe a game of darts?"

She fluttered long eyelashes. "That wasn't really what I meant. I was kinda thinking we could get outta here."

"And go where?"

Her smile turned downright dirty. "We could go back to your place, and you could show me your stick."

The suggestive line shocked him, rendering him momentarily speechless while things began shifting south of his belt ... even though he didn't want them to. Having a dick sometimes had its downside, like when it got a mind of its own and broadcast how certain words or actions affected you, even if you wished otherwise.

Yeah, her signals were clear: she was looking for a good time, and Marty could fill the role tonight if he chose to. He chose not to. Instead, he excused himself and headed toward the men's room. He had some beer to get rid of anyway.

He picked a urinal a few over from the next guy and was surprised when someone stepped beside him.

"Hey, I'm sorry." Zach unzipped and proceeded to relieve himself. "I didn't mean to monopolize her. If you want to change places with me—"

Done, Marty zipped up. "No, it's all good." *She seems way more into you anyway.*

"So you and Megan seem to be hitting it off." Zach's eyebrows rode up and down his forehead.

"We're just having a good time. Nothing there."

"You sure about that?"

Marty was *definitely* sure about that. With a shrug, he stepped away. "She's nice enough, but I think I'll head home."

"What, you mean now?" Zach finished and joined him at the sinks, giving him a bug-eyed look in the mirror. And no wonder. Marty's inner self was giving him the same look and asking what the fuck he was doing passing up a chance at the hot brunette.

"I'm beat."

"Well, shit. Want me to go with you?"

"Do you want to leave?"

Zach's eyes held Marty's in the mirror. "No. I'd like to stay."

"Then stay." Marty shrugged again, going for casual, but the move more closely resembled a shoulder jerk.

Zach studied Marty's reflection. "You sure?"

"I'm sure. Have fun."

For a fleeting instant, Marty contemplated whether his moment of grace would prove to be misguided, but he quickly dismissed it.

Chapter 3

I'll Take That Bad Boy to Go

Claudia Campbell threw herself onto the secondhand leather couch and released an extended sigh. Though it was nearly two in the morning, she wasn't tired. At. All. Too many thoughts were rollerblading through her mind, and most of them included the charming hockey captain with the dimples, dirty blond hair, Delft-blue eyes, and easy laugh.

A yawn from her roommate's doorway startled her, and she pulled herself up on her elbows and winced with contrition. "I'm sorry. Did I wake you? I was trying to be quiet."

Sleep-disheveled, robe hanging open to reveal a pale chest sprinkled with dark, curly hair, Rex Small wandered into the cramped living room and plopped into a dilapidated armchair. He rubbed one eye behind his glasses lens. "I was sleeping light anyway, waiting for you to come home. You usually don't stay out without us."

His tone held no reproach, but she scanned his expression anyway. A slow grin spread over his face. "Have fun with the hot hockey player? But not too much fun, I hope."

"Is that your subtle of way of finding out whether I cashed in my V-card?"

"Who cashed in her V-card?" Megan's sleepy voice drifted from the hallway.

"Good grief, did you *both* wait up for me? If I wanted this kind of supervision, I'd still be living at home," Claudia scoffed, keeping her voice low so she didn't wake up Alice, who was no doubt snoozing in Rex's bed.

Meg scratched the back of her head, making an even bigger bird's nest out of her dark brown hair. "No, you wouldn't. We're way less smothering than your mother could ever be. And a lot more fun." Being an only child hadn't merely been lonely, it had been at times suffocating. Megan had filled the role of sister—and Rex as brother later on—but Claudia hadn't been able to escape her widowed mother's heavy thumb, reinforced by her equally strict aunt. Double coverage, born out of nothing but concern for their "little CC." Not that Claudia didn't love them, but she'd been busting at the seams to escape their overprotective restraints. The "experiment"—their expression for her living somewhat independently—had proved extremely successful, in her opinion. Ask her mom and aunt, though, and they'd parrot, "Not so much." They were counting the days until she graduated and moved back under their roof—and digits—again. Though they didn't know it yet, Claudia was destined to crush their hopes of being a trio of single women huddled together every Saturday night, munching popcorn while they watched rom-coms.

Megan's voice brought her back to the living room. "As for waiting up, TV was boring, and I figured whatever you had to share would be way more entertaining. Where did you guys go? What did you do? Inquiring minds want to know."

"Nosy minds, you mean."

"Yeah, those too."

Rex looked on, a sleepy half-smile on his face—his usual expression when Megan and Claudia played verbal volleyball.

Claudia sat up, swinging her legs to the floor to make room for Megan on the couch. She absently patted the seat beside her. "Well, I hate to disappoint you, but there were no shenanigans. We didn't do what you're thinking we did. We went dancing at the Stompin'

Grounds for a few hours, then ended up at the Daily Grind for coffee, where we talked and talked. That's it."

Rex steepled his fingers in that way he had when he was contemplating something deep. Meg's eyebrows crawled up her forehead, and her eyes gleamed in that way *she* had when ferreting out salacious details. "Talk? Really? What a waste of a hunk! Not even a good-night kiss?"

Heat rushed to Claudia's cheeks, her unavoidable "tell."

Megan pointed a triumphant finger. "Ha! I knew it. With tongue?"

"Would you stop it?" Claudia huffed. Her lack of sexual experience always blazed through in a blush. Megan probably knew every time Claudia had kissed a boy these past fifteen years. That inexperience, however, wasn't due to absence of interest; it was from an absence of opportunity. Maybe that would change soon. Being an almost-twenty-year-old virgin was becoming embarrassing.

Meg nodded at Rex. "Definitely with tongue."

Rex's expression darkened, telegraphing he wasn't nearly as amused as Megan. His dark hazel eyes caught Claudia's. "Do you plan on seeing him again?"

"I don't know. Maybe. He wants to go out tonight." And she wanted to go out with him. He was *so* cute—maybe too cute—but more importantly, he was confident, a trait that sucker-punched her every time. Confidence in someone else had a way of canceling out her own insecurities, especially if they turned a bright spotlight of their attention on *her*. It made her feel more worthy somehow.

"Do you like this guy? A lot?"

Claudia stared up at the ceiling as she pondered Zach Pruitt. "He's easy to be around, although he's also a little easy with the compliments, which is good and bad. Good because, well, he's fun. Bad because I saw how the girls were drooling over him tonight. I suspect he's one of those bad-boy heartbreakers. I haven't fallen for one yet, and I'm not planning on falling for this one. However ..."

Rex cleared his throat and leaned forward. "Look, I know this is none of my business—"

Megan laughed. "Translation: he's going to stick his big, fat nose where it doesn't belong."

Despite the back-and-forth at *her* expense, Claudia couldn't help but love her two best friends. They knew where she came from, what and who had shaped her, and they *got* her. They didn't judge her, and they loved her in spite of her flaws. They were her family. Where would she be without them? They were the Three Buccateers, a nickname their drama teacher had given them after they had appeared in their high school's production of *The Pirates of Penzance. All for one, and one for all ... or something like that.*

"Let me put it this way, Rex. I enjoyed spending time with him more than I thought I would. He might be a smooth talker, but he's also funny and has lots of interesting things to say. He's upbeat; he smiles a lot." She loved being around positive people, and she loved guys with effortless smiles. "Megan, I think he'd be a good match for you."

Meg shook her head vigorously. "No way."

Claudia blinked in surprise. "Why not? He's tall, blond, and cut. Your type."

"We're too much alike. I would always be competing with him for attention." Megan let out a fluttering sigh. "I liked his friend much better."

Something uncomfortable dug at Claudia's gut. She had wanted to spend more time with Marty, peel back his layers, and find out what lurked beneath his dark, wavy hair and espresso eyes, what he hid behind his easygoing yet mysterious exterior. He had intrigued her; she sensed an abundance of depth lived in him. But while they'd been playing pool, she'd witnessed the attraction crackling between him and Megan. That's when she had turned her full attention to Zach. And now, knowing Megan was attracted to Marty, Claudia told herself he was completely off-limits.

"And? Did anything happen there?" She held her breath, afraid of what was coming. Megan and Marty hadn't left together, but they'd seemed to hit it off, if their overt flirting had been any indication. Megan usually got her man, so hooking up was probably in their future.

Why did that thought niggle at Claudia? *Let it go.*

Megan puffed out a breath. "Yeah, something happened. I scared the shit out of him."

Claudia blinked in surprise. "Huh? How?"

"I asked him if he wanted to take me back to his place and show me his stick. He ran away." Megan shrugged.

Claudia burst out with an incredulous laugh. "You *what*?" In her peripheral vision, Rex choked on his own laughter.

A devilish gleam danced in Meg's eyes. "I asked to see his *hockey* stick. Oh gee, do you think he took it the wrong way?" She batted those ridiculously long lashes of hers.

"No, he took it the right way." Rex's tone was pure sarcasm. "Which explains why he ran away." His focus narrowed on Claudia. "Just be careful, huh? I've heard a little about this Pruitt guy, and it's not very good. He's a hell of a hockey player, but that aside, he uses it to his advantage."

Claudia straightened her spine. "I get it. He's a player, and I don't mean a hockey player."

"That's right. He's a—" Meg began but pressed her lips together when Rex held up a warning hand. Rex was a kind, gentle soul who wouldn't harm a flea unless it was sucking the blood of a beloved pet, but he never hesitated to throttle Megan back. He was their substitute big brother, and Meg's over-the-top side always heeled to Rex, unlike her behavior with her lovers or her real brothers.

"He uses his status as a hotshot hockey player to get the girls." Rex's explanation, aimed at Claudia, was filled with kindness.

"Lots of girls. He does a lot of sleeping around," Megan added helpfully. "There are rumors he's screwed half of BC's female student population—maybe even a few professors—and he's working on getting through the other half. In other words, he's a manwhore."

"I got it the first time, Megan," Claudia countered blandly. "Look, you guys, I appreciate your concern. But practically speaking, if I want to lose my virginity, he sounds like the perfect candidate." Her voice came out on the flippant side, and she gave herself an inner pat on the back.

Rex's eyes bugged out in horror, magnified by the glasses. "Why would you want to give a guy like that your ... your ...?"

"Need me to spell it out, Rexie? V-i-r—" Meg interjected.

"No, I don't." He narrowed his eyes at Megan.

Claudia shifted her gaze between her two friends. "From what you're saying and what I'm guessing, he's had a lot of experience. Who better than a guy who knows what he's doing? I mean, come on! I want my first time to be as enjoyable as possible under the circumstances." Wincing, Claudia paused. "How much does it hurt, Meg? Really?"

"It's been so long ago I don't remember." Megan inspected her fingernails. "Well, phew! I'm glad we reached a consensus at the ass crack of dawn."

Rex let out a lion-like yawn. "It's not dawn yet, and what consensus did we reach?"

Megan flipped her hand toward him. "CC keeps the hot captain, and I get the broody one."

"The broody one you chased off, you mean? How're you gonna make that work? And anyway, he's not broody," Rex countered. "He's just quiet. Thoughtful. Like he's observing, taking it all in, turning it over in his mind. Like me."

Meg nodded. "I bet he's really smart."

Rex beamed. "Also like me."

Claudia couldn't believe they were having this conversation. At two in the morning. "So what you're really saying is he'd make the perfect guy friend." Her thoughts darted to Marty's chestnut hair and intense brown eyes that could draw a girl into their depths. Physically, he and Zach were similarly built, though Zach had a few inches on Marty, but their coloring and personalities were polar opposites. Their differences brought to mind those between Megan and herself. Maybe that's what made the two guys best friends. They complemented each other, played off one another like she and Megan did.

Huh. Maybe Megan and Marty would make a good couple, which means ... Zach and me?

Rex stood, yawning once more as he pivoted toward his bedroom. "You can never have too many good guy friends, but don't forget I'm still your number one. Night, you two."

"Good night, Sexy Rexy," Claudia and Megan chorused.

Meg turned to face Claudia on the couch, crossing her legs in the lotus position. "Okay. Now that Tyrant Rex is gone, spill. And don't leave out a single detail."

"I heard that," Rex's voice drifted from the dark hallway.

"Oh, go to bed and bother Alice!" Megan waved her hand in his general direction.

"I'm sure he *wants* to bother Alice. That's all you've got, Queen of Zingers?" Claudia teased after Rex's door closed.

"At two in the morning? When I'm stone-cold sober? Yeah. That's all I've got, smartass."

"You thought it was the ass crack of dawn."

"Stop stalling and talk." Meg hunched her shoulders and leaned in.

"There's really nothing to tell, *smartass*," Claudia tossed back. "Like I said, we danced and went to the Daily Grind. That's it."

"That's not what I wanted to hear. Tell me about kissing him. Was it good?" Meg's face brightened like a kid on Christmas morning.

Claudia's cheeks blazed once more when she recalled the good-night kiss in Zach's Subaru that had turned into two, three, so many she lost count. Those had been followed up by one last scorching kiss at her front door. Yeah, the guy definitely knew what he was doing. *Best kisser ever*. Not that she had much to compare to. "It was ... nice."

"Nice? That's it?" Megan squeaked. "Deets, CC! Did your tongues swab each other's tonsils? Did his hands find their way under your sweater? Did it get your motor running? Curl your toes?"

"Stop calling me CC, and maybe I'll tell you." Claudia dipped a severe eyebrow. CC was the little girl who'd grown up in Salem, and Claudia had left her behind when she'd moved to Boston. She was a grown-up now, damn it!

Meg held up a three-fingered Girl Scout salute and gave her a pointed stare.

"He did not feel me up, he just kissed me. It was—"

"Come on. The truth now." Megan rolled her hand in a hurry-up motion.

Claudia let out a defeated sigh; her BFF would keep at it until she pried the truth from her. "Okay. Yes, tongue was involved, and it was really hot. The guy can kiss. As for getting my motor running, yeah, I thought about climbing him for a split second." Claudia paused until Megan stopped squealing and clapping. "Toe-curling, though? I wouldn't go that far. It felt more ... rehearsed, if that makes sense." She had yet to kiss a guy who curled her toes, though it was possible she would get there eventually with Zach.

When Megan's brows drew together in confusion, Claudia rushed on. "I don't know. I can't really describe it. I haven't had as much experience at this stuff as you have. Like I said, it was nice, but I got the distinct impression I wasn't special. I could have been any other girl he was kissing, like we're interchangeable."

"Huh. Okay. With that said, you'd still be okay getting it on with this guy?"

"Why not? Like I said, experience might come in handy. I doubt I'd be tempted to fall for him." Again, her answer was more flip than what actually ran through her mind.

Megan rolled her eyes. "Ever the practical one. So what did you talk about?"

Claudia shrugged. "The usual stuff. Growing up—he's from the West Coast—our families, high school, college, our future plans, that sort of thing."

"In other words, you covered your entire nineteen years and then projected into the future? I know all about your plans. What are his? Outside of getting you into bed, of course."

"He plans to play in the NHL. St. Louis drafted him high last year, but he opted to finish school. Now he's not sure he wants that degree after all. He might start playing professionally next year, but once he drops out, he's done with BC for good. On the other hand, there are no guarantees he'll earn a roster spot with the Titans, so he's weighing his options."

"What's his major?"

"Business Admin, I think. Or Management. I'm surprised you haven't bumped into him." Megan was studying Information Systems, another business discipline at the Carroll School of Management, where Zach attended.

"For me to bump into him, he'd have to attend class," Meg said dryly.

Claudia laughed. "What makes you think he doesn't attend class?"

"He's an athlete. Special rules apply."

"Maybe, although I got the distinct impression an education is not the reason he's here." She grabbed Megan's hand. "Meg, we need to go to a hockey game!"

Her friend's mouth curved in a sly smile, eyebrows wiggling with devilish intent. "Exactly what I told Marty. Maybe he'll show me his stick after a game. Or before. Or anytime in between."

"You wicked, wicked woman!" Claudia teased, though the humor wasn't quite there for queasiness that remained in her stomach.

"Ha! Jealous much? You know, now that I think about it, I'm a little surprised you didn't go for Marty."

I did. The admission startled Claudia, and she shoved it back down. "We don't have that much in common, I don't think."

"Are you serious? Neither of you is the impulsive type, he lost his dad, like you, and he loves plants as much as you do."

Glimpsing Marty with Megan had led Claudia to believe he was really into her. What if she had read the situation wrong? Now she regretted missing out on a chance to quiz him about his love of botany. "Well, that sounds boring as hell. It's high time I broke out of my shell and did the opposite of what everyone expects of me. Maybe I should live a little and go for the bad boy." The words didn't feel quite right tumbling out of her mouth. Maybe she was just tired.

"Well, that bad boy certainly goes for you." Megan's voice softened with concern. "I can understand the appeal of living on the wild side, girlfriend. You're wanting to break out of your protective shell and live it up, but be careful. Take care your heart doesn't get smashed to bits."

Claudia shrugged, masking a sudden irritation that bloomed inside her. "I'm a big girl, Meg, and I'll be just fine. I'm only in it for a good time anyway."

And steering in completely uncharted territory. I hope I don't get pulled under and drown.

Chapter 4

Hang a Tie on the Door

Two weeks later

Marty stared into the mass of writhing bodies on the dance floor at the Stompin' Grounds. He might as well have been staring into the bottom of a fifty-foot well for the details he neither registered nor gave a rat's ass about. But somewhere in that pulsing throng were Zach, Claudia, and Megan, the people he'd come with but had zoned out until they'd left him behind to stew in his juices. While he normally wasn't much of a wallower, apparently he was a masochist because he was packing in every reason for his dismal mood in one go.

He eyed the tequila shot he had yet to throw back, contemplating the reasons for his misery. He could start with the shitty Thanksgiving in his future. Coach was working them right through Wednesday afternoon. Once practice was done, he was on call with the restoration company for the rest of the holiday his friends would be enjoying with family. Sure, he had signed up for the hours, but it still sucked. Besides needing the money, he had no home to go to; his mom and sisters were heading to some mountain cabin they'd rented in Vermont for the week. Even if he had the time off and could afford the gas to put in his piece of shit Honda Accord—that might or might not make it—his mother's boyfriend would be in Vermont too. Richard, or "Dick," as the LeBrun offspring referred to him outside their mom's presence, was a greasy freeloader, and Marty wasn't sure he could keep from punching the guy. While Marty hadn't given his mother the entire reason he was skipping out, the disappointment in her voice when he'd told her still sat heavily in his chest.

Normally, he could lose himself in hockey, but thinking of the game brought up yet another gripe. He'd never been a flashy playmaker, nor did he kid himself that he'd miraculously morph into one. His role was as a defensive player, a two-hundred-foot forward, but he'd turned over the puck one too many times during their last game because of a nagging shoulder injury he didn't want to divulge. Those mistakes had not only cost his team the two-game series against Maine, it had also cost him ice time. He constantly reminded himself his professional future, if he had one, would likely be earned with his fists as a brawler. If he was lucky, he would muscle his way onto a roster as a bottom-six grinder. Working hard, pushing his limits, seemed to only net him microns of improvement, and at times he swore he was skating backward.

Which led to his next life gripe: he'd bombed a weighted English Lit test. Who the fuck needed English Lit in the real world anyway? If he didn't bring his grades up, he faced the very real possibility of losing his scholarship. What then? No hockey and no college left him with slim options at best.

Not helping his sour mood were Zach and Claudia, who were lost somewhere in the gyrating crowd on the dance floor. The pair had become inseparable, and Zach wouldn't shut up about her perfect this and perfect that. Marty already *knew* she was perfection personified. Zach was obviously obsessing over her, but did he have to talk about her *all* the time? Dropped in the midst of Zach's nonstop verbal diarrhea about her were the constant questions: Was Marty okay with Zach spending time with Claudia? Did it bother him that Zach was dating her? Was their friendship in jeopardy?

Marty had reassured him, repeatedly, that he'd changed his mind about Claudia that first night. Maybe Zach saw through the lie, and that's why he wouldn't lay off. Didn't matter because Marty was sticking to the deception, no matter what. If Zach found out how Marty *really* felt, it would be far worse, and Marty didn't want to lose his best friend, even if Zach *was* annoying the hell out of him constantly.

Tonight, for instance, Zach had been over-the-top handsy with Claudia ... and she hadn't pushed him away. Despite a telltale blush staining her cheeks, she seemed to enjoy the PDA. Marty couldn't figure out which irritated him more.

Claudia had hugged Marty a beat or five too long when they'd first met up, and her fragrance still clung to his shirt. Beyond throwing his clothes into the wash, he had no idea how to get rid of the haunting scent, fueling his aggravation.

Add to the mix the fact that Megan wouldn't leave him alone, and Marty was one grumpy customer. He told himself to just get it over with and sleep with her already, and he probably would have done just that if she wasn't the best friend of the girl he coveted. Meg was beyond attractive, and he could think of worse ways to spend a night. But having sex with her would make a sticky situation even thornier, and the last thing he needed in his crowded life was more drama. He liked Megan, but she wasn't someone he wanted to start anything with, casual or otherwise. Hell, no one at present rang that bell for him—except Zach's current crush.

As if she'd read his mind, a breathless Megan appeared beside him. She grabbed his hand and tugged. "Come dance, Marty. Please?" The song had just switched over to the rare slow one, and she gave him a little pout when he didn't budge.

He wasn't against dancing. Didn't shy away from it, like a lot of his friends did. Hell, he was just as bad as the rest of them, but he didn't give a shit and usually worked himself out of his awkwardness. Right now, though, he needed to keep his distance from Zach and Claudia's lovey-dovey act. The visual of them clutching and groping each other made his stomach turn over.

A sliver of guilt sliced him as Megan slinked away to the restroom with droopy shoulders. He needed to be nicer to her, but he just didn't have the energy tonight.

The waitress sidled up, and he quickly downed his tequila shooter and twirled his finger in the air, motioning for another round. She arched an eyebrow. "You sure, handsome? Your friends haven't even touched the last one."

His eyes drifted to her name tag affixed to a pleasantly rounded chest. "S'okay, Lora. They will when they come back."

"You're on the hockey team, aren't you? I've been to a few of the games, and I've seen you guys play. You're really good."

Whether she meant him or the team, he couldn't say, nor did he care. "Yeah, I'm on the team, so can I get that drink now? I'm really thirsty." He beamed her what he hoped was a winning smile.

With a sly wink, she pivoted and sashayed away from him. He studied the sway of her hips and the round ass nicely outlined in her short shorts until she melted into the crowd.

"Nice ass," Zach remarked beside him. Marty hadn't been aware of Zach returning to the table, and the surprise about shot him out of his seat. "She kinda reminds me of Claudia with that ass and her blond hair."

"Where the fuck did you come from?" Marty looked around. "And where's Claudia? You didn't leave her on the dance floor alone, did you?" *For other guys to paw at?* Marty had learned these past few weeks that Claudia *liked* to dance—a lot—and dudes *liked* watching her dance—a lot.

"Nah, when she saw Meg heading to the bathroom, she decided she had to go too. What is up with girls having to go to the bathroom together all the time anyway?"

"They're either exchanging secrets or plotting our demise."

Zach shook his head, ignoring Marty's attempt at humor. "I don't get it."

Marty's gaze returned to where the waitress had disappeared, although he wasn't looking for her. Zach apparently thought he was and elbowed him. "You dog! You planning on tapping that too?"

"What do you mean, too?"

Zach threw back one of the shots and chased it with a beer. "I'm talking about Meg, of course."

Marty snapped his head toward his friend. "What's she told you? I haven't slept with her."

"And why is that? What's wrong with you? Not only is she scorching hot, but she's hot for *you*, my man. So what are you waiting for?"

Marty snorted, preparing to protest. Never one to kid himself, he found it easy to keep his ego in check because most girls who showed an interest in him only wanted to get close to Zach. Marty accepted the fact. But even his humble ego couldn't deny the hunger in Megan's eyes when she looked at him. He was dumbfounded as to why someone who turned heads everywhere she went wasted time on someone like him. Maybe it was because he didn't return that interest and she was a sucker for what she couldn't have. During these last few weeks of being thrown together, she had done her damnedest to change his mind. And it was getting more and more embarrassing, not to mention annoying. He needed a way out.

He leaned forward in his chair. "Think I'm gonna take off."

Zach look genuinely puzzled ... and flustered. "Look, I was really hoping ... I mean, you and Megan seem to be getting along so well ..." Zach's eyes darted toward the girls' bathroom before returning to Marty's. "I, uh, was kinda hoping you'd help me out here."

Marty's eyebrows climbed his forehead. "Help you out how?"

"I was counting on you to be my wingman and keep Megan occupied for a couple of hours so I could spend some time alone with Claudia."

"Occupy Megan how, exactly?" Marty was pretty damn sure he already knew how, yet he pressed for every fucking detail, whether he wanted to hear it or not. Yep, a masochist.

Zach clapped him on the shoulder and gave it a shake. "Seriously? I need to lay this out for you? Take her back to their place and get her naked. Take her for a spin between the sheets. Fuck her brainless for a few hours." A smirk curled Zach's mouth. "Tough duty, dude. Poor you. She's totally down with you doing her, and you could use it too. Just saying."

"If you want to be alone with Claudia so badly," Marty snapped, "then just fucking take her back to our place now and do what the hell you're going to do. I'm not staying out all night to accommodate your jacked libido." The force of Marty's words caught him by surprise, though Zach didn't seem to register it. He merely nodded. Heart hammering in a chest that felt as though bands were tightening around it, Marty glared at his friend.

Zach gusted out a sigh. "It's gonna be our first time, and I wanted it to be special. I want to take my time. I don't want to rush anything."

"Fucking too much information, bro," Marty groused. "Why is this one so different anyway?"

Zach dropped his gaze for a beat. "I really like her, Marty. She's ... I don't know, different. Special. She might even be the one. That's why I wanted to make sure you weren't into her, that you were into Megan instead."

"The one? What the hell does that mean?"

Zach smoothed his nape. "I could ... I could see myself marrying this girl, bro."

Marty's mouth dropped open. Zach shrugged, and a sheepish expression lifted his features. "I know. Weird, huh? I haven't slept with the girl, and I'm picturing myself putting a ring on her finger someday."

"Are you seriously telling me you're going to limit yourself to this one girl? Is that even possible for you?"

Zach's head bobbed slowly, and he cast his eyes to the side, a faraway look overtaking them. "Yeah. I don't even notice other girls. She's the only one I see. Does that make sense?"

It made perfect sense. *She's the only one I see too.*

Marty swallowed, his ruffled edges sifting back into place as he marshaled another supreme lie. "Look, I, uh, I'm not into Megan, but I can be scarce for a while. There's this girl—"

"The waitress?"

"Lora? No, not her. Someone I met ... in class. She invited me over to watch a movie, hang out, so I think I'll go see her." A girl in his class *had* invited him over—so it wasn't a total fabrication—but he'd blown her off.

"Oh yeah? Do I know her?"

"No, she's someone new." Marty rose from his seat. "Tell the girls I said bye."

"Hold up a minute! Didn't you just order another drink?"

"Another round, as a matter of fact, but you can finish it for me." Marty slid his wallet from his back pocket and threw down a twenty—his last one.

Zach picked up the bill and thrust it at Marty. "I got this." When Marty began to protest—he hated handouts—Zach waved him off. "Let me show my appreciation for the favor tonight. Besides, it's not fair for you to pay. You won't be here to drink any of it."

Marty's feet itched with urgency. Anxious to clear out before Claudia and Megan came back and pushed him to stay—or for more information about his fabricated date—he decided to bite back his objection and escape while he could.

He drove home, where he tossed a pillow, a sleeping bag, and a bottle of Old Crow into his car. Minutes later, he pulled up to the library, remembering too late they had shortened their hours and were closed. Oh well. Trying to study would have probably turned out to be a huge waste of time anyway. Exhausted yet unable to sleep, he climbed back into his car, drove home, and parked at the end of the block, six houses down from their place. Zach's car was in the driveway, and Marty tried not to think about what was going on inside. He pulled the sleeping bag around himself, turned on the car radio, and took several long pulls on the bottle of Crow.

After long, uncomfortable hours, he quietly dragged his ass into the house, relieved when nothing but quiet and Zach's closed bedroom door greeted him. After sliding between his cold sheets, Marty stared at the ceiling until he finally drifted off in a restless, tormented sleep filled with a sweet, flowery fragrance and dreams of a beautiful blond woman with shimmering brown eyes.

Chapter 5

Some Questions Have Thorns

Claudia awoke in a tangle of legs and sheets, surrounded in warmth and strange—but pleasant—Zach smells. Musk and day-old cologne emanated from the man sleeping beside her on rumpled sheets. His head was turned away, and she took advantage by blatantly running her gaze over his shoulders, following the length of his bare back where it tapered to a narrow waist. His muscles were relaxed, but she could still make out their definition, and a warm little wave washed over her. When she'd first met him a few weeks ago, he had struck her as every inch the bad boy, but since then, he had endeared himself by revealing a tender side. Admittedly, she'd been put off at first by all that charm. He'd pursued her relentlessly, which, while flattering, had been borderline annoying and exhausting. Now that she was catching glimpses of the guy behind all those dimpled smiles, though, she was letting him worm his way into her heart.

Last night, when she had told Zach she'd never been with anyone before, he'd been surprised but oh-so-sweet. First, he had placed a towel on the sheet beneath her, then he had taken things slowly, carefully, concern making him stop every time she had let out a gasp. Most of the gasps had been of the pleasant variety as sensations had rushed over her, but an errant wince or two had also escaped with the not-so-pleasant ones.

Now it was done, and she was bone weary and deliciously sated. Did she harbor regrets that she hadn't held out for Mr. Right? Zach could be in the running for Mr. Right, even if she hadn't been struck by a lightning bolt the first time she had laid eyes on him. She cared about him, and she was pretty sure he cared about her. Even if she had read him wrong and he ended up clipping the wings from their fledgling relationship, she was pleased with her choice of "the first." No disappointment, no shame. Still, lingering doubt had her wondering how he'd react to her this morning.

Scooting to the edge of the bed, she became aware of an ache between her legs. Zach rolled over with a sigh and caught her arm in his warm hand. "Hey, babe. Where are you going?" His eyes were closed, his voice thick with sleep, and in that instant any doubt fled from her mind.

She let a smile form on her lips. "I just thought I'd get dressed and scrounge around the kitchen for some coffee. Is it okay if I make a pot?"

"Yeah, that would be great. Make extra for Marty too."

A frisson of panic snaked through her chest. "Marty's here? I thought he was spending the night with a girlfriend."

A smirk tugged at Zach's lips. "Guess he changed his mind. I heard him come in sometime in the middle of the night."

The panic blossomed, spreading through her limbs. What if Marty had heard them? They hadn't exactly been quiet. Then again, did it matter what Marty thought? "I'm not going to run into him in the kitchen, am I?"

"Maybe, maybe not. Why?"

"I don't think he likes me very much, and it could be awkward."

Zach's eyelids fluttered open. "Not sure where you got that idea, but Marty likes you. A lot."

She blinked. Several times. "What?"

Zach rolled onto his side and dragged her next to him. "Oh yeah," he chortled. "That first night we met you? He bet me for a chance to talk to you first."

Claudia swallowed a surprised breath. "Bet you how? When?"

"Remember the dart game he lost?"

"You can't be serious!" *Marty was interested in ... me? If I'd known, would things have been different?* She shooed the thought from her mind.

"Dead serious. I won the bet, and I got the girl."

"I can't believe you guys actually did that!" She couldn't decide if she was flattered or offended.

Before she could ponder it further, Zach continued in his dozy tone. "Honestly, I was a little surprised myself. That's not exactly Marty's style."

"But it's your style, huh?" Good grief, she hadn't deluded herself about Zach's reputation, but she never expected he would place bets on getting girls.

"No, not really my style either. But I did what it took to get you. And now I've got you, right? I mean, last night was pretty special, wasn't it? I know it was for me." He craned his head and peered at her, his expression hopeful.

The swagger was gone from his voice, replaced by a boyish uncertainty that tugged at her heartstrings. *Okay. Definitely flattered.* She sighed. "Yeah, of course it was special." *It had to be. It's not every day I give up my virginity.*

He pulled her to him and kissed the top of her head. "I'm glad *I* was your first, babe. So we're together now?"

Not what she had expected from the campus king of one-nighters, and she was touched. "Are you asking if we're exclusive?"

"Yeah, something like that. Boyfriend and girlfriend."

Oh. So much for him not wanting to take it further. She laid a soft kiss on his mouth. "Yes, we're together." Giving his hip a squeeze, she wriggled from his grasp. "I'm going to go make that coffee now. Are you getting up?"

"What time is it?"

A digital clock glowed dim red numbers from where it sat on a dresser. "A little bit before seven."

"Way too early," he groaned, flopping onto his back with his arm flung over his eyes. "Do you mind if I sleep in for a bit?"

"No, of course not, sleepyhead."

She rose from the bed, gathered her clothes, and scurried into the bathroom, where she quickly dressed and tried to make herself presentable before slipping through Zach's bedroom door. Smoothing her clothes into place, she tiptoed down the hallway and into the kitchen, pulling up short at the sight of Marty seated at the counter. His head was bowed, and he was studying an open textbook, a steaming cup of coffee beside him. He was dressed in a short-sleeved T-shirt that showcased his sculpted torso and a pair of gym shorts that rode up his tree-trunk thighs. He was barefoot. She stood rooted in place, calculating whether she could flee before he caught sight of her. But she was too late. His eyes flicked up to her face, surprise widening them.

A blaze raced up her cheeks, broadcasting her embarrassment. "Uh, sorry ... I didn't realize you were out here ... I'll just go ..." She jabbed her thumb over her shoulder toward Zach's bedroom.

"No need. Want some coffee?" He was watching her from beneath hooded eyes, but she couldn't read what thoughts streamed behind them. He jerked his chin toward the coffee maker, jarring her out of her stupor. Then he stood, walked around the counter, and plucked a mug from inside a cabinet before she could answer.

"Yes, I'd love a cup. That's why I came out here. I was going to make a pot, but it looks like you beat me to it." She let out a nervous laugh. What was wrong with her? *Marty bet a dart game ...*

Wordlessly, he poured the coffee and held the mug out to her. "Black okay? I think we've got some milk, and I can probably find some sugar. We don't buy the flavors or cream shit some people put in coffee."

"No, black is fine. That's the way I like it too."

An awkward beat passed before they dropped their gazes, and Marty headed back to his stool. Claudia leaned against the wall and tested the hot brew with a small sip.

He downed a big gulp from a cup labeled with the Greek symbols of a campus sorority. "You seem surprised to see me here. You know I live here, right?" There was a teasing quality in his voice that relaxed her shoulders a tick.

"Yes, but Zach said you spent the night with a girlfriend. I guess I didn't expect you here quite so early. I figured you'd either still be at her place, or you'd be sleeping in, like Zach. Is she in a sorority? Is that where you got the cup?"

He peered at the mug as if he'd never seen it before. "No. I'm not sure where this cup came from. And I didn't spend the night with a girlfriend. Just wanted to give you guys some privacy, so I stayed away until I was too tired, then I came back here and climbed into bed."

Oh wow. How sweet is that? She took an overly loud sip of her java. "I never heard you come in."

He seemed to contemplate her for a moment, as if calculating carefully what to say next. For a breathless moment, she felt as though they were on some telepathic plane, where their minds were open to one another and they could read each other's thoughts.

He gave her a reassuring half-smile. "You didn't hear me come in because you were probably sound asleep. It was real quiet when I got home."

Thank you for that. Claudia's shoulders relaxed on a sigh. Marty hadn't heard them, and he hadn't slept over at a girlfriend's house. *Wait. What?* She couldn't untangle which scenario gave her the greatest dose of relief ... or why she would feel relieved at his not sleeping with someone in the first place. *For Megan's sake, of course. She'd be bummed if he was sleeping with anyone besides her.* "I guess that makes sense." She righted her mental self and decided to steer the conversation in a different, more benign direction. "Why are you up so early?"

"I need to get a jog in, and it's the only time I can carve out in my day."

"Do you and Zach usually jog together?"

He snorted. "Nah, I've given up trying to get his lazy ass out there with me. If he goes for a run, it's usually later in the day, and by then I'm either studying or getting in extra practice."

"What do you mean, extra practice?" She took another slug of the coffee, marveling at how good it tasted. Either she was more tired than she realized or they invested in the good stuff. Knowing Zach and how his parents doted on him, it was probably a gift from them.

Or, in true Zach fashion, he splurged with whatever money he had. He liked to spend; the word "saving" didn't exist in his vocabulary.

"When you've got limited talent like I do, you have to put in extra work so you can contribute to your team."

"You don't think you have the same level of talent as your teammates?"

Marty shrugged. "I know I don't. For instance, most of them have already had their rights picked up by an NHL team."

"You mean like ..."

"Yeah, like Zach. He's probably told you that the St. Louis Titans signed him a while ago. He could go pro after our college season's over if he chooses to."

She had watched the BC Eagles play, and while she was still learning the ins and outs of hockey, she had noticed that Zach was often on the ice more than Marty was. "Double shifting," Zach had called it. Their style of play was entirely different. Whereas Zach was speedy, had the puck on his stick often, and passed it to a teammate or shot it on net himself multiple times in a game, Marty was usually muscling guys off the puck or shoving at them against the boards. Both roles, Zach had explained, were important to the success of the team. But like people usually noticed the lead singer in a band without acknowledging the musicians who supported him or her, fans noticed the flashy guy on the ice. In other words, they noticed Zach.

"So what does a guy like you, who wants to break into the NHL, do?"

Marty took a thoughtful sip. "You pray a lot." A warm smile spread across his rugged features. "Seriously, you finish out your college years, get as much playing experience as you can, and then either put yourself out there as a free agent or see if you can get tryouts with different teams. If you don't get picked up by an NHL team, then you might take a stab at a roster spot in one of the other leagues. And if that doesn't work out, you fall back on that diploma you just earned."

"Other leagues?"

"Yeah, like the AHL."

"Is that like a farm team in baseball?" She felt a warm little flutter of satisfaction in her chest when he nodded approvingly at her question.

"Exactly. In the meantime, you stay in as good a shape as you possibly can, practice like hell, and you keep your nose clean. Don't give a team an excuse to pass you by."

She nodded. "That takes lots of discipline. I imagine keeping up that kind of effort can be tough." *Especially when your best friend has already been drafted.*

His brown eyes zeroed in on hers, their intensity firing off wobbly butterflies in her stomach. *I get why Megan is so hot for him.* "Which is why I have to jog." A wistfulness dropped a cloud over those eyes.

"Can I jog with you?" she blurted.

His expression transformed into one of shock.

"I don't mean right now," she stammered. "But I like jogging, and I don't have anyone to go with. I don't feel comfortable by myself around campus, but if I had a big strapping guy like you running with me, I'd get out and do it more. I really enjoy hiking too."

Shut. Up.

"Yeah, I remember. Jogging club and choir," he chuckled. "Are you an early riser?"

"Always have been. Mama says you miss the best part of the day when you sleep in."

"Another pearl you picked up, huh?"

"Maybe she's scattered more pearls than I realized." Claudia bit her bottom lip.

He darted his eyes out the window and held stock-still for several quiet heartbeats. At last, he turned his gaze back to her and nodded. "Yeah, you can come along." One corner of his mouth tugged upward. "How about we start tomorrow? I'm dying to see if you can keep up."

"Ha! You're on, hotshot." For reasons she wasn't sure of, her heart lifted a few inches. Marty had a way of making her feel relaxed, even in the most awkward situations. No, the light feeling had to be because of what she was arranging for Megan, Claudia told herself. She would convince her friend to come along, and she could play matchmaker for Meg and Marty. Never mind that Meg had never shown interest in exercise in any way, shape, or form. She now had a really good excuse to start.

When Claudia returned home later that morning, Megan was lying in wait, her eyes gleaming. “So how was it?”

Claudia had prepared herself for this very question, even if her answer didn’t show it. “It was ... nice.”

“Nice?” Meg screeched. “That’s it?”

“Well, I was so busy thinking about what went where and if I was doing everything right that I forgot to just relax and enjoy it. And then it was over with.” Cuddling and talking and caressing had followed, and she had loved them all. No one had ever taught her about these perks of intimacy—not sex ed, and certainly not her overprotective mother. Girlfriends focused on “it,” and guys ... well, she had never asked any. She’d been too shy to bring up the subject around boys in high school, and besides, they wouldn’t have been able to give her any insights from the female perspective.

“Well, that sounds ... disappointing.”

“No, it was—”

“Nice. Yeah, I get it.” Megan was the one who seemed disillusioned, and Claudia tried not to laugh out loud.

They headed for the kitchen, where Meg picked up a half-empty glass of OJ. Claudia opened the refrigerator door and stuck her head inside. “I’m not sure I got the full effect. I mean, I’ve read about orgasms, and of course I’ve heard you describe them”—*ad nauseum*—“but I don’t think I had one.”

“You’d know if you had one. It feels like an earthquake. Did you at least fake it so he thought you had one?”

“If I’ve never had an orgasm, how would I know how to fake one?” Claudia deadpanned.

“Okay, okay. So you didn’t reach the O zone this time, but you’ll get there. You just need a little more practice. How was it otherwise? Did it feel good?”

“Other than the burning sensation, you mean? Yeah, it did feel good. There were parts I really liked.”

“Such as?”

“Such as getting to see and touch all those muscles. Oh. My. God.”

"I wasn't talking about his body, although if you want to describe that in detail to me, I'm down for it. I was talking about the foreplay and what positions you guys tried. You know, the good stuff."

Claudia dipped an eyebrow at her friend. "Meg, you've been my best friend for nearly my entire life, but there are certain limits, and this is one. Let's just say I definitely would like to do it again."

"And I'm sure you'll get your chance."

Claudia grinned. "Yeah, probably tonight."

"You guys going out again, huh? This is getting hot and heavy." Megan's eyes went wide. "Tell me you're using protection. I mean, you should always have condoms in your purse in case he doesn't."

"Doesn't what? Have condoms in his purse?" Claudia's grin widened.

"Haha, so funny. You can make up for your bad jokes by setting me up with his best friend."

Claudia clapped her hands. "Actually, I have a plan." She filled Megan in on her jogging appointment with Marty in the morning. "So squeeze your butt into some tight booty shorts and come with. While we're running, you can take off ahead of us and give him an eyeful. That should get his motor running."

Megan groaned. "You know I *hate* running, especially if I have to get up early to do it. Or any sort of physical activity, for that matter, that doesn't involve sex."

"I do, but you've been drooling over Marty for weeks now, and I figured it would be a small sacrifice to put on some cute clothes and dazzle him with that bod of yours. Think of it as foreplay or running for sex. It's the warm-up to the main event." Claudia burst into a laugh.

"Ugh! If you weren't my best friend, I'd fire you." Meg stuck out her tongue.

"I love you too."

"Seriously, Claud, I appreciate you trying to set me up with him, but it's obvious he's not interested, so I'm moving on."

"Really? You hate jogging that much?"

A wicked gleam lit Megan's eyes. "No, I found someone else on the hockey team I'm interested in. Maybe you could have Zach introduce me."

An unexpected rush of relief caught Claudia by surprise when it rose up from her belly. She told herself it was merely a by-product of Megan turning her attention to someone who might actually return it. In other words, the relief she felt was all about her BFF. Yeah, that had to be it, and Claudia had no reason to examine her motives further. She placed the thorny question into the dusty cupboard of her mind and slammed the door shut.

Chapter 6

THE OCCASIONAL CASUAL

Three months later

It was an unseasonably warm February day when Marty nosed his Honda against the curb at Chestnut Hill Reservoir, behind Claudia's POS Nissan Pathfinder. As he killed his engine, he glanced out the window and saw her stretching in the distance. She was wearing that tight-fitting spandex stuff that accentuated her curves beautifully. Tucking his keys and wallet into his gym pants, he locked his car and jogged toward her.

She looked up when he caught her eye and gave him a brilliant smile. "There you are! I was wondering if I was about to be stood up."

"I'd never do that to you." He went into a walking lunge beside her.

"Things must be serious with this new girlfriend if she's making you late for our jogging dates."

"She's not the reason I'm late." *And she's not a girlfriend.* "She" was Lora, the waitress from the Stompin' Grounds. A senior, she was graduating in a few months, so her interest in long-term matched Marty's. In other words, she wanted nothing from a relationship beyond the physical perks. When he'd bumped into her at the library weeks after first meeting her, she had been very friendly and let him know she was interested in being friends with benefits. Discovering they shared that commonality, they had hooked up a few times. Nothing permanent, and so far it worked. As long as they each got out of it what they wanted and didn't change their minds about keeping things light, they would continue seeing each other until she left in a few months.

"No? What's your excuse, then?" Claudia braced her hand on his shoulder—he was extended in a deep lunge—to execute a standing quad stretch. He'd been taken aback the first time she had used him as a wall for her warm-ups, but now that he'd grown accustomed to it, he liked it. Made him feel ... useful.

"I had to turn in extra credit work for Chem."

"Oh, that's right. Is that the last of it?" She tugged at his shoulders as if trying to pull him to his feet.

"Can I help you?" he quipped.

"Yes, stand up so I can do my leg swings."

"Of course, Your Highness. And how many lumps of sugar in your tea?" He stood obediently.

She flattened her palm against his chest. "Yukity-yuk. Maybe I should give *you* two lumps."

"Not a good idea. You'd lose your mobile stretching wall."

"Good point." Her leg flew high in front of her. "So how's English Lit coming? Need any more of my help there?"

While he *loathed* English, Claudia loved it. More importantly, she excelled at it and had helped him over the rough patches. He had no doubt she would rock at being a teacher.

"Nope, I'm good."

Her head swiveled toward him. "So you think you'll be able to keep the scholarship?"

"Let's put it this way: my adviser is more optimistic now than he was a few months ago."

She stopped her leg swings to clap and pump her fist. "Yes! I'm so relieved."

Her antics spread warmth through his limbs, and he grinned. "*You're* relieved? How do think *I* feel?"

Now she placed both palms against him and started her hip abductor swings. He covered her hands with his to steady her as if it was the most natural move in the world ... because it was. Her eyes sparkled with mischief when she looked up at him. “So tell me about this girl you’re seeing. You’re being terribly enigmatic.”

He dipped an eyebrow at her. “You’re using awfully big words.”

“You’re not going to respond, are you?” she prodded.

“Nope.”

They headed for the trail and began their run, their timing perfectly choreographed.

“We’re going to run the circuit a couple times, yeah?” she said beside him.

“Yep. One circuit doesn’t give me enough time to harass you.”

She laughed. “I think it’s my turn to do the harassing.”

“You’ve got nothing to harass me about.”

“Ha! That’s where you’re wrong. I want to know about this mystery woman in your life.”

“Why?”

“I have to know if she’s good enough for you.”

Why he didn’t open up to Claudia about Lora baffled him. He had nothing to hide, but Claudia looked up to him, like a big brother, and he didn’t want to expose the shallow side of himself and risk disappointing her. Claudia’s admiration, if he could call it that, was a treasure he hoarded more than he was willing to admit. “I’m not going there, so don’t even try.”

She ignored him. Of course she did. “Zach says he hasn’t met her yet but that you’ve been seeing a lot of her. Is it serious?”

He sidestepped a divot in the path. “Haven’t seen that much of her, and it’s strictly casual.”

“But you like her?”

He gave her a sidelong glance, taking in her profile and the little ponytail gathered on the crown of her head like a golden topknot. “Shit, you’re nosy.”

“You like her.” A little grin tugged the corners of her mouth. “Of course you like her, or you wouldn’t be sleeping with her! Is she coming to the Beanpot Tournament? Do I get to meet her?”

“She won’t be there.”

“Why not?”

Because I didn’t invite her. “She’s not really into sports.”

"Wait. She's dating a hockey player, and she doesn't like sports? What do you two talk about? Oh, I get it. You don't talk, do you?"

"None of your business," he huffed. "Besides, my mom and sisters are going to be there, and I want to spend time with them."

"Ah. I guess introducing her to family might convey the wrong idea, like she's more than a fuck buddy. Am I right?"

"Crass, but correct. And for the record, she's happy with the arrangement."

She puffed a few breaths as their pace picked up. "I think this is the first girl I've heard about since I've known you. You don't do serious, do you?"

"With everything I've got going on, I don't have time for serious. I barely have time for the occasional casual."

A pair of joggers was headed toward them, and Claudia sprinted ahead of him single file, her ponytail bobbing as she went. "You want a family someday?" she called over her shoulder.

He caught up to her. "Yeah, I want all that. I just don't see it happening any time soon, so there's no point in looking."

"Sometimes it just happens whether you're looking or not."

He arched an eyebrow at her. "Are you trying to tell me something about you and Zach?"

"Nope. Just saying."

They ran in silence for a while. He was always surprised by how perfectly in sync their footfalls and breathing were, and today was no different. Whenever he wasn't on the road with the hockey team, he looked forward to these morning runs with her. She had lagged a little at first, but now she had no trouble keeping up with him. Zach never joined them, and Marty was glad for the time he got to spend alone with her. In the beginning, he had held his breath, waiting for a jealous shoe to fall, but it never came. "We're bros. I trust you more than I trust anyone else with her," Zach had said when Marty had asked him if their running jaunts bothered him.

"I haven't checked in with Zach about this in a while, but is he still okay with us jogging together?" Marty ventured.

"Why wouldn't he be?"

"Oh, I don't know. If a girl of mine was out every morning with another guy, it might bother me."

"Except we're only jogging, and you're like my brother. If it bothers him, he can come along and supervise. So far, I haven't been able to talk him into it, so I've stopped inviting him." She let out an extended sigh. "Maybe one of these days ..."

I hope not. "Maybe. Now shut up and jog."

Marty's mind meandered to his best friend, who was garnering a shit ton of attention as their team prepared for the Beanpot in a few days. Four major college hockey schools in the area would meet for the next two Mondays at the Fleet Center. After the Beanpot final, they would ramp up for NCAA playoffs, and while BC lagged this year, Zach's skills seemed to be getting sharper. If the Eagles made it to the semis, it would be because Zach put the team on his back. His play was stirring a frenzy, and with the heated attention, Zach had been spending a lot of time talking to his adviser-slash-agent lately.

He'd confided to Marty that he had yet to make up his mind about the next move, but Marty would be shocked if his buddy didn't leave school and enter the NHL at the end of BC's season. With all that money being bandied about and the prestige of making it to the big league, the lure would be overwhelming. Much as Marty wanted to complete his college education, he probably wouldn't pass up the opportunity himself—not that he would ever have that decision to make. No one had taken a sniff at him.

So Zach was cruising on Easy Street, with a bright future ahead. He was no fool; that future looked to include the woman jogging beside Marty, which surprised Marty as much as it did anyone who knew Zach and his ladies' man persona. His buddy had settled into a semblance of domestic bliss with Claudia. Marty applauded him for it, though he had had to grow a skin over his heart that mostly obscured his feelings from himself and from her. And thank fuck he had, or he never would have been able to languish in the friend zone. Yeah, Marty kept few secrets from her, but that colossal one overshadowed anything else he had to hide. And if she found out? He wouldn't let that happen. As it was, she had become one of his best friends, as he had become one of hers, and he couldn't fathom losing that closeness ... especially since that was the only way he could ever have her.

Days after their reservoir run, Claudia found herself seated in the Fleet Center stands between Megan and Danielle, Marty's eighteen-year-old sister. Beyond her sat their mom and his sixteen-year-old sister, Alexis. Claudia had witnessed an icy, awkward vibe pass between Marty and his mother, and she was grateful to have bubbly Danielle insulating her from the dour matriarch.

The teams had just taken the ice and were flying around its perimeter as they warmed up. Claudia's gaze searched out and found Zach, but Marty caught her attention when he skated by and waved. Like automatons on a string, their group of five all waved back.

She turned to Danielle. "It must be a treat to come watch your brother play."

"It is." Her face was bright with a smile as she watched the players skate. "I've always loved coming to his games, but now that he's going to school here, I hardly ever get to see him play, so this is extra special."

"Sounds like you miss him."

Danielle's brown eyes twinkled as she bobbed her head. "Oh yeah, I miss him a lot. I know that older brothers are supposed to be annoying, but Marty's not."

Genuinely curious, Claudia cocked her head. "What's he like?"

"He's funny, he likes to laugh, and he cheers us up all the time. He's generous; like, he always brings us little things, even though he doesn't have any money. He's always asking if we have everything we need, and he doesn't let anyone mess with us. He ... I always feel safe with him around. He's a good big brother."

Claudia's eyes returned to the ice, and once more she sought out Zach's frame. She spied him as he glided by a corner at the opposite end of the rink. His head turned toward the crowd that was pressed against the glass at ice level, and he paused to flick a puck over the glass and send them a smile and a wink. Her stomach turned over. Besides a smattering of little kids and parents, the majority of that audience was made up of young women—and they were holding up signs.

"Zach! Call me!" A phone number in huge block letters followed.

"All I want for my birthday is Zach Pruitt's baby."

"I bet my brother that Zach would date me. Help me win that bet."

In her mind's eye, every single girl was a supermodel. She leaned her shoulder against Megan's and whispered, "I'm not sure I have enough confidence to handle this."

"Yes, you do. You're way prettier and smarter than any of those girls." She cocked an ear. "And who did I hear Zach went home with last night? And who is he going home with tonight?"

Claudia rolled her eyes. "Me."

"That's right. He's not even looking at those girls. Well, except when he's doing the PR thing, which comes with the job. Now repeat after me: 'Zach Pruitt loves only me.'" Meg dug an elbow into Claudia's ribs, making Claudia yelp. "I can't hear you."

"Zach Pruitt loves only me," Claudia singsonged under her breath. "Happy now?"

"Delirious."

Danielle swiveled her head and gave Claudia a curious look. "You're Zach's girlfriend?" When Claudia nodded, Danielle's eyes strayed back to the ice. "Omigosh, you're so lucky. He is *so* cute."

And every female on the planet agrees with you.

"Have you ever met Zach's parents?" Zach had told her a week ago they wouldn't be coming. They lived in California with his sister, and his dad was a big-time executive who couldn't get away.

Danielle shook her head. "No, they never come that I know of. At least, I've never met them. They didn't come watch his sports in juniors either. But Marty says they follow his games and are really proud."

Huh. Zach rarely spoke about them, and it seemed to Claudia that he had either lived with other families or on his own since before he was a teen. She had never picked up any animosity, just more of a void that made her heart hurt for him.

"Will you be coming to the second round next week?" Claudia asked.

Danielle shook her head. "No, Mom needs to get back. How about you?"

"Unfortunately, no. I have a really important test that day."

"Well, I guess we'll just have to wait and find out from the guys how they did."

"If they win, it might take a while to hear about it," Claudia laughed. These boys liked to celebrate.

The teams left the ice, and Claudia sucked in a breath as she glanced up at the game clock. Fifteen minutes, and the tournament would be on.

Danielle must have felt the excitement building because she squealed, "I hope they win!"

"Me too. Either way, this is going to be a lot of fun."

Danielle tapped Claudia's arm and opened her mouth as if preparing to say something, but she hesitated for a beat.

Claudia shoulder-bumped the girl playfully. "What is it?"

Danielle let out an irrepressible giggle. "I'm glad you're here and that we got to meet you."

"Aw, thank you. That's a really sweet thing to say. I feel the same way." And Claudia meant it too. Meeting Marty's family gave her a more complete picture of him and his origins. Differences with his mother aside, he went out of his way to be sure his family was comfortable, and the way he and his sisters interacted warmed Claudia's chest. He was *so good* to them. Consequently, nothing Danielle had said about him surprised Claudia. He *was* a good guy.

Now if she could only fill in the blanks looming around Zach ...

Bad boy with a bit of an entitled attitude, lofty goals, and a sweet underbelly. She often pondered why he had picked her out of all the girls on campus. *Because he's in love with you,* she chided herself. But was Zach the kind of guy who committed for a lifetime, or was he more likely to fall in and out of love? *No idea.* He had dated her longer than he ever had anyone else, so maybe he loved her enough to settle into long-term with her. Then again, was *she* ready for that commitment? *I think so. Maybe.*

Was she ready to cast her lot with him and hope he would stay by her? *A tougher question, but not one I need to decide right now.*

She was caught off guard when Danielle whispered, "I wish you were Marty's girlfriend."

Had she meant for Claudia to hear her? Claudia decided to let it lie, but an errant thought popped and bobbed in her brain. *Had he won that bet, things might be different now.*

Marty stood outside his mom and sisters' room, knuckle poised to knock, when he froze. Angry female voices rose and fell behind the door, though he couldn't make out what they said.

The door flew open, revealing a tearful Danielle in the opening, a coat and purse clutched in her hand. Her watery eyes widened.

Sirens wailed in his head as he peered over her head to his mother, who stood by the window, fists perched on her hips and face twisted with frustration. He shifted his gaze back to Dani. "What's going on?"

"Will you talk some sense into your sister?" his mother barked at the same time Dani howled, "She says I can't go to MSU!"

Nudging his sister back inside, he closed the door behind them, steeling himself for the buzz saw he was walking into. "Let's not broadcast to the entire hotel, okay?"

Alexis jumped up from the bed, where she'd been sitting cross-legged with her mouth hanging open. She rushed into Marty's arms. He gave her a quick squeeze and stroked her head. "It's okay, Lexi. Maybe you and your sister can go to Starbucks and grab us some fancy coffee drinks."

Lexi wrinkled her nose. "I don't like coffee."

He pulled out a twenty. "Then a smoothie for you and coffees for the rest of us." He flashed her a smile he didn't feel, but she smiled back and plucked her coat from a chair and hustled Danielle to the door.

"Let me talk to Mom alone for a few minutes," he said to Danielle.

With a bob of her head and a swipe of her cheeks, Dani followed Lexi out the door.

His mother crossed her arms and let out a long-suffering sigh. "I just told Danielle it would be better if she attended community college for her first two years and lived at home, and she went all hysterical on me."

Wait. What? "Why community college? I thought she was all set for Michigan State."

"MSU is too expensive, and she refuses to understand simple economics." His mother flipped out a hand. "It will cost half as much if she just stays home and attends there. You need to talk some sense into her. She'll listen to you."

He wrestled a semblance of calm into his voice. "I don't understand why she has to give up MSU. The money's there, and she was promised—"

"I never promised her that." The indignant tone in her voice raised the hairs on his neck.

Whoa! Calmness melted away. "Yeah, you did, Mom. I was there. And she's had her heart set on it."

"Well, things change." His mother raised her chin and sniffed.

"What do you mean by that? Dad had money set aside for our educations, and there should have been plenty for the girls since I've hardly touched any of it." Another reason that scholarship was so important—it meant a bigger pot for his sisters.

"I had to use some of it."

The agitation inside him came out in his voice. "For what?"

"Don't you yell at me, Marty LeBrun."

He pulled in a cleansing breath and dialed down his volume. "I'm not yelling. It's just that I'm a little caught off guard by what I'm hearing. Where did the money go, Mom?"

"It didn't go anywhere." She strode to the phone. "I'll call Richard and let him explain—"

Marty blinked. Why the fuck was *Richard*, who was some seven hundred miles away in Michigan, involved in this conversation? "No, Mom. This is none of Richard's business. I want to hear from *you* why there's no money for Dani to go to MSU."

"I asked him to review my finances, and he thought it would be a good idea to hold back on any big expenses until he can familiarize himself with the entire picture."

What the actual fuck? To Marty's knowledge, the guy had no professional financial qualifications. He was a deadbeat, probably a con artist, but he was no adviser. "Why the hell is he familiarizing himself with your finances?" he growled.

Her condescending composure slipped a tick. "I get confused about these things, and I needed help."

Marty jabbed his thumb into his chest. "Why didn't you come to me for help, Mom? I can help." He refrained from adding, *And I don't have any ulterior motives.*

She huffed out the kind of breath she reserved for times when she was especially exasperated with Marty. "You're busy with school and your hockey. Besides, these are private matters."

"Private from *me*? I'm your son! Why the hell aren't they private from a stranger?"

Squaring herself up, she faced him. "Richard is *not* a stranger. He's simply trying to help me, and your hostile attitude isn't helping one bit. He was right to tell me I couldn't trust you."

Marty's head snapped backward from the verbal blow. "He *told* you that? And you *believed* him? This is something we, the family, discuss. Richard is not a part of that," he ground out.

"Richard *is* family," she hissed, "so this *does* involve him. You need to show him—and me—some respect. I'm entitled to a little happiness, you know." Tears shimmered in her eyes.

Marty's lungs deflated. "I never said you shouldn't be happy, Mom. I want that for you, but—"

"But what? Why are you so ... so unkind to him?"

"The truth?"

"Yes, please." She plucked a few tissues from a box.

Oh man, he was climbing out on a limb, but he needed to get this off his chest. He pulled in a fortifying breath. "I don't trust him. I think he might be after the estate." Before he could get out the rest of what he wanted to say—namely, that his primary concern was for her and his sisters—the limb cracked.

Her voice quavered as her words came out accusingly, haltingly, flaying him alive. "How could you say he's after me for my money? He loves me, Marty, which you may find hard to believe because he's not your father. You're not being fair to him or to me. You'll have to get used to the idea of him in our lives, or else."

"Or else what?" he asked softly.

"Or else ... I don't know. You've upset me, and I can't think straight."

"Then maybe I should go."

"That might be best." She dabbed at her nose and turned away.

Absolutely lost, heart and limbs leaden, Marty headed for the door. Being at odds with his mom wasn't a position he was used to, and he couldn't think of a circumstance he hated more. Did having a relationship with his mother mean he needed to suck up to a man he trusted less than a coiled snake? Where did it leave him if he couldn't? Those questions, along with, *What just happened?* swirled through his head as he exited the room.

Coffees in hand, his sisters rounded the corner and came to a standstill.

Dani gaped at him. "Marty? Is everything all right?"

He had no idea.

Chapter 7

PERKS

Marty stepped into the bar and squinted as he waited for his eyes to adjust to the dim interior. He heard his teammates before he spied them, overflowing a back corner where they celebrated winning the Beanpot. The party was well underway, and he needed to catch up after taking time out to call his sisters and share the news of the victory. He had talked to them frequently since the fallout with his mother a week ago, trying to keep his tie to them from becoming brittle and breaking. That phone call had gone longer than he'd planned, and that was okay. But now he was ready to join his team and party his ass off. They had all earned this. While their chances of getting into the NCAA semis might be growing slimmer by the day, this triumph was in the moment and all theirs to savor.

Apparently, the rest of Boston wanted to bask in the victory too because its entire college population seemed to be crammed into that raucous corner. He ambled over, and a few of his teammates lifted their chins and grinned. A crowd five people deep was knotted around a table, their backs to him. As he wound his way toward them, they raised their glasses to someone who was obscured from his view. They began to chant, "Pru-itt! Pru-itt!" followed by, "MVP! MVP!"

No surprise. Once more, Zach had proved why St. Louis had taken him so high in the draft. He'd played brilliantly in today's win, potting four of their five goals and leading them to this very celebration.

Marty shouldered his way through, eager to join in, but he stopped short at the sight that greeted him. Zach sat in the midst of the crowd like a king holding court, a girl Marty didn't recognize perched on his knee. Her arms were looped around his neck, her tits pressed against him. In his right hand, he held a nearly empty beer, and his left hand was snaked under Loopy's crop top, resting on her bare waist. The grin Zach sported split his face from ear to ear as he looked from the girl to the crowd.

Marty pushed air through his lungs. The celebration was gone, sucked from him, and his joy had evaporated. In its place swirled disappointment and anger.

His first instinct was to shout at his dumbass of a friend, but he held it in check. His next urge was to leave, but what if Marty was the only barrier keeping Zach from blowing what he had with Claudia? Zach loved her—he'd admitted as much to Marty. But too much booze combined with a lot of happy—with no Claudia around—could add up to a horrible decision with irreversible consequences that Zach would forever regret. It was clear that brain cells were in short supply in his arsenal at the moment, and he needed someone to keep him out of trouble. That someone was Marty. Yeah, Claudia would no doubt flip if she was here and got an eyeful of the scene, but honestly, Zach hadn't strayed too far afield. He hadn't had time. *Maybe he wouldn't go there even if he did have time, but why take the chance?*

Marty took a step back to marshal a plan, but at that same moment, Zach's eyes landed on him ... and widened. His shit-eating grin instantly transformed into a guilty O ... as in, *Oh shit! I'm busted.* He lurched to his feet, and the girl hit the floor. She cursed a blue streak at him as she floundered on her side. Ignoring her, Zach sidestepped and parked his hands on his hips, as if to say, *Wasn't me. That girl was in some other dude's lap.* Helped by a few people surrounding her, the girl climbed to her feet, threw a few more choice words at him, and stomped off. Under any other circumstances, Marty would have found the situation comical, and he would have enjoyed a good chuckle over it. But these weren't any regular circumstances.

Zach latched on to Marty's arm before Marty could pivot and go. "Hey. Glad you finally made it." The fake casual tone grated like sandpaper.

"That so? Looks like my showing up spoiled your fun."

Shifting from foot to foot, Zach ran a hand through his hair. "Hey, uh, that wasn't what it looked like."

The anger Marty had been holding back surged through him. "No? Then tell me what the hell it was, dumbass."

"Look, can we do this somewhere else?" Zach cuffed his arm again, but Marty shook it off.

Without a word, Marty strode outside, Zach right behind him. Marty turned, crossed his arms, and faced his friend. "Want to tell me what was going on in there?"

Zach smoothed his nape repeatedly. "I was just ... I got carried away is all, and you happened to walk in right after she climbed into my lap."

"You make it sound like she tied you down and gave you no choice."

One side of Zach's mouth lifted. "Hey, now *that* sounds like fun." Marty glared at him, and a look of contrition overtook Zach's features. "Bad joke. I was just trying to lighten things up."

They stood in charged silence until Zach finally ended it. "Are you gonna tell Claudia?" Marty had already made up his mind, but he held his tongue while he appraised his best friend. Zach couldn't hold up under the scrutiny. "Look, I know you and Claudia are besties and all, but I wish you wouldn't. She might blow this out of proportion. Nothing happened. Nothing was *gonna* happen." He blew out a breath. "I don't want to lose her, Marty. She's the best thing that ever happened to me."

Zach's heartfelt plea turned the tide of Marty's exasperation. His anger dissolved faster than powdered sugar in hot water, and he let his arms fall to his sides. "Yeah, she is, asshole, and don't you forget it. If you want to keep her, then no more flirting, no more 'weak moments.' Stay away from the jersey chasers." He poked his forefinger hard into Zach's chest, and Zach stumbled back a step.

"You're right. Won't happen again, I swear."

Marty wanted to believe him. He convinced himself Zach would follow through on that pledge, but a nagging doubt had taken root.

Six weeks later, the BC Eagles' season came to a close. Despite the team's last-minute Herculean push and Zach's unrivaled play, the boys ran out of runway, missing the semis by one heartbreaking point.

"Good thing we lost. Now I have time to work on that English Lit essay," Marty joked as he ran beside Claudia a few mornings after the loss. It was a gorgeous late March day, and though his disappointment sat like a rock in his gut, he felt lighter than he had in days.

"Are you gonna pass, do you think?"

"Yeah, I think I will. I'm rocking a D-plus now."

She held up her hand for a high five, and he obliged her with a slap to her palm. "Congrats. It may not be pretty, but it's definitely a passing grade. Or do you have to score higher to maintain the hockey scholarship?"

"No, I'm good."

She pivoted, running backward. "I'm proud of you, Smarty Marty."

A broad grin bloomed on his face. "Why, thank you, CC."

"Why doesn't it bother me when *you* use that nickname?"

"I pack more charm behind it. Now turn around before you fall on your cute ass and I have to explain the road rash to your boyfriend."

She shot him an impish smile. "You think I have a cute ass?"

He returned a fake glare. "No, I don't. It was a slip of the tongue." He groaned inside, battling the myriad visuals bombarding his brain.

Cocking one eyebrow, she turned and fell in beside him without uttering another word. *Thank fuck.*

They ran in companionable silence, and when they were done and piled into his car, he offered to buy her a coffee.

"Not this time, thanks. Besides, you're broke, and you shouldn't be offering to buy me drinks."

"Who says I'm broke?"

"Zach does. Your sisters do."

"Nah, my mom's sitting on a small fortune, and I'm first in line to inherit." Sarcasm dripped from his tone.

She barked a laugh. "This isn't the Middle Ages—you'll have to share that small fortune with your sisters despite their gender—and I'm pretty sure your mom's got a lot of years left."

"Yeah," he grumbled, "and that dickhead is going to take all the money anyway. If he outlives my mom, he'll pass it on to *his* kids."

"How can he pass on anything to his kids if he and your mom aren't married?"

"Not married *yet.*" According to Danielle, Dick had proposed, but his mother had been mum when Marty prodded her for information. In fact, his mom was mum whenever he tried to talk to her. The fences that had blown down during their confrontation needed a whole hell of a lot of mending, and he couldn't see those repairs happening anytime soon.

"Oh no. I'm so sorry. Do you want to talk about it?" Claudia's tone soothed his soul. She had a way of doing that.

He turned on the engine and pulled away from the curb. "Not now. I'm having a good time, and I don't want to ruin it."

He could feel her eyes on him. Finally, she faced forward. "Okay. But I'd like to understand someday, when you're ready to tell me."

"Deal." *If that day ever comes.*

When they turned into her complex's parking lot, Marty spotted Zach's light green Subaru Outback. It hadn't been there when he'd picked her up.

She peered out the window. "Huh. I thought he was sleeping in this morning. Wonder why he's here?"

"Let's go find out." Normally, Marty merely dropped her off, but this morning his curiosity took over, and he parked the car, locked up, and followed her up the stairs to the apartment she shared with Rex and Megan.

Before they reached her door, it flew open. Zach stood in the doorway, a smile stretching from ear to ear. "Guess what?" Before they could answer, he scooped Claudia up and swung her around.

"Zach, you're making me dizzy!" she laughed. "What's going on?"

He set her on her feet and pecked her lips. "You're looking at the latest addition to the St. Louis Titans roster!"

"What?" Claudia and Marty gasped at the same time.

Nodding, Zach sprouted a cocky grin and spread his arms wide. "That's right, boys and girls, I'm going to the Show. The team contacted my agent as soon as BC was out of the playoff picture, and we agreed to terms a little while ago."

Claudia clapped her hands over her mouth, muffling a shriek. "When do you start?"

"Two nights from now. I catch a flight tonight, meet with the coaches in the morning, then practice with my club after that, right before we get on a charter for an away game. I'm traveling with the team and might get my first shift against Winnipeg the next night. How sweet is that?"

"Oh my God!" She rushed into his outstretched arms, and Zach wrapped her up tight, sending Marty a wink over her shoulder.

Marty stood rooted in place, a maelstrom of emotions twisting inside him: joy for his friend, sadness at seeing him leave, hope that he might follow him into the NHL one day. In the mix were undeniable dejection and envy, and he shoved the toxic cocktail down.

By the time Claudia and Zach released each other, Marty had recovered himself enough to get his mouth moving again. He pulled Zach in for a bro hug and a clap on the back. "That's awesome, dude. You beat the odds. You made it!"

Zach grasped his shoulder as they pulled apart. "Yeah. Dream of a lifetime, and I gotta admit it feels fucking fantastic. Wish you were coming with me, though."

Marty forced a laugh. "So do I."

Claudia swiped at her moist cheeks. When had she started crying? "But, Zach, what about school?"

Zach gaped at her. "What about it?"

"Does this mean you're done?" Marty asked.

"Yep. I'm going to be a college dropout."

Claudia's voice came out in a shrill pitch. "What if things don't pan out, or you get injured?"

"Baby, this is Zach." He pointed at himself. "Nothing bad is going to happen. And with all the money I'm raking in, I don't see any reason to waste my time on classes I'm never going to use."

"But you've been attending school all year. Why drop out now? You could finish the last few weeks instead of throwing away the entire year."

He placed his hands on her shoulders and gave her an indulgent smile. "Trust me, it doesn't matter. Now can we celebrate? I have to leave in a few hours, and after I tell you how big my signing bonus is, you are going to want to drag me into bed before I go."

She side-eyed Marty, a pretty blush decorating her cheeks. He shuffled his feet, suddenly more awkward than he'd been a moment before. "I'll just, uh, get going." He whacked Zach's stomach with more force than he intended. "Zach, my man, well done. Don't forget about us little people when you're signing autographs and hanging with celebrities."

Marty turned to go. Claudia's soft voice drifted behind him as Zach led her into the apartment. "Everything is about to change, isn't it?"

He never heard Zach's reply, but it didn't matter. The answer was as blinding as sunlight on a frozen pond.

Claudia stood in a stupor beside Zach's bed, folding and refolding the same T-shirt. Meanwhile, he buzzed about his bedroom, packing with an eerily calm efficiency she found unnerving. In fact, the calmer he was, the more agitated she became. It was as if this had been the plan all along and he was embracing it full on. Then again, he had been ready for this his whole life, hadn't he? *Of course he's embracing it.*

She was thrilled for him. She was scared for him. She was anxious about *them*. They had been bouncing along in their happy bubble, and she'd been blissfully unaware how his going pro would affect her or the relationship they'd built. Something colossal had just shifted, and she was running atop quicksand, afraid of sinking but afraid of what waited on solid ground beyond the quagmire where she couldn't see. Exactly where—and how—did she fit into Zach's new life?

"Hey, babe, are you done folding that shirt yet?" Zach reached out his hand, and she passed it to him. "You okay?"

"I don't know. I think I'm still in shock."

"You're shocked that they signed me? I thought my woman believed in me." He smirked. "Oh, ye of so little faith."

"That's not what I meant. I always thought you would make it into the NHL, but I didn't realize it was going to happen ... now." *And I'm not ready.*

He dropped the T-shirt on the bed and pulled her against his chest, wrapping her up in a warm hug. "It's gonna be fine. We're gonna be fine." He set her apart from him and peered at her. "In fact, I've been thinking. Once I get settled in a week or so, I want you to join me."

"You mean, as in move to St. Louis?" she squeaked. "Permanently?"

"Yes. They're putting me up in an apartment with a few of the boys, but we can find our own place so you don't have to live with a bunch of guys. Whatever you want. I can afford it."

"Zach, I want to finish my education."

He shrugged. "So finish it in St. Louis. It'll give you something to do while I'm on the road."

"But I have two more years to go on a four-year scholarship *here.*"

He held her head in his hands. "Did you not hear what I said? I'm making a fuck ton of money. I'll pay your tuition. I'll buy you food, clothes, a car—whatever the hell you want. Just say yes and move with me."

"Zach, this is important to me. It's a goal I worked hard for all through high school, and I need to see it through. I need to do it for *me.*"

His hands slid from her face abruptly, and he stepped away. When he spoke, his voice rose. "What about me? Doesn't what I want count?"

"Of course it counts! But it's ... I ..." she stammered, completely flummoxed. *How do I answer that?*

He puffed out a breath. “Never mind. That wasn’t a fair question. I just assumed that you’d jump at this chance. Guess I was wrong about how you feel.”

“You weren’t wrong about how I feel. I love you, but this move is a huge shift for both of us. So much can happen. Do I have to jump at this chance now? Do I lose it if I don’t say yes right away?”

He shook his head dejectedly. “No, of course you don’t lose the chance. I want you with me, whether it’s now or in two years.”

“And I want to be with you, but it’s not that long, especially if we see each other in between. I can fly out there, you can come here, we can spend the summer together. We can work it out so we’re with each other a lot. In the meantime, you can focus on your career, and I can concentrate on my studies.” She would miss him, but the time away from him might prove positive; he had become a huge distraction, and her bombing GPA proved it. Marty wasn’t the only one struggling with grades, and her scholarship set a high bar. She didn’t want to lose it.

“Fine.” Zach’s tone carried a bite, but he countered it immediately with a lopsided grin. “I guess I just want what I want when I want it.”

“I’ve known that about you since I met you,” she quipped.

“Can’t help it. It’s the way I’m wired.”

I’m afraid I know that too.

Chapter 8

So That's How the Other Half Lives

A month goes by

Marty exited St. Louis's Lambert Field, having just arrived on a flight paid for by Zach. His eye immediately caught on a sign with his name on it being held by a guy in a crisp suit. The dude stood in front of a shiny black Lincoln Town Car, also courtesy of Zach. His friend was pulling out all the stops for this quick visit, no doubt in an effort to impress him.

Well, he was definitely impressed.

After introducing himself to the limo driver, Marty climbed into the backseat, feeling a bit awkward about the luxury treatment. He couldn't recall ever being chauffeured before—unless it was by his mom.

The driver caught his eye in the rearview mirror. "My instructions are to take you straight to the arena."

"What do I do with my bag?" Marty had only brought a carry-on for his two-day visit with his best friend, but he didn't want to lug it into the arena with him.

"That's all been handled, Mr. LeBrun. After I drop you off, I will deliver your bag to one of the staff, who will make sure it finds its way into Mr. Pruitt's vehicle."

All righty, then. I guess the details have been attended to. Apparently, they did things a little differently in the bigs.

When the limo arrived at the players' entrance, a woman stepped from the shadows and greeted him. "I'll show you to your seat, Mr. LeBrun."

"You don't need to do that. I'm sure I can find my way. I've been to more than one arena in my life." He had meant it as a joke, but judging from the woman's expression, he'd completely missed the mark. So he kept his mouth shut and let her escort him to a prime rink-side seat at center ice. From there, Marty watched the game, his eyes especially riveted on Zach whenever he took the ice. The air held an electric quality when Zach had a shift, and Marty wasn't sure if it was only him or if the whole crowd felt the buzz. Whatever it was, Zach rose to the occasion and played out of his mind, scoring two goals and being selected first star of the game.

As first star, he executed a flashy pirouette on the ice before giving an interview to the lady reporter, with the crowd cheering him on in the background. In Zach fashion, he flashed a dimple-popping smile and waved at the fans still in the arena. He had obviously taken to his newfound celebrity, just as the fans had taken to him.

Marty went to the friends and families area, where he'd been instructed to meet Zach after the game. Zach walked out, dressed to the nines in an expensive-looking suit, laughing and joking with one of the veteran players who had been Marty's idol for years. Zach introduced them, and Marty kept his foolish fangirl inclinations in check. When he and Zach were finally alone in the parking lot, Marty let his excitement show. "Shit, I can't believe I just met Bob Cramer!"

"Yeah," Zach laughed, "I thought you were going to wet yourself."

"Because I was! Thank God I was too tongue-tied to ask the guy for his autograph."

"You want his autograph? I can get it for you."

"No, it was just a knee-jerk reaction." Zach strolled up to a sleek black BMW M3, and Marty gaped. "Whoa, this yours?"

"Yep."

Marty was sure his eyes were bugging out of his head, but he didn't care. The vehicle was gorgeous, and he flashed back to the many times he and Zach had sat around and dreamed about the kinds of cars they would buy once they got that big paycheck. Well, this was no longer a dream for Zach, and an all-too-familiar pang of envy jabbed Marty's chest.

"She's pretty sweet, isn't she?" Zach opened the back door and tossed his bag inside. Marty caught a glimpse of his own bag.

"I tried to buy Claudia a sweet 911 when she was here, but she pitched a fit, so I backed off." He guffawed. "She's so damn stubborn, but so am I. I'm going to buy her one anyway and surprise her with it."

They climbed into the vehicle, and Marty's eyes traveled around the luxurious interior.

"Hey, you can take her for a spin," Zach offered. "As long as you don't leave your mouth hanging open the whole time you're driving. I don't want drool on my seats."

"I think I can manage to keep my mouth shut, and yeah, I'd totally love to drive this baby."

Zach shot him a sidelong glance. "In the meantime, let's go enjoy some of St. Louis's nightlife." Zach had the day off tomorrow, which was one reason they had picked this particular time for Marty's visit. "There's this great sushi place I want to take you to. Claudia loved it when she came to visit, and we both thought you'd enjoy it."

"Sounds great."

"Have you seen her lately? How's she looking? She seemed a little skinny when she was here."

Zach's question jarred Marty out of his gawk-a-thon. *Skinny?* Claudia's curves, in Marty's opinion, were just right. "Other than being bummed out about Rex and Alice moving to Japan, she's doing great." She had been devastated when Rex had dropped the bombshell on her and Megan that he and Alice were going over there indefinitely to tutor English. But to Marty's delight, she had bestowed *him* with the "best guy friend" designation. He had one more year of school and plenty of opportunity to fill that role for her. Plus keep an eye on her—for Zach's sake, of course.

"Oh shit, that's right. I totally forgot about that," Zach said absently.

Marty darted him a curious look. He had been in the room when she'd told Zach the news over the phone, and she'd been in tears, nearly inconsolable. How could Zach forget her heartache? *He's been busy, dumbass.*

"She's signed up for next year's classes, and she's excited about that."

"That was this week? Forgot about that too, I guess." Zach shook his head. "Damn, I wish I could talk her into putting this school thing aside and coming to live with me. I just don't get it."

"This school thing." Marty and Zach had had this discussion before. In fact, Marty had had the same discussion with Claudia, and while he understood exactly where she was coming from, Zach seemed to be having trouble accepting her desire to keep going and earn her degree in education.

Marty let the subject drop, focusing instead on Zach's eye-popping performance since he had joined his new club.

"So for a rookie, you're killing it. Hell, you'd be killing it for a non-rookie! How has it been so far?"

Zach's posture behind the wheel was as relaxed as Marty had ever seen it. A permanent smile seemed to be etched on his face. "It's a gas, man. Better than I ever dreamed it could be. I'm having the time of my life."

When they pulled up to the restaurant, Zach flipped a valet his keys and a wad of bills.

The kid grinned and gave him a two-finger salute. "Thanks, Mr. Pruitt! Great game tonight."

Zach grunted in the kid's general direction.

Inside the restaurant, the hostess beamed at him. "Hello, Mr. Pruitt. We're so delighted to have you back. Would you like to sit at the bar or at your usual table?"

"The table would be great, sweetheart. Thanks." Zach winked at the girl, and she gave him a sly smile with a few extra eyelash flutters thrown in. To Marty, he said, "It's hard to eat at the bar sometimes.

Fans see you, and they want to talk to you, get your autograph. It's a parade of interruptions."

Wow. One short month, and he's got the world eating out of the palm of his hand.

They spent dinner talking about their favorite subject: hockey. The playoffs, the league's latest rules, the officiating, the goalies and their damn big pads, the new equipment hitting the market.

After they'd polished off so many platters of sushi Marty lost count, he leaned back and patted his stomach.

"That was fucking amazing. And so is all this." Marty swiveled his head and waved his hand in the air. "I'm in awe. You truly are living the dream."

Zach flashed him a knowing grin. "You can too, my friend."

"I'm not so sure. You've taken it to a whole new level, and you're having a ton of success. I'm still floundering in the NCAA."

"So what do you plan to do if no team picks you up by the time school's over next year?"

Marty pushed out a breath. "I don't know. Maybe try out for an AHL team?"

Zach poured the rest of their Kirin bomber into their glasses. "Why not put yourself out there as a free agent? Lots of college guys get picked up that way."

"No, they don't. And those that do are way better than I am. I may have a shit ton of passion for this game, but I don't have the skill set to match. I'm not sure I ever will." And there it was: Marty's biggest fear—that he would never be able to make a career of the game he loved more than his next breath.

"You keep talking like that, and you definitely won't make it. If I were you, I'd do everything possible to get myself noticed this upcoming year and see where that takes me because you are definitely good enough. And if no one came knocking on my door, I'd get my agent to set up some PTOs for me. If it comes to it, I'll see if the Titans will give you a look. Think how that would be, playing on the same team again ... in the bigs!"

Easy for Zach to say. Had he gone that route, teams would have been lining up to have him show up for a professional tryout. But, of course, guys with talent like his never *had* to go that route. "Well, if nothing else, I might make a good scout or—"

“Coach. The way you yap when we’re in the middle of the game, telling us what to do and what our assignments are, I think you have the chops to be a coach.”

The possibility had not occurred to Marty before. He gave a nonchalant shrug. “Maybe. Still, my first choice is to go big league and live high off the hog, like my best friend.”

Zach laughed. “In the meantime, you’re welcome to live vicariously through me.”

The rest of the evening became a blur of bars and clubs—and a whole lot of alcohol. Marty had no clue what time they staggered into Zach’s apartment. When he woke up the next morning, his head pounded, and his mouth felt like someone had stuffed cotton in it. He looked around the luxurious guest suite Zach had put him in and decided he needed to pound plenty of coffee, water, or both. He skinned on a pair of jeans and stumbled into the kitchen. Zach shared the apartment with a couple of his teammates, and Marty expected to see maybe one of them there. To his surprise, what he saw instead was a woman in little more than tiny shorts that exposed her ass cheeks and a tank top that revealed more than it hid.

She grinned at him. “Well, good morning to you. Where did you come from?”

He fought to keep his eyes on her pretty face and not let them stray to her high beams barely contained by the skimpy top. “I’m, uh, a friend of Zach’s.”

To his further surprise, she said, “You’re Marty. I’ve heard all about you.”

You have? So how come I haven’t heard about you? “I’m afraid you have me at a bit of a disadvantage.”

“Ooh, that sounds interesting. Is that like having you in a compromising position?” She sat down at the kitchen counter and cupped her chin in her palm, letting her eyes run all over him, stopping at his bare chest.

He crossed his arms. “Uh ...”

“I’m Trixie.”

Of course you are. “It’s nice to meet you, Trixie.”

“Zach never mentioned how cute you are.” Her eyes took another uncomfortable tour of his body.

“And who do we have here?” came a feminine voice behind him.

He spun, his eyes landing on another knockout who wasn't wearing much more than the first girl. *What the actual hell?*

Trixie inspected her nails. "This is Marty."

The woman who wasn't Trixie came up beside him and scraped long fingernails down his bare back. "Good morning, Marty. I was wondering if I would get to meet you."

"I saw him first, Brenda."

Brenda's mouth curled up as she continued running her nails up and down his back, seemingly ignoring Trixie. Marty quelled the shivers that wanted to speed through him, but he couldn't hide the goose bumps that erupted on his skin.

"I think he prefers blonds, Trixie, so why don't you make yourself scarce?"

Before Marty could counter with the thought running through his head—namely, that he wasn't enjoying these girls licking their chops like he was a piece of meat—Zach ambled into the kitchen, pulling the girls' attention to him. Like Marty, he was bare chested, and Trixie blatantly roamed her gaze over him before giving her lips a slow lick. "You're looking yummy today, Zach."

Zach yawned. "As usual, Trix. Maybe it's time for a new line, huh?" He jerked his chin at Marty. "Want to grab some breakfast? There's this great place down the street."

God, yes!

Brenda pouted. "Well, aren't you a party pooper."

Zach's eyes strafed her chest, and a slow grin spread over his face. "You can't always get what you want."

Trixie narrowed her eyes at him. "Are you quoting song lines now?"

Marty's head spun. Who the hell were these women, and why the hell were they in Zach's apartment dressed the way they were? "Yeah, just let me pull on a shirt—"

"Oh, what a shame to cover that." This came from Trixie.

"—and get some socks and shoes. Then I'm ready to go." *So ready.*

He was grateful to escape the twin vixens' examination, and when he and Zach sat down in a diner a block from Zach's apartment, Marty couldn't hold back what had been streaking through his mind.

"Who the hell are they?" *And I better not find out you spent the night with either of them, or I'm going to be obliged to kick your ass.*

Zach waited for the waitress to take their orders before answering Marty's burning question. "They're just a couple of girls who come around whenever the guys are home. And don't be surprised if a few others are there when we get back."

What? "Which guys?"

"My roommates, man. The girls sorta came with the place, kinda like the furniture. I'm not exactly sure what the arrangements are, but they float from bedroom to bedroom on the regular. They don't seem to be particular about *whose* bedroom, and they're very accommodating. I'm sure any—or all—of them would indulge you, even though you're not a pro. Or are you still seeing that waitress?"

The cavalier remark about Marty not being a "pro" stung. His mind then leapt to how Zach knew how "accommodating" the bunnies were. He fought to keep his voice even and not betray how hurt and how damn flabbergasted he was. "No, she left a few weeks ago, and that was a good time to end things. It was never going to go anywhere anyway."

"Same old story with you," Zach chuckled.

"What does *that* mean?" Marty's defenses were in full array.

"Nothing. Only that you hook up for a while, and things burn out. It's not a dig against you, bro."

The server clattered a few cups on their table and poured steaming coffee from a carafe. Marty pounced on the cup closest to him when the server left. "Thank fuck," he muttered.

Zach doctored his brew, then lifted his eyes to Marty's. "If you're worried I'm tapping any of that action, then don't. I don't partake. In fact, I find them a little annoying. They seem to be there all the time, eating our food and drinking our booze. I've been thinking I should get my own place, but then I circle back to Claudia staying in Boston, and I lose my motivation." He shrugged. "I don't know. Maybe when the season's over, I'll work on getting a nice place by myself where she'll want to stay."

Marty's knotted gut began to uncoil, and he took a sip of his coffee.

Zach gave him a salacious grin. "You're probably strung a little tight since your girl left. If you want to dip your wick, the boys won't mind, and I sure as shit won't hold you back."

"No, I'm good." Marty would hold *himself* back, with little trouble. "What did Claudia think of Trixie and Brenda when she came to see you?"

Zach gave him a hard stare. "Claudia doesn't know about them, and I'd like to keep it that way."

Marty scoffed. "How did she miss them? Didn't she stay with you when she visited?"

"Nah, we didn't stay there. I mean, I showed her the place when no one was around because she wanted to see where I live, but I got us a nice hotel room, and that's where we spent all our time."

The coils in Marty's stomach cinched tight once more. "So you could keep her from knowing about the bunnies?"

Hot plates of scrambled eggs, sausage, and hash browns arrived, and a wave of nausea rolled through Marty's stomach. He stared at his meal, unsure he could eat it.

Zach piled a forkful of food and shoveled it in his mouth, chewing for a few beats before he answered. "No, it was more to keep her away from my pervy roommates. I didn't need to see them eye-fucking her, and there's no doubt in my mind they would have—every chance they got." He pointed his fork at Marty's plate. "You gonna eat that?"

"Yeah, yeah. Just waiting for it to cool off." *A total lie.*

Zach finished off another bite. "Those pervy roommates of mine got me thinking."

"About?"

Laying his fork on the table, Zach leaned back and crossed his arms. "I think I'm going to ask Claudia to marry me."

Marty gripped his own fork to keep from dropping it. "Say what?"

"I've been giving it a lot of thought. I know you're looking out for her, but I don't want some asshole turning her head and stealing her away. Guys already hit on her all the time, and with her living thousands of miles away ..."

"Is this so you can get her to move here?"

"No, let's just say I don't want her to get away. I'm thinking we get engaged now and get married next summer when she's done with school. What do you think? Too soon? I want to lock her up, but I don't want to scare her."

Marty opened his mouth, but nothing came out.

"Yeah, I know," Zach chuckled. "When the thought hit me, it surprised the hell out of me too. Who'd have thought? But she's the one for me. I'm positive about that."

Marty sat paralyzed, unable to find words. Every single one of his circuits was blown. He felt as though a fist was wedged in his throat, but at last he choked out, "Congratulations, man. That's ... great news." Looking at his plate, he pushed it away. His appetite dissolved in the bile churning inside.

Chapter 9

THE PROMISE

Two months later

Claudia walked into the new apartment she shared with Megan and was greeted with a shrieking demand. "Lemme see! Lemme see!"

Behind Claudia, Marty cleared his throat. She spun, and he hoisted her bag a foot off the ground. "Where do you want me to put this?"

He had picked her up from the airport—at the gate, no less—claiming Zach had threatened him with bodily harm if he didn't. Claudia didn't believe him. Knowing Marty, a threat hadn't been necessary. He was always there, willing to help without being smothering about it, and she loved him for it. He was the perfect male bestie.

"Here is fine." She pointed to the rare space devoid of moving boxes.

Megan grabbed Claudia's hand and gasped. "Oh. My. God! Did Zach steal the crown jewels? This thing is huge! How do you hold up your hand?"

"I was wondering the same thing." Marty's voice was dry as he deposited her bag.

Claudia laughed. "You know Zach. Nothing but the biggest will do."

"Well, this is definitely the biggest diamond I've ever seen," Megan chuckled.

Claudia dismissed the blush creeping into her cheeks. "It is beautiful, but it's definitely on the clunky side. It'll come in handy if someone tries to mug me, though. I'll just hit him with it and probably knock him out in the process."

"So it's a weapon and a source of light," Megan quipped. "I think I'm gonna need my sunglasses to look at it."

Claudia extended her hand and stared at the ridiculously large pear-shaped diamond. "Yeah, I'll wear the bling this summer when I'm with Zach, but I plan to lock it up when school starts this fall. I don't want to be a target." She pointed first at Marty, then at Megan. "And you guys are sworn to secrecy. No telling Zach I'm not wearing it twenty-four-seven."

Meg mimed locking her mouth with an invisible key and throwing it away. Marty merely stood in place, hands in his pockets.

Claudia narrowed her eyes at him. "Do I have your word?"

He nodded, but something unreadable passed through his eyes.

"Thanks again for the ride. Will you stay for a bit?"

"Yes, Marty," Megan chirped. "Why don't you hang out with us for a while? You can help us unpack, and I'll fix you something really special after." The hopeful look in her eyes was unmistakable. Megan was still angling to get Marty into bed despite having an excess of guys buzzing around her.

In typical Marty fashion, he didn't acknowledge Meg's pointed offer, glancing at his watch instead. "No, I need to get going. Game starts at seven, and I still need to get home and pick up my gear."

"When do Megan and I get to come watch one of your games?" Claudia wiggled her eyebrows. Marty had joined a men's league—affectionately known as a beer league—for the summer, which he somehow fit into his work schedule at the restoration company. He had only begun playing the previous week, and she looked forward to watching his games. Zach, in the meantime, was healing after a deep run in the playoffs *and* moving stuff into his new apartment.

He and Claudia would share it when she eventually moved to St. Louis permanently and during her visits between now and then. He had picked a gorgeous penthouse in the same building where he'd been living with the teammates she'd never met. In two weeks, she would return to St. Louis to fix up the apartment and explore the city with him for the rest of the summer. And she couldn't wait.

"Oh, anytime you need a good laugh, just stop on by." A smirk sprouted on Marty's clean-shaven face.

As he turned to go, Megan rushed toward him with a devilish smile. "Hey, I'm around all summer if you want to get together sometime. I'm even willing to take CC's place as your jogging partner."

"I'll remember that." A quick escape through the door, and he was gone.

Megan closed the door behind him, sagging against it as she faced Claudia. "Did that sound too desperate?"

Claudia pinched her thumb and finger together. "Maybe just a teeny-tiny bit."

"Oh well, you can't blame a girl for trying." Puffing out a resigned sigh, Megan picked up Claudia's hand once again and inspected the ring. "Yowser. Hard to say no with this thing blinding you."

Claudia frowned. "Are you saying I'm blind? I should have turned him down?"

Megan leveled her gaze at Claudia. "Not exactly, though this engagement seems uncharacteristically sudden for you."

"Considering I've never been engaged before, I'm not sure how you can say that." While Claudia's tone was bland, it harbored a modicum of irritation.

"You know what I mean. You tend to be the cautious type who weighs decisions carefully. In my humble opinion, whether or not to marry someone tops the list of life's *most* important decisions."

"You don't approve."

Meg pursed her lips. "I didn't say that. I just want to be sure my best friend is making the right move." She pushed herself from the door and strolled to the kitchen, where she pulled two mismatched ceramic mugs from a box and filled them with chilled chardonnay. "Let's toast to you getting engaged and me being your maid of honor."

Claudia dismissed the tiny tendrils of doubt sparked by Meg's comments. "Ooh, you're going all out with the fancy crystal, I see."

They clinked their cups and drank. Megan set her drink on the counter littered with packing materials and crossed her arms. "So tell me about the proposal. Did you accept right away?"

"It was a simple proposal, just the two of us in a luxury hotel suite he had rented for the occasion. I admit I was a little shocked, but I didn't need to think about it before I said yes." So many things had rushed through her brain when he had casually popped the question. Some of those thoughts probably hadn't belonged there, like: Would he be crushed if she said no? Was seven months long enough to know if they were a lifelong match? Even now, those questions buzzed through her head inconveniently, and she found herself constantly corralling them and putting them aside.

Megan lifted her cup to her lips for another sip and looked at Claudia thoughtfully over the rim. "So exactly when did you know he was the one for you?"

"I'm not sure I can put my finger on a precise moment. Things have been building between us for a while, and maybe his move got them moving a little faster. Getting married wasn't anything I was focused on. I hadn't really thought about it, to be honest. It was similar to how we ended up together. It just sort of happened. I was having fun, and then poof! I was in a serious relationship, and then I was getting married."

"It's the virgin effect."

"What's the 'virgin effect'?"

"It's where you pledge your eternal devotion to the guy you gave your virginity to." Meg laced her fingers under her chin and batted her eyelids dramatically.

Claudia hmphed in response.

"Aren't you at all curious about seeing what it's like with other guys before settling on just one?"

"Absolutely not." *I'm not you, Megan.*

"Not even a teeny-tiny bit?"

Claudia felt her rising defenses locking down. Where was Megan going with this? "Why are you asking me all these questions? Why would I be marrying him if I didn't want to spend the rest of my life with him?"

Megan gave her a small smile. "I just ... You know I love you, and I want you to be happy."

"But I am happy! What makes you think I'm not?"

"Nothing. I just want to be sure you know what you're doing, that you've thought it through. It's a lifetime, and you're both so young—"

"Everyone keeps saying that!"

Megan's eyebrows knotted together. "Like who?"

Claudia gusted out an exasperated sigh. "Like Mama, for one." Sheepishness heated her cheeks. "She was not pleased when I told her the news. I get it, we're young. I'll be twenty-two and he'll be twenty-three when we get married next August, but we want to get started with our lives and build a family. Besides, with all the attention he's getting, I don't want someone else to snap him up." She had promised to marry him. It was the right thing to do. Besides, who wouldn't want to marry a hot, fun pro athlete who lavished her in love and luxury? She would have been crazy to pass up the chance.

"Is that the real reason? You're afraid of the competition?"

"God, you're annoying sometimes, you know that?"

Megan grinned. "That's what best friends are for."

Claudia drained her wine and handed her cup back to Megan. Myriad thoughts sped through her brain, vying for attention. "When I was there, he treated me like a queen. He went all out, pulled out all the stops. He took me to all kinds of elegant places, overspent on me, and introduced me to everyone." Add to that list him dropping a lot of money on clothing and jewelry for her, and he had swept her off her feet.

Megan's eyes widened. "You finally met his roommates?"

And now they were broaching a touchy subject. Zach had been reluctant to introduce her to his roommates. "No, but like I've told you before, he said they're rude and crude, and he didn't want to expose me to that. It's one of the reasons he wanted to move into his own—our own—place." Claudia drew in a steadying breath. "Look, I know Zach's a little wild right now. He'll settle down. You'll see." *God, I hope he does.* He had gained a little more swagger in his step since breaking into the NHL, but wasn't that to be expected with the constant attention he had received as an overachieving rookie? The excitement would wear off, and he would settle in. Eventually, he would tune out all the babble.

"Do you hear yourself?" Megan chuffed. "You're caught in the classic, 'I'll tame him.' Think about it, Claudia." Megan reached over and rapped Claudia on the forehead.

Claudia swatted her hand away. "Ow! I don't *have* to think about it. I'm fine with him just the way he is. I accept him, warts and all."

Megan smirked. "You mean muscles and all." She then closed the distance between them and engulfed Claudia in a hug. "I'm sorry. I didn't mean to be a buzzkill. Can I still be your maid of honor?"

Claudia leaned into her embrace and sighed. "Of course. You're my best friend, and I wouldn't have it any other way."

After reassuring Megan, Claudia spent a few inner moments reassuring herself.

I'll be there to guide Zach as he grows up and becomes steadier, like Marty.

Whoa, what am I saying?

She loved Zach. He loved her. He needed her; he'd even admitted it. Everything would work out.

A few mornings later, Marty was enjoying one of his last jogs of the summer with Claudia. While she'd been off getting engaged to Zach last week, he'd missed her more than he could have imagined. The prospect of not having her company until September stabbed at something deep inside he couldn't—and didn't want to—identify. Unsurprisingly, he had been torn over the news of their engagement. It had set off all those uncomfortable, polarized emotions again ... not that it had been news. Zach had told him he was going to pop the question and had, in fact, dragged Marty along with him to select the ring during Marty's last visit.

Small consolation, but Marty had been right. The ring was way too big for her small hand, but Zach hadn't listened. "I want something that'll tell everyone she's taken," he'd insisted.

"No one will see it because they'll be blind," Marty had tossed back at him. The usual "Fuck you" had followed, and Zach had bought the huge-ass ring anyway. Did she even like it? She hadn't had a say in the size or the style.

Not how I would have done it. Of course, the only ring he could have afforded would have been a plastic one from a bubblegum machine.

"So what do your mom and aunt think of the engagement?" he ventured.

Claudia pulled a face. "I'm not sure Mama likes him."

"Why not?"

"Because he didn't ask her for my hand. Stupid, huh?"

His lips quirked. "I get that. Makes total sense."

"You do? It's kinda old-fashioned, if you ask me."

"Nothing wrong with old-fashioned." He side-eyed her as she kept pace beside him. Her ponytail was longer now, and it swished in time to their steps. "Are you growing your hair out?"

Absently, she reached for the ponytail and gave it a tug. "As a matter of fact, I am. Zach says he likes long hair." She shot Marty an embarrassed look.

"No need to look sheepish on my account. I think it's nice that you pay attention to what he likes and are willing to do that for him." *And speaking of paying attention to what your significant other likes ...* "What do you think of the ring?"

Claudia held her hand in front of her and stared at the two-plus-carat diamond on her left ring finger. The rock reached her knuckle.

"I think he went a little overboard. Please don't tell him, but I would've been happier with something smaller and a lot less showy. Did you know about this?"

"I saw it coming."

They ran on, quiet except for their panting breaths. As they rounded a bend in the circuit, Claudia broke the silence. "There's something that's been bothering me. I'm not sure if it's because Meg keeps nagging me about it or what, but it's about Zach's roommates."

Uh-oh. "What about his roommates?" *Please don't ask me for any details about what goes on at that place.*

When Marty had last stayed with Zach, the revolving door of jersey chasers had been even more eye-popping than during his first visit. More troublesome had been the level of flirting exchanged between Zach and the girls. And damn Zach had been mostly shirtless when they were around. On purpose. Marty suspected it had to do with the level of attention he got over his abs and his pecs—which he seemed to enjoy *way* too much—but when he had pressed Zach about it, Zach had once more insisted he hadn't touched any of them and that the attention was just part of the "pro perks package." Then he had accused Marty of being jealous and told him to mind his own fucking business. So Marty had.

Now Marty's internal conflict was once again rearing up on its hind legs, and he wrestled with the notion of being completely honest with Claudia. Should he tell her? What if it wrecked her and Zach's relationship? Zach denied sleeping with any of the girls, and Marty believed him. Besides, he had no proof beyond what he'd observed, which was mostly harmless. Flirting did not translate into infidelity. And there was the question of Marty's own motivation: Was it pure? After all, he was in love with Claudia himself, a fact he kept hidden from view ... sometimes from even himself.

She puffed out a breath, yanking him back to the running track. "I hardly ever saw his place, and I never did meet the roommates, which seemed odd. Like he was trying to hide something."

"Did you ask Zach about it?"

"Yes. He says he just wants to keep me away from them because they're a bunch of slobs. Have you met them? What are they like?"

"I've met them, but we haven't hung out. They strike me as typical hockey players, interested in the kind of crap hockey players are interested in." *The game, partying, women ...*

"Oh well," she laughed. "I'm probably just being paranoid, and Megan's suspicious mind doesn't help. I'm not sure I would have even thought about it if she hadn't planted the seed."

"That's probably true."

A lump formed in his chest. Unlike the secret he harbored about her ring, the activity in the apartment was a veritable can of worms, and if she found out what he knew, he would likely lose her trust and her friendship. Then again, the likelihood of her finding out—especially now that she and Zach had their own place—was minimal, which left him in the clear. If only that soothed his conscience. Her next comment didn't help.

"You do know that besides Megan, you're my best friend, right?"

He tried not to squirm. “I do. Do I lose my place when Rex returns?”

She shook her head. “No. Rex isn’t coming home till next year. Besides, though he and I have known each other a long time, he and I weren’t as close as you and me.” She turned to him and smiled. “You might have ousted him as number one even if he’d stuck around.”

Well, shit.

Eyes forward once more, she said, “Did Zach tell you he might get a shampoo endorsement?”

“In addition to the endorsements for hockey gear?”

“Uh-huh. Also, some company’s trying to hire him to do a shaving cream commercial.”

Marty didn’t mask his surprise. “No, haven’t heard any of this.”

“I swear, everything he touches right now is golden. Must be his boyish charm and good looks.” She guffawed. “He’s even getting attention from rock stars. The Fleet Fighters gave him a shoutout on their most recent tour, and some members of The Barge have been attending games and talking about how much they love his play. They even sang some off-the-cuff ditty about wanting to be like Zach Pruitt. I’m trying to get my hands on a copy.”

Whoa! The Fleet Fighters were a wildly successful American grunge band, and The Barge was a popular rock band from St. Louis. Holy hell, his best friend had really arrived, and at head-spinning speed.

They finished their run and went into their post-run stretching routine. Claudia gave him a tentative smile. “Can I ask you something?”

He rolled his eyes. “I hate it when you start out like that because you’re going to ask me to do something I don’t want to.”

She placed her hands on her hips. “Well, geez. It isn’t that bad. Besides, it should be something you *want* to do.”

“All right. Hit me with it.”

Casting her eyes down, she started in a small voice, signaling this was serious. “I know you and Zach have been best buddies forever, but I consider you a best buddy too. I would want my best buddy to tell me if my boyfriend was two-timing me, and I’d like to believe you would.”

Marty stopped stretching to gape at her. "You don't seriously think—" *Shit. Maybe she* does *know about the ladies lounging at the apartment.*

"No, I trust him, but he's Zach, and he's getting the kind of attention that could make him ..." She paused to chew on her bottom lip.

"What?" he prodded gently.

Her eyes locked on his. "I worry his head will get too big, and he'll lose sight of the important things. I'm not stupid. He's always drawn women to him like paper clips to a magnet, and now that he's a celebrity ... temptation is everywhere. He definitely eats it up, loves the lifestyle, so I can't help but wonder what else he might take advantage of."

Shock, with a generous dose of guilt, roiled inside Marty. He gathered his wits. "Well, stop wondering, because you have nothing to worry about."

She pulled in a big breath. "You would tell me if he strayed, wouldn't you?"

The look on her face—so trusting, so damn innocent—gutted him. "Of course I would, but honestly, Claudia, you're concerned over nothing."

"You're probably right. I mean, I do trust him." She gave him a warm smile that had the ability to wrangle anything from him. "Nevertheless, I'd like that promise."

"Then you have my promise."

If there is a God, please, please never make me have to live up to that promise.

Chapter 10

THE HIGH LIFE

Seven months later

With the holidays over and spring semester still a few weeks away, Marty was looking forward to focusing solely on BC Eagles hockey before his academic surge to the finish line and the team's push toward the playoffs commandeered all his attention. He had just finished cleaning up after hockey practice when, to his surprise, his coach stuck his head in the locker room and asked Marty to stop by. Questions running on his mind's racetrack, Marty entered Coach's office, closed the door, and sat when Coach instructed him to.

"So how's it looking for you? Any sniffs from the NHL? Has your agent put out any feelers?"

Marty's "agent," who was technically an uncompensated agent-slash-adviser—per NCAA rules—had worked her ass off trying to get an NHL team's attention without much to show for it.

"Nothing so far." Marty tried to keep the dejection out of his tone.

Steepling his fingers, Coach leaned back in his chair. "Have you considered the AHL? ECHL? CHL?"

Marty shook his head. "Haven't gone that route."

"Why not?"

Marty gave him a mirthless smile. "I guess some part of me feels like I'm admitting I'm not good enough for the NHL if I do."

Coach leveled his gaze at Marty's. "I'm not going to sugarcoat this for you, son. I'm not sure you *are* good enough for the NHL, and I'm not knocking your work ethic or your passion. Those are both strong. I do believe you have a chance and could make a nice career for yourself in the AHL, though. And let's not forget the AHL can be a gateway into the NHL."

The AHL held way more appeal than either of the other two leagues. The AHL was the highest league in North America right after the NHL, while the others ranked a tier or two below. The pay reflected those differences.

Marty nodded. Where was his coach going with this?

As if the man had read his mind, he continued. "The reason I ask is I have a few friends who coach AHL teams, and I've been talking to them about you. Ever heard of the Springfield Falcons? Or the Rockford Ice Hogs?"

Marty sat up a little straighter. "Yeah, of course I have."

"Well, if you can get your butt on a plane, I can arrange a meeting between you and the Ice Hogs head coach this week. The coach for the Falcons would like to see you next week, but first I have to know if you're on board."

Marty's thoughts scattered in myriad directions, from what airlines flew to Rockford to how soon he could get laundry done to whether his lone suit was decent enough to wear. "I think I can arrange that."

Coach slapped his desktop. "Good. Make your arrangements and give me the details. I'll set up the rest."

Marty remained glued to his seat until his coach arched an eyebrow at him. "Thanks, Coach. Is that it?"

"Is that not enough?" One corner of the man's mouth twitched as though he fought a smile.

"More than enough, sir," Marty blurted. "Thank you for the chance." As the magnitude of the meeting dawned on him, excitement percolated in his bloodstream.

"I'm glad you're willing to consider this possibility. Every NHL team needs muckers and grinders, but if they can't see you play, they'll never know about your two-hundred-foot game."

Marty left Coach's office striding a few inches off the ground. Maybe he should have been let down that the truth had been hung out there for all to see: he would never be more than a bottom-six player. But somehow he couldn't muster the disappointment. He would take this chance and run with it.

After gathering up his gear, he strode to his Honda. The first person he wanted to tell was Claudia, knowing how excited she would be for him. She was, bar none, his most enthusiastic fan, cheering for him at all his home games—sometimes she even made the road trip to away games, if they were close enough. But Claudia was in St. Louis with Zach for Christmas break.

So he called Zach instead. "Looks like I'm going to have a sit-down with the Ice Hogs coach in Rockford, Illinois, in a few days."

"No shit? I'll be playing the Blackhawks in Chicago in a few days! How about you rent a car—I'll pay for it–and drive down so we can get together? I'll even throw in a ticket to the game! What do you say? It's been too fucking long, man."

In the background, Claudia's voice rang out. "Go, Marty, go!" Apparently, she had been listening in.

Her cheer made him bust out a smile. This opportunity was becoming more promising by the second.

"This is my favorite bar in Chicago." Zach grinned as he held the door open for Marty.

Two days had sped past since Marty's meeting with Coach, and it seemed like decades ago. He'd traveled from Boston to Rockford to Chicago, where he had just taken in a playoff-style game between two powerhouse NHL teams. And though the Titans had dropped the contest to the Blackhawks, they had put on a wildly entertaining spectacle that showcased Zach's talents. Marty was happy for his buddy.

As they stood just inside the door, Marty's eyes adjusted to the gloom.

Zach pulled off his cashmere coat and tucked a silk scarf into its pocket. "I want to hear all about your meeting with the Ice Hogs."

Marty unencumbered himself from his Michelin Man down coat, a gift from his mother three Christmases ago. He'd grown since then, and he wrestled the too-tight coat from his torso. "Not a whole lot to tell, and I'm reserving judgment until I sit down with the Springfield Falcons next week. If it comes down to a choice between the two teams, I prefer the Falcons. They're closer to Boston, and if I get called up, they're the farm team for Arizona. I would *love* a chance to visit the desert, *especially* in the middle of a Massachusetts winter."

"Yeah, but Illinois is closer to Michigan. Don't you want to be closer to family?"

"Not with Dickhead in the picture. Besides, Massachusetts is home now. I think it would be a more comfortable fit overall."

A waitress in a skimpy outfit approached, her heavy-lashed eyes riveted on Zach. "Hey, sugar. It's been way too long since I last saw you." She gave him a flirty smile.

"Well, I'm about to fix that now," he said smoothly. "Where's your section, Crystal?" She pointed to an area at the back of the bar. "Perfect. Now I know I'll get the best service in the house." He matched her sly smile.

"Don't you always, sugar? You know I aim to please."

"And so you do, sweetheart. So you do. Bring two of the usual for me and my friend, okay? And this is on my tab." He sent her a wink before leading Marty back to a vacant table.

They sat down, with Zach taking a seat that placed his back against the wall.

Marty looked around. "What—besides Crystal—makes this your favorite watering hole in Chicago?"

"It's a favorite hangout for visiting athletes. That fact draws the most spectacular eye candy in the city, and with the abundance of women on the hunt for the next notch on their bedpost, the ratio of women to men definitely tips the scales for the dudes. Plus, as you just saw, the service is top grade."

Marty blinked, reining in the urge to ask Zach exactly what kind of service he had in mind. "Since when is that type of ratio important to you?"

"I'm not talking about me, my man. I'm thinking of *you*." He reached over and playfully whacked Marty's arm, then sat back with a smirk. "Although I do enjoy looking." His head swiveled to a TV that hung above their table. "Just like I enjoy looking at that." He pointed upward, where his face filled the screen. He was in his Titans away jersey, sweat pouring down his face as he spoke into a mic wavering below his chin. "They're having me do a lot more postgame interviews." He grinned, and his eyes followed the closed-circuit lettering crawling at the bottom of the picture. "I think I do a pretty good job, which is probably why they keep throwing me out there to talk to the reporters. People can't get enough of the new guy."

Marty frowned. "You're not exactly the 'new guy' anymore."

Zach turned his head back toward him and narrowed his gaze. "What difference does that make? My city sure thinks I am. So does the rest of the country, for that matter. Just ask the hundreds of sports talking heads clawing for a chance to interview me."

Marty let his disgust bubble to the surface. "Is this the part where I throw up, or is this the part where you tell me this is an act and you're not really as full of yourself as you sound?"

Zach threw his head back and laughed. "You don't seem to understand that you're out having drinks with a celebrity phenom."

"You're right. I don't," Marty replied dryly.

"Nothing like my bro to bring me back to earth if I float too high." He slapped the top of the table "Fuck, I've missed you. And I am, in fact, pulling your leg."

Crystal delivered their drinks, along with an eyeful of cleavage aimed in Zach's direction. He rewarded her obvious display with five twenties and a wink. "Looking awfully good tonight, Crystal." He leaned to her ear and loudly whispered, "Good enough to eat." He wiggled his eyebrows suggestively, and she shimmied in response, pushing her boobs so close together Marty thought they might spill out of her uniform. With a tee-hee and a twirl, she walked away, her hips swaying dramatically above her high heels. Zach's eyes followed her the whole way. "See what I mean about the eye candy? And she's just staff!" He waved a hand around the room. "Have a look. They smell blood, and they're coming in thick."

Marty glanced over his shoulder. Sure enough, the place was jammed with mostly short-skirted, high-heeled, twenty-something knockouts. "Guess you're right."

Zach held up his drink. "To friendship, something that can't be bought."

Marty raised his glass, clinked it against Zach's, and took a sip. His eyes popped wide. "What is this?"

"Pretty fucking good, am I right? Unlike friendship, excellent whiskey *can* be bought."

Marty savored the smooth, smoky burn that glided down his throat. "I don't think I've ever tasted anything even *close* to this good before. What brand is it?"

Zach waved a dismissive hand. "Something called Glenmorangie. Enjoy, my friend. And after this, we're indulging in the best steak around before we hit the hottest clubs in town, where you will see the hottest women Chicago has to offer."

Marty took another sip before setting his whiskey down. "Don't you need to be on a plane early tomorrow?"

"Nah, not until ten."

"You do this a lot? Party late after game night?"

Zach pointed at his chest. "This twenty-two-year-old body can take it, and I'll keep doing it until it can't."

As if to drive his point home, Zach took him to so many nightclubs after their steak dinner Marty lost count. He also lost count of the time and how many drinks he and Zach tossed back. Fortunately, Zach had hired a limo to drive them from one hot spot to another, and after closing down the last club at 4:00 a.m., they piled into the car that sped them through Chicago's deserted streets.

Marty's head rested against a window, and as he took in the cityscape beyond, his mind meandered to what it might be like to enjoy this kind of luxury on a permanent basis. The finest clothes, high-end restaurants, best nightclubs, top-shelf liquor, most beautiful women, and a ride home in a limo at the end of the night. He would likely never know. While he might be good enough to earn a spot on an AHL team where the pay was decent—but not even a tenth of what Zach made—it would never afford him this sort of extravagance. And maybe that was okay.

Vague recollections of dancing amid pulsing groups of young women floated pleasantly through his brain, shifting from one dance floor to the next. He recalled kissing more than a few, putting his hands in places maybe he ought not have—though he'd been invited to do just that and more—but he hadn't crossed the line. The overwhelming temptation had been beyond challenging to put aside, though. He found himself puzzling over how Zach managed to control his impulses night after night, given the nature of his lifestyle and his personality. Zach relished indulging, and he had the bank account to match ... and women noticed.

His friend stirred on the opposite side of the bench seat. "Fuck, I miss my woman!"

Probably because you had too many bumping and grinding around you tonight and your dick was paying attention. Judging from Marty's observations, Zach had mostly behaved himself. *As it should be. Don't want to have to keep something like that from Claudia. She's my best friend,* he thought drowsily.

"You'll see her in a few days after your road trip, bro," Marty pointed out logically.

"Want her *now*!" Zach turned a bleary-eyed stare on Marty. "I'm going to get that girl pregnant right away. I want her to have my babies. Lots of them."

The comment startled Marty out of his drunken haze. "You're not going to wait?"

"No. Nothing welds a woman to you like having your kid," Zach slurred. "Or so I've heard."

"You want her *welded* to you," Marty repeated. "You think she won't stick around otherwise?"

"No, she's faithful, dude. Loyal and true. I think."

"What do you mean, you *think*?"

"I don't know, man. Sometimes I have inappropriate thoughts about other women, and I wonder if she has the same about other guys." With that, Zach slumped against the window and began snoring.

Marty's alcohol-soaked brain couldn't process. Soon he too slumped against the window and closed his eyes.

"Are we going out after your game tonight?" It was a dreary, frigid Friday as Claudia strained to lift weights beside Marty in the gym. Over two weeks ago, he had flown to Illinois to meet with a team. He and Zach had gotten together in Chicago afterward, but Zach had had little to say about the encounter. "We had a few drinks, a steak dinner, and called it a night." Marty had been equally uninformative, and Claudia hadn't pushed. The Ice Hogs hadn't followed up, and neither had the Falcons. Since then, Marty seemed adrift, aloof. She didn't know how to reach him other than to go on being his friend.

He slid her a sidelong glance. "You're doing it wrong again." He put down his own free weights, stood, and took up position in front of her, removing the dumbbells from her hands. "You're not watching your form in the mirror. You hold them like this." He demonstrated.

She rolled her eyes at him. "That's what I was doing!"

"No, it wasn't. Here." He handed the weights back and stood behind her, so close she could feel the heat radiating off his body, and placed his hands on her hips. Their eyes caught in the mirror. "Keep your hips straight, like this. You're flopping forward. Now lift. No, not like that. Like—that's it. See how different that feels?"

No, I don't, she wanted to shout. But he was doing her a favor, helping her get toned for the strapless wedding dress she pictured herself in a summer from now, and she didn't want to irritate him more than she already had.

She pumped her arms a few times while he stood to the side and watched. He nodded approvingly. "Much better. I don't know why you think you need to do this, though. You're in great shape already. Besides, you have over a year to go. Eat the bonbons now while you can."

"Haha, very funny. And I'm doing this because my arms are flabby," she huffed.

"No, they're not. You're per—you look fine the way you are."

"You're just saying that because you don't like me working out with you. I know I'm a pain in the ass ... which is why I need to know if we're going out tonight. I want to buy you dinner to thank you." She grinned at him in the mirror.

"Maybe. I don't know. I might have a date."

"Oh. I didn't know you were seeing someone."

"Why did you stop lifting? Keep going. As for the date, I'm not exactly seeing someone. It's just a possible last-minute thing."

"Oh. Well, she could come with us."

He smirked. "And have her meet Megan? No, thanks."

"Meg will behave."

"Last time you said that she hung on my neck and stuck her tongue in my ear all night. Not only did I get swimmer's ear, but it scared off every girl within a mile."

"She was protecting you."

"Right," he snorted. "That kind of protection I don't need. It's tough enough getting anyone to go out with me when I've got nothing going for me."

She couldn't picture it. Girls she barely knew were constantly approaching her about meeting that "good-looking, dark-haired hockey player" she hung out with. "I don't believe you, Marty LeBrun. You have *plenty* to offer. You're just fishing for compliments."

He racked his weights. "I don't make any money, and my future prospects are slim. Girls go for the flashy guys with money. This is a well-known fact."

She dropped her arms. "You're talking about Zach."

His eyes widened in the reflection. "That's not what I meant."

Putting the dumbbells down, she grabbed a towel and dabbed at her neck while he stood stock-still, staring at her. She straddled the weight bench and passed him the towel. "Then what did you mean?"

"Nothing. I guess I'm just sour grapes because I may be playing my last competitive hockey game ever at the end of this season." He tossed the towel onto the floor.

"It's really eating at you, huh?"

"Yep."

"Then let's go out tonight and have some fun. Just you and me. Unless your date comes through and you want to get lucky, of course." She wiggled her eyebrows, eliciting a twitch of his lips, which warmed her all over. She loved that she had the power to pull him from a mood.

"Going out with you *is* getting lucky."

"Aw, that's so sweet. But don't tell Zach. He'll take it the wrong way."

He nodded. "Our secret."

"Promise?"

"Cross my heart and hope to die."

Chapter 11

Times Are A-Changin'

Six weeks pass

The BC Eagles' season was done. Finished. And so was Marty's career as a hockey player. He thought this team might eke its way into the Frozen Four, but they had been eliminated. Again.

The time had come to remove his gear, pack up his locker, and finish his good-byes, but he was dragging his feet as though his skates were filled with a hundred pounds of ice.

He rummaged around in his hockey bag absently, not paying attention to what he was doing, and noticed a handwritten "While You Were Out" message tucked under a corner of the bag. Stepping into the weight room for privacy—he didn't need to worry about the din because losing dressing rooms were as noiseless as a graveyard—he dialed the number on the pink slip and held his breath.

One short conversation, and his world went from being in the crapper to bumping along in the clouds. And the first person he thought to call? Claudia.

He dialed her number, and relief flooded him when she picked up on the second ring. "Hi, CC."

"Hey there, Smarty Marty. Are you going to let me take you out and cheer you up tonight? Just you and me. Meg's out on a date. I can be outside Kelley Rink in a jiff." Her voice sounded tentative.

"You don't need to cheer me up. But you can come celebrate with me. And *I'm* buying." He couldn't keep the grin from his voice.

"What are we celebrating?" she said in a breathless rush.

"The Falcons want to sign me."

"What? Are you kidding me? Omigod! That's fantastic!" She shrieked the last word.

He laughed. *That's my girl ... who's not my girl.* "I'm not kidding, and you're not getting another word out of me until I'm done here."

"Then hurry up already! Why are you talking to me on the phone?"

"My question exactly."

Before returning to the locker room, he owed Coach a visit, so he walked down the hall and tapped on the door. Coach invited him in, his voice as low as Marty could remember. He craned his head around the door. "Coach, I—"

"Well, there's a bright spot!" Coach had been leaning back in his chair, feet propped on his desk, but he vaulted upright when he laid eyes on Marty. "I just heard the news. Congratulations, son!" He clapped him on the back and gave him an awkward half hug.

"Thanks, Coach. I couldn't have done it without your help."

"I disagree. You've got more going for you than most young men your age I know. And LeBrun?" He cocked an eyebrow.

"Yes, sir?"

"If things don't work out for you in the minors, give some thought to coaching. Leagues at every level need good, young coaches." With that, he gave Marty's shoulder one last pat.

Huh. That's the second time I've heard that.

An hour later, Marty was cozied up at a table with Claudia in a corner at the Pint Pot. The place was hopping—no one seemed to be mourning the Eagles' loss, including the smattering of players who were present—and Marty had to lean in close every time he and Claudia spoke. Yeah, that wasn't so terrible. Never mind the cloud of perfume he continually inhaled that left him dizzy. *The very best smell.*

"Do your mom and sisters know?" Her breath feathered his ear, and chills shot up his spine.

He nodded. "Called Dani a little while ago and got to talk to Alexis too. I think they're going to come stay with me for a while this summer after I get settled."

"How soon do you think that'll be?"

"I'm not sure yet. I'm checking out some clinics Coach recommended. I want to spend the summer getting in shape for training camp, but I also have to find a place to live and a temporary job. I might just give the girls keys and let them stay without me there. Shit. First I have to graduate."

"You'll graduate. I'd like to help out with the girls, although I'll be in St. Louis most of the time. I can check on them when I'm in Salem visiting Mom and Aunt Bev." She laid her small hand on his forearm, and a spiderweb of sensation warmed his skin. "You're really worried about the situation at home, huh?"

"Yeah." His mom hadn't been around when he called, not that she would have talked to him anyway. Danielle said she had been off with *Dick* somewhere the last few days, which had been a relief for Dani and Lexi. The situation sounded toxic, and it rubbed him sandpaper raw.

"I'm sure you'll get it all worked out. You're so good that way. In the meantime, though, they must be so excited for you!"

"Almost as excited as you," he chuckled.

"Have you told Zach yet?"

"Not yet." *Although I'm not sure why.*

"Hmm. Probably because he's focused on the playoffs, and he doesn't see or hear anything else."

He pulled back and grinned at her. "How do you do that?"

"What?"

"Read my mind. I was just wondering why I hadn't told him yet."

She smirked. "I know everything that lurks in your mind."

He scanned her lovely face. *Not everything.*

"I'm sure he'll be happy for you." Biting her lower lip, she cast her eyes down before raising them back to his. Brown and luminous and beautiful. "Speaking of Zach ... do you think he's changed?" The shift in her demeanor—from teasing to troubled—was breathtaking.

"Maybe." He let out a long exhale. "Sometimes I wonder if he's letting himself get carried away with all this newfound fame."

She tilted her head. "Like how?"

"Just some of the stuff I hear him say. When he's talking about how everyone wants to interview him or—"

"But everyone *does* want to interview him. He's not bragging. He's just stating the truth." She straightened, pulling herself upright.

Uh-oh. The hackles in her voice told him not to push it. Obviously, she wasn't looking for an honest answer—she wanted reassurance. She wanted to hear that Zach wasn't any different than before he'd turned pro, and Marty wondered what had happened that allowed doubt to creep into her mind.

He decided to give her what she was looking for, and he marshaled diplomacy. "He kids a lot. Sometimes he's so good at it I can't tell what's a joke and what's not."

Her features softened, and she scraped something on the scarred tabletop with her thumbnail. "There's actually something I've been wondering about." *Uh-oh. And here comes my answer.* She flicked her eyes to his, and he gave her a subtle nod to encourage her. "The last time I was there, I bumped into a couple of girls who looked like they were models. I hopped on the elevator, and we got to talking. They noticed the floor I'd come from and asked if I knew Zach. When I said yes, their eyes lit up and they talked about him like they knew him well and had been to parties with him. They wanted to know if I was his girlfriend. It was really weird. What's weirder, though, is when I asked Zach about it later, he had no clue who I was talking about. He said fans pull shit like that all the time trying to get close to a player, but I believed them. They seemed sincere. I guess I'm just naïve." She paused a beat and gave him a thoughtful look. "Do you think I'm naïve?"

"No, I think you're very sharp."

"Did you ever bump into them at Zach's apartment when he lived with his roommates?"

The familiar pang of guilt gave Marty a quick jab. *I have to back up my buddy. I'm his wingman.* Just where that left his allegiance to Claudia, he wasn't sure. Why was life a blurred palette of grays?

"Not that I'm aware of, but as I told you, the few times I visited him before you two moved in together, he and I didn't stay at his place much." He swallowed. "His roommates might have had some girlfriends there. But I was so hungover, I'm just not sure." He sagged, the weight of his lie sitting heavily on his shoulders.

She dipped an eyebrow. "You don't remember if there were girls that looked like supermodels in Zach's apartment? You must have been *really* hungover."

He shrugged. "Zach's right about all the crazy shit fans pull. I've seen it the few times I've been with him after a game. So I wouldn't put too much stock in what those women said."

She regarded him for a long moment, as if trying to decide whether to accept his lie or not. Finally, she relented. "Oh well. Now my other man is turning pro. Let's drink to that!"

Her other man. He probably shouldn't have liked the sound of that as much as he did.

Claudia had been right about Marty graduating, he pondered as he donned his cap and gown. Not long after, he strode across the stage and collected his diploma cover to the cheers and whistles of his own private peanut gallery sitting in the audience. He waved the holder at them after exchanging handshakes with a line of faculty he didn't recall ever seeing before.

Claudia sat beside Megan and his sisters, cheering the loudest. His mother hadn't been able to get time off for reasons that eluded him, but he shoved his disappointment into a corner and basked instead in the attention his small crew lavished on him.

The following week brought a whirlwind of apartment hunting in Springfield with his sisters in tow—they had to approve the place if they were going to visit him, they argued—interviewing for temporary jobs, and checking out training programs. Touring the Falcons' facilities and meeting his new coaches and some teammates put a tickle in his belly. This was really happening.

Next came moving day, which went rather easily, considering his meager belongings and the help of some BC teammates. Once everything had been dragged up to his second-floor two-bedroom and he'd returned the rental truck, he flopped his sweat-soaked self onto his couch and threw back a cold one. He surveyed his four new bare walls and felt an unexpected pang. As exciting and exhausting as the activity of the last few weeks had been, sitting in this unfamiliar place was unsettlingly quiet. And weird. And lonelier than he could have imagined. Boston had been home for so long that he'd practically grown roots there, and now he was uprooted and teetering. His sisters had gone back to Michigan, and Claudia was in St. Louis with Zach. Marty's anchors were pulled up and stowed, and he was adrift. He even missed Megan, who had returned to Salem.

His pity party lasted the one night, and he threw himself into organizing his place, learning his new city, and connecting with teammates. He also watched as many playoff games as he could and kept in close touch with his sisters and friends ... especially Claudia.

Zach's season had ended in mid-May when the Titans fell to Dallas in the semis. Once more, Zach had turned in a stellar performance, climbing the NHL's leading charts: most goals, most assists, most points.

Contact between Zach and him had shriveled, but he kept up through Claudia, who, between weekly phone calls, was a prolific email writer. She often referred to Marty as her pillar, her rock—steady and reliable. Apparently, Zach wasn't taking the playoff exit well and was drinking through his frustrations, insisting he needed to "blow off steam." Claudia speculated the reduced level of attention was fueling his foul mood. All that love and praise had fed him throughout the season, and without it, he was starving.

Sometimes his liquor love affair kept him out with his friends until the bars closed, and while Claudia told Marty she worried about Zach's physical and mental health, she didn't dwell on concerns about his faithfulness. No more talk of the Brendas and Trixies of the world. He never broached the subject, but one of the few times she did, she was dismissive.

"He only comes home smelling like a distillery, not some other girl's perfume," she laughed on the phone. Though her tone held a blithe quality, her confidence seemed to drain a little more every time he talked to her. She was obviously struggling to convince herself everything would be all right, and he hoped for her sake that things *would* turn out. He wanted her to be happy above all else.

Soon he had little time to contemplate her happiness or much else because the buzz of training camp and a new season grew louder in his head and the team's dressing room. The fit with his new club was more seamless than he had expected, and in his first real game appearance, the crowd cheered him as loudly as they did his teammates. The noise was startling, and he acknowledged fans with a wave before trying to lock out the noise and quell the springs bouncing in his stomach.

As he pulled in a series of breaths during the singing of "The Star Spangled Banner," he smiled to himself. Despite not having Claudia in his everyday life, this was going to be a hell of a year.

The first time Marty saw Claudia after his move was during Thanksgiving break, when she stopped in Springfield to catch one of his games on her way to St. Louis. She had arrived after warm-ups, and he couldn't keep his eyes from straying to her beaming face in the stands. His game held an extra spark that night. He skated as though lightning bolts powered his boots, checked with the power of a freight train, and when he got into a scrap with an opponent, his fists flew without mercy. After the game, he took a few extra minutes showering and shaving.

The first thing she did when they met up afterward was to cradle his hand in her small ones. Her big brown eyes raised to his. "Does it hurt?"

"Jesus, your hands are cold! No, it doesn't, and don't I get a hug first?"

Laughing, she threw herself into his arms and squeezed his neck. He buried his nose in her hair and whispered, "I've missed you."

She pulled back but didn't let go. "I've missed you too. My jogging's sort of fallen off, as you can tell." She stepped back and swept her hands down her body, her expression morphing into a grimace.

His eyes traced her form. She was perfect. "I think you look great. Don't change a thing."

She swatted his chest. "Smooth talker."

I was telling the truth. He grinned at her like an idiot.

A few of his teammates jostled them, and he didn't miss how their eyes widened when they took her in. Yeah, she was gorgeous, and an air of elegance clung to her. Her hair was down, and it cascaded over her shoulders like a golden waterfall. She had also upgraded her wardrobe, and besides the rock on her finger, a few new pieces of jewelry glittered from her ears, her neck, and her wrists.

"Let's move out of the way." He tugged her against a wall.

Her eyes ran from his toes to his damp hair. "You look good too. You've put on some muscle, and I swear you've grown an inch or two. You looked really good out there. Strong. Powerful."

Heat flared in his cheeks. He had put on weight, all of it muscle, and the fact that she had noticed warmed him all over. "So what do you say we—"

"Marty?" a familiar voice called.

He looked up, and a frisson of disappointment shot through him. "Oh hey, Hope."

The blond woman walked toward them, her eyes fastened on Claudia, where they remained. "This must be the *friend* I hear so much about."

Claudia smiled faintly and extended her hand. "Hi. I'm Claudia—"

"Campbell," Hope interrupted. "Yes, I know. And I'm Hope Morris." Hope stepped beside him and wrapped up one of his arms possessively. "I'm Marty's girlfriend."

He refrained from rolling his eyes. Hope worked for the Falcons' PR firm. They'd met at a team party and had dated a few times. Slept together once. While he liked her, he wasn't liking her laying claim to him in front of his best friend.

Claudia's smile broadened. "Marty and I are heading out to dinner to catch up. Are you joining us?"

"I'm afraid I can't make it. Maybe the next time you're in town, hmm?"

"I'll be around tomorrow until I have to catch my flight. Maybe we can—"

"I'm driving you," Marty interjected. Claudia's eyes darted to his, and they harbored a question. Yeah, this was news to him too. "We need to leave early, so I thought we'd catch breakfast on the way.

Also, you're staying with me tonight. It'll shave some time off the drive."

"Oh, but I have a hotel—"

"I know. I canceled it. Forgot to tell you. My bad." *Shit. I need to look up that hotel and cancel her reservation.*

Hope's hands slid down his arm. "All righty, then. You two have fun, but not *too* much fun. Claudia, nice to meet you. Marty?" Hand gripping his lapel, she yanked his face to hers and laid a hard kiss on his mouth. "Tomorrow night, right?"

"Uh, yeah. Sure." *Jesuuuus!*

As they walked to his new used Chevy Blazer, he blew out a breath. "I'm sorry about that. We've only dated a few times, so I'm not sure where the claws came from."

"You like her, though?"

"Yeah, but—"

"I know. It's *casual.*" Claudia gave him an impish smile. "Does *she* think it's casual?"

He frowned. "Maybe there's a little miscommunication there. Either way, I didn't expect—"

"Her to stake her claim on the hot hockey captain? Can't say I blame her."

One corner of his mouth quirked. "You noticed the *C* on the sweater, huh?"

"Of course I did."

"It's not a big deal. Our regular captain went down early with an injury, and they've been rotating the captaincy."

"And they picked *you*, and you haven't even been with them a full season. That *is* a big deal, so stop being so humble." At the car, she canted her head. "You wear it well."

His heart beat a little faster. "Thanks."

He stowed his bag, and they climbed into the vehicle. She turned her head toward him. "About me staying at your place ..."

"Yeah, sorry I kinda dropped that on you suddenly. Hope that's okay."

"It's fine. I actually prefer it because I want to see your place, but I didn't want to presume. But let's not tell Zach, huh?" A shadow passed over her face.

"I won't mention it." He turned the key in the ignition, and the engine sputtered to life. "Everything okay between you two?"

"I think so," she sighed. "He's just been kind of ... I'm not sure how to describe it. It's like these clothes I'm wearing. He now has a personal shopper for both of us."

He shot her a sidelong glance. "She's doing a good job. I think you look great." *But then, you always look great.*

"Thanks, but my point is he's kind of taken over my appearance. I mean, I don't really mind—I love having the nice outfits—but it's a little ... weird. For example, if there's something I like clothes-wise and he doesn't, it stays on the rack. My hair needs to be a certain way. And this jewelry." She shook a bracelet on her wrist. "I'm not big on bling, but he wants me wearing a certain amount whenever I go out. They're tasteful, but they're still more than I would normally wear."

"Does he say why?"

She nodded. "He says I'm a reflection of him, and he wants 'his woman' to look good." Marty could practically hear her eyes roll in her head.

He bit back the comment dancing on the tip of his tongue: she would be stunning in anything or nothing at all. "That doesn't sound like Zach," he said instead.

"Well, I think we're dealing with New Zach." She shook her head. "Things that didn't matter before seem to be important now, like giving a rat's rear end about fashion. He's even inserted himself into the wedding planning. He says it's because some of his teammates and their significant others will be there, and he doesn't want to look like a yokel. Whatever that means." She flipped a hand in the air.

"But you're still excited about the wedding, right?"

A zap of energy seemed to enliven her, and her enthusiasm blossomed. "Oh yes."

They arrived at the restaurant, and after they were seated, she ran on for a while about the venue, the music, the flowers, the tux fittings, and her dress. He caught the word "strapless" as he gazed at her across the table.

"Which is why I need to start jogging again," she laughed. "The dress has to fit on my wedding day."

I bet you'll be beautiful in it. "I'm sure it will." It occurred to him that her excitement had caught him up too. He was genuinely happy for her, and he gave himself a mental pat on the back. Distance aside, he was still looking after her as Zach had asked him, but somewhere along the way he had moved into the friend zone permanently. And he was okay with that.

"All this planning is a little nuts—on top of it being my senior year—and sometimes I forget to eat, which is actually a good thing. You're lucky you just have best-man duties. You don't need to plan anything for a few months yet."

"I'll get on that right after the first of the year. Did Zach tell you I'm staying with him for a few days in early February?"

"Yeah, right after the all-star break. Your AHL all-star game is at the same time as the NHL's, right?"

"Yep. I'll be in Michigan visiting Dani and Lexi, and I'll stop off in St. Louis on my way back."

"What if you get picked to go to the game?"

"No way," he scoffed. "Even on the off chance I do, I'd bow out. I need to check on my sisters more than I need to party with other AHLers."

They paused as a server delivered a glass of red wine for her and a mid-grade bourbon on the rocks for him.

After they toasted one another, Claudia dropped her voice. "Is the situation with your mom any better?"

He grimaced. "No. If I catch her when I call, she talks to me for about two seconds, then puts *him* on the line. What the hell? I have nothing to say to him. I want to talk to *her*. The only reason I talk to him at all is the old saying 'Keep your friends close and your enemies closer.' Except he's as elusive as an eel." He paused his rant to catch a breath. "She and I used to be close until *Dick* came along. It feels like the son of a bitch is driving a wedge between us on purpose. She swears he's not living there, but she's obviously lying because he's at the house around the clock. I have to ask myself if she knows she's aiding and abetting or if he's got her so twisted she has no clue."

"How do you know he's living there?"

"Dani keeps me in the loop."

The blame for the ever-widening rift between Marty and his mother rested squarely on her asshole boyfriend's slimy shoulders.

Dani was as unhappy about the gigolo as Marty was, but their shared contempt did nothing to unclip the guy from their mother's belt loops, and Marty was out of solutions.

"Could it simply be because he's in love with her and wants to be with her?"

"No. And why isn't he out working at a job? Where does his money come from that allows him to just hang with my mom?"

Claudia took a dainty sip of wine. "What's he like?"

Marty gusted out a breath. "He flips from syrupy sweet to a pompous windbag in the blink of an eye depending on who he's manipulating for what."

"So you want to get your sisters out of there."

"Absolutely. I don't make a ton, but Springfield is affordable, and I'd figure out how to take care of them. But Lexi's in her senior year of high school and doesn't want to move. Dani's going to community college and living at home to keep an eye on Alexis. Once Lexi graduates, I want to move them here. I can't stop my mom doing what she's going to do, but I can help my sisters."

"Are you worried about ... abuse?"

"Danielle says nothing's going on, but if he lays a finger on either of them, I will cut off his balls and feed them to him. And I'll enjoy every minute of it." What he didn't mention was his worry over Dickhead marrying his mom and getting control of not only her finances, but an underaged Alexis.

Claudia reached across the table and squeezed his hand briefly. "I'll be moving to St. Louis permanently this summer. It's not so far. I can go visit them. Or better yet, why don't I have them stay with Zach and me until you can get something worked out? If it takes a year, then so be it. I would enjoy their company."

"Aren't you planning to get a teaching job?"

Her eyes darted around the room. "I-I'm not sure. Not right away, I don't think."

He sat back, stunned. "Why not? It's been your dream for as long as I've known you."

She returned her gaze to his, and in her eyes he saw a mixture of sadness and sheepishness. "Zach says we'll be buying a house, and he wants me to spend my time fixing it up."

"You can't do that and teach too?"

She shrugged. “Apparently not.”

Placing his weight on his forearms, he leaned forward. “Are you okay with that?”

“Yes, of course.” She tossed her hair behind her shoulder.

“CC, this is me you’re talking to. I’m your number one, remember? You can tell me.”

“I’m fine with it. It’ll be an adventure, a big change.” She made an exploding motion with her hands. “You and I are becoming adults, aren’t we, Smarty Marty? Soon things are going to be very different.”

“Yeah, they are.”

I just hope those changes don’t run us over like a runaway locomotive.

Chapter 12

WHO CARES IF THEY'RE REAL?

February the following year

The sun was dipping below the horizon when Marty strolled out of St. Louis's airport. He wasn't greeted by a chauffeur holding a sign this time. Instead, Zach stood on the concrete island beside a white limousine.

A grin split his face from ear to ear. "Hey, LB! Over here, dude."

When Marty reached him, Zach pulled him in for a vigorous thump on the back that nearly had Marty stumbling. Marty caught a whiff of alcohol. Apparently, Zach had started the party early.

"Damn, it's great to see you!" Zach blared.

In return, Marty squeezed Zach's shoulder with his free hand." It's great to see you too, man. It's been way too long."

"Let me get that." Zach grabbed the bag from his hand. "What's it been? Six months?" He whistled, and a man in a black cap and dark suit Marty hadn't noticed stepped up to the curb and took the bag Zach thrust at him.

Without acknowledging the man, Zach shoved Marty into the back of the limo and climbed in after him. "Ready for a great time?

You better be because we are painting the town red—make that purple!"

Marty smirked. "Looks like you started without me."

"Hey, the all-star break's almost over, and then it's back to the grind. I'm just packing it in while I can." Sliding his Bulgari sunglasses down the bridge of his nose, Zach waggled his eyebrows, and Marty got a good look at the bloodshot eyes behind the rims. Besides the designer frames, his friend was dressed in an expensive-looking black knit sweater under an even more expensive-looking leather jacket. A gold Rolex flashed on his left wrist, and on his right was a gold bracelet made up of heavy links.

Marty found himself hitching up his old gray slacks and straightening the collar of his one light blue button-down under his puffy winter coat. He pointed at the bracelet. "Nice bling."

"Gotta look the part, man." A smirk decorated Zach's face. "Not that you know about that. Yet. But someday, if you make it to the Show, you'll understand."

Was that a dis? Maybe it's the booze talking. A sense of dread nudged the excitement Marty had felt at seeing Zach again. His friend seemed ... different. Was this the "New Zach" Claudia had talked about?

The limo glided away from the curb, and Zach reached for a bottle of Woodford Reserve nestled beside two crystal tumblers in a sleek bar. The bar, which was tucked behind the driver and ran the width of the vehicle, was stocked with more liquor than Marty's favorite watering hole in Springfield. It held glasses, a small fridge, and an ice dispenser. Zach splashed the brown liquid into the glasses and handed one to Marty, clinking his against it. "*Salut!* Welcome back, my friend. We're going to have us a hell of a party tonight." He tossed back half of the contents and wiped his mouth with the back of his hand. "A teammate of mine is throwing a party, and that's where we're headed. Should be a blast, man. And if it isn't, we'll blow his place and go find fun somewhere else."

"Sounds great." *Except I have a whole hell of a lot of catching up to do.* Marty took two quick swallows.

Zach sat back. "You look like you're staying in shape and eating your Wheaties. So how's life in Springfield?"

Marty filled him in on skating in the AHL, his teammates, and his three-year contract with the Falcons.

"So you like it?"

"Yeah, I like it. It's a good group of guys. They play hard, and they play with heart and grit."

Zach took another long sip. "I see where you have to tune them up on the regular. You always were a good fighter, though."

"Not really what I want to do, but it fills a role. I can protect my guys and get a decent amount of ice time."

"But the money. Shit, you have a way to go before you can afford something like this, huh?" Zach waved a careless hand.

"Yeah, asshole, rub it in."

Zach threw an arm around his neck and put him in a quasi headlock. "I'm sorry. That was a shit thing to say." He kissed the top of Marty's head and released him. "You know I love you like a brother. I'd do anything for you."

Marty quashed his annoyance and finished his drink. "Speaking of doing anything, we need to plan your bachelor party. You do want a bachelor party, right?"

"Hells yeah! And I want it to be epic." Zach glanced out the window. "We're here. We'll talk about my party later. I have lots of ideas."

They pulled up to a ridiculously large mansion with a circular drive around a big-ass fountain almost as wide as the limo was long. *Like pulling up to a luxury hotel.* Not that Marty had much experience with that. *Time to see how the other half lives.*

The interior of the mansion was as impressive as its exterior. Guests mingled in and around the place, and among them were faces Marty recognized from Zach's team, as well as players from other local sports teams. There was also a passel of little kids, which made sense since most of the guys were family men. Zach steered them toward a cluster of young guys and introduced them as his teammates.

He threw his arm around one dude's shoulders and dragged him in for a bro hug. "And this here is my main man, Steele. Steele, you remember my best friend, Marty LeBrun."

Marty recognized the big blond as one of Zach's previous roommates—one who liked to keep the party going and also made

Brenda and Trixie the happiest. Marty shook his hand. "Hey, man. How's it going?"

One side of Steele's mouth curled in a wicked grin. "That's right. And you were the hungover guy Trixie and Brenda couldn't stop talking about."

Zach clapped Marty's shoulder and wiggled his eyebrows. "They still live in the building. I run into them all the time. I'm sure they'd looooove to see *you*," he snickered.

"I'm, uh, seeing someone." *Sort of.* He and Hope were bumping along a rocky road he wasn't optimistic would smooth itself out. She had wanted to spend the ten-day break with him. When he'd told her he needed to head home for a visit, she had asked to tag along. The suggestion had set alarm bells clanging in his head that must have shown in his expression because her face had fallen. He'd felt terrible, but taking her home to meet his family would not only have been awkward—he hadn't known what awaited him—but it was a line he was unwilling to cross. He liked Hope a lot. They had hockey in common, and he liked having someone to do couples stuff with. She was a plus-one to go to parties with, to invite to team dinners, to cheer him on. She was easy on the eyes, and they had fun together. And having someone to share his bed regularly was a welcome bonus. But with her wanting to take it to the next level and him wanting to coast in casual mode, the comfortable relationship was coming to its inevitable conclusion.

"That's right," Zach laughed. "Marty is a serial monogamist."

Drinks were magically replenished, and soon the group was talking hockey, cars, and female celebrities they'd like to date. Marty's attention floated in and out of the conversation that sometimes slid into adolescence. Zach's friend Steele, especially, verged on juvenile. Marty had seen his type before, and they were always troublemakers.

He laughed at himself. *Am I turning into an old man worried about who my friends associate with?* He put the thought aside, and time passed—he had no idea how long, but it was pitch-black outside when Zach pulled him aside.

His buddy leaned into Marty a little too heavily, as if he was trying to prop himself up. "What do you say we get outta here? It's kind of boring, we've done our duty, and the boys are restless. They want to hit the clubs."

"Which boys?"

"Steele and the single guys."

The sound of two people arguing rose from a solarium. The cluster of guys peered through a French door that opened onto the sunroom, and Steele covered his mouth with his fingers and let out a high-pitched laugh. "Oh. My. Fucking. God! They're at it again."

"Who's at it?" Zach rose up on the balls of his feet to look over Steele's shoulder, and Marty stepped to the side to get a look at what was causing all the fuss.

A statuesque platinum blond in stilettos, tight black leather pants, and an even tighter red sweater that showed off her very ample assets stood arguing with one of the players.

"Who is that?" Marty asked. The two were leaned in, gesticulating wildly, yelling over each other, looking like a rabid pair of dogs going at it.

"That's Donny and his wife, BB," Zach said out of the side of his mouth as his gaze remained fastened on the dueling duo. "Liquor those two up, then sit back and watch the fireworks."

"Yeah, and I've heard those fireworks carry into bed later," Steele guffawed.

Marty was a bit befuddled. "They do this a lot? And they don't care that people are watching them air their dirty laundry?"

Zach folded his arms over his chest. "Nah, they're in their own world. But it allows us to spectate and have fun at their expense."

"What does BB stand for?"

Zach glanced at him and smirked. "Take a guess."

Steele, who flanked Zach's other side, held his cupped hands to his chest. "Big Boobs."

Marty blinked.

Zach whacked Marty's arm. "He's just kidding. It's short for Bluebelle or something like that."

They all broke into raucous laughter.

The husband and wife swiveled their heads toward the window where everyone was gawking at them and moved off somewhere private.

"Show's over. It's time to go anyway," Zach announced. To Steele and the crew, he said, "We'll see you at the Purple Pussycat."

As they strode toward the front door, Marty shook his head. "Jesus, that guy must be humiliated after having his personal drama on full display in front of his teammates."

"Nah, he's a lucky bastard."

"How do you figure?"

"She may be a handful"—Zach paused to make a squeezing motion with his hands and laughed at his own stupid joke—"but fuck me, look at her! She's sizzling hot. I'd put up with her shit too."

Marty slid him a stink-eye.

"What? Don't tell me you wouldn't tap that if given half the chance."

"I wouldn't tap that if given a complete chance," Marty replied dryly.

"Seriously? Who are you, and what have you done with my best friend?" Zach threw his head back and laughed.

Marty might have asked himself the same question about Zach.

He told himself they'd club a little, then get back to the apartment Zach and Claudia shared part-time and wind down. After hearing so much about it from her, he was looking forward to putting his feet up in a place that would feel like home as soon as he walked in. Tonight and tomorrow would be filled with hockey, hanging out with his best friend, and getting some wedding details out of the way. It wasn't every day your best friend got married. Marty was committed to doing everything in his power to make sure he and Zach were on the same page so that Zach got the celebration he wanted.

The rest of the night was a whirlwind of exclusive clubs with lots of alcohol in the mix. Zach seemed to be in his element everywhere he went, with patrons acting as though the party had finally arrived when he made his grand entrance. Any time he took the dance floor, he was the focal point, with an entourage of groupies surrounding him. Obviously, Zach was a regular at the places they went. Long lines might snake their way to bouncer-guarded entrances, but Zach bypassed them all. With a mere bob of his head or a knowing smile, doors magically opened for him and his buddies. Inside, a roped-off VIP table always awaited.

As they made their way to the door of one club, Zach was mobbed by a group of women all wanting his autograph—or some other piece of him, as demonstrated by the occasional grope a girl slid in. Zach flirted outrageously with each and every one but kept it PG-13. As he stood back and watched, Marty wondered how this was going to play when Claudia moved to St. Louis permanently. *It's not your problem.*

Five or six nightclubs in, Zach extricated himself from a gaggle of girls on the dance floor and stumbled to their table, where Marty played wingman amid a half dozen of Zach's adoring fans. The women, who were seated on a dark couch, scooted over, and Zach plopped between them and rested his arms along the back of the couch. Sweat beaded along his hairline, and the black leather jacket was long gone, along with the black sweater, leaving him in a molded black T-shirt the women kept touching and cooing over.

An instant after he'd sat down, Zach jerked his chin at Marty and lurched to his feet. The women protested, and he blew them kisses. "Be right back, ladies. Don't panic."

Marty fell in beside him as they wound their way to a corner of the bar. Zach swiped a hand across his forehead and signaled to the bartender. His jaw muscle twitched, and his hand drummed his thigh. He'd been amped up all night, as though he'd been pounding Red Bulls—and he'd continually hit the head. "Fuck, it's hot in here."

"Not if you're not shaking your ass on the dance floor."

Zach glanced over his shoulder. "Yeah, but it's hard not to. Those chicks are smoking hot, yeah?"

Marty smirked. "Absolutely. More pro perks?"

"Some of the better ones." Zach grinned roguishly. "What do you say we blow this place, go home, and get more shit-faced? I've had enough for one night. You?"

"What about all your 'fans'? Won't you break their hearts?"

"They know I'll be back. Meanwhile, Steele and the boys can fill in adequately. Looks like they're trying their best right now." Zach lifted his chin toward the dance floor, where Steele and his buddies were swarmed by a passel of very friendly girls. "It's tough to fill the Zachinator's shoes, though."

Despite the buzzing in his head, the word registered, and Marty gave him a sidelong glance. "The *Zachinator*?"

"That's what they call me." He jabbed a thumb at his chest.

"Somehow I don't see Claudia fitting into all this," Marty blurted. *Or calling you the "Zachinator."*

Zach stared at him for a beat. He shrugged and turned to the bartender, who shoved a credit card receipt at him.

Hours later, they lounged on Zach's leather couches, finishing off the dregs of a fantastic Japanese whiskey whose label Marty couldn't recall.

"Fuck, I love my woman!" Zach suddenly yelled. "She is the sweetest, the most caring, the ..." He grunted a word Marty couldn't understand. Marty peeked at him between splayed fingers. Zach sat up and parked his elbows on his thighs. He wagged a finger. "Although, there's one thing that would make her even more perfect than she is."

Seriously? "What's that?"

Zach cupped his hands against his chest, as he had done earlier at the party. "Her tits, man. She needs bigger tits. Help me convince her to get a boob job."

"No way, bro. Do *not* drag me into this." Marty's hand slid from his face. "Why the hell would you want her to do that in the first place?" He was sober enough to refrain from adding that she was perfect the way she was.

Zach spread his hands wide. "I want to show her off."

"You don't show her off now?"

"Yeah, but she's only a 34C. I want to take her to parties where she's in a slinky red dress cut down to there, and her gorgeous, round double-D's—or maybe E's—are about to bust out. She'd put BB's rack to shame, and I'd be the envy of every guy there."

Marty shook his muzzy head. At the same time it occurred to him that Zach had shared way too much personal information about Claudia's anatomy, he realized Zach wanted to display that anatomy for all to see. When he ordered his thoughts, his tongue was thick and slow. "Wait. Are you talking about making her look like Big Boobs and then dressing her for everyone to ogle?"

"Fuck yeah!" Zach made a jacking-off motion over his crotch, and an unnatural, manic gleam shone in his eyes. "Now you understand why Donny puts up with his woman's shit and doesn't give a flying fuck if she embarrasses him at parties. It's all worth it because he gets to go home and fuck her tits. Every. Single. Night. God, what I wouldn't give to be in his shoes! I mean, who cares if she's high maintenance when she's built like that? Totally worth every fucking penny."

An unsettling greasiness crept through Marty's gut, and he sat up, grasping the back of the couch to steady himself. Was it the booze making him feel sick? "They're not even real, dude."

"My point exactly! You can buy them, and they look amazing! Fuck, I want Claudia to get implants."

"Do you hear yourself? What's gotten into you, you perv? You make it sound like you want to marry a porn star."

Zach's eyes widened. "Did I *say* that?"

"No, but you sure as hell implied it." Marty swayed to his feet. "I'm going to bed."

Zach waved a hand at him, drawling, "Fuck you."

Marty realized he was unfamiliar with the apartment's layout. "Wait. Where am I sleeping?"

"I don't give a shit. Sleep in the elevator for all I fucking care. Or better yet, crawl into the same bed as Brenda or Trixie. If you time it right, they'll be in the same fucking bed and make a man sandwish, uh, sandwich, out of you. Your dick could use a little of their magic, my friend, because Steele was abso-fucking-lutely right. Best fucking blow jobs on the blanket, uh, planet. And there's other dirty shit those girls do too."

Marty blinked. "You know this how?"

Zach gave him a bleary-eyed smile. "A li'l birdie told me, that's how I know."

Chapter 13

My Moral Compass Is Tilted

Marty woke up with a head-pounding hangover, a condition that was becoming commonplace whenever he spent time with Zach. A glance at a clock told him it was two in the afternoon. He dragged a hand across his sandpaper jaw as bits and pieces of their late-night ramble floated back to him. Had he actually heard Zach say he wanted Claudia to get a boob job? *Nah. I had to be hallucinating*. And had Zach actually implied he had firsthand knowledge of Brenda's and Trixie's talents? *No, I'm reading that all wrong*.

He dragged his smelly hide out of bed and cranked on the shower, standing under its hot spray until he began to feel human again. Afterward, he dressed and staggered into the penthouse's immense open living room, where floor-to-ceiling windows revealed St. Louis's skyline. Zach—bare-chested, as always—sat hunched over a marble counter reading something. The smell of rich coffee filled the air, and Marty followed the aroma.

Zach gave him a sidelong glance and grinned. “Well, fuck me, it lives!”

“How long have you been up?” Marty picked up the carafe and began pouring the brew into a waiting mug.

“A couple hours now.”

“Are you serious? How do you party like that and wake up without any effects?”

“Oh, trust me. I feel the effects. I just wear them better than you do,” Zach snickered.

Marty took a tongue-burning sip. “So what’s on today’s agenda?”

“Steele and the boys are having a little get-together at their place later, sort of a last-gasp celebration before we start back up again. I told them we’d stop by.”

“Huh. You like hanging with those guys? I thought you were sick of them after living with them.”

“They’re okay guys. They’re single, so they’re more fun to hang out with than the married guys. And the married guys really don’t hang out unless we’re on the road. They’d rather be with their families when they’re home.”

“Makes sense to me.”

“Yeah, whatever. So we need to order some grub to soak up this alcohol. What sounds good? Cheeseburgers? Pizza? Chinese?”

“Yeah, sure.” After a gallon of coffee.

When they had polished off gourmet burgers and double orders of onion rings from a local restaurant, they sat down to kill each other in a Half-Life-a-thon, which Zach surprisingly won. Surprising because Marty usually bested him at non-hockey competition, and because Zach had been drinking straight brown liquor since their burgers had arrived. Marty wondered at his friend’s capacity. Not only was Marty’s body still processing what he’d imbibed the night before, but the thought of booze made him want to retch. Plus, hockey started in two days, and the toxins had to be purged from his system. Zach seemed to be going the opposite direction, pre-loading on alcohol.

His buddy stood and teetered. “Whoa! Room’s spinning.”

“You all right?”

“Think so.” He staggered to a console table that held a phone and an answering machine. “Actually, no. Looks like I have two voicemails. Probably Claudia," he grumbled. "Shit. Guess I have to call her." He trundled off to his bedroom and slammed the door.

Marty was still frowning at Zach's door when he emerged five minutes later. "That was quick. Were you able to get ahold of her? Is everything okay?"

"Everything's fine. She just wanted to talk. You know how women are." He gave Marty an epic eye-roll. "Hey, we still need to figure out my bachelor party. I do know one thing: it's going to be in Vegas."

Marty leaned back and rested an arm along the back of the couch. "Don't take this the wrong way, but are you sure you should be getting married?" He had intended it as a joke, though when the words left his mouth, he realized there was nothing funny about his concern.

Zach's eyebrows shot to his hairline. "Why the fuck would you ask me a question like that? Of course I'm sure."

Going for nonchalant, Marty shrugged a shoulder. "I don't know, man. You really seem to enjoy living it up. There's nothing wrong with that, but I wonder how that's going to play when you're married and Claudia's here twenty-four-seven. Is she gonna wanna party all the time too? Are you going to keep clubbing with your buddies and leave her home alone? If you give up that lifestyle, will you miss it and resent her?"

Zach's mouth quirked.

"They're serious questions, Zach. And I'm not looking for answers from you, but you might want to be sure you have the answers yourself before you say, 'I do.'"

Zach's hands went to his hips, and he blew out an extended breath as he tipped his head to the ceiling. "I love her, Marty. There's nobody else for me. I'm ready for this. So I go a little hard sometimes, but I'm just getting it out of my system. It's my last hurrah." Zach leveled him with a hard gaze. "Once I'm over it, that's it. I'll be ready to settle down."

But are you going to be "over it" before those vows?

The right words were coming out of Zach's mouth, but they were at odds with the behavior Marty had witnessed. His friend danced on the edge of being the bad boy. Like a little kid trying to see what he could get away with, he tested limits, pushed against boundaries without stepping over the line. Maybe what Marty was seeing was exactly what Zach said it was: a case of overindulging before his life changed, like a person binge-eating right before starting a diet.

Zach gave Marty a chin jerk. "Let's go see what Steele and the boys have going on."

"When do you want to talk about the bachelor party?" *And how the hell am I going to afford Vegas?*

"We'll do it when we get back. C'mon. Those guys might eat all the food or kill all the booze before we get there."

Thirty minutes later, as they stepped off the elevator onto Steele's floor, Marty could hear the party before they even rounded the corner that led to the end unit.

Zach grinned at the door. "Sounds like we're getting here just in time." He turned the knob and pushed open the door. A sensory overload of music and people crammed together made Marty's aching head throb even more.

"Hey, close the fucking door before the neighbors call the police!" someone hollered. Zach obliged and wound his way into the fray with a couple of handles of booze, calling out greetings as he went. A wave of cheers rose up. He was in his element.

Marty had been to plenty of parties and done his fair share of wading right in, but at this moment, he was a gasping fish out of water. He pushed his way toward the kitchen—having a drink in his hand, even a soda, would make him feel less like he was standing on stage naked—and tried not to glance around like a tourist. Dancing bodies spilled over into every space, a lot of them in some state of undress. He plucked a root beer from a cooler.

A pretty redhead caught his eye and smiled at him. "Is this your first time at a Steele party?"

"I look that out of place, huh?"

She twirled her hair and giggled. "You do look a *little* awkward."

"Gee, thanks?" He popped the top of his soda, noticing she fisted a full beer bottle.

"Did you come with someone?"

Glancing around, he was surprised—yet not—that a shirtless Zach was dancing in a throng of women. Marty jerked his head toward him. "Yeah, I'm here with Zach. Do you know him?" He took a bubbly sip.

Her lips tipped up in a predatory smile. "Not as well as I'd like to. Maybe you can put in a good word for me? He's a regular at Steele's shindigs, but I haven't had a chance to talk to him yet."

Marty ignored the *good word* bit. "Does Steele host a lot of these?"

She shrugged. "When he's not on the road, at least a couple of times a week."

How in the hell does the guy stay in game shape? "That's a lot of parties."

"And they're always crazy fun." Her auburn eyebrows rode up and down her forehead.

"Crazy how?" *Do I want to know?*

"Let's just say anything you want, you can get at a Steele party. See ya later." She raised her bottle before disappearing into the crowd.

Two sodas later, Marty had settled into an inconspicuous corner, trying to keep his eyes to himself. The place was devolving into a drunken orgy, making him uncomfortable mentally *and* physically. Meanwhile, Zach continually disappeared down a darkened hallway that led to the bedrooms—sometimes alone, but most times with at least one scantily clad woman—seemingly unaware Marty was in the room.

So Marty left. The chorus from "Mama Told Me Not to Come," an old favorite of his mom's, replayed itself in his head.

Letting himself into Zach and Claudia's apartment, he pulled in the cool, undisturbed air and breathed. *Sanctuary.* He plopped onto a couch; his eyes roamed around the space. Claudia's touches were everywhere he looked, including a collection of droopy plants. Apparently, Zach wasn't babying them the way Claudia would.

Claudia and Zach. An utter mismatch.

Marty busied himself watering the pots while his conflicted emotions battled in his head once more.

Should he have insisted Zach leave with him? *Probably.* Was Zach partaking of the overt debauchery—and that hidden behind closed doors—at this very moment? Marty didn't want to know.

Where did his loyalties lie? To whom did he owe what?

The stillness of the apartment began to grate. He needed to talk to someone. Couldn't talk to his mom, and he didn't want to reach out to Hope and revive the dying relationship. He definitely couldn't call Claudia. How would he parry her questions about what he and Zach were up to? Instead, he dialed Danielle and blew out a relieved breath when she picked up on the second ring.

"You're home!" he barked.

"Yes, I'm home. What's up? Didn't I just see you yesterday?"

His back sagged into the couch cushions. "Nothing's up. I just wanted to be sure you and Alexis are okay."

She trilled, and the sound lifted his heart from its despondency. "Wow! Missing us already, huh? How's the visit with Zach going?"

"I—it's been an eye-opener." *I'm re-evaluating my friendship with my best friend.*

"Sounds very serious. Does this have to do with your dream of getting into the NHL?"

His mind tumbled through his thoughts. "Yeah, I think it does. I used to think I wanted the money, the glory, but now I'm not so sure." *Will I sacrifice my integrity and transform into the spoiled, overindulgent athletes upstairs?* "The AHL may not be at the top, but I *like* the guys I associate with. They're humble, respectful, and they love the game for what it is, not for the big paycheck. They're so appreciative of what they have, and I like being part of that. It suits me."

"Then maybe you've found a home and your work family."

Maybe I have.

"Dani, let me ask you something. Say you had two really good friends, and one of them did something bad, and you knew about it. Say they asked you not to say anything to the other friend because it would hurt them. What would you do?"

"Did you actually witness the one friend doing the bad thing, or did you just hear about it?"

"I didn't see it, but the evidence points that way." If he didn't know, he couldn't definitively say Zach was doing anything wrong, could he? Yeah, he was a coward.

"If it's going to hurt my other good friend, I wouldn't say anything without hard proof, Marty. And even then, I'd tread carefully and weigh whether tearing someone up is worth it. Is this about Zach doing something bad?"

"No. Just a hypothetical I heard someone talking about." *Me. Talking it out in my head.*

Chapter 14

MUDDY WATERS

The front door banged open with a reverberating *thud*, jarring Marty upright from where he'd been dozing on Zach's couch.

"There you are! What the fuck happened to you? One minute you're there, and the next you're gone, and no one knew where you were." His friend's hair and clothing were disheveled, his eyes on the wild side.

"I have an early flight and needed some shut-eye. You were having a good time, and I didn't want to pull you away." Marty infused calm into his voice to keep Zach from becoming more excitable. He planted his feet on the floor and rested his elbows on his thighs. "What time is it?"

"I don't know. Eleven? Midnight? The party's still going strong." Zach's tone was sullen.

I expect it is. "I've only been back for a few hours." Marty narrowed his eyes at his friend. "Are you high?"

"What? No!" Zach ate up the distance from the front door to the kitchen with wobbly paces and began rummaging around in the big-ass Sub-Zero.

Marty ambled in and leaned his hip against the counter. "Buzzed?"

Hand on the fridge door, Zach wheeled, his face red. "What are you, my den mother? Do I need to check in with you every time I have a drink? Why the fuck does it matter?"

Marty pursed his lips in an I-don't-care fashion. "It doesn't. Just trying to figure out why you're so amped up."

Zach slammed the fridge door and ran a hand through his hair. "I'm not amped up. I was just ... I don't know." He scowled. "I need a drink. Want one?" Without waiting for Marty's answer, he headed out of the kitchen to an open butler's pantry that served as a full-blown bar.

"Sure. But maybe we should eat something first." Marty was no chef, but he was adequate when it came to plating a meal.

"Not hungry." Zach poured two drinks, handed Marty one, and sank into a black leather couch, where he repeatedly tapped his thumb on his knee.

Marty took a seat in an armchair opposite him and twirled the amber liquid in his glass. "I noticed a lot of traffic disappearing down the hall, and I couldn't decide if people were sneaking off to do coke or each other." *And you were part of that traffic.*

Zach snickered. "I'm sure it was both." A bulb seemed to wink on in his eyes. "You don't think *I'm* taking part in that shit, do you?"

"I don't know. You were one of the people I saw disappearing, and you're a little twitchy right now."

Zach threw back the contents of his drink and stood for a refill. When he returned to the couch, he had the bottle with him. He took a long tug from his glass and leveled Marty with a hard stare. "Maybe I'm twitchy because my *best friend* is putting some not-so-subtle accusations out there. Look, you need to understand something. Playing in the bigs puts a lot of pressure on a guy. Pressure to play well every fucking night, pressure to grind it out through the injuries, pressure of living in a fishbowl."

"I get that."

"Maybe at the AHL level," Zach scoffed. "NHL is a different beast."

Marty bit back his irritation. "That may be, but players at all levels, including the lowly AHL, have similar stresses. Well, with the exception of women gunning for a baby daddy. We don't make enough to have that particular bull's eye on our backs."

To Marty's satisfaction, realization seemed to dawn in Zach's eyes.

"So like I said, I *do* get it," Marty concluded.

Zach flapped a hand at him. "Okay, okay. What I was trying to say is that when the pressure's lifted, like it was this past week, I unwind. And I unwind like I play: balls to the wall."

Marty raised his hands in surrender. "As long as it's not balls deep in some of Steele's friends."

"Goddamn, you're like my fucking conscience or something. Who assigned you that job?"

"Sorry. Just worried about you, bro, and about Claudia." A thought popped into his brain. "How come you didn't spend your time off visiting her in Boston last week?"

Zach cocked an eyebrow. "Why? Did she say something to you?"

"No, I was just wondering. Seems like it would've been a good time to see her."

"I *just* saw her. Besides, she'd just spend her time with her nose stuck in her books. What fun would that be? And speaking of fun, let's talk about my bachelor party." His shoulders eased, and a smile curled one side of his mouth. He poured himself another drink and held up the bottle to Marty, who shook his head. "You still have plenty of time to line up what I want, but understand that I'm paying for everything."

"But—"

"Not arguing about it, LB. I want my party my way, and you can't afford it." He held up a hand. "No offense. Just stating the obvious, and I think you'll agree when you hear what I have in mind."

Marty pushed out an exasperated breath. "All right. Let's hear it."

"I want two nights with my tribe, and it's gotta be Vegas. I have about a dozen guys in mind."

Marty narrowed his eyes. "Why Vegas?"

Zach broke out in a salacious grin. "Because what happens in Vegas stays in Vegas, baby."

"You're not—"

"Oh hell no, Marty. Jesus fucking Christ, lighten up! If the other guys want to get hookers, they can do it on their own time and their own dime. I just want to have a little fun, see the sights."

"Sights?"

"Yeah, doofus. Titty shows. Get with the program. I'll just be looking, so don't get your panties in a wad. No harm, no foul." Zach polished off *that* pour and refilled his glass. His speech grew more slurred. "Listen up. So here's what we do. We rent luxury suites on the same floor of a new high-end hotel. Maybe the Bellagio. We can share the suites, but each guy gets his own private bedroom and bath. Got that?"

"Got it. Two nights, suites, a dozen guys, and private rooms."

"And a limo to take us everywhere. No one drives. Now the first night, we go out, have a nice dinner, maybe see a show and gamble. The next night is when we cut loose."

"Can't wait to hear this."

Zach flung out an arm, nearly toppling his glass. "Would you fucking get over yourself already? Just because you're not getting any doesn't mean you have to shit all over everyone else's parade."

Marty put down his untouched drink and steepled his fingers. "Whether I'm getting laid or not has nothing to do with your bachelor party." Why did he feel like he was the only adult in the room?

"Fine," Zach scoffed. He brought his drink to his lips, and the liquid dribbled down his chin. "Fuck, all this talk about getting laid is making me horny."

"*Drinking* makes you horny. It always has." *And with the amount you're putting away, you've got to be ready to explode.* No way was he letting Zach return to Steele's debauch-a-fest, especially in his current condition. "Let's get back to your bachelor party."

"Okay. Okay." Zach set his drink down, sloshing some over the sides. "You're my best man, and you have to give me the kind of party I want."

"Thought we already established that."

As if he hadn't heard him, Zach ran on. "And I want two things." He flicked out his forefinger. "Like I said, I want it held in Vegas." He added his middle finger. "I want private strippers. That's plural, not singular. Three's great, but six would be better. And private means we're not sitting in a strip joint with a hundred other dudes.

They're dancing for just us. And they have to have big tits. The bigger, the better."

Marty sat forward. "Are you shitting me? *Six?" And what's with the sudden fascination with big tits?* Zach had never expressed an interest in large breasts before. Women, yes, but the whole package. He'd never singled out one anatomical feature.

"Hey, I'm paying for it. I just want you to coordinate it and herd the cats. That's what best men do. And this stays between us. Claudia will know nothing about any of these details. This party is for *me.*" Zach jabbed a finger against his chest. "I don't need her stamp of approval. The Zachinator is about to be taken out of circulation, shackled to the old ball and chain. Women around the world will weep."

Marty executed a mental headshake. He wasn't sure which sickened him more: referring to Claudia as "the old ball and chain" or Zach's inflated opinion of his impact on womankind—or any number of the scenarios Marty had witnessed and would need to bleach from his memory banks.

He pulled in a steadying breath. "So what does Claudia have planned for her bachelorette party? If I know Megan, male strippers are involved." Marty couldn't help himself.

Zach shook his head, and Marty wondered if the motion made him dizzy. "Nah, Claudia's not into that shit."

"Maybe, maybe not. Megan definitely is."

"What the fuck are you trying to do here? Huh? What is your problem? Hey! What happened to my drink? Oh. There it is." Zach's unsteady hand brought the glass to his lips, and he slurped what was left.

"You do realize you're indulging yourself in a double standard here. It's okay for you to have strippers—*plural*—but what's good for the gander isn't good for the goose?"

"If I ever thought Claudia ... Nah, she'd never do that to me. Hell, if it's Chippendale dancers she wants, let her have 'em. I know my girl. She won't be taking any of them home. And if she does, she doesn't deserve me." He nodded as if to punctuate the statement.

Yeah? What about you, Zachinator? For not the first time, Marty pondered whether being a hotshot in the NHL had pushed his friend over to the dark side, where excesses turned Dr. Jekyll into Mr. Hyde.

Zach rose and swayed in place. "Well, I think we're done here. I'm going to bed. I'm taking you to the airport tomorrow, so wake me if I'm still asleep."

As Marty watched his drunk friend stagger to his bedroom, a saying he had read once came drifting back: money doesn't change a person; it merely amplifies their character. If you're a good person, you grow into a better one. But if you're a bad person, you become a worse person.

Had this drunken, excess-driven slob been the real Zach Pruitt all along and Marty was seeing him without blinders for the first time?

No clue.

He'd do his duty as best man, but after that, he wasn't sure what would be left of their friendship.

Sadness crept in overnight, and it settled inside him early the next morning as he wrote Zach a brief note and tiptoed out of the apartment to grab the cab he had ordered.

When Marty picked up Zach's call later that day, he got an earful. He made his excuses about not wanting to wake Zach up, then brought the conversation to a quick end. It was time for practice anyway, and Hope was waiting rink-side. Her body language told him the end of their relationship was imminent and there was no getting around it. He would have to pass her before taking the ice, and he pulled in a cleansing breath as he approached.

Damn.

She looked up at him when he reached her. On skates, he was a good foot taller. "Enjoy yourself on vacation?" Her voice was frostier than the sheet of ice waiting for him.

"It was okay. It was all family time." Zach was family, right? Forget about the shenanigans—she didn't need to know those sordid details. *No one* needed to know those details.

"We need to talk."

He nodded. “When?”

“Tonight.”

“Want me to pick you up?”

She shook her head.

A sinking sensation set in, but after a mere ten minutes of practice, hockey was the only thing occupying his mind. A heartbeat later, focus snapped to excruciating pain in his left arm. He dropped his stick and doubled over, grasping his arm.

Fuck!

Could life deal him any more setbacks? Turns out it could. An errant slapshot had caught him in the wrong place, and after an examination by the medical staff, his arm was declared broken. He was done for at least four weeks.

The injury didn’t deter Hope from breaking up with him several days later. Though he had expected it, it still felt like another shovelful of shit being heaped on the growing pile that was his life. Consequently, when his coach pulled him into his office that same day, Marty braced himself for the worst—and was pleasantly surprised by the bright side that showed itself instead.

Coach flicked a finger at him to take a chair. “What would you think of standing behind the bench and helping me coach the next sixteen or so games?” One of the assistants had been called away on a family emergency, and Coach needed someone to fill the vacant slot during his absence.

Marty gave him a bug-eyed look. “I don’t know anything about coaching.”

Coach chuffed. “No? Then why is it your teammates are always looking to you on the ice? You’re the one encouraging them, telling them what to do, how to position themselves. You’re running plays out there. Not sure what you call it from where you come from, but I call that coaching.” Coach leaned back with a smug smile.

“Yeah, okay. I’d be honored.” A thrill ignited in his belly and spread outward.

He left Coach’s office stunned ... but the pain in his arm was all but forgotten.

Chapter 15
COMMENCEMENT

Three months later

Finally, it was over! Claudia bent to pick up her cap from the grass, where it had landed after she had tossed it in the air along with the rest of her graduating class. She wasn't used to the heavy Rolex on her left wrist—a graduation present from Zach—and it weighed her down as she retrieved the cap.

"Hey, I'm going to take off," Megan called behind her.

Claudia straightened, spun, and clutched her friend in a tight hug. "I'll catch up with you later, huh?"

"Absolutely. As soon as I'm done with the obligatory family thing. They did pay for my education after all." Megan pecked her cheek and ran off.

"Feel any different?" a familiar male voice said.

Claudia shaded her eyes as a tall, broad form dressed in a suit strolled toward her. She launched herself into Marty's open arms and hugged his neck. "Thank you so much for coming."

"Hey, someone had to represent the male side of this group."

Neither Rex nor Zach had been able to attend. Rex was half a globe away, and Zach was in the thick of playoffs. Both airtight excuses, but she'd felt let down nonetheless. Being with Marty dulled the pang of disappointment. "Well, I'm glad it was you!"

He set her apart and scanned her from her strappy heels to her updo. "The robe looks good on you. Gives you that judge-on-a-high-pulpit look."

She swatted his arm. "You're joining our little celebration, right?"

"Try and get rid of me." He held out a colorful gift bag he had apparently been hiding behind his back. "A little something for your graduation."

"You didn't have to." She took the bag from him and peeked inside, pushing aside the haphazard man-arranged tissue paper.

"I know, but I wanted to."

Squeaking with pleasure, she pulled out an indoor herb garden kit.

He seemed to be holding his breath. "Like it?"

"I love it! Thank you!"

He grinned. "I wanted to get you a live one, but with you moving to St. Louis, I thought this would travel better. You can set it up in your apartment by the—"

"The window in the breakfast nook!"

"Exactly."

"Oh, this is the perfect gift! You know me so well. You really are my bestie." She leaned in for another hug and caught a pleasant whiff of woodsy man. Such a nice smell.

At dinner a few hours later, Marty had her mother and Aunt Beverly giggling like a pair of schoolgirls. He was polite, friendly, and seemed fascinated by everything they had to say. Of course he was. She had always been able to depend on him to do and say the right thing at the right time, and she loved him for it. A thought popped into her head. Did Hope know how lucky she was to be dating Marty?

Afterward, as Claudia walked her mom and aunt to their motel room door, her mother gushed, "What a nice young man! Can we see him again for brunch tomorrow? It'll be our treat."

Claudia feigned outrage. "So the only reason you're offering me brunch is to see Marty again?"

"No, CC, dear. You're not invited." Her mother and Aunt Bev burst into a fresh round of giggles.

Claudia shook her finger at them. "You're both naughty." Then she grinned. "I'll ask him. I'm sure he'd love to, but I'm coming along to be sure things don't get out of hand."

Her mother sighed. "If he's your Zach's best friend, then I'm sure we'll like Zach too."

A breath hitched in her lungs. They still hadn't met Zach, which was a source of embarrassment for Claudia. The timing never seemed to work. Then again, she hadn't met his parents in person either. The first opportunity would come at the rehearsal dinner.

"I'm sure you'll love him, Mom." She kissed both women good night and began her amble back to the parking lot, where Marty waited in his Blazer. She glanced at her fancy new watch, disappointed she hadn't heard from Zach all day. No messages, no missed calls. He was probably on the team plane heading to the next city and the next game. No, they had just finished the first of two home games, so he should have been around.

By the time she slid into Marty's passenger seat, she had put aside an unsettling feeling and plastered on a smile. "My mother and aunt have crushes on you. They want to take you to brunch tomorrow."

One corner of Marty's mouth quirked. "I'm flattered. You're coming along for protection, right?"

"Of course. And speaking of protection, are you ready to carry on the celebration at the Stompin' Grounds with Megan?"

He tapped his clean-shaven chin thoughtfully. "Hmm. That depends. Is she going to try to climb me again?"

"She'll behave. She knows you have a girlfriend in Springfield." When he didn't speak or make a move to start the Blazer, doubt welled inside Claudia, and she side-eyed him. "Is Hope coming with you to the wedding?"

He shook his head. "We broke up a few months ago."

An odd wave of sadness mixed with relief rushed through her. Hope had been so pretty, so ... perfect, but somehow she hadn't been right for Marty. *And I'm basing this on a five-minute meeting? Ha!* "I'm so sorry. Are you seeing someone else?"

He swiveled his head toward her. "Nope. I was actually thinking of inviting Danielle as my plus-one for the wedding, if that's okay with you. She's going to be staying with me for a while. I didn't want to mention anything to her until I spoke to you, but I know she'd love to come."

"Of course! I'd love to have her there. Will Alexis be with you too?"

"No. She wants to stay with our mom. She's getting married, you know." He let out an extended sigh.

"To Dickhead? Or should I use his formal name, Richard Cranium?"

A ghost of a smile played across his mouth. "Yeah, to Dickhead."

"Oh, ouch. When?"

"Right around the same time as your wedding, which gives me a great excuse not to go. That's assuming I'm even invited." He let out a grim chuckle, and her heart hurt for him. "I hear the wedding's small and Lexi will be in it. Another reason she's staying behind." He turned the key in the ignition. "How are your plans coming?"

Claudia got it—he wanted a change of subject. "Everything's handled, I think. Meg's been great at helping me organize, and of course Mom and Aunt Bev are buzzing around like busy bees. I think all I have to do is show up and play queen for the day."

He eased the SUV out of its parking spot. "I don't think I've asked you this, but are you taking Zach's last name?"

She barked a mirthless laugh. "No, and he's not happy about it. But it'll be easier for me because when I apply for teaching jobs, the name on the application will line up with the transcripts." A lame excuse, but she would continue to wield it, damn it. It was better than confessing that she didn't want the notoriety that came from being married to a superstar. Besides, sharing his last name would make it hard to maintain the separate identity she had carved for herself these last four years.

"And how's finding that teaching job coming? Have you applied for anything in St. Louis?" Checking over his shoulder, he nosed the car onto the street.

Her heart sank a little, but she forced a smile. "Not yet. Thought I'd wait until the wedding's over to get a lay of the land."

"Which means you won't be teaching this next school year." His tone was flat, no judgment, but his statement rankled just the same because he sparked a flaring nerve. She couldn't abide Marty being disappointed in her—to her knowledge, he never had been—but she sensed his disappointment in her for caving to Zach's surprising macho demand. No, it had been a request. *That felt like a demand.*

In truth, she was disappointed in herself, but she buried the feeling and brilliantly trotted out a new reason for abandoning her dream—temporarily.

"It's okay. A few of the wives are recruiting me to help with the team fundraisers, and that's going to keep me busy. I may not be teaching munchkins right away, but there will be opportunities to engage with kids playing hockey and stuck in the hospitals. I'm really looking forward to that."

Several silent beats passed before he spoke. "Yeah, those hospital visits are really important—to the kids and the players too. It's one of my favorite things to do in our community."

Turning her head toward him, she studied his profile. "Facing those little patients has to be rough."

"It's heartbreaking, yeah, especially when you consider you might not see that kid on your next visit—and not because they went home. But when their faces light up, and you know *you* did that, that you brought a little joy into their lives and took their minds off their shitty situations, it's ..." He pressed the heel of his hand into an eye. "It means a hell of a lot." These last words came out in a hoarse whisper.

Her heart squeezed, and tears pricked her eyes, blurring her vision. She laid a hand on his bicep. "Why does that not surprise me about you, Marty LeBrun? You have such a huge heart. You'll make a great dad someday."

He cleared his throat. "How soon are you and Zach going to have kids?"

She slid her hand from his arm. "I'm not sure. Not for a while." Zach had been pushing for her to go off birth control, but she was resisting for reasons she didn't quite comprehend herself.

"What are you doing for your bachelorette party?"

"No idea. Megan says it's top secret. All I know is that we're spending the night somewhere, and she's packing an overnight bag for me. I'm a little nervous—you know Megan. How about the bachelor party? Have you got the strippers lined up yet?"

He snapped his head to her. "What strippers?"

"Ha! You just gave it away. I was only fishing, but it's a logical guess. A bunch of rowdy guys at a bachelor party in Vegas. A strip club is definitely in the mix somewhere. Just be sure the bachelor doesn't get any handsier than stuffing a few bills here and there. So where are you holding it?"

"Like Megan, I'm sworn to secrecy."

"Coward."

He slid her a grin. "Yep. Ready to get drunk?"

"But you're driving."

"I wasn't talking about me. I was talking about you, graduate."

She turned sideways in her seat to better watch him. "Okay. Promise to hold me up on the dance floor if I fall down?"

Eyes on the road, he nodded. "You can lean on me."

"Will you hold my hair back if I have to puke?"

"Always."

"And will you pour me into bed later if I can't do it myself?"

Another nod. "Of course."

"Wow, you truly are a best friend. Do I still have to go jogging with you in the morning?" She grimaced.

"Absolutely."

She gave him an eye-roll. "Well, that puts a damper on things."

"We won't start until ten. How's that? Then we'll meet your mom and aunt for brunch after."

She clapped her hands. "Sounds like we've covered our bases. Let's do this!"

Marty's eyes lifted to the rearview mirror before sliding over to her. "You have to promise me one thing, though."

"After all the promises you just made me? You've got it, whatever it is."

He turned his eyes back to the road. "Don't tell Megan I'm single?" The wince was obvious in his voice.

She let loose a laugh. "On my honor as a friend, I will not say a word. Then maybe you can relax and enjoy an evening where she doesn't hang all over you."

"I don't mind a little hanging. It's just that when Megan gets on a track, she's hard to derail."

"And I expect her hanging on your arm could physically hurt." She drew in a silent breath. "How was the end of your season? Is the arm healed?"

"It's getting there. I need more PT to get my strength back."

"Sitting out must have sucked."

He stopped at a red light, his eyes focused somewhere beyond the windshield. "I got a few games in at the end, though I didn't help us get into the playoffs. Sitting out wasn't as bad as I thought it would be. Coach had me work with him behind the bench as a defensive coordinator while I was on the IR. Totally different perspective, and I learned a ton. I enjoyed it. I think it'll make me a better player when the season starts up again."

"And you'll be playing for the Falcons this year?"

The light turned green, and he surged forward. "Unless they trade me. I have another two years left on my contract."

"I wish St. Louis was closer so I could come to your games. They're more fun than Zach's. Things are a bit looser."

"You just like the fighting," he chuckled.

"Nothing like sweaty men beating the crap out of each other to get a girl's motor running, I always say."

He turned his head toward her, and the shadows playing on his face accentuated his strong jaw and full mouth. "Really? That's what you say?"

She giggled, feeling lighter than she had in hours. They were in for a fun night, just like old times, and soon she'd be able to put aside the empty feeling left by Zach going dark.

Zach's words from his phone call a short while ago ran on a loop inside Marty's head as he stood knocking at Claudia's apartment door: "Watch out for my girl. I wasn't able to talk to her last night, and she hasn't picked up her phone this morning, so I'm a little worried."

I'll always look out for your girl, Marty had nearly blurted. Taking care of Claudia any way he could was as natural as breathing.

"We had *a lot* to drink last night, Zach. I'm sure she's still sleeping it off. I'm picking her up in fifteen minutes for a jog, so I'll give you a shout if she's anything but fine," he had answered.

"I'm glad you were there to celebrate with her. Wish I could have been."

"I'm pretty sure she does too." Claudia had rallied and put on a good show of enjoying herself, but there had been no mistaking the sliver of sadness in her eyes whenever Zach's name had come up during their celebration last night.

"I'll make it up to her when the season's over. God, I can't wait to see her in a few days, and I can't wait for the wedding."

"No cold feet?" Marty had joked.

"No, sir. My feet are sizzling, they're so hot. I'm putting on my dancing shoes when that day comes. I'm so ready to make it official."

The tension that had crackled between them during Marty's visit in February had eased, and thank God. But for the physical distance, their friendship was back on track. Zach told Marty he'd given up booze, and the shift in Zach's personality was unmistakable. The fact that he was looking forward to tying the knot rather than fixating on other women's anatomy had flooded Marty with a sense of relief too.

The world was as it should be ... except no one was answering his knocks. He rapped again and shouted through the door. "Hey, sleepyheads. This is your 10:00 a.m. wake-up call. Get up."

Megan, her dark hair disheveled and only one eye open, cracked the door as wide as the security chain would allow. "Goddamn, if it isn't the bluebird of happiness chirping *way* too early." The smell of sour alcohol wafted through the opening.

He grinned. "Ten o'clock is *not* too early for birds to be chirping."

The door closed, and the sound of a chain sliding preceded her opening it wide. She turned and walked away from him, giving him the back view of a baggy men's BC T-shirt that barely covered her ass. "Well, go chirp at CC, then. I'm going back to bed."

His gaze roamed to the hallway and Claudia's closed door. "Is she even awake?"

"Beats me." Meg shuffled to her bedroom and shut the door. Simultaneously, Claudia's door opened.

Hair up in a long ponytail, she was dressed for running, but shadows smudged the skin below her half-lidded eyes. "I'm ready," she croaked. Instead of alcohol, the smell of soap and something fresh drifted off her.

"Did you just get up?"

She looked up at him, the slight move making her wince. "No, I've been up for five minutes."

He laughed. He couldn't help himself. "You sure you want to do this?"

She nodded. "I have to. I only have a few months to be a knockout in that strapless dress. I don't want to give Zach any excuses to run from the altar."

Marty leaned his arm on the wall by her door and tugged her ponytail with his free hand. "There's no doubt you'll be a knockout, and Zach won't be looking for excuses to run. If he's stupid enough to make one wrong move, I'll beat his ass, and then I'll take his place."

She gave him a bleary-eyed smile. "I can always depend on you to do the right thing, Smarty Marty."

A frisson of sorrow caught him off guard, wrapping its tendrils around his heart, but he shook it off. "Yes, you can, CC, bride-to-be." *Count on it for the rest of your life.*

Chapter 16

THE SECRETS THAT STAY IN VEGAS

Two and a half months later

Marty stood frozen in place, unable to pull his eyes from the scene in front of him. It couldn't be happening. It had to be a nightmare. An inner head slap ripped the curtain from that illusion: this was real. He had been thrust into a no-man's-land, torn between right and wrong, between what to do and whether to do anything at all. Where did his allegiances lie?

The first day of the bachelor party had started out tame. They had spent the morning golfing, the early afternoon drinking in the clubhouse, followed by gambling and dinner at Bayette's. A group of twelve guys having a good time celebrating a wedding six days away. Had it been Marty's bachelor party, he would have been satisfied to stop right there. But it wasn't his party, and, as the actual bachelor continually reminded him, it was Marty's job to make sure Zach got whatever Zach wanted: the best fucking party ever.

Countless cocktails and a dozen bottles of wine with dinner had turned the benign celebration rowdy, and the party had been obliged to leave the steakhouse. From there, the "herd of cats"—led by Steele, the tom of the group, and his willing accomplice, Zach—had prowled the nightclubs until they had settled in the one where Marty currently found himself. Marty, together with Rex—who had flown in from Japan only the day before—had switched to nonalcoholic beverages. Rex because he was a light drinker and jet-lagged, and Marty because he needed his wits about him in order to collar Zach, the elusive Energizer Bunny.

Even before the evening had gotten away from him, Marty had decided it sucked being sober when everyone around you was smashed. It also sucked that he was an abject failure at keeping tabs on his best friend, as evidenced by the shenanigans on full display.

The multi-leveled, cavernous space was bathed in dark blues and violets, and a smoky haze softened strobes and spotlights. Liberally scattered throughout were clear floor-to-ceiling tubes that stood upon neon-pink-banded pedestals. Inside the cylinders, women in silver thongs and platform heels gyrated to the pulsing beat. But the titillating displays hadn't been enough to satisfy New Zach. The dude's Energizer Bunny self had been ramping up while grinding Marty down to a state of exhaustion before disappearing into the dark recesses of the club.

And now Marty had found him ... in a secluded hallway that held semi-private cubicles where people could talk. Or engage in activities like the one Zach was currently engaged in.

The *bachelor*, his shirt unbuttoned, sat in a chair braced against one of the booth's walls, lending Marty an excellent side view. Zach, however, had no idea Marty stood within eight feet because his head was thrown back and his eyes were closed. A well-endowed dark-haired woman in a red-and-black lace bustier, a tight black skirt hiked around her hips, and red stilettos straddled his lap. She was grinding down on him as he palmed her exposed tits.

What. The. Actual. Fuck?

Despite the nude tube dancers, they were in a nightclub, not a strip club, yet Zach had gotten himself a lap dance.

Stunned stupid, it took several beats before Marty's brain kicked into gear and his mouth moved.

"Zach! Jesus Christ!" he bellowed, his voice cutting through the pounding beat of the music. They whipped their heads toward him and froze. Zach stared at him wide-eyed as the woman clambered off his lap, adjusted her bustier, and exited the booth, brushing against Marty without acknowledging him.

Just another day at the office?

Marty stepped into the booth. "What the fuck was that?"

Zach shoved his fingers in his hair. He leveled a fierce glare at Marty. "What did it look like, dumbass?"

"What about Claudia?" Marty snapped.

"What *about* Claudia?"

"What would she think if she walked in and saw what I just saw?"

"What exactly did you see?" Zach tossed back.

"A chick giving you a lap dance. You feeling her up and getting off. That's what I saw."

"Jealous much?" Zach let out a mirthless laugh. "And I didn't get off." Marty could have sworn Zach grumbled, "Thanks to you."

"What the fuck is the matter with you, Zach? You're getting married in less than a week!"

"Nothing's the matter with me, but Jesus, Marty, this den-mother act is fucking annoying," Zach slurred. "Lighten up already! We had our clothes on. Nothing was going on. I didn't even kiss her."

"You call that *nothing*? Who are you, Bill Clinton?" Marty could feel a vein throbbing in his neck.

Zach stood up, calmly rearranged his fly, and buttoned his shirt—which was when Marty noticed flakes of white powder on the dark fabric and a trace below his left nostril. Now Zach's behavior made a little more sense.

"She was a little drunk and got friendly, that's all," Zach continued. "What was I supposed to do, push her off my lap? It's not like I fucked her or had her blow me. I sure as hell could have done either, but I kept it under control. Satisfied?"

Not at all.

Zach patted his shoulder, and Marty shoved his hand away. Zach smirked. "Let it go, dude. I'm just acting like any other twenty-three-year-old pro athlete who's making a shit ton of money. I'm taking advantage of the perks while I can, living in the moment, sowing my wild oats. That's all. I wasn't going to take that chick home and screw her. Fuck, I didn't even know her name."

"And that makes it better?" Marty couldn't stop himself. "Not only do you disrespect *your future wife*—who would be utterly humiliated if she knew—but you discount that girl like she's nothing more than a prize you're entitled to." He pointed at Zach's shirt. "Your good time is showing."

"Whoa, bro. Is that the real problem here? I'm more than willing to share." Zach looped an arm around Marty's neck. "C'mon, LB. Let's get you some happy powder. You're not having enough fun, buddy."

Marty broke Zach's hold. "No, thanks."

Zach snorted. "I never realized what a prude you are."

Marty's jaw clenched. "I'm no prude, but you are way out of line tonight."

A few beats passed with Zach looking at the floor and Marty's chest heaving with angry breaths. Zach propped a hand on his hip. "Maybe." He offered Marty a conciliatory half-smile. "Having the time of my life. I mean, this is the best, and I just got a little carried away. It doesn't mean anything."

And where were Zach's thoughts of Claudia in the midst of this shit-show?

Zach continued. "I guess I didn't think about Claudia—just me and the moment—and I should have. I love her. I don't want to hurt her. Ever."

Marty's head spun. Who was this guy standing beside him?

Lights flickered on, their glare harsh. Zach puffed out a breath. "Looks like it's closing time. Maybe we should call it a night, huh? I'll do better tomorrow, bro. I promise." He held out his hand for a shake, and Marty was slow to take it.

Zach had two personalities: New Zach, the guy brimming with a helluva lot of swagger and entitlement, and Old Zach, the dude who didn't take himself too seriously and who cared about his friends.

Which Zach would emerge in the end?

If Marty thought he had seen the worst of New Zach, he'd been sorely mistaken. The next night, after another day of golfing, drinking, gambling, and more drinking, a high, shit-faced Zach had been so amped up before the strippers arrived that Steele joked he should jack off first so he wouldn't embarrass himself when the show began around ten thirty.

Zach, Steele, Rex, and Marty shared a palatial four-bedroom suite, but the party was being held in one of the other suites Marty had rented, which was equally large and lavish.

As it had been the entire time, the booze was top-shelf and plentiful, and now Zach didn't bother hiding his latest vice: the nose candy heaped on a glass countertop in one of the suite's many bathrooms. Turned out that was top-shelf too.

Zach pulled Marty aside several times, asking if he was behaving well enough to pass Marty's den-mother test. The act grated. When Marty gave him a little shove and told him to shut up, Zach laughed it off. "You know I'm only giving you shit, right? C'mon. Have a drink, do some blow. Loosen up. If you're lucky, you might get a different kind of blow later, assuming one of the girls is willing." He'd waggled his eyebrows devilishly.

"Is that what *you're* hoping for?" Marty had thrown back and held his breath.

"I'm an almost married man. Just thinking of my friends. I'm generous like that."

They had spent the next little bit partying and talking about old teammates and friends when Zach had blindsided Marty. "Speaking of friends, what's up with you and Megan?"

The abundance of whiskey in Marty's bloodstream had done little to help him jump back on track. "What do you mean?"

Zach had guffawed. "Dude, seriously, why aren't you tapping that?"

"Not interested," Marty had chuffed. "Why the hell is everyone so dead set on me sleeping with her?" God, but he was so over the Megan setups.

Zach had lowered his voice conspiratorially. "I don't know about 'everyone,' but I want you to do the deed so you can tell me how it is."

Marty had given his head a little shake. "'Scuse me?"

"What are you, blind? That girl is *smoking* hot, and she's dying for you to fuck her, you lucky bastard." Marty's rising bemusement had likely shown on his face, though Zach apparently hadn't picked it up because he had run on. "So give her what she wants and bone her, just once, then tell me what she's like. I bet she's one fun fuck. I've imagined screwing that chick for a *long* time."

Impaired as he had been, Marty had been sickened, and he'd spluttered, "Dude, she's your fiancée's best friend! Show some class. That's just ... wrong."

Zach had simply thrown his head back and laughed. Before Marty could marshal another piece of his mind, the doorbell had rung, and Steele had opened the door to a group of gorgeous women. Though Zach was paying, Marty had done his research and ordered them up for tonight. He had taken his title of best man seriously.

And what a great job he'd done, according to the boys who had congratulated him and slapped him on the back. The bachelor had gotten what his heart desired: six very hot, well-endowed strippers who pranced for him and fawned over him. Zach was the grand sultan presiding over his harem. And he had loved it so much he talked the girls into staying when their act was over. A more apt description might have been that he had hauled out his fat wallet and bribed them, but the girls hadn't complained, and the guys had whooped their delight.

Everyone had been happy with the outcome. Well, most everyone.

Hours later, here Marty sat, a little nauseated over the debauchery he'd organized, in a suite brimming with drunk, coked-up, horny guys and six topless dancers moving their bodies in ways that made him squirm. His dick and his brain had gone two separate ways. His dick was doing what came naturally when there was a little too much drink, a little too much dancing, a little too much feminine skin on display. But his brain was fixed on Claudia and his promise to her. *You will tell me if Zach ever strays, won't you? You're my best friend.*

God, what would she think of him if she got an eyeful of this room right now?

Technically, though, Zach *hadn't* strayed—or so Marty argued with himself. Strippers, lap dances, and suspicions aside, Marty hadn't caught his friend *in the act*, and Zach had sworn he hadn't committed *the act*. Marty decided to leave the cocaine out of the equation because Claudia had never specifically asked for that kind of intel.

His eyes tracked two of their group and one of the dancers heading to the bathroom, as they'd been doing all night. Besides coke, his mind leapt to what else they might be doing in there.

Shit, would it just stop already?

"Dude, you look like you just lost your best friend," Zach laughed, his eyes hooded and his speech slurred.

"A little beat, that's all."

Marty had lost track of time. A glance at his watch told him it was past three.

A stripper in nothing but a thong parked her bare ass on Zach's knee, and to Marty's relief, he kept his hands in the PG zone. The woman tipped a glass of bourbon to Zach's lips, and he gulped it and licked his lips.

"That's nice, baby," he purred. He took the glass from her and held it to *her* lips. Watching her mouth closely as she sipped, he distractedly mumbled to Marty, "If you're tired, go back to the suite." Then the woman cupped Zach's face and pulled his mouth to hers, and they were all thrashing tongues as she deposited the liquor into his mouth. A moan rumbled in Zach's throat.

Can't do it.

Zach pulled away, a little breathless. "If you think you need to keep an eye on me, don't worry. The girls' time is about up." Zach's eyes lingered unabashedly on the woman's tits before lifting to the coy smile on her face. "What lovely, large knockers you have."

She looped her arms around his neck and let out a throaty laugh. "Why, thank you, doctor."

Young Frankenstein *is now officially ruined for me.*

Rex, who had looked more shell-shocked tonight than last night, faked a yawn. "I'm beat too, Marty. Let's head back."

Zach's eyes strayed across the room to where Steele was bumping and grinding between two girls. "Steele and I will get them paid and come back to the room in just a few. Promise." The look on Zach's face was pure earnestness, so different from the wolfish one from only moments before. *Dr. Jekyll, Mr. Hyde. Old Zach, New Zach.*

"I'll do you one better, LB. I'll knock on your door so you know I'm back. If I don't, you can come drag my ass back."

Shit, I'm so damn tired. Zach can't get into too much trouble with just a few minutes left on the clock.

Rex jerked his head toward the door. "Works for me. Let's go."

Marty wobbled to his feet, anxious to leave. "All right."

He and Rex trudged back to their suite and exchanged good nights before retreating to their respective bedrooms, which were down a hallway on the opposite side from Zach's and Steele's rooms.

Marty stripped down to his boxers, climbed under the sheets, and scrubbed his hand down his face. Thank fuck this bachelor party was over! Tomorrow they'd board planes and head to their respective homes. Marty would fly to Hartford—the closest airport to Springfield—while Zach and Rex headed to Boston. Marty would grab Danielle and drive to Salem, where they'd all focus on the wedding taking place on an estate bordering the harbor in Salem in just a few days.

The sooner Zach married Claudia, the better. Marty felt as though he was handing off an unruly teenager, and he was glad to be done with the responsibility. As he stared at the ceiling, a knock jarred him from his thoughts.

"S'me," Zach announced. "Thanks for these couple days, buddy."

"You're welcome. Get some shut-eye."

"Yep."

Relief flooded Marty's body. Yeah, Zach had pushed the envelope for sure—more like shoved—but Marty could tell Claudia her fiancé had remained true and do so with a clear conscience. Tired as he was, though, the night's activities kept him from a deep sleep. He drifted along the edges of dreams where men laughed and women giggled.

Chapter 17
Those Pesky Gray Areas

The night was short—too short—and Marty dragged himself from bed, pulled on a pair of jeans, and trundled into the common area to fix some coffee. Why hadn't he thought to order it through room service? Didn't matter now. As he fiddled with the filter, a tiny cough sounded from behind him. He whirled, startled to see the woman who had been swapping spit with Zach last night standing behind him in a Titans T-shirt with Zach's number on the shoulder. The hem barely skimmed the tops of her bare thighs.

Confused, he blurted, "Do you want something else to put on?"

She smiled. "I think you've seen it all already, haven't you?"

"Just thought you might be cold," he said lamely. *Where did she come from?* He turned back to his task, though he'd forgotten what he was supposed to be doing. "Uh, didn't realize you came over last night."

"Mm-hmm. I hope we didn't wake you. Zach said you were sleeping and to keep it down. Kinda hard to do, if you know what I mean," she giggled.

"We?" He spun and nearly dropped the bag of ground coffee. Next to the first stripper was another one, dressed much like the first one but sporting Zach's golf shirt. Normally, Marty adored women

who weren't hung up on modesty, but this was not that kind of moment. His heart raced, and not because two beautiful, mostly naked women were looking him over.

Oh no, oh no, oh no.

"So, ah ..." He cleared the squeak from his voice. "You spent the night with Steele?" *For fuck's sake, please say yes.*

Titan T-shirt shook her head. "No, but Miranda and Sugar did. The other girls stayed with the guys in the party suite."

"That was one kickass party," Golf Shirt said.

Yeah, someone's ass is getting kicked.

Rex ambled out, and his eyes went wide behind his glasses. "Uh, hello." The girls pivoted, giving Marty perfect ass stereovision. Rex's eyes darted from the girls to Marty and back again. "Where did you two come from?" he rasped.

Right there with you, dude.

"Zach's room. Did we wake you?"

Just kill me now.

Marty couldn't get his tongue working, but Rex asked the question Irish step-dancing its way through Marty's mind: "So, you, uh, were here all night?"

"You're cute," Titan T-shirt said. She slid Golf Shirt a sly smile. "There wasn't much night left, but we squeezed the most out of it, didn't we?"

They tittered.

Just then, a yawning Zach in boxers emerged from the hallway. He took in the scene and swallowed hard. Titan T-shirt bounced over to him and plastered herself against him. His arms encircled her, but he appeared confused.

Maybe he didn't screw her.

That hope was dashed the next instant when she loudly whispered, "That was fun, especially the third time. Ready for more, Romeo? Maybe your friends would like to join us." She glanced over her shoulder, apparently feeling the need to explain. "We usually get the ugly, flabby guys who can't get it up, so it's a real treat for us to be with someone who's hung and knows how to use it." She turned back to Zach and caressed his face, adoration shimmering in her eyes.

Golf Shirt nodded behind her. Marty's and Rex's mouths dropped open. Zach's gaze fastened on Marty's.

Marty held up his hand. "You can't explain this one away."

Zach swallowed. "Then I won't try. But you can't tell her. It'll destroy her." A pained look overtook his features.

"You should have thought of that *before* you did irreparable damage."

"We need to talk. Just hear me out."

Two dickheads were getting married this week. Marty hadn't been able to stop one. He had been responsible for the other one and had totally blown it. *Fuck me.*

"You are such an asshole!" Marty glared at Zach from across the table. They sat in a diner, where breakfast dishes clinked and clanked harshly around them. Plates of pancakes, eggs, and bacon sat steaming in front of them, but Marty couldn't muster an appetite. Apparently, Zach could because he was shoveling food in his mouth.

Guess I'd be hungry too if I had just fucked two women three times over the course of a few hours.

Zach looked up at him. "I get it. I'm an asshole. But isn't it better I did this now instead of after Claudia and I are married? When I make those vows, that's it."

Marty sat forward, horrified. "You're not going through with the wedding, are you?"

"Why wouldn't I?"

"Seriously? You just cheated on her! Not once, but at least twice."

"How do you figure?"

Marty held up two fingers. "Two women."

"Yeah, but it all happened in the course of one night, so that equals one time."

"I'm not going to argue semantics with you. You. Did. It. After promising me—and her—you wouldn't."

Zach sighed and sat back. "I got caught up. I love the game, the chase, the newness, the excitement. Always have."

Marty narrowed his eyes. "How is sleeping with two hookers *chasing* them? You paid them to do it."

"Well, no, I didn't. I paid them to *strip*. Sex was their idea. They wanted a piece of the Zachinator, and I couldn't disappoint them. They threw those particular services in pro bono. Or is that 'pro boner'?"

Marty didn't miss the snicker Zach fought to hide. "Do you hear yourself, douchebag?"

"Guess you didn't like my little joke. Look, I screwed up. I got drunk and let things get out of hand. But I'm a guy with a boatload of steam to blow off. And there's nothing wrong with that."

"There's plenty wrong when you're incapable—or unwilling—to control it and you end up betraying a woman you supposedly love."

Zach scratched the back of his head and locked his eyes on Marty again. He dropped his voice. "Let me explain. I've *always* wanted to get it on with two girls at the same time. It's been a fantasy of mine since I was a kid and first started beating off. The opportunity was there, and I took it—*any* guy would. I'm only human. I figured it was better to get it out of my system now than let it consume me later. It doesn't make me love Claudia any less. And now it's done and out of the way." He laid his napkin on the table.

"I'm not sure *any* guy would." *I sure as hell wouldn't have, not if I were days away from marrying the most beautiful ...* "So you're telling me that at Steele's parties you never—" Marty swallowed the rest of his question. He didn't *want* to know if Zach had had sex with Brenda and Trixie—together or separately. "Never mind."

Another question that continually tumbled through Marty's mind surfaced once more. *Who and what are you, Zach Pruitt?* How many times had he imagined being in Zach's skates? A world where Claudia was *his*? He couldn't imagine looking at another woman, much less sleeping around, if Claudia waited at home for him. She would be the only woman he wanted. Was that a flaw in him or in Zach?

"Marty, if you tell Claudia what you saw, it'll ruin everything. She won't understand, and she'll be hurt. And it'll be for no good reason because I never plan on doing that again. I'm taking my vows in four days, and I will never betray them. She'll have a husband who will give her the world and who will take care of her. Are you willing to blow that up because of one indiscretion?"

"How is this suddenly *my* fault?" Claudia's tearstained face streaked through Marty's mind, and his heart constricted. Could he take knowing he'd caused the heartache behind those tears? He would be the messenger, however, and not the one who actually shattered her trust. Would she resent him for it? Would the adage "Don't shoot the messenger" come into play? Could he bear it if he lost her friendship? And what about Marty's own culpability when he had to admit to her that Zach's betrayal had come on *his* watch? That he had unwittingly aided and abetted?

Zach locked him in a hard stare, ignoring the question. "You envy me. You always have, haven't you?" Zach's voice held an edge Marty didn't like.

Marty sat back, his eyes staring out the window without seeing. "I thought I did once. You're at the top of the heap, tearing it up, playing in the best league in the world, earning tons of money. Everywhere you go, they roll out the red carpet for you." He turned his gaze back to Zach. "I used to think I wanted that. But watching you, I'm not so sure anymore."

One of Zach's eyebrows dipped. "What the fuck does that mean?"

"I believe all that fame has gone to your head and that you think it's okay to give in to your impulses. My worry would be that I'd get caught up just like you and lose who I am. 'I can't help myself' is your mantra. You blame it on booze; you blame it on other people. You don't take responsibility for your actions because somewhere along the way you've come to believe that you're entitled to behave badly. The money and fame have warped you, Zach. You're not the same guy I knew in juniors."

"I haven't been that guy in a while," Zach scoffed. Several beats went by. "Isn't this really more about you envying me Claudia? The fact that I won the prize and you missed out? That I *beat* you?"

Marty didn't mask his surprise. So much was packed into that statement that he had no idea where to start unpacking.

He marshaled his defenses. "If you're asking me if I wish I had a woman who was gorgeous and smart and fun waiting for me at home, who also worshipped the ground I walked on, then the answer is yes. But let's face it. Neither of us deserves Claudia."

A sigh gusted from Zach, and the fight seemed to leave his body with it. "You're right about that, LB." He rested his elbows on the table and held his forehead for long minutes. When he looked up again, guilt lurked in his eyes. "Bottom line is: I love Claudia. I need her so I can be a better man, so I can fly right. I want to build a life with her. I want to make her happy, live up to her expectations, be the guy she sees when she looks at me. I won't get that chance if you tell her what happened. I admit last night was a mistake. But last night is also ... nothing to me. I don't even remember most of it. It's gone, done, out of mind, like putting a loss in hockey behind me." Zach's eyes grew teary, and the look on his face twisted Marty's gut. "Please, Marty. I don't want to lose Claudia, especially over something that means nothing. Don't take this chance from me. I'll do whatever you say. No more drugs, no more alcohol, no more women who aren't her. I *need* her."

Marty wasn't sure Zach *knew* the meaning of love. For that matter, neither did Marty. But he was sure his moral compass was straighter than Zach's. Or was it? If Marty hadn't been so disgusted by Zach's behavior last night, would he have partaken in more than a few lines of coke, a few drinks, and a lot of ogling? The answer wasn't clear.

Zach wiped moisture from his eyes. "We've been friends a long time, Marty. Please."

Too many grays clouded Marty's vision. What was right? What was wrong? Where did his fidelity lie? If Zach was telling the truth, that he had needed to sow the last of his wild oats and his oat bag was now truly tapped, did Marty have the right to ruin two people's happiness?

His emotions, like his thoughts, were on a wild roller coaster ride with no end in sight.

Not telling Claudia meant he ran the risk of losing her trust and her friendship, and squandering either would feel like he'd severed one of his own limbs. Not to mention carrying Zach's secret could gut him. Yet telling Claudia meant that the friendship he had shared for the last decade with the guy sitting across the table from him would be irretrievably lost.

Who should he preserve, Zach or Claudia? Who came first? He had more history with Zach, had gone to battle with Zach, and Zach had shown his loyalty in spades when they'd been younger. Lately, though, Zach's priorities had shifted, and while his loyalty extended to his teammates, it didn't seem to apply to the one person who deserved it most: his fiancée. Then again, Zach had promised to never cross that line again.

Rock, meet hard place. Evils, I'll pick the lesser of you ... but which one is that?

The questions bombarding Marty's brain congealed into one: Was Marty willing to deliver heartache at Claudia's doorstep four days before the wedding she'd been looking forward to the past year? Not if he could help it.

"You've got to stay away from guys like Steele." *So I'm negotiating now?*

Light brightened Zach's watery eyes, as if he'd just caught a lifeline that would pull him to safety. "Done. Claudia doesn't like him anyway, so I don't see that friendship continuing. Besides, word on the street is that he won't be sticking with the team."

"What about the shit you said about Megan last night?" *Yeah, we need to clear that up too.*

"Fuck. What did I say?' Zach cast his eyes to the table. "I was so wasted I don't remember. You've known me a long time, Marty. Sometimes I just vomit out shit that has no relation to my brain. It doesn't mean anything."

"Your words better start meaning something, dude—*now*—or you're going to get burned ... or worse, burn someone you care about." He didn't hold back his disdain, though it might have easily been directed at himself for his part in the cover-up.

Rex intercepted him later as he strode into the suite. "Where's Zach?"

"I left him downstairs to settle up the hotel bill. Why?"

"I'm not sure I can look him in the eye. Are you going to tell—"

Marty cuffed Rex's arm and steered him toward the bedroom. "I've gotta finish packing. Why don't we talk while I'm doing that?"

Once inside the bedroom, he latched the door and gathered his bag. "I just spent the last hour with Zach, and he swears last night was a case of him sowing the last of his wild oats and that he has it out of his system now. He begged me not to say anything because he's in love with Claudia and still wants to marry her. He promised to be faithful from now on."

Rex folded his arms over his chest and watched him from the other side of the bed. "And you believe him?"

Marty paused his packing. "I believe he *means* to. I believe he *wants* to. I believe he genuinely loves her."

"So what are you going to do?"

Marty pushed a breath through his lungs. "I'm not going to tell her." There. He'd said it out loud, so his decision was made.

Rex's eyes widened, and his jaw went slack. "But what if—"

"Rex, you've been her best friend for a long time. Do *you* want to watch her go through that kind of heartbreak? Her engagement to the guy she thinks is Mr. Right will be off, the wedding she's been planning all year will be off, and she'll be humiliated in front of her friends and family. What would *you* do?"

Rex stroked his stubbly chin. "You make a valid point."

"As long as there's a chance Zach follows through on his promises, Claudia won't get hurt. If I tell her now, she's definitely going to get hurt. For what it's worth, he also promised to stop the drinking and drugs and hanging out with guys like Steele. If he can keep his nose clean, there's a good chance he'll keep those promises."

"Yeah, I have a feeling Steele is Eddie Haskell."

Marty frowned. "Who's Eddie Haskell?"

Rex gave him a sheepish smile. "Alice loves reruns of *Leave it to Beaver*. Eddie Haskell is this kid on the show who's always coming up with these schemes, and he eggs the other kids on. They end up doing his dirty work and getting caught while he gets away slick as a whistle."

Marty tossed a pair of socks into his bag. "Except, unlike Zach, Steele's got nothing to lose, and he's right in there with them doing the 'dirty work.' So I ask you again, what would you do?"

Rex raised his eyes to Marty's. "I'd probably go the same route you're going. I'm not sure I'd have thought to extract the bargains from him, so good on you for thinking of it."

Extract the bargains. Why did Marty feel as though he had bargained with the devil?

The wedding day arrived with minimal drama, and Marty was lauded for carrying out his best-man duties smoothly. Well, most of them anyway.

Like the first time he had seen her, Claudia had seemed to be surrounded in light as she walked down the aisle on her mother's arm. Her beauty had so captivated him that he'd almost missed his cue for the ring and fumbled. Beyond the near miss—which had the congregation chuckling—he had made the perfect toast, danced with the mothers, aunts, and bridesmaids, and had seen the bride and groom off on their ten-day honeymoon to Belize.

Yeah, he'd done a great job. Too bad he got no joy from it. While people continued dancing and celebrating, he sat alone with his back to them at one of the guest tables, drinking yet another whiskey in a long line of whiskeys. If he drank enough, he would fill the hollowness that had been building all day and was on the verge of swallowing him whole.

The wedding had been a jolt to Marty's system, like the death of a loved one. The bonds were set in ink, and Claudia would never be more than a friend to him. Finality had hung in the air the entire day, nearly suffocating him. Guilt and sadness sat heavy in his chest.

No amount of telling himself he didn't care or that he was happy for his best friend dulled the ache, and the more he drank, the more the alcohol ripped down the barriers he had erected these past years. The truth glared at him from behind the rubble of his barricade: he loved Claudia with a boundless passion, and he would never have her.

A light touch on his shoulder made him turn. "Hey. Still tuxed up, huh?" Danielle slid into the empty seat beside him.

"Guess I forgot." He loosened his bowtie and unfastened the top few buttons of his shirt. "There. Now I'm relaxed."

Dani laughed. "It's a start, but you have a long way to go."

He held up his mostly empty drink. "Six more of these will help."

"Drink those, and you'll never find the room."

The venue's mansion had been converted into a B&B, and Zach had booked the entire place for the wedding party. Consequently, Marty's stumble to the room he shared with Dani would be a short one unless he got lost, which was a definite possibility. "You'll be here to steer me in the right direction, and then you can pour me into bed."

"Except I'm not going to be here."

He arched an eyebrow. "You're not? Where are you going?"

Danielle jabbed a thumb over her shoulder. "See the girl over there?"

"The one you've been hanging with all day?"

"Yeah. She and I started talking, and we hit it off. Her parents are friends of the Campbells, and her dad is a district court judge in Salem. Anyway, they're headed to their vacation home on Cape Cod for a few days and invited me to join them. They'll drive me to Springfield after, so you don't have to come get me."

What could he say? She was nineteen. "Okay, then have fun, I guess. Leave me their contact info."

She nodded just as two slender hands slid icy drinks on the table; one drink was clear, the other brown. Marty's gaze traveled up the arms attached to the hands and landed on Megan's grinning face. She nudged the brown drink over to him. "You look like you could use a refill."

"God bless you," he slurred and threw back the dregs of his whiskey, exchanging it for the fresh one.

Dani stood and leaned in to peck his cheek. "I leave you in Megan's capable hands. I'll see you in a few days."

Megan's eyes followed Danielle's exit. "Where's she off to?" He filled her in. A gleam lit Meg's pretty green eyes. "So I have you all to myself tonight, huh? Lucky me."

He chuffed. If she thought she was going to break down his defenses tonight, she was mistaken. Fortunately, she didn't push it. After congratulating each other for carrying out their best-man and maid-of-honor duties with ease, they moved on to benign topics: her recent move to Chicago for her first *real* job, his coming season. Miraculously, a few more drinks appeared, and each one seemed to go down easier than the last.

As he watched her talk, Zach's lewd words about Megan floated and bobbed in Marty's consciousness. Zach was right: the girl was smoking hot. She always had been. What had Marty found objectionable about her? Why had he resisted her all these years? The answer lurked in the gray areas until it bolted into his brain, and sadness reared its head again. *Claudia.*

Megan excused herself, and he looked around. Rex and Alice were clutched together on the dance floor, swaying to a fast song. Very few dancers remained, and those that did bopped to the beat around them. Shadows had grown longer, and the crowd had thinned. Megan came into his line of sight, and he watched the sway of her hips and the way the silky fabric of her dress accentuated them. Her hair was down, and it caught light and shifted over her shoulders. In her hands, she held fresh drinks. Feeling woozy, he loosened another shirt button and threw back the contents of his last drink before she reached him.

The familiar devilish gleam glistened in her eyes, and she laughed for reasons he didn't understand.

He ran a hand through his hair. "You're laughing. Do I look funny?"

She set the glasses on the table and gazed down at him. "Not at all. In fact ..." She surprised him when she plunked herself in his lap and threw her arms around his neck, her face mere inches from his. The pleasantness of her warm breath cascading over his skin was nullified by the alcohol on her breath, and he searched his muddled brain for a way to get her out of his lap politely but quickly. She gave him a classic Meg pout, apparently picking up his psyche's response to her.

She sighed and pressed her forehead to his. "Why don't you like me, Marty?"

"I like you, Meg." And he wasn't lying. There had always been a barrier between them, but he struggled to recall why. His gray matter was once more filled with shifting shades.

She rearranged herself so she perched on only one of his knees, and his hand went to her hip to steady her. A sly smile spread over her face, and he realized she had misunderstood the move and that he needed to correct that misunderstanding pronto. But then she leaned in and brushed her lips over his, and something inconvenient stirred. She lingered, kissing him softly. Unwelcome visions of the strippers' undulating, nude bodies, of the lusty woman in red lace sensuously riding Zach in a dark booth, of Claudia floating down the aisle in strapless white, her skin smooth and pearly and perfect, all converged in Marty's head. He found himself not only returning the kiss but taking control, deepening it as he gave himself over to unbridled need.

Megan responded with a moan and dug her nails into his back, through the fabric of his shirt.

He pulled away, his breathing ragged. Maybe he had found a way to fill the hole draining his soul. "Where's your room?"

He awoke the next morning with a massive hangover and a sinking feeling. He lay naked in a strange bed, with a body tucked beside him—also naked—the ends of her dark brown hair tickling his chin. Had they had sex? There were no condom wrappers in sight. Jesus fucking Christ, had he been so wasted that he'd had unprotected sex? With *Megan*? He *never* got that wasted; he also never forgot getting it on with someone. But if he couldn't remember *sex*, what else had he forgotten?

Gingerly, he inched his body to the edge of the bed and retrieved his boxers from the floor. As he pulled them on, he ransacked his memory banks but came up empty. He glanced over at her sleeping form, pondering how the hell to find out if he'd had unprotected sex—without offending her—and then how the hell to bolt without ... offending her.

Megan rolled over with a moan. One half-lidded eye fixed on him. "Morning," she mumbled.

"Morning," he croaked.

"We need to talk." She shuffled to the other side of the bed, holding the sheet to her chin.

Oh. Shit.

He leapt from the bed as though she'd goosed him. "I'll just, uh ... I'll get dressed, and we can talk over breakfast."

Thirty minutes of awkward silence passed before they faced each other across a restaurant table. She sipped fresh coffee and moaned. “Omigod, do I need this!”

His brain leapt to whether she had moaned like that last night, and he winced inside. *Why can’t I remember?*

She leveled her bloodshot greens at him. “What do you remember about last night?”

“Uh, to be honest, things are a little fuzzy from the time we got to your room.”

Her mouth twisted to the side while she regarded him for a beat. “We didn’t have sex.”

Simultaneously relieved and puzzled, he blinked. “We didn’t?” Had his cock wilted from the copious amounts of whiskey he’d imbibed?

She smirked. “You were ready to go, so that’s not what stopped us.”

He slugged a sip of coffee in a bid to mask his growing discomfort. She was going to drag out the torture, wasn’t she? “So what *did* stop us?” he prodded.

“You called me ‘Claudia.’”

His head jerked. “I *what?*”

“Needless to say, that sucked the air right out of my tires.”

Okay. So he deserved to be tortured ... and much, much more. “Are you sure that’s what I said? What if I actually said *clown car* or *Counting Crows*?”

Her eyes narrowed. “Hmm. I’m pretty sure that would be even worse. Either way, I know what I heard, and you said *her* name. You know, I’ve been called a lot of things, but this is the first time in my life I’ve been called my best friend’s name by the guy I’m naked with.”

He sat back with a gust of air. “I don’t know what to say ... other than I’m really, really sorry.”

She cupped her chin in her hand. She really did have pretty green eyes. “That’s one of the things I like best about you. You’re not full of yourself, and you’re sincere to a fault. Damn, I wish you were a jerk.”

"Gee, thanks?"

She twirled her mug on the tabletop. "I have a theory."

Uh-oh. "Do I want to hear this?"

"I don't care if you do or not. I'm telling you anyway. I think you're in love with Claudia, and you have been since day one. You were wishing it was her in that bed instead of me."

He reared back. *"What?"*

She sprouted a smirk.

He leaned across the table and tapped her forehead with his middle finger. "You've lost it, haven't you? Working with all those numbers and computers has sucked the brain right out of your head."

"Haha. Funny, Marty. But you know what? You don't fool me. I've had a few epiphanies since last night." Her thumb went up. "One, you light up every time she walks into a room, and you don't pay attention to anyone else when she's there. When you think no one's looking, you steal glances at her." She flicked out her index finger. "Two, you open up to her. You talk to her like no one else, and you seem ... happy, relaxed when you're around her." Her middle finger popped up. "Three, yesterday, when she was walking down the aisle toward Zach, you got this indescribably sad look. Or maybe it was an 'I wish that was me' expression. I hadn't put it all together before, but now it's clear as day."

The painful stab he had dulled from yesterday reared up and gave him a lung-crushing jab. He sucked in a breath. "That's it. I'm calling the loony wagon."

She laid her hand gently on his forearm, and compassion hovered in her eyes. "Hey, between you and me? I think she should have married you instead of Zach."

That makes two of us. Then again, he asked and I didn't. "Too late now."

Chapter 18

SOMETHING'S ROTTEN IN ST. LOUIS

Six months later

Claudia leapt for the phone. Zach had left for the road days ago, and she wanted to hear his voice and know everything was okay. Her heart sank a little when she read the caller ID.

"Hi, Meg."

"Wow. Let's not go overboard with the excitement, huh?"

"Sorry," Claudia laughed. "I thought you might be Zach. I haven't talked to him for a few days."

"When does he come to Chicago next? Maybe he and I can meet up."

"I'll have to check the schedule, but I don't think it's for a few months yet. Speaking of meeting up, though, he'll be in Boston the end of this month, and he might squeeze in one of Marty's games."

"Hmm."

"That's it? I expected to hear your gears clicking, your eyelashes fluttering, and talk about crashing their mini-reunion so you could jump Marty's bones." Claudia was still trying to puzzle out what, if anything, had happened between her two best friends at the wedding. Ever since Claudia had returned from her honeymoon, Megan's relentless pursuit had turned arctic and become encrusted with ice so thick it had freezer burn.

"I told you, I'm not interested anymore," Meg huffed.

"Yeah, you told me, but I still don't understand why."

"I'm tired of chasing a guy who's obviously not interested. My confidence was taking too big a hit, so I've turned my sights on other targets."

Claudia snorted. "Anyone in particular?"

"Nope, but I'm having fun trying out different candidates. Let's just say sex is on the menu nightly, if I want it. So enough about me. Let's talk about you."

"Oh, let's not." Claudia laughed harshly to mask her discomfort. Talking about Meg's love life had taken her mind off her own, and she preferred to keep it that way.

"Oh, come on! You're only six months into a marriage to Mr. Hot Hockey Superstar. You two must be burning up the sheets on the regular. Before long, your bed will be a heap of ash."

Claudia hesitated, unsure what to say next. Tell Meg the truth? That the sheets were tepid? That Zach had been distancing himself? That he denied it whenever Claudia brought it up?

It's just a phase. He's under a lot of pressure. No point exposing the dirty laundry.

Instead of confiding in her bestie, she forced another laugh. "Yeah, living with a hockey hottie is one funfest." *A little too much sarcasm maybe. Hopefully Meg didn't pick it up.* Claudia recovered and sped ahead. "He's always in demand. For instance, when he gets home in two days, we attend a teammate's party. Then it's more parties or dinners nearly every night until he leaves again. Our social calendar is full, full, full." Never mind that Claudia would have preferred cozying up on the couch, eating pizza, and watching a movie instead. Zach seemed to want the opposite.

Maybe Zach's aloofness lately stemmed from her broaching the subject of work again. Talking about her teaching always put him off, but he'd have to get over it because she would soon be on the hunt for a job. She couldn't bear to sit around forever, and she wasn't ready to pop out babies like he wanted her to. Helping with the fundraisers occupied some of her spare time, but it didn't fulfill her. Besides, she wanted a life of her own, *outside* of hockey.

She steered the conversation away from her marriage and got lost in Megan's stories about life in Chicago and their childhood memories. Those recollections always lifted Claudia's spirits.

"Did you get Rex's email?" Meg asked. "It sounds like they're coming home for good in a few months."

"I wonder where they're going to settle?"

They spent the next fifteen minutes arguing playfully about which of their two cities was the best one for the couple to live in. When Claudia finally hung up, it was seven o'clock. If Zach had tried to reach her, their call waiting would have beeped. But there had been nothing.

She paused to admire her flourishing herb garden. How poignant that in the midst of the luxury surrounding her, Marty's simple gift was the possession she most treasured.

After pouring herself a healthy glassful of red, she settled on the couch, her legs curled under her as she stared out the windows at the twinkling skyline. How could something so beautiful feel so cold?

"How did I get here?" she asked herself aloud.

Two glasses in, she hadn't found the answer, so she put herself to bed. Tomorrow would probably bring an achy head, but at least it would dull the ache in her heart.

Claudia's world mostly righted itself when Zach came home, she mused as they pulled up to his teammate's house. Inside, the party was warming up but seemed to jump a full gear when Zach walked in. He was exceptionally handsome tonight, and she fell back to observe the heads turned toward him, as though he was a sun god blessing his following by simply being among them, by shining on them.

He disappeared almost immediately, and she found him minutes later at the bar, a drained drink in hand, talking to a group of men and women as he got himself a refill. She told herself she was a big girl and could get her own beverage, though he usually fetched one for her and spent time with her throughout the evening—especially at the beginning, when she was the least comfortable. But she didn't let the oversight ruffle her feathers. He'd been gone, she was happy he was home, and they were going to have fun, damn it.

The next instant, he *did* ruffle her feathers when he extended his arm and pulled her snug against him, addressing the cluster of mostly familiar faces. "You've all met Claudia, right? The future ex-Mrs. Pruitt?" He gripped her a little tighter to lock her in and looked down his nose at her. "Oh, wait. You can't be an *ex-Mrs.* since you're still a Campbell." Their audience laughed politely. She did not.

Was she recognizing a new wrinkle in his personality, or had she been blind to his machoism this entire time?

The question spun in her mind as she doused her anger and pretended to join in the conversation. Zach soon excused himself, and for the rest of the evening, he disappeared and reappeared but mostly left her on her own.

The party eventually wound down and she was ready to leave, but she couldn't find Zach. She went searching and found him in the host's deserted office, alone with BB, a beautiful blond in a tight, low-cut black leather dress that revealed a lot of cleavage. And BB had a lot of cleavage to reveal.

Cloaked in the hallway shadows, Claudia observed BB and Zach standing several feet apart, talking, though Zach's gaze rested on the woman's breasts instead of her face. BB was a teammate's wife who often ended up in explosive arguments with him, or so Claudia had heard. She had never exchanged more than a greeting with the woman and hadn't witnessed any drama firsthand. Still, the significant others buzzed with envy whenever they spoke about her, and Claudia understood why. The woman was centerfold-worthy.

Claudia mustered her confidence and strutted in. Zach shot her a startlingly irritated look. Under his breath—but loud enough to hear—he said, "Uh-oh. Mom's here. Guess I'm in trouble."

BB—bless her—turned and offered Claudia a warm smile. "And here's your lovely wife you've been telling me so much about. I'll just scoot and leave you two alone. Nice talking to you, Zach."

His eyes trailed BB out of the office until she disappeared from sight. He turned to Claudia. "Hey, baby. Where have you been? I've been looking all over for you." He tucked her under his arm, his speech slurred.

"Liar. You've been busy chatting up Busty BB." She said it half-teasingly, trying to pin back her annoyance. Jealousy was not becoming, her mama had always said.

"Just being friendly. She was alone, and I felt bad for her."

"Huh. I've been alone too, but I don't recall you showing any concern for me."

He didn't seem to pick up on her snark. Instead, his gaze dipped to her chest and lingered. "I've been wondering. What would you say to getting breast implants?"

She burst out with a humorless laugh. "You're kidding, right?"

He blinked. "No. I think you could use a little more ... more."

She wiggled out of his hold and parked her hands on her hips. "I thought you liked my boobs the way they are." *You certainly couldn't keep your hands off them before.*

One eyebrow dipped, and he pointed at her chest. "They're okay, but you've been looking a little skinny lately." A grin formed on his face, part leer, part sneer. "A nice pair of double-D's. Something a man can smother himself in. Then I could really show you off, baby."

His words cut through her like a knife and carved out a chunk of her soul. Hot tears pricked her eyes. "Not funny, Zach."

"I'm not trying to be funny. I'm dead serious. If it's the money you're worried about, trust me. I can afford it."

All of her wanted to fold over and hide herself from his mocking appraisal, but anger steeled her spine. "I'm not worried about *anything* except how much you've had to drink." Alcohol was behind his comment. It had to be. He would never say anything so awful if he were sober, would he? Yet a veneer she had been clinging to was wearing off, and her anger couldn't conceal it. Alcohol might be the reason he criticized aloud, but it also had a way of revealing the truth. It pained her too much to admit he found her inadequate.

She pushed out a breath and said it was time to go home.

"I'm not done yet," he retorted.

"Yes, you are, Zach," she bit back.

"Ooh, I like it when you get all feisty like that. Tie me up and whip me, baby. I've been a bad, bad boy." He grabbed her ass roughly and growled, "Mine."

As she drove them home, he was over-the-top grabby.

"Stop it!" she snapped. "You're going to make me crash."

He slumped into his seat with a grumble.

They walked into the apartment, and he pounced, pinning her against the wall, laying sloppy kisses on her neck. Groping her under her blouse, he murmured, "Hey, baby, I have this idea about spicing up our sex life."

She gritted her teeth. "I didn't realize it needed spicing up."

He pulled back and smiled. The smile bordered on greasy. "It can be so much better. What would you say ... What if we tried a three-way?"

Her mouth dropped open. *A three-way?* Recovering herself, she tossed back, with exaggeratedly feigned innocence, "Oh! Like you, me, and another guy?"

His face transformed with shock, and the priceless look gave her a victory boost. The astonishment slid from his face, and he threw his head back and laughed. Then he leaned over her, renewing his assault on her neck and breasts. "No. You, me, and another woman. Wouldn't that be so fucking hot?" he mumbled against her skin.

She slid away from him and narrowed her eyes. "No, it wouldn't be hot. At. All! Wait. Just who did you have in mind?"

He opened his palms in a placating manner. "Don't be like that, CC. You know I was only kidding."

"Don't call me that, please." *I'm not fond of the nickname to begin with, and I especially don't like how it sounds coming from you.*

"CC, CC," he taunted. "Where's your sense of humor? You take everything I say so seriously sometimes. You know you're the only girl for me. Now come here and take your clothes off so I can feast my eyes on your beautiful body. Come on, baby. A nice, slow striptease. Do it for your Zach."

Disgust balled her stomach, and she fled to the guest room, her head spinning from the maelstrom of emotions.

She plopped on the bed, numb. After six months of marriage, they should have been lingering in the honeymoon phase, right? He should have still been infatuated with her and *only* her, just as she was. Not as a *Hustler* babe romping on the bed with him and another woman.

Those sheets were tepid because what they did between them was no longer lovemaking. The intimacy was gone, and the act was purely sex for the sake of release. Maybe if they could revive that connection, she would be less sensitive to his flirting. Once upon a time, it hadn't bothered her. Of course, that was before he'd become so overt. Even if she could resolve herself to that part of him, the sting of not measuring up in his eyes wouldn't go away.

Was she so unappealing? Or was the man she'd pledged herself to transforming into someone she didn't recognize—and didn't like?

Fully clothed, she crawled under the covers and let the tears come until she had no more to shed.

Marty looked up from his plate of cannelloni, his eyes taking in his best friend across the table. Zach continually glanced over his shoulder, seemingly disinterested in the food in front of him.

"Hey, you all right over there? You seem a little ... on edge."

"Huh? No, I'm good, man. Everything's great. Wonder when they're going to bring my other drink, though? I ordered it long before they brought our food." Zach sat upright stiffly, as if he was in pain.

Thought you'd given up booze.

The drink came, and Zach seemed to settle down, attacking his food like a man on rations. Tension ratcheted down a few clicks, and they talked hockey.

"You looked good out there tonight," Zach said. "Still don't know why you're not in the NHL."

Marty chuckled mirthlessly. "Tell that to management, huh? I watch the kids going up, but I haven't gotten the nod yet." *Not sure I ever will.* "You're having another kickass season, I see. Good on you."

Zach grinned. "Yeah, I'm doing all right, huh? They've got themselves a bargain right now. At the end of this year, Zach gets a *big* pay raise."

"Do you want to stay in St. Louis?"

Zach shrugged. “Don’t care. I’ll go wherever they’re willing to pay me every dime I’m worth.”

“How does Claudia feel about that? Will she mind picking up and moving?” The thought occurred to Marty that Zach hadn’t mentioned her once tonight.

“Claudia? She’ll be fine with it. When the kids come, though, that’ll be a different story,” Zach chuckled.

Marty’s heart registered an unexpected jab. “Yeah? Are you telling me there’s a little Pruitt on the way?”

Zach poked at his salad. “No, not yet. I’m doing my part, though.” A knowing grin spread over Zach’s face, and Marty cast his eyes back to his meal.

They continued eating in silence; Marty couldn’t recall this palpable awkwardness between them before. “So how *is* Claudia?”

“Claudia’s fine. You should give her a call. I’m sure she’ll fill your ear with the latest riveting details about the team’s fundraisers.” Zach rolled his eyes and made a “blah, blah, blah” gesture with his hand.

A most unflattering representation of his wife.

“You say that as if it’s a bad thing. I’d be proud of a wife who puts her career on hold for me and throws all her energy into something as worthwhile as that. Beats her sitting around, complaining that I’m not home enough.” *I’d be even more proud of her if she were teaching elementary kids.* His mind wandered to that bright-eyed sophomore he’d met all those years ago, eager to get her degree, joking about the smaller kids being easier to catch.

One of Zach’s eyebrows dipped, and his mouth became a firm line. “How is this any of your business?”

Whoa. “Sorry. I thought we were having a friendly conversation here.” Marty sat back and swiped his napkin across his mouth. He pointed at Zach’s empty drink. “Last time we talked, I thought you were giving that up.”

“Well, I guess I changed my mind, didn’t I?”

Fuck. Marty had a bad, bad feeling about this. He leaned in, forearms on the table. “What’s eating you, man?”

Zach threw down his napkin. “Shit, and here I thought I was going to have a pleasant time tonight, catching up with an old friend over dinner. Whoops! Disappointed again,” he mocked.

"No need to be an asshole, dude."

Zach hung his head. "I'm sorry. Christ, it's been a long road trip. I want to go home. I didn't mean to be a dick."

"Look, if you need—"

Zach held up his hand. "I know what you're going to say. You're going to tell me that if I need to talk, I can count on you. I know that, LB. I always have. You've been my best friend since we were sixteen. And while I appreciate the offer, I don't need anyone."

With a suppressed sigh, Marty turned the conversation back to Zach and his prowess on the ice, the only subject that brought a smile to his friend's face. As Marty listened with half an ear, he vowed to call Claudia in the morning and get the real story.

Claudia turned the table on him when he reached her the next day because suddenly they were talking about Megan, a subject he'd never intended to bring up. He was still conflicted about the night of the wedding and what had happened—or not happened—between them. Selfishly, he was beyond relieved that they hadn't done the deed, but he had hurt her. And as much as Megan had driven him crazy over the years, he felt bad that he'd undone their friendship. He hadn't spoken to her since their revealing breakfast the morning after.

"I like Megan," he heard himself say. "She's fun, smart, and a solid friend."

"So what exactly happened between you two?"

Alarms blared in his head. "Isn't that kind of a personal question?" How much about that night *had* Meg told Claudia?

"Absolutely, it is. But she's my best friend and so are you, which gives me nosy rights."

"Good to know." He paused his breathing. "Is *she* saying anything happened?"

"No, but it feels as if you two had a breakup and aren't telling me."

“We didn’t ‘break up’ because we were never together. She’s probably met someone she’s far more interested in than me, and that’s what you’re seeing.”

“Yeah, that’s what she said. So tell me about your sisters. Danielle’s living with you?”

He released a silent breath of relief. *Dodged that bullet.* “She is. Alexis may join us soon, but I’m torn about that development.”

“Why?”

And there he was, spilling his guts to her. It appeared Dickhead was trying to isolate his mother from friends and family. Lexi was one of the last stakes tethering his mother to them, but it placed his sister in a precarious situation Marty wanted her out of. Forget the inheritance he had once felt entitled to. All he cared about now was keeping his sisters whole. Dani had gotten out, and she wouldn’t turn back, though she still pined for her mom. So did Marty, but that mother was gone, despite his efforts to haul her back to them. She had made her choice, and that choice was the toxic, all-consuming relationship between her and her new husband. Marty didn’t want it spilling over on his young sister. But how could he spring her if she didn’t want to be sprung?

As he talked it out with Claudia, his shoulders eased a few inches. She always had that effect on him, and he was grateful to count her as a friend.

Chapter 19

LATE NIGHTS

A month later

Zach's name glowed on the caller ID, and Claudia's lips lifted into a smile. The regular season was done, and playoffs loomed. In that sliver between, they seemed to have struck some sort of equilibrium. Not exactly rock-solid, but a pad beneath them just the same. She was grateful for the chance it afforded them to breathe.

"Hey, handsome."

"Hi, babe. Hey, we're not doing anything tonight, are we?"

"Why, are you planning to come home and ravish me from dusk until dawn?" *Please say yes. We need some drought relief here.*

He barked a laugh—far from the smooth, purring "yes" she longed to hear. The night before, she had teased him about the honeymoon being over before their first wedding anniversary, but he hadn't responded to her little joke. Now she found herself wanting to throttle the little voice squeaking in her head that perhaps it wasn't a joke after all.

"Here's the thing. You know that car show I was telling you about?"

She shook her head, even though he couldn't see her. "No, I don't remember that."

"What? I swear, you don't listen to half of what I say anymore. The honeymoon *is* over!" He was kidding, though a hint of irritation ran through his voice. God, had she really been turning a deaf ear? She couldn't fathom it, not with the way she hung on his every word, a stroke to his ego he seemed to need and she tried to feed.

"I'm sorry, sweetie, but it must have slipped my mind."

"Then you're definitely going to have to give me this one. So Steele and I—"

"Steele, your old teammate?"

"Yeah. He's in town, and he thought it'd be fun to get together like old times."

She frowned. "Old times, as in his revolving door of women?"

"That's just a bunch of BS," he scoffed. "The guy gets a bad rap. If you'd give him a chance, you'd see that he's decent." The thread of annoyance was unmistakable this time.

"I didn't know I was being offered the chance. Are you bringing him home?"

"No, not this time. He and I are going to head over there now and check out the cars. Maybe I can find one of those cute sixties models convertible Corvettes you like so much and buy it for you."

Zach had taken to lavishing her with gifts lately, a puzzle she was still trying to solve. It wasn't their anniversary yet, and her birthday had come and gone. She should have been delighted and left it at that, but they weren't exactly gifts she'd wanted—more jewelry she didn't wear, an odd piece of art glass that didn't fit in, expensive perfume that wasn't her brand—and the way he'd sort of casually tossed them at her made them feel like an afterthought.

"Aw, that's so sweet." When had she mentioned wanting a vintage Corvette? "You want me to delay dinner for a little while?"

"Nah, we'll grab a bite to eat afterward. I know you've got a big day tomorrow. Don't wait up."

She had a breakfast meeting with the other SOs to organize a food drive that would dovetail with the start of playoffs. Nice that he had remembered, but a tiny alarm bell rang deep in her gut. She pushed it down, telling herself she was being an idiot. "Okay. I probably won't fall asleep, but if I do, you'll wake me up when you get home?"

Happy voices chattered in the background, though Claudia couldn't place them. It didn't sound like the usual locker room racket. "Yeah, sure. Hey look, gotta go."

"Don't I even get an 'I love you'?"

He responded with an exasperated sigh and dropped his voice low, as if he didn't want anybody to hear him. "You know I do. Do I have to say it every time we talk?"

Hurt sparked in her soul. "Um, no, of course not. I was just teasing. Have a good time."

"Christ, I'm sorry, babe. It's just that the guys are harassing me, and I really gotta go. I do love you."

Kinda hard to tell sometimes.

She went through the motions of making dinner anyway, more to give herself something to do than because she was hungry. As it was, when she sat down to eat alone, she found she could only take two or three bites. A debate raged inside of her, one side thinking way too long and way too hard about Zach's tone during the phone call, while the other side admonished her for sliding farther down the insecurity scale.

Her hypersensitivity over the past few months was making her brain record things that simply weren't there, and she needed to stop.

After a healthy glass of wine, losing herself in a rom-com, and slipping into silky PJs, she crawled into bed with her mind relatively calm and blank. She was awakened from a dreamless sleep by Zach's hard, hot body pressed up to her back. His body wasn't the only thing that was hard. Alcohol and shampoo drifted off of him. His tongue was licking a wet trail up her neck to her ear, and his hands were kneading her breasts through the satiny fabric. While she normally welcomed his sporadic advances, this one had an edge to it she couldn't warm to.

She lifted her lids, and the digital clock told her it was past three in the morning. How long had he been home? She turned in his hold, and her fingers wove through wet hair.

"When did you get home? And did you take a shower just now?" The scene was a bit fuzzy around the edges, and the thought occurred that maybe she was dreaming. But no, there was nothing dreamlike about his hands tugging at her bottoms.

As he continued his clumsy seduction, he murmured, "I've been home for a while, but I fell asleep on the couch. I smelled like cigar smoke, and I didn't think you'd enjoy that, so I took a shower. God, I'm so hot for you right now."

Confusion whirled in her mind. At home, he never took showers at night unless he was with her and they were engaging in sexy time—which hadn't happened in a while. And cigar smoke? Zach didn't smoke cigars. But he did drink—at times heavily—and the sour smell of alcohol currently oozing from his pores collided with his shampoo freshness. Add in the way he was attacking her clothes and the fact he was already naked, his usual bed attire of boxer briefs and T-shirt missing, and she wasn't sure the right man had climbed into her bed.

He shoved her bottoms around her knees while his hands frantically yanked at the hem of her top. She gave his chest a small shove. "Zach, what are you doing?" The words tumbled from her before she realized how stupid they sounded.

Undaunted, he continued wrestling with her top. "Isn't it obvious? I'm making love to my beautiful wife."

"This doesn't feel like lovemaking," she huffed, trying to inject humor she didn't feel into her words.

"That's because you need to loosen up. I've been thinking about you all night, and it's made me so fucking horny. I want you, Claudia." He latched onto a nipple, biting down hard enough to make her cry out.

She wriggled beneath him. "Ow! That hurts!"

"Come on, baby. Let's get down and dirty. You know you like it."

"Not if you're going to hurt me, I don't."

He stilled, peering down at her, a hard glint reflected in his eyes. He had pinned her arms above her head, and she was vulnerable. Exposed. This version of Zach was wild and unsettling, and it frightened her. *He* frightened her.

His expression suddenly softened, as did his hold. "I'm sorry, babe. I didn't mean to get carried away. It's just that being near you drives me fucking insane sometimes." He dropped his head into the crook of her neck and began laying soft kisses along her throat to her ear, where he paused to lavish her earlobe. "I need you, Claudia. I need you bad. I'm about to explode."

The plea in his voice gave her pause. She should have been overjoyed that her husband wanted her so desperately, but something felt off. He kissed her jaw, her mouth, and a moment later he sank inside her with one powerful thrust.

"Oh, thank fuck!" gusted from him.

The whole episode ended quickly, and he rolled off of her, flopping onto his back, immediately falling into a deep sleep. She inched away from him and pulled up her bottoms. Tucking the covers under her neck, she stared up at the ceiling, one question revolving through her mind: What the hell had prompted *that*?

A half-hour later, her eyes were still trained on the ceiling, and different scenarios played out in her head as the question tumbled around and around. She had no answer, but she did have a mantra which she repeated until she fell into a fitful sleep: *He wanted me. He came home to me.*

Waking before he did the following morning, she slipped from the covers and hurried through her morning routine so she could make it out the door before he woke. The urge to escape was a new feeling, one she couldn't quite comprehend.

As she was gathering her purse and notebook in the kitchen, Zach appeared, leaning against the door frame. In his usual boxers and T-shirt, he was a disheveled mess, his bleary eyes half-lidded and shot through with spiderwebs of red.

"Hi," he rasped.

"Hey."

His brows furrowed in a frown. "Are you mad at me?"

Straightening her spine, she placed a hand on her hip and fastened her gaze on him. "No, I'm not mad at you. Just a little confused about what happened last night."

He folded his arms across his chest. "What do you mean, what happened last night?"

"Never mind. I've got to get going." She hoisted her purse on her shoulder.

With no choice but to exit through the doorway where he now stood, she approached, intending to brush past him. As he encircled her wrist—presumably to hold her back—her eyes landed on two dark purple marks on his neck, just below his ear.

She sucked in a pained breath and lifted her chin toward his neck. "What are those?"

He immediately clapped a hand over the marks. "What are what?"

"The hickeys on your neck you're trying to cover up." She let the purse slide from her shoulders, and she crossed her arms, preparing for battle. Emotions tossed inside her like a stormy sea, pain and anger tearing at something deep and primal.

"You must have given them to me last night."

She shook her head. "Wasn't me." *You didn't give me the chance, even if I'd been inclined.*

"Actually, those aren't hickeys. I got hit with a stick," he countered.

"I must have missed that. When did you get hit with a stick?"

"In practice. Why are you being so paranoid? What, you think that because I spent the evening with a buddy that I've been out getting my neck sucked by some chick? I wouldn't do that to you, and you know it. Besides, if I was with someone else, why would I come home so horny for you? I swear, Claudia, you're making shit up, looking for trouble where there isn't any." One side of his mouth quirked. "Or maybe you think Steele was sucking my neck? Wait till I tell him!"

"You're not seeing him again, are you?"

"I told him I'd meet him for breakfast this morning before I fly out with the boys. That was before I realized I had to ask my wife for permission first." He placed his hands together in a mock praying gesture. "Please, Mom, may I have a written permission slip?"

"You're behaving like a class-A ass," she snorted. "Where exactly did you go last night?"

He rose to his full height. "And you're giving me the fifth degree. I told you. I went to the car show with Steele."

I am not backing down. "I mean after that."

"We went out for dinner, just like I said we would. How many times do I have to answer the same goddamn question?" His tone was edged with flinty defensiveness, which told her so much more she didn't want to know.

"And dinner lasted until 3:00 a.m.?" Too bad if she sounded like a shrewish wife; he already thought she was one anyway.

He rolled his eyes. "No, Claudia, dinner didn't last until 3:00 a.m. Steele wanted to hit some of his favorite haunts, so I gave in. It's not like I wanted to go, but he insisted, and I would have been a douche if I'd said no. Is that what you want? For me to act like a douche?"

"Why didn't you just say you went to the clubs in the first place?"

"Why didn't you ask?"

Her head spun. Every time she raised a question, he twisted it around on her. She was exhausted from a sleepless night. Mentally exhausted from the mind games. She looked at her watch. "I've got to go. Will I see you when I get home?"

"I've got to get ready for this trip. You know, hockey? It's what I do for a living. It's the reason you get to live in this nice place and wear a Rolex." He waved his hand around the space dismissively.

Her spine went ramrod straight. "When did you turn into such a jerk, Zach?"

He bared his teeth in a mock smile. "Right after *you* turned into a bitch, Claudia."

"I don't deserve this. I'm out."

She slammed the door behind her and climbed aboard the elevator, her thumb jabbing the button for the underground garage. "Come on, come on, come on!" The doors closed just as she heard Zach calling, "Hold up!" On the elevator ride down, she struggled not to hyperventilate, praying all the while for an uninterrupted descent—if someone clambered aboard with her, they might panic and call 911.

After piling into Zach's latest gift, a Mercedes S-Class, she screeched out of the garage. She had gotten herself under some semblance of control by the time she pulled into the restaurant's parking lot.

I am not going to think about him right now. I need to focus on what I'm here for.

Apparently, her emotions were still showing. One of the wives, a dark-haired beauty named Alana, approached and rested a hand on her shoulder, a concerned frown etched in her features. "Is everything okay?"

"Yes, of course. I guess I'm just a little flustered from the traffic, that's all." Claudia's shallow breathing added to the effect, and the woman seemed to accept her feeble excuse.

Claudia sat through the meeting without registering much of the discussion; she simply nodded and smiled at the appropriate places and took the assignments she was handed. Her mind churned and chugged through the exchange with Zach until she thought she might burst. She needed to talk to someone. Not Megan, though. Her bestie would commandeer the conversation and issue orders, whether those orders made sense for Claudia or not. Having to fight on two fronts was more than Claudia's emotional arsenal could handle.

Maybe she should call her mother. Her mom knew what it was like to navigate the choppy waters in a marriage, but Mom continued to doubt Claudia's choice in Zach in the first place. Again, Claudia was too drained to defend him in exchange for her mother's wisdom.

Maybe she should call Marty. But he was busy, and he was Zach's best friend too. Other than fishing for his affirmations that she wasn't insane, what could she gain by putting him in the middle of their conflict?

As she weighed her dismal options, the meeting came to an end. Her body was leaden, reluctant to return home but unsure where else to go, and by the time she got herself moving, only Alana remained.

The woman offered her a tentative smile. "You look like you could use a friend. I'm available if you need to talk."

Claudia contemplated her for an instant, recalling rumors surrounding her own rocky marriage.

"How about if I order us a couple of mimosas and we grab that corner table over there?" Alana tilted her head toward a private corner booth. It was all the encouragement Claudia needed.

Soon they were huddled together, sipping the refreshing drinks. Any kind of alcohol during the day was not usual for Claudia, but the champagne eased some of the kinks in her stomach. She drew in a fortifying breath. "Zach's been acting a little off lately, and I don't know what to make of it."

Alana placed a comforting hand on her forearm. "That's not unusual this time of year. The stress of the long season and gearing up for playoffs does funny things to their psyches. Some men who are normally perfect darlings turn into snarling beasts we want no part of."

"Do they blow off steam by staying out until the clubs close?"

"Sometimes, though I've found that Dirk prefers tinkering in his workshop when he's stressed. I've learned to leave him alone when he goes in there until he emerges a few hours later. By then, he's ready to engage with me, but it took me a while to figure that out. We've been much happier since I made that discovery." Alana sipped her mimosa. "Does this have anything to do with the car show last night?"

Claudia couldn't mask her surprise. "How do you know about that?"

"Dirk went with Zach and the other guys, but he came home early. They were looking for extra fun, and he was done. And with Steele in the mix ... Let's just say hanging out with Steele always ends in an out-of-control party." Alana's smile transformed into one of sympathy. Claudia's insides turned greasy.

Extra fun? "What aren't you telling me, Alana?"

"I only know what Dirk told me, which wasn't much. He seemed annoyed, and when I prodded him, he mentioned that some of the models—you know, the gorgeous ones in sequined, tight-fitting evening gowns who play Vanna White beside the cars?—had joined their group as the show wound down. He'd seen all the cars he'd come to see, and he didn't want any part of whatever Steele was cooking up, so he left. One thing you need to understand about Dirk is he's not big on partying like he used to be. It's one thing to hang out with his teammates and their families, but he gave the rest of it up a while back. It saved our marriage."

"Does he miss it?"

"He says he doesn't, and I believe him. He seems happier now. Calmer too."

"If you don't mind my asking, was he ever unfaithful?"

"No. There was a lot of flirting—some of it maybe not so innocent—but he never crossed the line. If he had, there wouldn't have been any going back for me."

"Zach came home last night with hickeys on his neck," Claudia blurted. *Never mind that he felt compelled to take a shower and that he was beyond aroused—and not, I'm sure, by me.*

"Did you ask him about it?"

Claudia blew out a long breath. "Thank you for not saying it's no big deal or I must have imagined them. I did ask him this morning when I first noticed them, and we ended up arguing. First he tried to deny they were there, and then he told me it was nothing." The fire simmering in Claudia's belly all morning reheated. "Another woman's lips on my husband's neck is not nothing. Even if it didn't go beyond that, I have to ask myself why and how she was able to get that intimate with him."

Alana gave her arm a squeeze. "I'm so sorry. Steele is not the best influence."

"But Steele is no excuse. Zach's a big boy who can make his own decisions. I doubt anyone held him down. He either wanted it or, at the very least, he let it happen." Tears suddenly surged and stung her eyes. "I don't know what to do."

"This reminds me of the rough patch Dirk and I went through when we first got married."

"How did you resolve it?"

"A lot of tears and a lot of talk. Ultimately, he decided our marriage was important enough for him to make some changes."

When Claudia returned home, she breathed a sigh of relief knowing Zach would be gone for several days. Two minutes later, the concierge called to tell her she had a delivery, and she asked him to come up. He arrived, his small frame lost behind an enormous bouquet of roses. Attached to the flowers was a hand-painted card with Zach's recognizable scrawl:

I'm so sorry for what I said. I have no excuse, so I won't even try to blame it on anyone but myself. You are my only girl, and I love you with my whole heart, even though I don't always act like it. I need you. I want you. Please forgive me. Let me make it up to you when I get back.

Making it up to her usually involved an extravagant gift, and her mind tallied the expensive presents he'd lavished on her lately. *I wonder what a pair of hickeys equals? Diamond earrings?*

For the next hour, she paced around the apartment, tidying up to expel some of the nervous energy crackling in her body. As she stooped to pick up the slacks he'd worn the night before, she puzzled over why he had chosen the dressy pants over his jeans. The corner of a white piece of paper protruded from the pocket, and her heart went into overdrive when she plucked it out. The portrait of a beautiful woman smiled at her. The shot had been taken up close, showcasing her long blond hair, bright blue eyes, and her assets cresting the top of a strapless gold evening gown. Beside the woman's photo were her name—Kandi Kane—her email address, and a local phone number. On the back of the card, in handwriting Claudia didn't recognize, were written the words, "Don't forget to call me, Kandi." A tiny heart dotted the *i*.

"Aw, Kandi Kane with a heart. It would be adorable if it weren't so cliché," Claudia growled to herself. The turmoil in her gut pitched once more. She swallowed the urge to retch as she picked up an incoming call from Zach.

"Hey, babe. Did you get the flowers?" His voice was cautiously eager.

She called upon all her will to stuff civility into her next words. "I did. They're beautiful." Had he written the lovely note himself, or had he used a canned apology he'd found on the Internet?

"So? Am I forgiven?"

"I'm not sure I have that much forgiveness in me, Zach. Right now I'm staring at Kandi Kane's business card. Oh, and she wants to be sure you don't forget to call her. Is she the one who put the artwork on your neck?"

"You're not going to let that go, are you?"

The exasperation in his tone unleashed the unholy mix that had been roiling inside her. *How dare he!*

"Let it go?" she screeched. "If you can give me a plausible answer as to why another woman was putting her lips on *my* husband's neck, then maybe I'll be able to *let it go!*"

The sigh he released mimicked a puff of wind. "Okay. The truth."

"Now *that* would be a refreshing change."

Ignoring her sarcasm, he ran on with his tale. "We were getting ready to leave the car show, and these girls asked if they could come along."

"The gorgeous models, you mean," she rejoined in the blandest tone possible.

"I didn't want them to, but Steele said, 'Sure, come on.' You know Steele."

Oh boy, do I! She pressed her lips together as he continued. "Later, after we'd had a few drinks, Steele put one of them up to a dare. That's how the hickeys happened, but I swear, it was nothing. In fact, I forgot all about them until you saw them this morning."

"Now I understand why you were so worked up at 3:00 a.m. She got you hot and bothered, and you used me to get off. Wow. Don't I feel special. Tell me, Zach, were you picturing her the entire time?"

"No, of course not! I came home to you, didn't I? You're the one I wanted. I wasn't horny until I got home and saw you lying in bed. Babe, you've got to believe me."

Why? Silence crackled on the phone line.

"Baby? Did you hear me?" His voice was strangled, bordering on desperate. "I made a bad decision."

"You made several, starting with spending the evening with Steele."

"I don't disagree. For what it's worth, I told him to go fuck himself. Baby, please." Desperation was replaced by dejected resignation.

Her trust, once so freely given, lay in tatters around her. She loved him, but could she trust him?

"I think I need to get away for a while, Zach." *I need to not see you everywhere I look, and I need to sort through this painful debris.* She swallowed the tears clogging her throat.

"What do you mean, get away?"

"Meg's birthday is coming up, and she's invited me to stay with her for a few days. After that, I might go home and see Mama. It's been a while." Squeezing her eyes shut, she drew in three calming breaths.

His tone reflected a hint of outrage. "What about me, Claudia? Playoffs are about to start! You say our relationship is important, but you're running off during the most important time of the year."

Resurging anger choked off her tears. "Most important time of the year for *you*, Zach. Not me." She recoiled a bit at her own harsh words.

"I don't want to come home to an empty apartment!"

What you mean is, you don't want to have to take care of yourself.

"Claudia?" he pleaded. "Please don't go. It won't happen again, I swear."

"You're right about that, Zach, not if you want to stay in this marriage. In the meantime, I need to get my head straight. I think a break will do us both good."

"Baby, please don't do this. I love you. How am I going to get along without you?"

"You should have thought about that before you let a stranger suck your neck."

She hung up and counted to ten. Three times. Then she called Marty.

Chapter 20

Read the Signs

By the time Marty realized Claudia had called him, it was eight o'clock the following morning. He had been exhausted after attending their final team dinner that marked the end of the season, and he hadn't bothered listening to voicemail that probably held consoling messages from friends and family. He had made it a late night, not wanting to come home and face his four walls of reality. Another hockey season was over with nothing to show for it. A few days to wallow, and then he would go to work at the restoration company where he'd taken a temporary job. In this moment, life was one big sucking swamp.

Whoopee! The future's so bright, I gotta wear shades.

Part of him wanted to call Claudia back, but the part that didn't want to talk to anybody right now told him he didn't have to; he gave himself permission to sulk in a corner instead. Danielle had left for her waitressing job at a local diner, but she'd left him a half pot of coffee. He poured himself a cup, relieved to be gloriously alone with his miserable thoughts. Until his phone rang.

Hand hesitating over the receiver, he debated whether to pick up Claudia's call. But when he reminded himself that it was only seven o'clock her time and something might be wrong, he quickly answered.

"Hey, what's up?"

"Hi, Marty. I left you a voicemail yesterday, but I forgot you were already at the rink. I also forgot that it was the last day of your season. How did you guys do?"

Her voice sounded off. Couple that with the fact she had forgotten it was his last day—something she never did—and sirens blared in his head.

"We lost." *Of course we did.*

"I'm so sorry to hear that."

"Well, what do you expect after the shitty season we had? It just sort of put a punctuation mark on the whole damn year." God, he hadn't meant to whine to her, except that was exactly what he was doing. "But I'll bounce back. How about you? What's going on?" *Why are you calling me at seven in the morning?*

"I need to talk about Zach."

The sirens in his head climbed to a high pitch. "Okay. I'm here."

"I think he might be cheating on me."

Coffee cup raised to his lips, he set it down to suck in a silent breath and marshal his thoughts. "'Think' and 'might' tell me you suspect rather than actually know. So tell me what makes you suspect."

"There are signs that I would be a fool to ignore."

"Like what?" Did he really want to know? *No.* The subject made him cringe inside. He hadn't talked to Zach since the wedding, and he had absolutely no feel for whether Zach had held to his promise to be faithful to Claudia.

"Like he took a shower before he crawled into bed at 3:00 a.m. the other night. This was after he'd been out with Steele."

Marty kept his voice steady. "And taking a shower is a problem why?"

"Because he never does that."

"Maybe he just wanted to smell good for you."

"Do *you* do that? Take a shower before you go to bed at night? When you've already showered that day?"

"Yeah, sometimes."

"When you're alone?"

He chuckled mildly. "Yes, even when I'm alone, which, by the way, is ninety-nine percent of the time."

"Oh, I get it. When you're alone, they're *those* kinds of showers, huh?" she snickered. He took it as a positive sign.

"They're not *those* kinds of showers, and even if they were"—*and you're the star player*—"you're getting *way* too personal. You know what I think? I think he was hoping to get lucky, and he knew waking you up in the middle of the night might piss you off, so he made sure he at least smelled good."

"Sounds like you're speaking from experience." A beat later, she sighed. "Seriously though, how come it sounds so reasonable when you say it?"

"Because it is reasonable." He was not about to raise the specter of Zach washing off perfume that didn't belong on him, a thought not so far-fetched, considering Steele was part of the scenario.

"Well, I haven't told you the half of it yet." Marty braced himself as Claudia described finding hickeys on Zach's neck—*the son of a bitch!*— and a model's business card with a cutesy message written on the back. He refrained from asking whether she was well-endowed. Instead, he asked if he and Claudia had talked about it.

Her sigh vibrated through the phone. "No, we had an argument yesterday before I had to leave. Then he flew out later in the morning with the team, so we haven't had a chance to hash it out. But he did send me a huge bouquet with a note of apology. He's called a few times, but I've let the calls go. I'm trying to figure out what to say to him."

Then she went on to describe some of his behavior of late, like insulting her in front of friends and flirting outrageously with other women.

"And there's the Four Seasons hotel card key the cleaners found when I took in his suit jackets," she said quietly.

"And? He stays at a lot of hotels."

"That's what he said. But the team never puts them up in Four Seasons, and certainly not the one in his hometown. I don't know where it came from, and he denied knowing anything about it when I asked—then again, he denies a lot of stuff these days," she muttered. "Later, he blew up and called me paranoid, insecure, and a few other choice adjectives I won't repeat. I haven't told anyone else because it hurts too much to think about, but I keep wondering—"

"Don't go there," Marty barked, realizing too late how harsh he'd sounded. His reaction had been of the knee-jerk variety; he'd been motivated to protect her, and he'd acted like someone warning a child not to touch a hot burner. But it was more than that. The bark had also been meant for Zach, and if his buddy had been there, Marty would have been sorely tempted to rearrange a few of his body parts. *Goddamn him!*

Recognizing that Claudia needed calm, Marty told himself to keep a lid on his own emotions, and he adopted his most soothing tone. "You know Zach. He loves a good time, and he's the life of the party. The drunker he gets, the stupider he acts. That doesn't mean he's spending time with anyone else." *How can I convince her if I can't even convince myself?*

"That doesn't add up to staying out until 3:00 a.m. and treating me like I'm a noose around his neck."

The old ball and chain.

Marty dragged a hand over his unshaved jaw. What to say? "He doesn't mean anything by it," he hedged.

Her soft sniffles fractured his heart; at the same time, the anger boiling inside him threatened to break his placid surface. What was wrong with Zach? Marty would *never* have treated her like this. *You would know every single fucking day how much I love you if you were mine. There would be no doubt ... about anything!*

Zach had more than most men could hope for: a beautiful woman with a big heart who worshipped the ground he walked on. In her eyes, Zach could do no wrong. Well, once upon a time that had been the case, but maybe she was opening her eyes to what had been there all along.

A voice sounded off in his head. *Tell her! Tell her everything so she understands what she's dealing with. That's the only way she can make an honest decision about her future. Hiding the truth from her will only hurt her worse.*

Keeping Zach's secret was one thing, but standing by while he treated Claudia like shit? No, that exceeded any promises Marty had signed up for.

He pulled in a breath of courage. "Claudia, it's no secret Zach likes women—"

"So do you, Marty, but I don't see you using your charm on other women when you're in a relationship."

He pounced on an opportunity to lighten the moment. "Because I don't have any?"

Without acknowledging his terrible joke, she barreled ahead. "What's wrong with me, Marty? Why can't he just be happy with me? I was talking to one of the player's wives, and she explained how she and her husband went through a rocky time. When I asked if he'd been unfaithful, she said that if he had, she wouldn't be with him. I totally get that. Once that trust's destroyed, it's gone and there's no getting it back. But I keep wondering if she didn't look very closely. You know, if you don't have proof, you can deny it's true, right? If she knew that her husband actually had cheated, she would have been devastated, so she decided not to dig too deep. Not knowing is a protective barrier of sorts; you're safe in your little cocoon. And I don't blame her one bit. I'm not sure *I* could handle knowing if it was true."

Well, shit.

She let go a sigh. "So maybe I don't want to know. Does that make me a coward?"

She's talking in circles. What does she really want from me? The truth or reassurance so she can hide in her cocoon? Which way should he play this?

The tug-of-war that had been going on since the day Marty set eyes on her raged inside. The selfish side of him considered that if she knew the whole truth about Zach, Marty might finally have his chance. But at what cost? The other side of him, the side that adored her, didn't want to see her hurt. Worse, if he confessed what he knew about an event from six months ago, he might destroy the trust she had placed in *him*. And he didn't want to lose her friendship. So the side that loved her beyond measure won the fight.

"Look, Zach loves you. A lot. He's told me more than once you're the only one for him. But maybe it's time you pushed back a little and let him know how much it hurts when he says certain things about you or flirts in front of you. He probably doesn't even know he's doing it, so set him straight. Make him see it from your perspective.

Show him he's out of line and how it affects you. I know Zach. He'll wake up and say, 'Oh hell. I didn't realize I was doing that.' And don't forget that you're the one he comes home to because *you're* the one he wants to be with, Claudia."

Another sigh escaped her. "You always know the right things to say. You're a good guy, Marty."

His guilt-riddled conscience wasn't so sure it agreed.

Marty's conversation with Claudia had been over for less than thirty minutes, yet here he was, dialing her number. When she picked up, he burst out with the news he had just received.

"I got called up by Arizona!" He hooted, hollered, and repeated his news before finally letting her get a word in.

She let out a delighted laugh. "What? When? How?"

"One of their top six forwards went down with a knee injury, so they're filling his position from the bottom up, which leaves an opening on the fourth line. Since my season's over, they called me up to fill that role."

"Is it at wing?"

"Who cares?" he laughed. "I'll fill in at right wing, left wing, center, defense, goal. Anywhere. Hell, I'll even drive the Zamboni if that's what they want."

"When do you leave?"

He glanced at his watch. "In about three hours, so I've gotta get going. But we're doing an East Coast swing, so I'm catching up with them on the road down in Florida before we head up to Boston. Jesus, I can't believe I finally get to go to the Show."

"It's because they've watched you, and they know how good you are. Oh, Marty, I'm so happy for you! Maybe I can schedule my visit home so I'm in Salem the same time as your Boston game. Then I could come watch you play in your big-boy sweater!"

"That would be fucking awesome! I'd love to see you."

"Rex and Alice are also going to be in town visiting family. We could all come!" She squealed on the other line. "This could be so much fun!"

Excitement bubbled in his bloodstream. At last, here was his chance to break into the big league! “I really do need to go. I’ll call you from the road.”

“You better! And Marty?”

“Yeah?”

“You deserve this more than anyone I know. Good things are about to happen to you, Marty LeBrun. I can feel it.”

“So can I.”

Could life get any sweeter?

“Oh my God, Meg, did you see that?” Balancing a bowl of popcorn between her crossed legs, Claudia shoved Megan’s arm. They were propped against Megan’s couch, riveted to the TV, watching Marty play in his second NHL game.

Claudia howled. “He flattened that guy!”

“Oh, believe me, I did see it. All that hard, sweaty man taking down another one gives me goose bumps.”

“Of course you would say that. But what about that crushing check? Oh! Oh! And now look at him! He’s driving to the net.” Claudia gasped and clutched Meg’s arm. The shot went wide, and her shoulders dropped as her lungs deflated. So close. The game was nearly over, and his team was ahead by one, but she wanted so badly for him to score his first NHL goal.

“Would you stop doing that? You’re making me spill popcorn everywhere,” Meg laughed.

Claudia ignored her friend, focused solely on Marty skating to the bench and hopping over the boards. He squeezed in between a few teammates, and one of them patted his helmet. Marty ducked his head, but Claudia didn’t miss the little smile tugging his lips.

Her heart suddenly soared, and tears stung her eyes. *He did it! He’s finally playing in the NHL!* She couldn’t wait to talk to him and tell him how happy and how proud she was. While he hadn’t had much ice time—only about six minutes each game—his presence on the ice definitely made an impact. A tenacious forechecker, he was also fearless on the back-check, hitting guys who outweighed him by a good twenty pounds. Some of their star players began to shy away when he was on the ice.

She and Meg were not the only ones impressed with his play.

"Oh mercy! Did you see that hit?" the TV color commentator said.

The play-by-play announcer replied that he had. "He's playing bigger than his size."

The color man agreed. "And that was a clean, solid hockey hit. Where did they find this guy?"

"He was an undrafted college kid who played at BC. Arizona might have found that extra grit they need to go deep in the playoffs."

"Well, he's really electrified his team. He's not getting a lot of minutes, but he's taking advantage of every single shift."

"Yeah, he really brings a lot of energy to their fourth line."

Claudia elbowed Megan again. "Go, Marty, go!"

Megan snatched a handful of popcorn and chucked it at her. "Lucky you, you get to go watch him play in Boston."

A Mitsubishi commercial featuring hip people bopping to a funky tune inside a car filled the screen. The boys were on a TV timeout. "I've been thinking about that. I may head home instead." Claudia's heart, which had been dancing in her chest only moments before, sank like a chunk of moss rock. She had ignored Zach's calls, and the guilt was piling up like garbage in a city enduring a trash collectors' strike.

Megan turned to look at her. "Have you talked to him?"

"No, not yet, but he's been calling every day." *And leaving sweet voicemails, his typical MO when he's screwed up. At least he's trying*. "I should go home so we can work through our issues. Now that I've had a day or two to think about it, I realize I was being childish."

"Childish how? I don't see where you did anything wrong."

"I ran away," Claudia sighed. "I should have stuck around and hashed it out with him."

Meg tossed a few pieces of popcorn into her mouth. "You needed to get away and clear your head. And that's what you've done."

"I did, and it's clearer now. I want to see Marty in Boston, but patching things up with Zach takes priority. Fortunately, I held off telling Mama I was coming home, so I don't need to deal with disappointing her. And Marty will understand."

A few beats passed before Meg ventured, "Do you think your issues can be patched up?"

"I think so, but I don't have the answers yet. I just know I have to try to find that connection again. Once this game is over, I'm going to call Zach and let him know I'm driving home tomorrow."

Megan's eyes locked on hers, so many thoughts obviously streaming behind them. "I'm going to miss you. It's been nice having you here. You know you can come back if you need to, right? My door's always open."

Claudia threw an arm around Meg's shoulders and pulled her in for a hug. "I can't thank you enough for being my safe harbor."

"Always." Meg's voice cracked, and she released Claudia. "Now let's watch Marty get that goal!"

Marty didn't get a goal in the remaining four minutes, but knowing him, he didn't care. What mattered most to him was that he was there and he was contributing. Claudia couldn't wait to watch his next game in two days. Meanwhile, the thought of returning to St. Louis energized her, and she hopped up to call Zach.

She dialed their home number, and the answering machine kicked on. "Hi, honey. It's me. I miss you, and I'm coming home. I'll start out in the morning, so I should be there by early afternoon. Can't wait to see you." Then she dialed his cell phone, and when she didn't reach him there, she left the same message. Between the two, he would learn about her plan before she arrived home. And if she timed it right, she would beat him there before he came home from practice.

As she packed her car that night, she called Marty. "Megan and I caught your game tonight. You looked great! Have you wiped the smile off your face yet?"

He laughed, and she felt warm all over. She had missed that sound. "No, I think they're going to have to surgically remove it."

"Well, you've certainly made fans out of the announcers. They were gushing."

"Gushing? I don't think I've ever made anyone gush before. Although when you get here, I can show off and maybe make you dribble your drink on your chin."

She pulled in a breath. "About that. I'm not coming to Boston after all."

"Why not?" The disappointment in his voice was palpable.

"I need to get home and work things out."

Fortunately, he didn't press. The episode with Zach still stung, and she simply wanted it in her rearview mirror. Besides, she worried she had caused a rift between the two best friends with what she had confided in Marty. She didn't want that rift to grow, and she certainly didn't want to be at the center of it.

She floated him a peace offering. "Are any road trips bringing you out my way before the start of quarterfinals? I'd really love to see you play in person."

"No, nothing planned."

"I'm so sorry. I could probably get my mom and Aunt Bev to take my place."

He laughed, and her shoulders eased. "It's okay. I'll have a few supporters in the stands." He went on to tell her how Dani would be there, as well as some old teammates and coaches from BC.

"If you can get your hands on a few extra tickets, Rex and Alice would really like to come."

"If you're offering up four people in your place, nice try, but it's not gonna work. No one can take your place."

Her heart melted a little. "For such a hard-nosed hockey player, you say the sweetest things."

"Only for you, CC. Only for you."

She didn't doubt he meant it.

Chapter 21

Double Vision

The drive back to St. Louis had been unremarkable, a mild mid-April day where the sun played peek-a-boo with the clouds. The Mercedes's clock read 2:05 p.m. when she pulled into the underground garage and parked beside Zach's BMW.

A giddiness she hadn't felt in a long time effervesced in her veins as she let herself into the apartment. She set her bag down by the front door and called his name. When she got no answer, she wasn't surprised. He often traded rides with teammates heading to the arena.

"Good," she said aloud. She had another hour to unpack, get herself cleaned up, and figure out dinner before he returned from practice.

Maybe I should check the fridge first in case I need groceries. Stepping into the kitchen, her spirits dropped. Under the window, her herb garden was a mass of crunchy brown leaves. Had she forgotten to water the plants before she left? Zach certainly wouldn't have noticed, and even if he had, he wouldn't have bothered. A single tear trickled down her cheek.

God, I loved that herb garden!

An instant later, she admonished herself aloud. "Oh, get over it already, you big baby."

She paused to check the answering machine on the kitchen desk. Beside the phone sat a mostly empty bottle of bourbon, which she brushed away from her consciousness. Listening to the messages, she heard her own voice telling Zach she would be home, along with messages from their insurance agent and a teammate's wife. With a headshake, she suppressed a smile. He had probably been going a thousand miles a minute, getting himself ready for playoffs, and had forgotten to check the machine. A twinge of guilt snapped like a rubber band inside of her. She shouldn't have run out in the first place.

Bag in hand, she ambled down the hallway toward the master bedroom. The door was closed, but she didn't think anything of it until she placed her hand on the doorknob. A moan sounded from the other side, then another, and she froze mid-turn. Her pulse skyrocketed. She told herself she was imagining the noise.

What she heard next shattered her world.

Zach's slurred voice rumbled, "Fuck, baby, I love being in your mouth. It always feels so damn good."

If she hadn't been standing outside her own bedroom door, she might have been overhearing one of her own lovemaking sessions with Zach. Reality sizzled through her like a lightning bolt, and the bottom dropped out of her stomach. Heart jackhammering against her ribs, her hand instinctively twisted the knob and opened the door.

The room was dim, and the first thing her senses registered was the reek of booze, weed, and sex.

As her vision sharpened, her naked husband came into view. Zach stood facing her at the foot of *their* rumpled bed, a woman with nothing but a thong kneeling in front of him, her head bobbing. He didn't see Claudia because his eyes were closed, his head turned toward a different woman—this one completely nude—who was pressed to his side, their tongues dueling. One of his arms was wrapped around her body, massaging her ass, while his other hand kneaded her bare breast. In turn, her hand alternated between pinching his nipples and strumming his chest, and the other one tunneled in his hair, holding his head to hers.

"Dirty girl," he groaned. He pulled away, his half-hooded eyes shifting to the woman sucking him off. "Can't get enough of my big cock, can you, Trix?" The woman let out a guttural grunt.

"My turn, Zach," the other woman purred. "You know she always chokes."

"Shut up, Brenda," the choker managed between bobs.

Zach let out a throaty chuckle like nothing Claudia had ever heard. "No fighting, ladies. There's plenty of the Zachinator to go around. Have I ever come up short?"

Nausea waved through Claudia as she stood frozen to the floor, gaping at the disgusting porn channel she'd landed on and couldn't change. A voice inside her head told her to run. As Zach was turning back toward the woman he'd been locking lips with, his tongue seeking hers, Claudia pivoted to flee, and she caught a glimpse of his eyes snapping to hers, wide with shock.

A feminine squeak sounded behind her, along with another voice rasping in a high pitch, "You said she was out of town."

Claudia grabbed her bag and fled her apartment for the last time.

Claudia lay on her childhood bed, curled in a fetal ball, exhausted yet unable to sleep. She'd been awake for thirty-six hours—or was it more? She stared at her wall, blinking away the tears that blurred her vision. Too bad they couldn't annihilate what she'd stumbled on in her bedroom. Why hadn't she died in a fiery car crash on her way to the airport? Or picked a plane that had exploded in midair? *No, no. That would kill other people too.*

God, she was tired of feeling ... of thinking ... of breathing.

"CC?" her mama's gentle voice called through the door.

Funny how the nickname she'd grown to hate as a symbol of her childhood boundaries held such a soothing quality now, a reassuring reminder of home. She wanted to wrap that reminder around her like a steel quilt.

The door opened slowly, its softly creaking hinges giving her mother away. Claudia squeezed her eyes shut, feigning sleep. The twin bed dipped as her mom sat on its edge. A little sigh, and then

Mama's hand was brushing Claudia's hair from her face. No words, just soft, loving caresses, and soon Claudia's refilled well of tears burst its seams again. She threw herself into her mother's lap and sobbed, her heart physically hurting. Her mother stroked her hair, murmuring comforting words Claudia didn't entirely catch. She did know, however, that none of them included, "I told you so."

"Zach has been calling," her mama said.

"I can't talk to him right now, Mama." Her thoughts were a scatter of birdshot, her emotions fractured and tangled. She needed every arrow in her quiver to be straight and true before she spoke to him, and that meant sorting out all the jumbled feelings writhing inside her.

"I told him you're sleeping and that you can't talk to him right now," her mother replied. "And I'll keep telling him that until you tell me not to. But in the meantime, there's someone here who would like to see you."

Claudia raised her head and snuffled.

Her mother gave her a sympathetic smile. "It's Rex, dear. When I told his mother you had come home for a while, she let him know. He and his girlfriend are staying with her right now." Mama finger-combed Claudia's hair. "I thought that seeing him might cheer you up. Is it okay if I let him in?"

Claudia hoisted herself onto an elbow and swiped at her wet cheeks with the back of her hand. "No, I'll come out there. Please tell him to give me a minute."

In the bathroom, she splashed cold water on her blotchy face and flushed her gritty eyes. It didn't help much, but this was Rex, who had seen her in everything from green avocado facemasks to her 4:00 a.m. I've-had-too-much-to-drink self.

As soon as she spotted him standing by the front door, talking to her mother, she rushed into his open arms and wept fresh tears.

After she got herself under control, he said in that soothing voice of his, "Hey, it's a beautiful day outside. Why don't we go sit on the porch swing?"

She gave him a numb nod, and he led her outside. Once they were seated, he rested an arm along the back of the swing. "What happened, CC? Your mom said you and Zach had a big fight and you caught the first plane to Boston. That's all I know. Megan's been calling me. She's worried too."

I need to call Meg. Claudia hadn't been able to bring herself to call her best friend because doing so meant walking through the pain all over again. She laid her head on Rex's shoulder and haltingly recounted the events of the last twenty-four hours—including every last depraved detail, none of which she had shared with her mom—along with some of the earlier red flags she had chosen to ignore.

An hour later, when she had exhausted her reservoir of tears—and Rex had told her over and over that Zach was a moron and a rat bastard—she slumped against him. "I'm gonna cut my hair and donate it to Locks of Love."

Rex craned his head and peered at her. "Why?"

"Because *Zach* wanted me to grow it out. For him. Just like he wanted to dress me up like a Barbie doll. I went along with it, but not anymore."

He squeezed her shoulder. "I don't know if you're up for it, but Marty's playing in Boston tomorrow night, and he left Alice and me some tickets. I'm sure he could wrangle one more, so what do you say? It could take your mind off your troubles for a few hours. We're planning to meet up with him afterward for dinner too. I know he'd love to see you. He told us how disappointed he was that you weren't going to make it."

Straightening, she sniffed through her stuffed nose. "Does he know I'm here?"

"No, I talked to him before your blowup with Zach, so he has no idea. Figured I'd leave that up to you whether you want to tell him and how much."

The thought of seeing Marty, of being surrounded by her two best male friends in the world, lifted her spirits a tick. *Why not?* What else did she have to do with her time but stew in wretchedness? And Rex was right—hockey, the sport she'd grown to love, *could* hip-check her miserable thoughts for a time. "Yeah, I'd like that."

"Great! I'll get in touch with Marty and set it up."

As she prepared to nestle back against Rex, an unfamiliar sedan screeched to a halt beside the curb. Her back stiffened when she glimpsed a disheveled Zach leaping from the driver's side and slamming the door behind him. He streaked up the sidewalk, and

Rex vaulted from the swing to face him. "Are you expecting him?" he growled from the side of his mouth.

Somehow she had expected Zach. Rising beside her friend, she tugged on his wrist. "No, but it's okay. I've got to get this over with sooner or later, and I'd rather it be sooner. Thanks for being here, Rex."

Zach came to an abrupt halt at the bottom of the short flight leading up to the front porch. One hand raking his messy hair and the other stuffed into a jeans pocket, he darted his eyes from her to Rex to the plantings beside him.

Rex pulled her against him for a quick hug, whispering, "Okay, but if you want me to stay, I don't mind."

She pecked his cheek, separated herself from his embrace, and gave him a tentative smile. "You're the best. But I think I can manage."

"Am I still your number one?"

"You might have to share that title with Marty."

Rex chuckled. "Hmm. Sharing top honors with a badass? Yeah, I think I'm okay with that. Especially since he's paying for the tickets and dinner."

Rex strolled down the stairs, pausing long enough to glower at Zach. Zach's eyes trailed him as he got into his car and drove away.

Claudia pulled in a deep, cleansing breath and braced herself.

Zach's sallow face was covered in an unflattering scruff, and his rumpled clothing looked as though he'd retrieved it from the bottom of the dirty laundry pile. In short, he looked like shit. He swung his bloodshot gaze to her. "Can we talk?"

"I think the time for that has come and gone." Her voice came out flinty and even, and she gave herself an inner pat on the back.

He opened his mouth as if to say something but was interrupted by the front door opening. Claudia's mother appeared in the doorway. She didn't acknowledge Zach, but to Claudia she said, "Your Aunt Bev and I are going to run some errands, so if you need privacy, we won't be back for a few hours."

Claudia nodded. Whether or not her mother had made up the errands at the last minute, she didn't know, but she found herself immensely grateful for the quiet house.

After several long, silent minutes, when Claudia was sure the two women had made their way out the back door to the detached garage, she jerked her chin at Zach and stepped inside, feeling the air shift as he entered the house behind her.

She swiftly took up position, leaning against the open doorway that divided the living room from the kitchen. The whole scenario should have felt awkward, but a new shaft of steel had sprouted inside her, propping her up and steadying her with fresh resolve.

Zach paced the living room like a caged lion, one hand continually tugging the hair at the back of his head. He stopped mid-stride and faced her with a familiar contrite expression. "I'm sorry."

"Okay." *Wait for it. His next line will be, "It wasn't my fault."*

"I shouldn't have done it, okay? But, baby, I missed you so much. I'd had too much to drink, and I—"

She threw up her hand, palm out. "Stop. Just stop." Her voice was tight, and outrage simmered in her gut.

"It was only a blow job," he whined. "They had this idea—"

"Only a blow job? Zach! First of all, stop lying. And stop blaming everyone else for a dick you're unable or unwilling to keep zipped up. I accepted your excuses in the past because I wanted to, because I was fooling myself. I didn't want to admit what was right in front of me this whole time, but my eyes are *wide* open now thanks to the porn show you and your playmates put on. And *do not* try to paint yourself as the innocent victim here. I *heard* what you said, Zach. It was clear this wasn't your first *ménage* romp with Barbi and Bambi." She paused to slow her shallow breaths. "I have only one question for you. Do I need to get a test?"

He cast his eyes downward. "No. I used protection."

"Well, wow, what do you know about that, boys and girls! He was a cheat, but a safe cheat. Thank you for your consideration, Zach Pruitt." She took a mock bow.

As swift as lightning, his face twisted with a glower. "It's the alcohol. If I hadn't been drunk—"

"Bullshit! Alcohol merely lowers your inhibitions. The thought, the desire is already there, and all the alcohol does is take away your thin thread of control. You have a problem, Zach, and it's not me. *Now* I understand why you floated the idea of a threesome—you were dead serious."

His brows drew down, thick and heavy. "There are lots of wives who enjoy that kind of play. And they enjoy keeping their husbands happy instead of getting all hysterical and blowing everything out of proportion. Lucky me, I'm stuck with a prude."

"Not anymore. I'm hiring an attorney. I suggest you do the same."

He let out a harsh laugh. "So you can bleed me dry? Too bad for you, Claudia. The signing bonus? It's gone. I'm up to my neck in debt."

Why am I not surprised? She wrestled the gaudy engagement ring off her finger and tossed it at him. It hit his arm and clattered to the hardwood floor at his feet. "That should help you pay off some of that debt. You can sell all the other jewelry too. And the clothes. And the Mercedes, which is at Lambert, by the way. I'll give you the ticket so you can pick it up."

Shock replaced his indignation. "You can't give that shit back."

"I never wanted *that shit* in the first place! And now that I realize the gifts were your way of relieving your guilty conscience, I don't want them anywhere in my line of sight."

He flung out a hand. "I just flew halfway around the country without any sleep to bring you home. You can't do this to me!"

"Watch me."

He shoved his fingers into his messy hair and yanked. "It was only oral sex. Baby, this isn't fair."

"Fair? You dare use the word 'fair' after what *you* just did? In the bed *we* shared?" she screamed. "Let's talk about fair. How would you feel if you walked in on me, buck-naked, straddling some guy who's eating me out? After all, it's only oral sex."

"I wouldn't like it," he grumbled. "But you doing that would be different."

"How?"

"You doing something like that would mean something to you. What I did doesn't mean anything to me."

Ah. There's the other line I was expecting. "Apparently, it meant enough that you were willing to throw our marriage out the window. You *humiliated* me, Zach, and you made a sham of our marriage. You violated my trust."

"I don't want to lose you, Claudia. I love you."

"And where were these grand thoughts of love when you were sticking your dick in someone else's mouth, Zach?"

He had the audacity to roll his eyes. "Crude, Claudia."

"And what you did is crude, Zach. Don't get all high and mighty on me."

"I couldn't help myself. C'mon. You know I'm wired this way."

"You *could* help yourself!" Claudia's voice was strident and clear. "Man up and own your mistakes!"

He dropped his head. "Okay. So maybe I have a problem. I can do something about it."

"You *should* do something about it—you really, really need to—but I won't be there. I'm sorry you came all this way."

"Please, Claudia. I need you with me." The plea in his voice matched the one in his eyes. How easily he shifted between indignant and pitiful. When one tactic failed, he tried another. She saw it all so clearly now. He didn't care about losing *her*; he simply cared about losing. The truth made her stomach roll over.

"You don't need me, Zach. In fact, it's painfully obvious you married the wrong girl, and I married the wrong guy. I believed I was getting the sweet, fun guy I met in college who cared about our life together, not a drunk, self-centered hedonist. I don't know *who* you are anymore, but you're not anyone I want to be with. I don't like you, Zach."

The stricken look on his face told her she'd wounded him. That expression, together with the bedroom scene, would be indelibly seared in her memory banks, even as she fought to stitch the open gash in her heart.

Chapter 22

TRUE CONFESSIONS

Relief imbued a calmness in Claudia, and her butt could have been floating an inch above the arena club seat where she sat cheering in ripped jeans, a favorite old sweater, and scuffed boots. The lightness bobbing inside her couldn't merely be explained by the missing weight of her hair either. She had finally climbed off the emotional roller coaster ride she had shared with Zach. A toxicity she hadn't realized she'd been dragging around like a pair of cement-filled galoshes had been flushed from her system. Suddenly, she could see a horizon of possibilities. For years, she'd conformed to *his* wishes and wants, and tonight, for the first time in a long time, she felt like ... herself. And while a part of her ached for him and would always care about him, she couldn't deny her newfound sense of liberation. Freedom.

"Go, Eleven, go!" she yelled as she latched on to Rex's arm. Her eyes tracked Marty's jersey as he took the ice. "He's got so much jump! Look at him line that guy up!"

The bone-crushing check he laid on the home team's top center reverberated through the arena, and the crowd let out a collective gasp.

"Whoa!" Rex laughed beside her. "That was a huge hit!" On his other side sat Alice, who clapped and shrieked, oblivious to the stink-eye the hometown fans were sending their way.

Too bad! We're rooting for our friend, not the team. "Ooh, look! He stole the puck!" Claudia held her breath as Marty sprinted up the ice, protecting the puck with his body while holding off a D-man on his flank.

Hit the net! Marty had yet to score a goal in the NHL, but according to his coach, the ability to put the biscuit in the basket wasn't the reason the team had brought him up. His talents didn't necessarily show up on the score sheet, and he was doing everything the club had asked of him.

He flung the puck toward the net off his backhand, and it squirted wide into the corner. He dashed after it, pulling two defenders with him who squashed him against the boards. Somehow he managed to fish out the puck and put it on a teammate's stick. The guy fired the puck at the net, and it bounced off the goalie's shoulder and in.

"He got a point!" Claudia squealed as Marty's teammates mobbed him against the glass. The smile on his face radiated pure joy, and her heart cartwheeled inside her chest. She reined in the urge to go overboard, though, because he and his team were the enemy, and the enemy had just gone up by two goals and silenced the building.

Arizona held on for the win, and as she, Rex, and Alice stood up, a Boston fan gave them a chin lift. "Our BC boy did good. He just came up from the minors, didn't he?"

"Yes, and he's been working so hard, and this is his first point since they called him up, and I hope they don't send him back down," she babbled. The guy laughed and wished them all a good night.

Later, seated in the restaurant where Marty would soon join them, she still percolated with excitement. "You were right, Rex. Coming tonight *was* a good idea. I've barely thought about Zach." *Or how he tearfully begged for another chance as he sat on my mom's couch.* The emotions were still raw, sending a jolt through her every time a thought brushed their frayed edges.

Alice looked up from the menu, her brows knotted in a sad frown. "I didn't want to bring it up earlier, but I just want you to know how sorry I am about what happened to you, Claudia."

Wistfulness took hold and gave Claudia a hard shake. "Zach was my first ... everything. I can't believe how blind I was."

Alice squeezed Claudia's hand. "You weren't blind. You were simply working at a marriage without knowing you were the only one in it. He didn't deserve you, especially not after what he pulled at the bachelor party. The writing was on the wall then."

Claudia did a double take. "What did he pull at the bachelor party?"

Alice slid sheepish eyes to Rex. "If you won't tell her, I will." Rex's lips pressed into a firm, bloodless line. He flashed Alice a warning look.

"Tell me what?" Claudia said.

Rex dashed his eyes to the ceiling and blew out a puffed-cheek breath.

Claudia bounced her gaze between the two. "What's going on, you guys? What did Zach do? It's safe to tell me. It's over between us."

Alice dropped her voice, and to Claudia's horror, she went on to describe a night of debauchery that ended with Zach in bed with two strippers.

Alice sipped her water. "Zach was into the *ménage-à-trois* thing back then."

Stunned, Claudia sat back. "Why am I just now hearing about this? I thought you guys golfed and gambled and *maybe* hit one strip club before you headed back to the suite and got shit-faced!" She narrowed her eyes at Rex, whose lips remained stubbornly pressed together. "Wait. Who hired the strippers?"

Alice and Rex exchanged looks.

"Not Marty," Claudia exclaimed, as if trying to convince herself Marty hadn't orchestrated it.

Now they nodded like synced bobbleheads.

"So Marty knew what happened?" *Of course he did. He was the best man. He arranged everything*. She lasered her focus in on Rex. "I. Want. The. Truth." She gripped the edge of the table so tightly her knuckles turned white. Inside, her gut boiled like a magma chamber ready to unleash its contents.

Rex seemed to squirm. "Well, yeah, Marty knew. It was hard *not* to know since we shared a suite. But neither of us found out until the next morning."

"When Rex got up, Marty was talking to the girls," Alice added helpfully. "Then Zach came out, and he and the girls disappeared into the bedroom again."

Claudia's mouth hung open. "And you all knew. This whole time."

Alice seemed to realize that "you all" included her. "Rex felt terrible about it. It's been bothering him ever since. But after talking to Marty that morning, they decided it was best to keep it to themselves."

"Whose idea was *that?"* Claudia reeled with the discovery.

"It was Marty's idea. Rex just went along," Alice blurted.

Rex fired another scowl Alice's way and pushed his glasses up the bridge of his nose. "Look, Claud, Marty hired the strippers for a dance that was supposed to last an hour. He didn't arrange for them to stay over."

"Six strippers. With twelve guys. In Zach's private suite," Claudia repeated.

"The number and location were all Zach's idea. In fact, he insisted. As for keeping quiet, Marty and I both decided it was best."

"But *you* didn't make me a promise," Claudia whispered as her world shattered all over again.

Rex leaned forward. "The extracurricular stuff was ... that was on Zach. Marty and I didn't participate." He looked at Alice as if trying to convince her. "All Marty did was coordinate what Zach wanted."

Like a pimp. Claudia ground her back molars. "I get that part. What I *don't* get is why everyone knew but me, why neither you nor Marty told me." *Especially Marty. He gave me his word! If he'd told me like he promised he would, he could have saved me a buttload of heartache! Instead, he was in on it.* "Don't you think I had the right to know?"

Hurt and humiliation raged inside her. Air fled from her lungs, and the world around her disappeared as her mind flipped through a series of unsettling images. Faith in the man she had trusted the most had earned her a kick in the teeth, and she wanted to double over and keen in pain.

Marty's betrayal ripped into her more savagely than Zach's had. Why?

Because deep down I expected it of Zach. I never, ever expected it of Marty.

Marty hurried toward the restaurant where Claudia, Rex, and Alice waited for him. Shit, he was on a high it would take a week to come down from! And soon he'd be celebrating that high with Claudia. What better way than to be with her?

Don't get carried away. It's only one game. Put it behind you and get ready for the next one. The words were the usual locker room mantra, but damn if he wasn't going to bask in the glow tonight!

The coach had given him more ice time and had complimented his play afterward. "We'll be starting playoffs soon, LeBrun, and we expect you to be part of that."

Finally, the stars were aligning! He had waited his entire life to play in the big league, and it looked like he was going to stick! *Don't jinx it, don't jinx it.* No matter what, he would give it one hundred percent every minute, every shift, every night because this might be his only shot. Ever.

He barreled around a corner and set his sights on the restaurant just ahead. A familiar form raced toward him, and he slowed up, confused by what he saw. Was that Claudia? With short hair? Running *at* him? Maybe she was as excited as he was and had spotted him. In another second, she would jump into his arms and congratulate him.

The closer they got, the more her face came into view, and he shifted from euphoria to panic. What was wrong? He came to a stop on the sidewalk, and she ran at him. He opened his arms for her, but instead of rushing into them, she launched herself into his chest and shoved—hard—sending him stumbling backward. A few people milled about, and they stopped in their tracks, apparently as stunned as he was.

"You lied to me!" she screeched and shoved him again.

He threw up his hands in surrender, and before he could spit out a question about what the hell was going on, she went into an expletive-laced tirade about him betraying her, that he was no friend, that he had caused her a world of hurt. Somewhere in there was a powerful invitation for him to go fuck himself.

"Wait! What did I do?" he spluttered as she paused to haul in more breath.

"What did you *do*? You not only hired a half dozen strippers, you had them sleep with my husband. And you never told me about it, even though you promised—you promised, Marty!—to tell me if he fucked someone else. Not only did you not tell me, but you *helped* him!" Fury dissolved into hurt, and her eyes glossed over. Her tone shifted to a quaver, her voice sounding strangled. "All this time, you guys kept his secret and were laughing behind my back." The fat tear that rolled down her cheek nearly gutted him.

"I didn't—"

"I don't want your excuses! It happened, and you were part of it. What else did you not tell me, huh? What about all the other women, the 'get-togethers' with his neighbors *after* we got married? Were you part of that too?"

What. The. Fuck? "Trixie and Bren—what are you talking about? Look, I'm not proud of it, but I admit I knew what happened at the bachelor party. Did I know that would happen? No fucking way. If I had known, I would have stopped it." He went on to plead his case, to explain how conflicted he had been, leaving out how he had talked it over with Rex and how they had agreed it was best to keep it from her. She seemed not to register a word, tapping her foot, looking at anything and everything but him. Sadness was swapped for anger, then reverted back. Every emotion showed on her face, including her disdain for *him*. But he had to keep trying to reach her. "As for any other stuff, I have no clue. Zach and I haven't exactly been close." *Because of what he did in Vegas.* "So what did he do?" *I'll tear him apart if—*

"Never mind what Zach did." She swiped angrily at a track of tears. "This isn't about Zach. It's about you and me. You hurt me, Marty. What you did is *worse* than what Zach did. I *trusted* you, and you absolutely destroyed me." Her lower lip wobbled, and more tears fell. He reached for her hands, but she wrenched them away. "I don't want anything to do with you ever again." She pivoted and speed-walked away from him, leaving him dumbfounded and hollowed out on a sidewalk in Boston.

A distraught Rex filled Marty in on Zach's latest antics, and Marty threw his head back and bellowed out a "Fuck!" *Jesus Christ, no wonder Claudia came at me!* And she had also known about his and Rex's collusion.

Marty tried calling her, over and over and over, for days. At first, it went to voicemail, and he left her pleas to call him so they could talk it through. Surely she would. Claudia rarely got upset, but when she did, her anger blew over. She always circled back to clear the air. But that was then. This was now, and as he sat in his San Jose hotel room preparing for game one of the quarterfinals, he tried one last time. When his call led him to a recorded message that told him he was blocked, he knew she was done with him for good.

Next, he called Zach, who picked up on the third ring with a drunken, "Yeah?"

"What the fuck, Zach? Don't you have a playoff game tomorrow night?"

"Which is why I'm celebrating. Oh. And I'm also wallowing because, apparently, I've lost my wife. Double whammy." His tone was maddeningly blasé.

"And what are you going to do about getting her back?"

"I don't know, Marty. What do you think I should do about it?" His sarcasm grated on Marty's shredded nerves. "I've tried everything, but that little bitch took off and ran like she always does. But hey, good news for you, my man. You can pick up the Zachinator's seconds."

Marty's blood pressure spiked. *Fucking douchebag.* "You're drunk."

"Whoa, one point to the minor leaguer!"

"Zach, you need help. Professional help. The NHL has a substance abuse program now, and you can participate without penalty. I think you should look into it before you blow your career."

"Marty, have I told you lately to go fuck yourself? No? Well, do us both a favor, and while you're at it, fuck the high horse you rode in on too." Zach hung up.

Marty dropped his forehead into his hands. Once upon a time, he had pictured his old friend congratulating him on breaking into the NHL. Never had he imagined their friendship in ruins like this. *Jesus, what have I done wrong?* First Claudia, and now Zach. Never mind that Zach was the linchpin in the triangle.

Two days later, as Marty was heading off the ice after morning skate, a trainer approached. “Hey, you’re good friends with Zach Pruitt, right?”

Used to be. “Why?”

“He was in a car accident.”

“Shit. Did he get hurt?”

“Don’t know. All I heard is he crashed his car, and he and a passenger were taken to the hospital.”

The illogical thought that Zach and Claudia had been together, maybe trying to patch things up, streaked through Marty’s brain, and his heart rate kicked into overdrive. “Do you know anything about the passenger?”

The trainer shook his head.

Marty quickly made his way to the locker room on skates, handing off his gloves, helmet, and stick to the equipment guy. Without bothering to shed his gear, he plucked his cell phone from his equipment bag and stared at it, unsure who to call. Finally, he dialed Megan.

“Whoa! Marty LeBrun is calling *me*? To what do I owe this unexpected delight?”

He stifled his irritation. “I just heard Zach was in a car accident. Is Claudia okay?”

“Um, as far as I know. I mean, her heart’s already been broken beyond repair by her slimeball of a husband, so I don’t think this latest episode could inflict any more damage.”

“So she wasn’t the passenger, right?”

“No. Another woman was in the car with him. Probably the latest bimbo in a long line of bimbos.”

“Son of a bitch.” He gusted out a breath that had been trapped in his lungs, and in its place relief rushed in. “Jesus, Meg. I don’t know what to say.”

“None of us does.” She sighed. “His wife leaves him because he’s unfaithful, and while he’s begging her to give him another chance, he doesn't miss a beat. Goes right out and finds someone else to fuck. A real prince, that one."

"He didn't used to be like that, though, did he?" he said almost to himself. Had Zach been this guy all along and Marty had never seen it? Or had fame, drugs, and alcohol twisted him into someone Marty neither recognized nor wanted to associate with?

Meg's voice brought him back to the present. "Claudia will get through this shit-show, even if I have to drag her out of it. She's strong, and she's gonna be okay. Eventually. I hate to see what she's going through, but I'm glad she reached her limit and dumped his ass before this accident. As bad as it is, it could have been so much worse. It could have been *her*, Marty."

"I want to call her ..." *So badly.*

"I wouldn't do that."

"Will you do me a favor? Just let her know, please, that I'm thinking about her and if she needs anything—"

"Not to hurt your tender feelings, Marty, but you might be the very last person on this planet she wants to hear from. She told me she would rather talk to Zach than you right now."

Shit. That hurts. "Fuck, I really screwed this whole thing up." *If only I could go back to the night of the bachelor party ...*

Meg's voice was laced with empathy when she next spoke. "Between you and me, I think she's wrong, but it doesn't matter, does it? It's her life."

And I have no place in it anymore.

After they ended the call, he battled the overwhelming urge to fold in on himself. He still had hockey, and playoffs were about to begin. The most exciting time of year, and he was going to be a part of it on the biggest stage on the planet. It was his time to shine, and he would throw himself into it with everything he had.

Determination flowed in his veins when his phone rang an hour later. Shocked by the name on caller ID, he picked up right away. "Mom? Is everything okay?" He hadn't spoken to his mother since last fall. She never called him, and he had stopped calling her because he was sick of trying to fight his way past her gatekeeper, his *stepdad*. Though their mother had cut off communication with Danielle too, Dani stayed in touch with Alexis, and information still trickled her way.

The sob greeting him on the other end banded his heart in fear. "What's going on?" His voice cracked with his rising panic.

"H-he took everything, Marty. *Everything!"* his mother wailed.

"Hold up. Slow down. Who took everything?" As if he didn't know.

"R-Richard. He moved all my funds over—every dime your dad left us—and now he's gone, and I don't know how to find him! Even if I could figure out where he stashed the money, I don't have access because it's all in his name! Marty, what am I going to do? I don't have money to pay this month's mortgage!"

Marty mentally tallied his bank accounts, calculating his meager funds. "I can wire you a little money, Mom, but I'll have to get the rest somewhere else. First, though, you need to close your joint accounts and open one in your name only. With you guys being married—"

She cut him off with a whimper. "We're not legally married."

"What?"

"We're not legally married, and Michigan doesn't recognize common law unions. He said he had some legal issues to resolve and insisted we go through with the ceremony and go on the honeymoon anyway—the ceremony and honeymoon *I* paid for. He promised that it wouldn't take long to work everything out, and when he did, we'd make it official at the justice of the peace. I believed him! But every time I pressed him, he put me off. Then I got suspicious and started digging. That's when he took off."

Marty pushed a cleansing breath through his lungs. "If you weren't married, how did he get his hands on your money?"

"I-I signed some papers giving him control. I trusted him, Marty. Oh my God, I've been so foolish!"

"We'll work this out, Mom." *No fucking idea how, but we have to.* "In the meantime, are you and Lexi safe? Do you want to stay with Dani and me for a while? I'm in San Jose with my team right now, but I should be back in a few days."

Another sob wracked her. "Y-yes, but I don't have any money."

"Like I said, I'll wire you some. You two pack whatever stuff you need in your car and start heading to Springfield."

She sniffled, "Okay," and they spent a few more minutes hashing out details.

His apartment was about to get a whole hell of a lot more crowded, but at least his family would be safe. Now, more than ever, he needed to earn that permanent roster spot so he could finally realize his dream of taking care of them forever.

Fate was a fickle bitch, Marty learned later that night as he was supported off the ice and into the training room following a heavy hit from behind that had sent him crashing headfirst into the boards. His first game in the NHL playoffs, and he hadn't even made it through the first period.

He lay on an examining table, sweat pouring down his face—and it wasn't only from the physical play moments earlier. The team doctor's fingers prodded, and Marty saw stars every time the man manipulated his collarbone. He winced, gasped, and quelled the nausea rolling through him.

At last, the dude showed mercy and stopped. He gave Marty a grim look. "I'll need imaging to confirm what I'm seeing, but I'm ninety-nine percent sure your collarbone is broken."

More beads of sweat—from panic this time—popped out along Marty's hairline. Terrified of the answer, he haltingly posed the question blaring in his mind. "What does that mean for the next game?"

The doc dipped an eyebrow. "Son, you won't see your next game before training camp next season."

Marty lay back and moaned as his future evaporated before his eyes.

Part 2

Chapter 23

Out of the Past

Ten years later – November, 2011

Marty lounged at his breakfast counter, sipping coffee and reading his latest copy of *The Hockey News*. In his peripheral vision, Renee darted in and around the kitchen like a sugared-up hummingbird as she got herself ready for work.

"So the usual practice for you today?" she said over her shoulder.

"Uh-huh."

"I'm heading to the grocery store after work. Can you think of anything we need?"

"Didn't you just go, like yesterday?"

"I did, but I wanted to pick up a few extra things to make us a special dinner tonight."

His senses went on high alert, and he glanced up from his paper in time to see her lean against the counter and cross her arms.

"Is there some special occasion I forgot about?" he said.

"No. I just thought it might be a good time to talk about where I'll be living in a few months."

He arched an expectant eyebrow. "Are you planning to move away?"

She turned from him so abruptly her blond ponytail swished from side to side, and she began rattling dishes in the cupboard. "Don't you remember me telling you my landlord is raising my rent in the spring? I was thinking ... I mean, rather than sign another one-year lease at the higher rate, maybe it's time I moved in here." She pivoted and leveled her gaze at his before running on. "I practically live over here anyway, and combining households makes a lot of sense financially. Your place is close to work for both of us, and we could save a gob of money. What I currently pay in rent would go a long way toward paying *your* rent and adding to the grocery budget."

He studied her for a moment, taking in the shape of her face, her hazel eyes, and the sprinkling of freckles across the bridge of her nose—her parts added up to an attractive sum, and it was that sum he had first noticed two years ago when he had moved to Loveland, Colorado.

"Or not." She spun away, but not before he caught the flash of disappointment in her eyes.

Once again, he hadn't meant to upset her, but he had needed a moment or five to process so he didn't blurt out the wrong thing. Her mind buzzed at a nervous pace he couldn't keep up with at times, especially when it flitted between various relationship land mines, such as whether she thought about him more than he thought about her, or whether his job was more important to him than she was.

His mind leapt, like it often did, to what emergencies might come up to keep him from a dinner he suddenly wasn't sure he wanted to eat. Had he forgotten a coaches' meeting? A players' meeting? As an AHL assistant coach with head coaching aspirations, he had to make himself available at the drop of a puck, and that often meant sacrificing personal time. Or maybe he had promised a kids' hockey club a skating clinic tonight?

He let out a silent sigh. After time in the rink's weight room and practice this afternoon, his schedule was wide open. "Sure, we can talk about it over dinner."

Renee's shoulders eased visibly. She had broached the subject of her expiring lease once before, and while it seemed like an event in the distant future, he needed to make up his mind about where he wanted this relationship to go. Obviously, she wouldn't be content to remain in stasis forever. He thought of the missed chances, the blown opportunities, and the fact that he was in his early thirties. Wasn't it time he settled down?

He studied Renee's efficient movements and let his mind wander. As candidates went, Renee Turner would be a good choice to settle down with. Several years younger than he, she was intelligent, didn't have any vices that he knew of, and she was a great cook. Her career as a dental hygienist ensured he would always have clean teeth, he jokingly told himself.

If only she had a hobby, some way to distract herself so she was more focused on her own life and less on his. With him being on the road half the year, having other interests could fill her spare time, give her a lift of confidence, and keep her from being unhappy when he was gone.

But that had to be her only flaw—if one could even call it such.

Renee and he shared similar interests, and she mostly supported his fledgling career as a hockey coach. The travel definitely bothered her, but she didn't seem to mind that he wasn't hauling in the dough—nor would he anytime soon. The path to his ultimate goal, head coach in the NHL, was both a long journey and a long shot. Until and unless he reached that pinnacle, his salary would remain in an unimpressive five-figure range.

When the time came, she would make a great mom. He wanted kids, especially after interacting with his niece and nephews and watching his buddies with their children. Teaching the little guys to skate, hoisting them on their shoulders, playing ball—all held an undeniable appeal.

The words of an old friend broke the surface of his mind's meanderings: "You'll make a great dad someday." Claudia Campbell's bright brown eyes and beautiful smile materialized, and a warmth he hadn't experienced in a while crept over him. When was the last time he had thought of her? Months? Years? Whenever he remembered back, he couldn't avoid reliving their gut-wrenching parting. Though time had dulled the ache, his stomach still clenched with the memory.

He had loved her with his whole heart once, but as the years had blurred by, he had come to realize what he'd felt had been an acute case of puppy-love. A violent crush. A hard fall caused by an unseen chemical reaction. Simple biology at work. Unreal and completely unsustainable. He did miss the closeness of their friendship, though, and he'd never replicated that with any woman since her.

I wonder what she's doing now? Probably teaching, married with a few kids of her own.

"So I'll see you around five?" Renee's words jarred him from his musings.

"Yep, I'll be here."

She leaned in for a kiss, and he obliged her. "Have fun with the boys." She flashed him a grin and was out the door.

As he made the eight-mile drive to the arena, his mind returned to Renee and what he thought was coming tonight. Once he agreed to them living together, the next natural step would be a walk up the aisle. Not that he was against moving in together permanently or getting married, but something inside him hitched, and a little voice yapped that he needed more time. "More time for what?" he retorted aloud. Renee loved him. He loved her. Maybe not in that combustible, lunatic way the movies loved to showcase, but he wasn't the kind of man to let recklessness rule him anyway. He was Mr. Steady-and-Boring. His single passion, the only one he had ever let catch flame, was hockey. Always had been, always would be.

He stopped at a red light and glanced at a car beside him, where a man and woman were locked in a heated embrace. When they pulled apart, they stared into each other's eyes for a long moment and shared a knowing smile. He was surprised they weren't a pair of teenagers—more like thirty-somethings, like him, or even forty-somethings. He had seen it before, plenty of times, and it always made him wonder. What was it that drew a person to someone else so fiercely they couldn't keep their hands and eyes off each other?

The light turned green, and he pulled ahead. When he had met Renee, he wasn't looking for long-term. He had told himself to hold out for that one woman who stirred him to madness, who made him want to leap from casual without second-guessing. The one who, when he took her to bed, shared a connection so deep it made the earth shudder and shake. Not that sex with Renee wasn't good, but it was no different than what he'd experienced before. The connection, while pleasant, was physical, the sensations fleeting. He had heard so much about that spiritual phenomenon, where two souls twined together on an otherworldly plane, yet he had no idea what that felt like. Would he ever know?

His mother—who might have been jaded on the subject—had told him repeatedly that the star stuff and romantic crap were BS, and he had mostly bought into her narrative. If a soul mate existed out there for him, he had yet to meet her, and at this stage in his life, he probably never would. Or she could be out there and he wouldn't recognize her because he was incapable of deep romantic love. Something inside him was shut off, nonfunctional. Or nonexistent. It was time he accepted these flaws in himself and moved on.

Ten years ago, he'd told himself he was too young, that his life wasn't stable enough for serious anyway. Yet he had managed to take care of his mother and sisters, and while those relationships weren't in the same realm as romantic ones, he had stepped up to the plate, youth and instability be damned. And now? The same worn excuses weren't holding up when it came to committing himself long-term.

He pulled his Chevy Suburban into a parking slot and nearly laughed out loud at one of his players swabbing his girlfriend's tonsils. Exiting his vehicle, Marty grabbed his bag and chuckled when the pair jumped apart.

"Ah, hey, Coach," the player, Seth Hughes, squeaked. Lip gloss sparkled on his lips and cheek.

"Hi, Coach," the girlfriend giggled. "Bye, Seth." She gave Seth a pinkie wave and hopped into her beater of a car. Seth watched her drive away, a moony expression on his young face. *Then again, maybe the romantic crap is real.*

"You can close your mouth now, Hughes."

Seth seemed to come out of his trance, and he grunted at Marty.

Marty squeezed his nape. "Let's go, Romeo. Save the clutch and grab for the ice, huh?"

Seth headed for the players' locker room, and Marty peeled off to the coaches' area. Before he opened the door and immersed himself in hockey, he circled back to his earlier thoughts about Renee. He pushed out a breath. Renee had said they needed to talk. Well, tonight he had something important to tell her too because he had decided it was time. Time to launch himself off the high dive, time to seize the chance and not let opportunity slip by.

Yeah, this'll work.

Within moments of being on the ice, stick in hand, whistle around his neck, Marty was in his element. A one-dimensional world where his focus was riveted on the players going through their drills, working three-on-three in the corners. He was still lost in the zone when they began to scrimmage, black on red, and he noted every nuance to their game while the head coach, Johnny Graham, barked out directions.

"Just chip it out! Don't get fancy. Simple plays win games, boys."

"And good defense," Marty said under his breath. Coach Graham seemed to hear him because he swiveled his head and nodded. Coach Graham was the main reason Marty had landed this job. He had coached under him in the East Coast Hockey League—the ECHL—and when a coaching position opened up with the Hawks, Graham had called Marty. The position was a step down, but that step brought him into a world with more opportunity for advancement than Marty had experienced before. Now in his second year, he had already shinnied up one vital rung from video coach to assistant coach.

Yeah, after what felt like endless aimless years, things were definitely on a stable upswing in Marty LeBrun's life, and he smiled to himself.

Seth charged into the O zone after missing a swat at the puck, forechecking his way into the corner to retrieve it. A hard hit on his opponent, and both players went down against the boards. Another player shouted and waved frantically toward the pair heaped on the ice. "He's cut! Seth's cut!"

Marty and the other coaches, along with a trainer, sped over to where blood—lots of it—pooled in stark contrast to the bright ice.

A few breathless moments passed, and the trainer declared, "Skate blade just missed his carotid artery, but it cut his jaw and cheek. He needs more medical help than I can give him."

"Call 911," someone yelled.

"It'll be quicker if someone takes him."

Coach Graham looked around, his gaze falling on Marty. "LeBrun! Get this kid to the hospital!"

The trainer, who was pressing a towel to Seth's face, looked up at him. "I'll get some compresses while you get out of those skates."

"I'll call his folks," another voice shouted.

Getting changed, situating Seth in his Suburban, and pulling up to UCHealth Medical Center of the Rockies' emergency entrance were one long blur that came to a halt only when medical staff had Seth on a table in an exam room. The kid had complained the whole way about missing ice time. *A real hockey warrior, this one.* Marty's admiration for the kid rose.

"You his dad?" one of the attendants asked Marty.

"No, his coach."

"Well, you need to step out—"

"He stays." Though a bit slurred, Seth's words were unmistakable.

"He's over eighteen," Marty pointed out.

"Okay. Someone will be in shortly to get an IV going and prep. We'll need to stitch the wound."

Next came an admissions clerk who collected Seth's information. When the room cleared, Seth began grousing again—about his bloody sweater this time.

Marty stepped beside his bed. "Buddy, you're lucky you only have stitches and a sweater to complain about. That skate came real close to nicking your throat. It could have been much worse."

More cursing from Seth.

As Marty opened his mouth to tell the kid how the stitches could only improve his looks and make him look like a *real* hockey player, a blond woman in blue scrubs decorated with white flowers appeared in the doorway. Clipboard in hand, she fastened her eyes on Seth. "Seth Hughes?"

Marty recognized those eyes, that voice, and his mouth swung open like an unhinged door. *"Claudia?"*

Claudia was so focused on the kid lying on the bed, his Hawks sweater caked in drying blood, that she hadn't noticed the man who stood beside him. *Hockey players*, she was thinking to herself with an inner eye-roll. But then the man said her name, and all other thought fled.

She raised her eyes to his, her brain trying to process the familiar face she was looking at. Soft brown eyes. Older, taller, squarer, broader, dressed in a dark track suit with a whistle hanging around his neck. But it was *him*.

"Marty LeBrun?" Her voice came out in a strangled choke. Memories came rushing back at her—some wanted, some not. "Oh my God, what are you doing here?" Her gaze darted back to the kid—*no, he's too old to be Marty's son*—and gears began clicking into place. "Well, I can see what you're doing *here*. You're obviously with Mr., uh,"—she glanced at her forgotten paperwork—"Hughes. What I meant was, what are you doing here in Loveland?"

The kid's eyes bounced between her and Marty—and who could blame him?—as Marty stood frozen with wide eyes and gaping mouth.

"Coach? You okay?" Seth Hughes said—or at least that's what she *thought* she heard. His speech wasn't exactly crisp.

"You're his coach! You're a Hawks coach!" She cringed at the sound of her own voice. She acted like a player in a game of *What's My Line?* who had just guessed the anonymous guest's occupation and was anticipating the grand prize.

Marty had yet to utter a word.

She waved her hand a little too frantically. "Hello? You in there? I didn't cause you to have a heart attack, did I? I mean, you are in the right place if that's the case, but—"

"Coach! Say something!" the patient urged.

Marty shook his head as if his spirit had just re-entered his body. "Claudia Campbell. Is it still Campbell? Are you married?" he blurted. His voice sounded just as strangled as hers had.

"It's still Campbell. Not married." *What now? Do I hug him? No, no. You have a patient to take care of.* A little woozy, she cleared her throat and drew closer to the bed on the side opposite from where Marty stood. "All right, Mr. Hughes. I have a few questions to ask before we can stitch you up and give you that Frankenstein look. It's all the rage." *Oh shit! Did I just say that?*

Seth Hughes chuckled. "Sweet. Coach says it'll improve my looks."

"Your looks are just fine, but I've heard chicks dig the scars," she quipped.

"Coach" had returned to silently gawking at her, so she tried to lock out his presence while she got down to asking Seth the usual alertness and orientation questions—did he know his name, where he was, when it was, and who the president was? Simultaneously, she struggled to quell the moths racing around in her tummy, splatting against each other and the walls enclosing them.

After she'd completed her interview, she struck her most professional demeanor. "Someone will be in to take care of you shortly, Mr. Hughes. Bye, Coach LeBrun. Lovely to see you again. Good luck to you and your team this season." She spun on her heel so quickly she nearly tangled up her legs and fell on her face. Then she rushed from the room, her cheeks heated, her heart throwing itself against her rib cage, and she dove for the cover of a computer alcove near the nurses' station.

Oh. My. God.

Her mind raced, scattering in a million different directions. How long had Marty been living in Loveland? What had he been doing the last ten years? Was *he* married? *I should have interviewed* him *while I was at it.* How come she'd never paid attention to the Colorado Hawks? Not that sports talk would ever focus on the coaches ... or that she would listen to the chatter in the first place. When she'd gone cold turkey ten years ago, she'd gone all out, to the point where her co-workers knew to zip it when she was within earshot and the subject was sports. Between her Netflix subscription and her sports boycott, she had successfully maintained her hockey vacuum.

But now she wanted to gather all the information she could about Marty. How was he? *Obviously, he is more than fine, judging by the look of him.*

Then the tough questions began circling. Had he forgiven her? Had she forgiven him? *Yes, long ago.* Could there ever be a bridge back to some semblance of the friendship they had shared?

God, Marty. I've missed you so much.

Chapter 24

ELEPHANTS AND COFFEE

I can't fucking believe the second question out of my mouth was "Are you married?" What the fuck is wrong with me?

"Whoa, Coach. Old girlfriend? She's hot," Seth half slurred, half snickered.

Marty glared at the mess of a player lying on the bed. "None of your damn business." *And yeah, she* is *hot. Really hot!* A few fine lines bracketed her mouth and eyes, lending her an alluring maturity. Silky strands streaked with reddish-gold pulled back in a braid, a little slimmer—though she filled out her scrubs very nicely—and those eyes still reminded him of glossy, melted chocolate he wanted to dunk his entire body in.

Marty's eyes strayed back to the doorway. Words like *starstruck, mesmerized,* and *tongue-tied* whirled in his head, blocking out all logical thought.

"Coach, I think you can close your mouth now," Seth joked.

"Huh?" Marty whipped his head toward his player, who sported a smile that resembled a grimace. *Yeah, Coach, get your head out of your ass.* "Did you let your girlfriend know you're here?"

Seth answered that he had texted her and she was on her way over.

"When they come to stitch you up, I'm gonna step out, okay?"

"Sure, Coach. Scared of a few stitches, or is there some blond reason?" Seth winked. Actually *winked*. The kid was enjoying his front-row seat to Marty's brain scramble.

The next few minutes dragged as they waited for the medical team. When they finally arrived, Marty dashed from the room. *Where the hell am I going? She's a nurse. Why is she a nurse? And where do nurses hang out when they're not working on patients?* He jogged down the hall toward the entrance, his eyes strafing staff, but he didn't see Claudia.

A concerned-looking security guard intercepted him. "Can I help you?"

Probably thinks I'm an escaped mental patient. "Yes. I'm looking for one of the nurses. There's a piece of information I forgot to give her. I think her name tag said Claudia Campbell."

The guard frowned. "What kind of infor—"

Marty shook his head, then dropped his voice conspiratorially. "This was very, ah, delicate and personal, and I only want to disclose it to that nurse. No need to spread it around the entire hospital, if you catch my drift."

The guard seemed to appraise him for a beat before jerking his head to one of the hallways. "Nurses' station, two-thirds of the way down."

Marty's blood fizzed. "Thanks, man. Appreciate it." He ran to the nurses' station, but it was empty. Damn! He began roaming the quiet hallway and was rewarded by a flash of blond hair and blue-patterned scrubs tucked into an alcove. He slowed his steps and approached. Claudia's focus was riveted to a computer screen. She looked up, and those gorgeous eyes widened. Not a stitch of makeup covered skin as smooth as cream. She hopped up from her seat and faced him, nearly toppling her clipboard.

Now that he had her in his sights, he had no idea what to say. He had been transported back to his BC days and the first time he had laid eyes on her across a pool table. She had radiated light in a hazy college bar, blinding him, and now she was doing it under the harsh glare of fluorescents.

Fortunately, she was quicker than he. *Always has been.* "Hi, Marty."

"Thanks for not throwing your clipboard at me, even though you're probably tempted to," he panted. *Shit! Why am I out of breath?* The short jog between Seth's room and the nurses' station wasn't enough to wind him.

Her mouth curved into a smile. "Funny. It didn't even occur to me, but now that you mention it ..." She picked up the clipboard and inspected it while simultaneously seeming to size up his head. Her eyes did that twinkly thing whenever she was considering some kind of mischief.

Maybe she doesn't hate me anymore. "You look great!" he exclaimed.

She set the clipboard back down and laced her hands in front of her. Her smile broadened. "So do you. I think you grew a few inches, maybe packed on a few pounds since I last saw you."

"It's all muscle. I work out all the time." *Jesus fucking Christ! Seth Hughes's lines are less lame than mine. And just why am I going for lines anyway?*

Her eyes made one long sweep of his body, and he found himself tightening his abs. "I can see that. 'Packed on a few pounds' probably wasn't the best word choice. What I meant was you've filled out your spindly twenty-something-year-old frame nicely."

"Spindly? You thought I was spindly?" *And why am I so focused on how I looked to her back then ... and now?*

"Lanky?" She let loose a laugh and flicked her hand. "I'm not doing this very well. Let's leave it at 'You look as though you're taking good care of yourself.' How's that?"

"That works." He grinned idiotically, his mind drawing another blank.

She rocked on the balls of her feet. "So ... how long have you been coaching the Hawks?"

"I'm an assistant coach. I took the job about two years ago after kicking around in a few of the other leagues."

"Playing or coaching?"

"Both. I—"

"Ms. Campbell? Are we all right?" came a crisp voice. Marty whirled and spotted a stout, middle-aged woman in black scrubs peering over the rim of her glasses at him. Judging by her expression, she didn't approve of what she saw.

"We're just fine, Ms. Norris," Claudia countered sweetly.

"Don't you have some paperwork to take care of?" Ms. Norris huffed.

Marty squared his shoulders. "I'm sorry, ma'am. This is on me. I saw Claudia, uh, Ms. Campbell, and followed her back here without her knowledge."

The woman's eyes grew to the size of pucks.

Jesus! Sounds like I'm stalking her. "We're old friends from Boston College days, and when I spotted her, I wanted to say hello."

Ms. Norris pursed her lips. "Yes, well, this is a hospital, not a social club." She tapped her watch, and to Claudia she said, "And if I'm not mistaken, your shift isn't quite over yet."

When it appeared that Ms. Norris wasn't leaving until he did, he turned back to Claudia. "When is your shift over?"

Claudia glanced at her watch, a plain thing with a slim black band. "In about fifteen minutes, but I've got patient charts to complete." Confusion must have been etched on his face because she followed this up with, "I'll be finished in about an hour."

"Can I buy you a coffee when you're done?" He looked over his shoulder at Ms. Norris. "So we can catch up outside of work hours?"

Calculations seemed to flit behind Claudia's eyes.

"I won't take up a lot of your time. Just long enough to drink a cup of coffee," he urged. *Please say yes.*

Claudia beamed him a dazzling smile. "I think we're going to need more than a few minutes to cover ten years, but sure, I'll meet you when I'm done."

"Great!" He spun, gave Ms. Norris a nod, and sped toward Seth's room. He needed to check on the kid and be sure his girlfriend could get him home.

She said an hour, but when is that? A clock ticking on a wall showed the time at a little before four. *Can that be right?* He stopped in his tracks and pulled his phone from his pants pocket to double-check. A string of text messages clamored for his attention, most of them from the trainer and the other coaches asking about Seth. *Well, damn!* Marty had been so focused on tracking down Claudia that he'd utterly forgotten the reason he was at the hospital in the first place. He ducked into a deserted waiting room and sent a reply-all, updating Hawks staff.

Scanning the rest of the messages to be sure he included everyone, he realized he'd missed one from Renee: *Could you pick up a bottle of red on your way home?*

Shit, shit, shit! In all the excitement, he'd completely forgotten about their "dinner." He dialed her number, sucking in a breath as he calculated what to say and how to say it. Relief flooded him when she didn't pick up, and he left her a voicemail.

"Had an emergency with one of the players, and I'm stuck at the hospital. He's going to be okay, but we might want to reschedule that dinner for another night. I'll update you when I can."

Renee was used to the myriad on-ice injuries that popped up during a season. She would understand.

Throwing his head back, he stared at the acoustic-tile ceiling. He hadn't exactly lied, but the gray areas had once more encroached and blurred the boundaries. *I'm a dick.*

Oddly, he couldn't muster much guilt. The little remorse he did feel was demolished by the sheer joy galloping through his veins.

An hour or so later, Marty sat in a booth at Mimi's across from Claudia. They had driven to the restaurant separately—after she had reminded him the local coffee shop he had wanted to take her to closed at 3:00 p.m.—and though they were tucked away, he couldn't help but continually scope the place out. Would someone recognize him and wonder why he was with a pretty woman who wasn't his girlfriend?

"Are you hungry?" His eyes scanned the menu without registering what was on it.

"I could eat a little something." She smirked at him. "This reminds me of the first time we met at the Pint Pot. Do you remember that? You were checking the menu, even though we had all agreed to get wings."

"Yeah, I remember." *I'll never forget that night. I lost my mind then too.* "I know I said coffee, but if you want something else, go ahead and order it. They have really good desserts here too."

"If I get one of their desserts, I'm going to have to run an extra two miles to burn it off."

I disagree. He laid the menu down on the table. "You still jog?"

"As much as I can. How about you? Oh, I forgot. You said something about working out all the time, so I expect you do. Probably comes with the job, huh?"

"Yeah, I can't let these kids show me up."

"It's so funny to hear you call them kids. The last time I saw you, *you* were one of those kids. So tell me how you got here from Springfield." With her elbows on the table, she laced her fingers together and rested her chin on them, as though she was settling in for a long listen.

"I spent a half dozen years in the AHL playing for a few different teams before an old coach talked me into retiring and working from *behind* the bench with him. I had some success in the other leagues before landing this job. It wasn't exactly a straight trajectory, but it led me here. And it got me away from having to work other part-time jobs."

"And the NHL? Did you play much?"

"I logged almost eight games. My last sniff at the NHL as a player was the first game of the playoffs with Arizona. I broke my collarbone, and that was the end of my season *and* my career in the bigs." He shrugged as if the memory didn't sting anymore, but he couldn't imagine the feeling ever going away.

She shook her head, sadness and sympathy reflected in her delicate features. Her hair was loose now, and it sifted around her shoulders. She wore jeans, boots, and a dark green CSU hoodie that complemented her eyes. "I'm sorry. I know how much making it to the Show meant to you."

"I can still make it. As a coach this time."

The server appeared at their table, ready for their order. Claudia ordered soup, salad, and a cup of decaf.

"Just coffee for me." He handed the server their menus.

"Aren't you hungry?" Claudia asked after the woman left their table.

"After today's excitement, I'm not sure I can eat." *My stomach is twisted in a knot, and it's got nothing to do with Seth's injury.* "Your turn. What brought you to Colorado?"

She leaned back and grinned. “Rex and Alice.”

“Say what?”

“Rex got a job teaching at CSU six years ago, and I came out for a visit. I fell in love with the Rocky Mountains, and I stayed.”

You’ve been here this whole time, and I never knew? “Are they still here?”

She gave him a slow nod. “Yep. They’re married, they live in Fort Collins, and they have two adorable kids I babysit. I’m known as Aunt Claudia in the Small household.” The smile on her face told him volumes about how much the title pleased her.

Apparently, she had forgiven Rex. Marty’s hopeful heart lifted. “I’m sure you’re great at it. Did you ever become a teacher?”

She wagged her head. “No, that never worked out. When I looked at my options for supporting myself ten years ago, I quickly realized nursing paid better, so I went back to school. And here I am.” She flipped out a presenter’s hand.

“So you went to your fallback. Do you like it?”

“Like any job, it’s got its good and bad points.”

“Is one of those bad points Ms. Norris?”

“Oh, she’s okay. She’s the charge nurse, and I only get her once or twice a week. She likes her nurses front and center at all times, whether there are patients or not. But it’s a good job, and it pays the bills. I work three twelve-hours shifts a week, and I have no problem picking up extra work whenever I need to.” She shrugged a shoulder. “So how are your sisters?”

“Doing well. Danielle and her husband live just up the road in Wellington—he works at Odell Brewing—so I get to see my niece and nephew a lot.”

Now her eyes popped wide. “Danielle has children?”

He bobbed his head. “Two, and Lexi has one, which makes me Uncle Marty in their households.” A proud grin sprouted on his face.

“Ha! Parallel lives. Well, kind of. Where does Lexi live?”

“With my mom back in Springfield. They kept my old apartment.”

“Is Richard Cranium—”

“Dickhead? No. He got what he came for and got the hell out of Dodge. Long, sad story that needs more than one cup of coffee.”

“I’m sorry.”

"Don't be. It worked out in the end. Mom and I have been close ever since, and if that's what it took, it was worth the price." So what if he was still paying for it? He, his mom, and his sisters had learned a hard—but invaluable—lesson, and he viewed the debt the same way he would a student loan.

"I'm glad to hear it. I remember how much that tore you up." Claudia sipped her water. "What do you do in your spare time? Are you still into plants?"

Chuckling, he shook his head. "My job doesn't leave a lot of spare time for plants or anything else."

Her lips quirked. "Twenty-four-seven hockey, then. Why am I not surprised?"

Unsure what to say, he was relieved when the server approached their table with the coffee. He thanked her and began doctoring his cup with cream.

"It looks like you've gotten fancy." Claudia lifted her chin toward his cup. When he frowned in confusion, she went on. "You used to take it black, remember? 'We don't keep any of that crap around here,' I think you said that first morning I had coffee in your kitchen."

"Well, it's amazing how your tastes change when you get a few extra bucks in your pocket," he chuckled. "So I know what happened to Rex and Alice. What's Megan up to?"

Claudia lifted her mug to her lips and blew. "She got married a few years ago. No munchkins yet."

His eyebrows shot to his hairline. "No kidding? I haven't talked to her for probably ten years." *Not since I called her to find out if you were okay.* "What's the guy like?"

Claudia cracked a huge smile. "He's a great guy who adores her. She adores him back, and they're a perfect match. He has this Rex-like zen about him that curbs her more bombastic side. He does it in such a sweet, subtle way that I don't think she even knows it."

"I'm happy for her. Tell her I said hello." He paused to glance out the window at the day's dying light reflected on a chrome bumper.

Claudia cupped her chin in her palm. "Meg had such a huge crush on you for the longest time. Of all the guys she liked, you were the only holdout. Did you know that?"

Recollections of the wedding and waking up naked beside Megan bubbled to the surface, and he squirmed inside. Had Megan ever told Claudia about that disastrous night? "No, I didn't know. Sounds like she found the right guy."

Claudia's food arrived, and she hovered her fork above the salad. "Sure you don't want any?"

"No, thanks. Go ahead."

He watched as she took delicate bites of her greens, then dipped her spoon into the soup. She had always eaten like that, he realized, with the same mannerisms. Christ, how many meals had he shared with her?

She flicked a finger at his left hand. "I don't see a ring, so I'm guessing you're not married. Are you seeing someone?"

Though he should have seen the question coming, it caught him off guard, and a sudden case of whiplash tied his tongue once more. "Uh, yeah. Kinda."

Kinda? Holy hell, Renee would flay me alive ... deservedly so.

A familiar impish grin curved Claudia's pretty mouth. "Why am I not surprised? Don't tell me. 'Kinda' is Marty LeBrun code for 'strictly casual.'"

He let out a hoarse laugh and fidgeted in his seat. Why couldn't he just tell her about Renee? Simply spit out that they'd been dating for nearly two years? That he was on the brink of taking it to the next level, but that doubt was holding him back? Because he was, in fact, having doubts, and he would have loved to talk them out with someone who wasn't Renee. Once upon a time, Claudia had been his closest female friend, someone he could tell anything without fear of judgment. Who would always listen, whose point of view he respected.

Her brown eyes seemed to appraise him as she dabbed at her mouth. "It's amazing how some things change and some don't. When I've thought about you over the years, I've tried to picture that one woman who could make you fall hard and hang up your 'casual' skates." *You thought about me?* "Guess you haven't found her yet."

I found her a long time ago, but she got away. Whoa.

He laughed again, and her eyebrow dipped. "Actually, ah, I've been seeing someone for a while now. We're talking about moving in together."

Claudia straightened, and unreadable emotion flashed in her chocolate depths. “Wow. Well, that’s great news. She must be one smart girl to have captured Marty LeBrun’s elusive heart.”

Yeah, she is smart, but ... But why didn’t she pull those deep-seated strings inside his so-called elusive heart? The ones he thought were dead or nonexistent. The ones being strummed at this very moment by the woman whose presence scrambled his brain and caused prickles to break out under his skin? He didn’t enjoy his body’s unsettling reactions to her.

It’s nothing. Just the excitement of seeing an old friend after such a long time.

Biology. Chemistry. An overactive imagination.

“How about you? Anything serious?” he croaked.

She shook her head, and a frisson of relief snaked through him. “No. I’ve tried over the years, but ... I don’t know. I’ve decided I’m not very good at picking partners, so I’m giving it a rest. I’m content hanging out in my condo with my two cats.”

Images of her embracing someone else made his roiling stomach churn with more acid. It was time to change the subject, if only to get out of his own head. “Did you go back to BC for your nursing degree?”

She stacked her empty dishes and lifted her eyes to the ceiling. “No, I went to DePaul in Chicago and got my BSN eight years ago.” Her gaze landed back on him. “It’s been good having something to throw myself into. It took me a bit to land on my feet.”

He frowned. “I always thought you got a big settlement. Big enough that you wouldn’t have to work if you didn’t want to.”

“I was talking about getting back on my feet emotionally. As for a settlement, I didn’t want anything, but when he offered to pay for my tuition and living expenses while I was earning my degree, I decided to accept that offer so I could stand on my own two feet afterward and never have to depend on another person.” Her eyes had always been expressive, and right now they were expressing an indelible sadness he wanted to wipe away.

The server appeared, waving a carafe of fresh coffee. Claudia placed her hand over her cup. “No, thanks. I’m done.” To Marty, she said, “I should get going.” Marty followed her lead and asked for the check.

Once the server left, Claudia bit her lower lip and cast her gaze to the side before leveling it at his. "It's been great seeing you. I'm so happy you're doing well." Was their time together over so soon? He braced himself for a good-bye he didn't want to hear.

Intensity shimmered in her eyes as she drilled them into his, unspoken words lurking there. "I, um, I owe you a long overdue apology. I'm so sorry about what I said all those years ago. I wasn't being fair." She paused for breath and rushed on. "It's funny how different things look after time passes, and I think I didn't want to see what was right in front of me."

"I screwed up—big-time—and your world had just been turned upside down. It happens. Your reaction was totally understandable."

"That's not what I meant. I was talking about the balancing act you were trying to negotiate. What a horrible position to be in." A sheen glossed her eyes, and helplessness locked him down. "There was no good option for you, but I didn't recognize it. Not then. I couldn't think, and I couldn't put myself in your shoes. I should never have blamed you for his bad behavior. I knew his shortcomings; the signs had always been there, but I chose to keep my eyes closed. This sounds strange, and as much as it ripped me apart to find him, um, the way I did, in retrospect, it was good it happened that way. I could have kept kidding myself for a long time, pretending the signs weren't there, but the appalling scene that last day tore off the blinders. There was no going back. And the whole situation was foisted on both of us by one guy."

One guy. The elephant in the room that they had both danced around the entire meal, and now that meal was over. Their *time* together was over.

After paying the bill, he walked her out to her car, a late-model silver Honda Civic. She raised up on tiptoe and looped an arm around his neck. His hands instinctively went to her small waist. A quick, fierce hug, and she pulled away, but not before a familiar fragrance that had haunted his senses for years cast a fresh spell over him.

"Thanks again," she said. "I'm glad you tracked me down today."

"What's the name of the perfume you wear?" he blurted. Maybe he could get Renee to wear it.

One corner of Claudia's mouth quirked. "I'm not wearing any perfume. Too many patients with allergies. It's just me."

"Oh." He stared down at her, his voice trapped in his throat.

"Before you go, please tell me I'm forgiven." She peered up at him, her eyes brimming with hope.

"You? Why would you need—" He held her gaze while he rummaged around in his brain. "No."

Her eyes widened.

"But if you meet me tomorrow for a run, I'll consider it." He fought a grin. "Or are you working?"

She burst out with a laugh. "You drive a hard bargain, Marty LeBrun, but no, I'm not on tomorrow, so name the time and place, and I'll be there to grovel."

"Has your number changed?"

"Yes."

"Better give me your new one so I can tell you when and where to grovel."

She did, and he wanted to pump his fist in celebration. *Yes! I got her number*. It occurred to him he had reverted to high school, but he didn't care. God, tomorrow couldn't come soon enough.

His mind leapt to Renee waiting at home for him, and his heart sank. No one had seen him with Claudia, and even if they had, he hadn't crossed a line. Now he needed to explain to himself just what he *had* done before he tried to explain it to Renee.

Chapter 25

Is That My Conscience Knocking?

As Claudia drove home, she found herself suspended in a no-woman's-land somewhere between giddiness and bewilderment. She had barely been aware of stopping at the grocery store, where she'd navigated the aisles oblivious to what she needed to buy.

Marty! Here in Loveland this whole time.

She looked at herself in the rearview mirror and winced at the sight that greeted her. No makeup revealed wan cheeks and dark pouches of sleeplessness below her dull, achy eyes. After all this time, it would have been nice to have some warning today would bring a blast from the past. She could have brought a more stylish outfit to change into after work. She could have put on perfume. She could have dabbed concealer under her eyes and hidden her other facial flaws with makeup.

How many times had she thought about Marty over the years, about the treasured friendship she had thrown away like so much garbage, about the way she had attacked him the night she had learned about the bachelor party? How she had hated him during those endless months when she'd languished in a black hole of despair, where her anguish-twisted mind had shifted the blame for Zach's shortcomings onto Marty's broad shoulders.

He hadn't deserved any of it.

She frowned at her reflection. "Not your finest moment." But at the time, it had meant survival.

When she had finally emerged from her fog of pain and blame, she had discarded the remnants of her life with Zach and moved on. Her friendship with Marty had been collateral damage, and when she had finally reclaimed her soul, she had realized her mistake. But it had been too late for apologies. Too late for so much, and the backlash against her psyche had been massive. How could she have treated Marty the way she had? The combination of shock, horror, and hurt—mostly hurt—in his expression that night was forever branded on her brain. Time and time again, she had thought about finding him and piecing together their relationship, but embarrassment and guilt had held her back. And then his number had changed. She knew because she had finally worked up the nerve to call and had reached a clueless teenager who was definitely *not* Marty LeBrun.

In the meantime, Marty had grown up too. He had always been in good shape, but he had the fully developed muscles of a grown man now. Square and chiseled. Broad, powerful shoulders that could probably carry any amount of weight she threw at them—not that she planned to find out.

She pulled into her driveway and opened the garage door. Grasping grocery bags in both hands, she wove her way around her makeshift workshop, where a stripped dresser awaited her attention. Several layers of ivory paint and a lot of elbow grease would give it that old-world feel she aimed for. *Next week.*

She hit the clicker, lowering the garage door as she wrangled herself and the groceries into her second-floor condo. A familiar meow greeted her, and she bent to scratch her calico's head. "Such a fierce guard dog, Miss Eggroll."

The cat fell in behind her, and they climbed her interior stairs to a bright, open living space that always made Claudia release a sigh of happiness. This was her sanctuary, a place where she could lock out the rest of the world. At a barstool beside her breakfast counter sat her indignant orange tabby. "I know you're happy to see me, Popcorn. Your snooty attitude doesn't fool me one bit."

Letting her backpack slide from her shoulder, Claudia kicked off her shoes and padded down the hallway to her bedroom to change into comfy sweats. She gave her office-slash-guest bedroom a passing glance, ignoring the big gap where the dresser belonged.

Next week for sure.

After feeding her cats, she poured herself a hefty glass of chardonnay and drifted back to her office. She gingerly sat in front of the computer, where she opened a browser and typed in Marty's name. For the next hour, she sipped her wine and lost herself in his coaching career, his accomplishments, and his accolades.

How had she lived in the same town with Marty and never known it?

He was huge in community service, a beloved figure donating his time for charity events and kids' hockey camps and clinics. He had arrived in Loveland two years earlier and taken the Loveland hockey scene by storm. The Colorado Hawks, the AHL affiliate to the NHL's Colorado Blizzard, had hired him for a video coach, and he had quickly worked his way up to an assistant coach. One former coach gushed, "His hockey IQ is off the charts. When it comes to X's and O's, he's a detailed person. The Hawks are lucky to have him."

She went on to read more articles written by fans of Marty LeBrun. "His approach to the game is one of the driving factors behind the team's overachievement last season," one declared. Another asserted, "His players love and respect him. The team needed an infusion, and he's the fresh blood that's bringing them out of their coma." Yet another article went on to speculate he would soon be a candidate for head coach and implored ownership to do whatever it took to hang on to him. *Wonder how that sits with the existing head coach.*

Claudia nearly laughed out loud with delight for him. *You deserve this, Marty LeBrun!*

She refilled her wine, started up her gas fireplace, and plopped onto her overstuffed couch. Eggroll immediately made herself comfortable in Claudia's lap. "I saw my old best friend today," she told the cat. "He's doing really well, and I'm so happy to see it." The cat peered up at her. "Are we going to be best friends again, you ask? I would love it if we could, but I wasn't very good to him. He's probably *still* damaged from being besties with me," Claudia chuckled.

She stroked Eggroll's head, and the cat's throat rumbled with contentment. "Besides, he's a busy guy, and he has a girlfriend now. I'm sure she would *not* appreciate another woman busting into his life, even if it is just friends. So I don't see how we'll ever be able to return to what we had."

As she uttered the last sentence, sadness crept over her. A moment later, her phone chimed with a text.

Marty: *Still up for running tomorrow? I'm thinking 9 a.m.*

His message was like a hit of helium to her heart, and it floated above her melancholy.

Claudia: *Wouldn't miss it.*

Marty: *Awesome! How about meeting me at Benson Sculpture Garden? Know where it is?*

Claudia: *Sure do. I live only a few blocks away.*

Marty's reply came quickly. *See you soon, CC.*

She let out a belly laugh that had Eggroll leaping from her lap and tapped out her reply. *Looking forward to it.* And she was—more than she had looked forward to anything in a long, long time.

Standing close to the park's shelter, Marty shook out his hands as he scanned Aspen Drive. Exactly why he was shaking his hands escaped him since the weather was mild for a November day, but he suspected it had something to do with the nerves that had been jumping in his system ever since he had finalized plans with Claudia last night.

After spending time with her, he had returned to the arena under the pretense of studying video. He actually had studied video, though he'd spent the bulk of the time rolling through virtual video starring Claudia. Guilt and relief had gone to war inside him when Renee had decided to do the rare overnight at her own place because she'd assumed he wouldn't be home until late.

No reason to tell her about Claudia just yet. Why upset her when he had no idea where any of this would lead? Then again, would Renee be upset if she knew? She wasn't the jealous type, but he'd never given her reason to be. The fact that he was even pondering possible jealousy caused him to question his true intentions regarding Claudia. Right now, though, his emotions were a jumbled mess of contradictions he had no interest in untangling.

Before he could give any of it much more thought, a familiar form appeared in his line of sight, walking briskly toward him, her ponytail swinging. When she spotted him, Claudia's face lit up with a dazzling smile that made his heart thump a little harder.

"Did I keep you waiting long?" she said when she reached him.

"No, I've only been here a few minutes. Where's your car?"

"Told you I lived close by. It's such a beautiful morning; I decided to walk."

"Getting extra exercise, I see. Maybe we can run past it later, and you can show me where you live. This loop is pretty short, but I didn't know how much you were up for."

"We could do that, or we could do this loop a couple of times like we used to do around Chestnut Hill Reservoir." She strode to a grassy area and went into a lunge.

Yeah, jackass. She doesn't want you stalking her—not that I would. I wonder if she'll want to use me as a human wall again? He cast the ridiculous thought out of his head.

They spent an awkward few minutes going through their warm-ups, followed by a stuttering start as they adjusted to one another's steps. Their equally awkward small talk couldn't keep his mind off how well synced they'd once been and if they'd be able to regain that rhythm, and he found himself mentally lost when she said, "Guess you don't want to tell me, huh?"

"Tell you what?" He'd totally missed whatever question she had posed.

"Does your girlfriend mind you running with me?"

"No, of course not." *Because she has no idea.* But if Claudia was going to stay in his life, he had to change that, and the notion made his insides feel a little slimy.

She cut him a sidelong glance. "What part of town do you live in?"

"Not too far from the rink, in Windsor. I rent a house in Water Valley."

"I have some friends who live over there. That's a really nice development."

They ran along in companionable silence and were nearing the end of the loop for the second time when she asked if he wanted to go around again. Other people milled about, but the park was relatively quiet, and he agreed. Without him registering it, they had fallen into the familiar cadence of steps and breaths, as if they hadn't missed a beat. He couldn't help but smile to himself.

She jarred him out of his happy place when she asked, "Have you stayed in touch with Zach?"

"No. We crossed paths a time or two early on, but ..."

Marty hadn't spoken to Zach in a decade, but his ears always perked up when he heard Zach's name. And his name had only come up occasionally in the hockey world, usually in conjunction with an injury or a trade rather than his substance abuse. Though Zach was in the twilight of his career, he could still contribute, bringing that veteran experience clubs sought, especially around playoff time. Anything else he'd done in his life was a mystery to Marty, and he was okay with that.

"I get it," Claudia huffed as they rounded a corner.

He hesitated several beats before venturing, "How about you?"

When she didn't answer, he admonished himself for overstepping the delicate truce between them he hoped to nurture.

She surprised him when they came to the end of their round. "Let's stop, and I'll fill you in." She drew in several lungfuls of air and stared off toward the mountains while he waited, his curiosity strung tight like a bowstring.

"I only spoke to him through my attorney at first," she began. "I had the dubious honor of belonging to the 'wives before they were famous' club, and I resented the hell out of it. It wasn't all bad, though. A few of us formed a small support group that met once a month." She shook her head, a wistful smile on her face, and flicked her eyes to his. "I think it was more an excuse to get together and get hammered."

He chuckled, and her impish smile spread over her face before fading. "At the same time I walked in on ... um, I stopped following hockey in any way, shape, or form. That's why I didn't know how your season ended, and I'm so sorry about that."

He took a swig from his water bottle and offered it to her, just as he had so many years ago, without realizing what he'd done. And just as she had so many years ago, she took a sip and handed it back to him.

"I dated a shrink for a while, and he made me realize how anger was holding me back," she continued. An inconvenient stab of envy embedded itself in Marty's chest and lingered. "Things didn't work out in that relationship either, but I'll always be grateful to him for teaching me to let go. I really believe the right people come into your life when you're ready for them, and he was the guy I needed at that moment in time. He helped me move on.

"Zach stayed in touch, even though I didn't respond. And while I still didn't follow the sport, gossip about him and some model or celebrity would sometimes pop up and spread like wildfire on social media. The 'news' always fizzed out a nanosecond later, but it still stung. I thought it was because I wanted him back." A shroud seemed to drop over her eyes, spurring him to rush in and comfort her, but he reined in the urge.

"Then, about five years ago, he got injured and had to have knee surgery. He asked for my help, so I took some time off and went to stay with him in Tampa, the idea being I'd nurse him back to health. That's when I knew for sure."

Marty's breath caught in his chest, and he arched his eyebrows expectantly.

She stared toward the west again. "I knew I could never go back—not that I'd been considering it, but still, you sometimes wonder. My future was on a completely different track, and it was a track I *liked*. And when he started up the drinking and abusing oxy and God knows what else, that sealed it." She let out a bitter laugh. "If he'd been mobile, he probably would have hosted a *ménage-à*-ten." She swung her gaze to Marty's, her brown eyes reflecting the light. "I knew I had to leave for my own sake. I found him some domestic help, told him I'd always care about him, and I left."

"What happened after that?"

"Well, we are talking about Zach, and he's relentless when he wants something. He *thought* he wanted me, but of course he didn't.

He simply wanted what he couldn't have. I had to finally change my number and jump through a few more hoops before my life quieted down nicely again." She held his gaze. "I was surprised to learn you guys didn't stay in touch, but then again, your lifestyles were night and day."

"There were a lot of times when I was partying right along with him. But the friendship had been on a downhill slide ever since he went to the Show. In fact, *I* was surprised he didn't replace me with Steele as best man at your wedding."

Claudia covered her mouth and the laugh trying to escape. "Oh my God, can you imagine what a fiasco that would have been? Of course, it might have saved me a lot of trouble because I couldn't have helped but see the dark side of Zach."

Her words clobbered him like a two-hundred-and-thirty-pound defenseman, and it must have shown in his expression because she rushed on. "I didn't mean that as a knock against you, Marty." She blinked up at him. "I need to grovel some more, don't I?"

"Yeah, and you can do that at the same time, same place, tomorrow."

She shook her head, and his heart fell.

"Can't. I work tomorrow from four a.m. to four p.m."

He mentally rearranged his schedule. "I could meet you in the late afternoon, when you're done, before the Hawks game." It would be a tight squeeze, but he would do it.

"That might work." She seemed to appraise him, and her scrutiny made him squirm inside. *She's probably wondering if I'm telling Renee about any of this*. But then she pointed to his eyebrow. "That's a new scar, isn't it?"

He touched his brow. "New to you, maybe. I got it about six years ago."

"Flying puck?"

"No, a fight. I won, in case you're wondering. It's on YouTube." He grinned down at her.

"I might have watched it last night. Is that the one where you threw down with the Hershey Bears enforcer?"

"You were checking out my fights on YouTube?" Why did the thought of her looking him up warm him all over?

Amusement danced in her eyes. "Maybe it popped up while I was looking up boy bands. Well, I better get going. See you tomorrow afternoon."

"Yeah, bye." He stood in a daze and watched her walk away, her hips swaying, her ponytail swinging. His mind raced to how he'd nearly pulled that ponytail and how he had lost his tugging right when he'd lost her friendship—the one he was suddenly clawing to get back. But was wanting an important friendship back so bad?

When his mind meandered to what Renee would think, reason kind of went off the track.

Shit! Am I as bad as Zach? Hanging with one woman while I have another one at home? No. I'm only sleeping with one of them. Although, given a choice ... Don't go there, dickhead.

Marty had never shared Zach's desire to sleep his way through the country two or six women at a time. He hadn't understood the appeal. Was it the bragging rights? Or was it trying to find perfection that didn't exist? Zach had had perfection in Claudia, and yet it hadn't been enough. Marty used to envy his friend, but that envy vanished the day Claudia dumped Zach's ass ... maybe before.

Even as his mind strayed to places it shouldn't, it wasn't that he pictured himself with Renee *and* Claudia. He only pictured himself with one of them in that moment—the wrong one. Thank God he was going on the road soon—he had a budding problem to wrestle into submission. Too bad it would be harder than throwing down with the Bears enforcer.

Chapter 26

A Fresh Perspective

One of the advantages of being a coach was how easily one became immersed in the job and the nuances of the sport, especially on the road. And the road was someplace Marty enjoyed being for a number of reasons—the focus on the game, the camaraderie, and the break from the home front. The time away might not have been as vital for Renee as it was for him, but he was convinced it made the relationship work. He knew this because during down times, like the all-star break and summer, tensions often built between them, and he found himself spending more hours at the gym or doing outdoor activities with buddies—like golfing or kayaking—to maintain harmony. And while he didn't exactly *miss* her when he was gone, he always looked forward to seeing her when the trip was over.

But this time he wasn't as keen on returning home, where Renee waited for him. The past week he'd spent zoned in on hockey to the exclusion of everything else, and consequently the fresh perspective he had hoped for on their relationship never materialized. He was no closer to figuring out what the hell he was doing than before the trip started. Adding to his distress was the uncomfortable fact that while he had stayed in touch with her via texting, the texts between himself and Claudia outnumbered those with Renee.

It's only because we're making up for lost time. He was in a relationship with Renee; he was simply trying to restore a friendship that predated her.

Marty's head still spun every time he recalled Claudia walking into the exam room over a week ago. It was as though she had walked out of the fog where she had disappeared years ago, like a time traveler in a movie or the *Star Trek* crew passing through portals.

Stepping into his house in the wee hours after a restless plane flight, he eyed the stairs leading to the bedroom. Normally, he was up those stairs and climbing into bed beside Renee, but a foreign reluctance had him stripping down to his boxers, grabbing a few quilts, and settling himself on the family room couch. Though he told himself she wouldn't appreciate him waking her up at 2:00 a.m., that stupid little voice inside his head reminded him she had never minded before, and they often ended up having sex. Which was when he realized he didn't *want* to have sex with her. Not right now, and maybe not tomorrow either.

What the hell was wrong with him?

He startled awake later that next morning to Renee brushing hair from his forehead as she perched on the edge of the couch in her robe.

"Why did you sleep here last night?"

Closing his gritty eyes, he yawned. "It was late, and I, uh, didn't want to wake you up."

She nuzzled his neck, purring in his ear, "That hasn't stopped you before."

He sat up abruptly. "Shit, I have to get to the rink. What time is it?"

Surprise chased by hurt flashed in her eyes. "But you just got home. Don't you have today off? You look exhausted."

"Not this time. I'm sorry, but we have to debrief after the trip, and I told Coach Graham I'd get things set up before the rest of the coaching staff shows up." All true, but he was more excited about getting to the rink than normal. Or was he anxious to get out of the house? He put *that* disturbing notion aside and told himself nothing had changed since Claudia had come back into his life.

Renee frowned at him. “I leave in a few days for a week at my folks’ place in Mexico, and it would be nice to spend some time together before I go. Will you be home for dinner?”

“I should be.”

“Maybe we can have that talk.”

“What talk?”

Her eyebrows inched up her forehead. “About my lease expiring?”

“When does it expire again?”

“March.”

“That’s still four months away. We’ve got plenty of time to figure it out.”

The vertical pleats between her eyes deepened. “You say that like it’s not important to you.”

“It’s important. It’s just that I owe the team a lot of my energy right now. You know how it is this time of year.” He kissed her cheek, moved her aside, and stood. “How about I grab some takeout on my way home tonight?”

She let out a long exhale. “Okay.”

He dashed from the room, dressed, and left before he had to see the look of dismay on her face one more time.

Yeah, his behavior baffled him. One thing he knew for sure, though. He needed to tell her about Claudia.

“I can’t meet you for our run tomorrow.” He sat in his office, talking on the phone with Claudia after five, most of the trainers and coaching staff gone. After arriving in the middle of the night and spending all day at the rink, he was running on fumes and needed sleep before he face-planted.

“That’s okay. I had something come up too. Hey, I told Rex and Alice about bumping into you, and they thought it would be fun for all of us to get together. Maybe this Friday night? Something simple at their place or mine, and bring your girlfriend. We’d all really like to meet her.”

"She's leaving town for a week, but I could come stag on Friday," he said smoothly. Half of him was distracted by the something that had "come up"—was Claudia going on a date?—while the other half debated introducing Renee to his old friends and vice versa. Better he saw them alone for the first time. Who knew what kinds of stories would surface, and he wasn't sure how many of them he wanted her to hear. Not that he had anything to hide, but something about blending his old and new lives made the new one seem ... superglued. Although Renee knew Danielle and her husband, and that didn't make him angsty. Then again, when he spent time with Dani and her family, he did it solo because, well, Dani didn't like Renee for reasons he didn't comprehend.

Claudia's voice jolted him back to the present. "That sounds great! What's her name anyway? I don't think you've mentioned it."

"Renee."

"That's a pretty name."

Wonder if Renee will say the same about your name?

An hour later, he stood in the kitchen sipping a 90 Shilling while Renee pulled out plates for the Chinese food he had picked up on his way home.

He cleared his throat. "Did I tell you about running into Claudia Campbell the other day? Talk about a blast from the past!"

"Who's Claudia Campbell? I don't think you've ever mentioned her before."

Marty kept his eyes fixed on Renee as she prepared the plates of food, trying to gauge her mood. "I didn't? I'm pretty sure I did."

"No, you've told me about some of your other girlfriends—"

"She wasn't a girlfriend. She was married to Zach Pruitt, my buddy from juniors. We were roommates in college."

"You and Claudia?"

"No! Me and Zach." He checked for a smirk on her face but didn't spot one.

"Hmm. It's funny that I know about Zach Pruitt, but I never heard about his wife."

He lifted his head and looked at her. *What did* that *mean?* Her question had sparked irritation inside of him, though he wasn't sure why. "Funny how?"

She handed him his plate, chopsticks, and a napkin. "I just find it curious, that's all. I thought I knew everything about you."

"It's not possible for two people to know everything about each other," he retorted, a little on the harsh side.

The frown returned to her face. "Okay. Sorry. Didn't mean to ruffle your feathers. I was just making conversation."

"No, I'm the one who's sorry." He took her plate from her and set it down at the breakfast counter before fetching his own. "I didn't mean for that to sound the way it did." He needed to get his brain back online. "Anyway, I had coffee with her, and she'd like to meet you sometime."

They both sat, and Renee carefully spread her napkin over her lap. "When was this? You've been gone for nearly a week."

He slid his chopsticks out of their paper sleeve and split them apart. "I bumped into her at the hospital the day Seth got hurt. We had coffee shortly after that." An hour later, in fact, but he needed to keep the timing vague since he had led Renee to believe he couldn't make dinner in time because of Seth's injury.

Jesus Christ, how do cheaters balance their lives? I'm not even cheating, and I can't stand the maneuvering. Having to keep the stories straight is stressful. But telling Renee the truth will upset her for no good reason.

She forked a bite of rice. "So some woman comes out of your past, and you have coffee with her, but you don't bother telling me?" Though she wasn't looking at him, something in her voicc set sirens wailing in his head. Was it hurt? Anger?

Better not tell her about us jogging together yet either.

"I'm telling you now. I didn't tell you sooner because it wasn't a big deal and I forgot about it." *Lies number one and two.* He puffed out a breath. "It was a long time ago, she was married to my friend, and we hung out a lot. When things between them fell apart, she disappeared." He recited these facts like a kid spouting out his multiplication tables. "I haven't thought about her in years." *Lie number three.* "After running into each other, we wanted to catch up, which we did over a cup of coffee." *Maybe if I say it enough times, it will take on the casual note I'm going for.* "Like I said, no big deal. I've had a lot on my mind, and I spaced telling you. I don't tell you every time Coach Graham and I grab coffee, and this was like that." Of course, sitting down with Claudia was nothing like coffee with his boss. *Lie number four*. He was reinforcing his fortress walls in preparation for a battle he wasn't sure was coming.

She side-eyed him, as if trying to make up her mind about his story that had more holes than a slice of Swiss cheese. "I guess that makes sense. So is she single now?"

He pushed his food around his plate with his fork. "We didn't really talk about her status. As far as I can tell, there's no one serious in her life right now."

Renee dropped her chin into her cupped palm. "Is she pretty?"

She's gorgeous. "Uh, she's okay. She looks about the same as before but a little older now." *Lie number four and a half.*

"Do I need to worry?"

"About what?"

Her hazel gaze shot to his. "About her stealing you away from me."

He rolled his eyes. "You've got nothing to worry about." That little voice inside his head whispered he might have told lie number five, and he warned it to shut the fuck up. Eager to cut short the stilted conversation that followed, he hurried through the rest of the meal.

After cleaning the kitchen, he trundled off to bed, leaving Renee to watch some true crime show on TV. As he drifted off to sleep, he told himself to tread easy. Renee wasn't typically hypersensitive, but her feelings did get hurt now and again—especially at times like these, when he was distracted. The last thing he wanted was for his actions to cause her pain.

As he put that inner discussion aside, his mind wandered to this Friday night, and a spark of excitement ignited inside him. He disregarded the inconvenient question of whether omitting to tell Renee about his plans qualified as lie number six.

Claudia jumped when her doorbell rang. "Shit! He's early. Or am I late?" She swiped pink-tinted gloss across her lips as Popcorn watched her in the mirror. After spending an hour getting ready for her date with Marty that wasn't a date, she still wasn't sure of her choice in attire. She had tried on four different outfits in various combinations, and the remnants of her indecision lay strewn about her closet floor, with Eggroll curled atop them in a sleeping ball.

One last perusal, and she gave her reflection a nod of approval. Charcoal jeans, chunky black ankle boots, and a strappy cold-shoulder top in a navy fabric that hugged her curves. Silver hoops adorned her ears. She slipped on a gray open-drape cardigan and smoothed her blond waves.

"Ready as I'll ever be. I hope I didn't overdo it."

Popcorn meowed.

"I'm taking that as a compliment," she called over her shoulder as she hurried down the hall from her bedroom, then down the flight of stairs to her front door.

A rap sounded just as she yanked open the door. Marty filled her door frame, his fist poised in mid-knock. He took her in and let out a low whistle. "Wow! You look fantastic."

Okay. Good choice on the clothes.

"Why, thank you. So do you." He sported a close-fitting black shawl sweater under a gray pea coat, jeans, and black Timberland boots. It was a good look on his muscular frame.

From behind his back, he produced a mixed bouquet of pink and purple flowers.

"Oh!" She took them from him and held them to her nose. "What are these for?"

"Well, I picked out a bouquet for Alice and didn't want to leave you out."

She waved him in. "I'll just put these in water, and then we can go. Thanks for coming to get me." He had *insisted*, leaving her little choice, but she was okay with that. It gave them more time to talk.

His eyes traveled up her stairs. "Yeah, no problem. So this is a second-floor unit?"

"Yep, with an inside garage entrance," she called over her shoulder as she led him up to the living area. "And it's all mine."

"You own it?"

"Well, the bank and I do." She pulled out a vase and began filling it at the center island sink. "Feel free to look around. Well, everywhere except my closet, that is."

“Believe me, I wouldn’t set foot in a woman’s closet without being invited,” he chuckled. “Still love your plants, I see.”

“I do. And I loved your herb garden so much I bought myself a new one after I moved in here.” She lifted her chin toward a row of clay pots on a living room windowsill.

He ambled in that direction, pausing at her fireplace mantel, his gaze fastened on a cluster of framed photos. He picked one up, and a corner of his mouth quirked. “This looks like you, Rex, and Alice in Boston.”

She arranged the stems in the vase. “It is. That was taken before your game that night when—”

Oh shit! Way to remind him right away about that awful night I lost it and tried to knock him on his ass. She abandoned her floral arranging and covered the short distance dividing them. Standing beside him, she studied the picture. “I like looking at it. It brings back good memories.”

“Like when you shoved me on the sidewalk?”

She raised her startled gaze to his. Amusement danced in his brown eyes, and relief washed over her. She shook her head. “Yeah, that. All these years later, and I’m still mortified by what I did.”

He carefully placed the picture back among the others. As he moved, she caught his familiar woodsy scent. Whether it was aftershave, him, or a combination of the two, she didn’t know, but she had always loved that smell. As the scent had in college, it conjured warmth, safety, and comfort wrapped up in a Marty bundle—now with a little spice thrown in. She pulled in the fragrance, holding back the urge to close her eyes.

He chuckled, breaking the spell. “You were pretty strong. Then again, I was spindly.” He slid her a sly wink.

She let loose a laugh. “I was a teeny-weeny bit insane that night, and I’ve heard insanity gives people superhuman strength. I can’t imagine trying to shove you backward now.” She swept his sculpted body with an appreciative once-over, and his eyes bored into hers. A charged awkwardness crackled between them, and she stepped back. *What was* that? “Well, I guess we’d better go. Don’t want to be late.”

Popcorn materialized and rubbed against Marty’s leg. Before Claudia could shoo the cat away, Marty scooped him up and began scratching his ears. The sweet sight warmed her all over. "I didn't know you liked cats."

"I didn't either. Haven't spent much time around them." He continued his gentle scratches, and Popcorn revved up his purr motor.

"Well, I think you've just made a new friend."

Minutes later, they were heading across town in Marty's Suburban, Claudia guiding him to their destination as they talked nonstop—just like it had always been. She couldn't help but steal glances at his strong profile. Had he always looked like that? *He's definitely gotten better with age.*

When they arrived at Alice and Rex's, Alice launched herself at Marty and Rex hauled him in for a bro hug while their two kids and one dog danced around him. He seemed at ease with all of it. After he handed off the bouquet to Alice, he passed her a bakery box Claudia had noticed in the backseat of the Suburban.

"Just a little something from B Sweet Cupcakes for the kids."

Alice slapped her hand to her chest. "Omigosh, now I'll never get them to settle down!"

"Well, there's plenty in there for the adults too, so we can match their energy." He ruffled the kids' hair.

Claudia's heart melted into a puddle of goo, and she was pretty sure her face was frozen in a dopey grin. *Cats and kids, flowers and cupcakes. He's kinda perfect. Then again, I guess he always has been. How did I not notice before?*

Alice waggled her eyebrows at Claudia as Rex took their coats and offered them drinks. Soon they were toasting one another, and Alice was dragging Claudia upstairs on the pretext of showing her a new comforter. "Bring your wine," Alice insisted and scooted up the stairs. Claudia rushed to keep up with her.

As soon as they entered the master bedroom, Alice shut the door and squealed, "Oh. My. God! When did Marty become such a stud?"

Claudia smirked. "I think he's always been a stud, but we were too busy gawking at Rex and Zach."

"I always thought you two would make a great couple, and now's your chance! Or are you going to stay strictly in the friend zone? I know it might be awkward to make that shift, but please tell me you're open to it." Alice peered at her with furrowed brows.

"It doesn't matter if I'm open to it. He has a girlfriend who's out of town, remember? And if she hadn't been, I would've been the fifth wheel tonight."

Alice's face dropped with disappointment. "Oh damn! I totally forgot. What's she like? Have you met her?" Claudia nearly laughed out loud at the transformation.

"Not yet, but hopefully soon. Let's say I'm very curious."

That curiosity got the better of Claudia when she was halfway through her second glass of wine and feeling its effects. While Alice and Rex busied themselves getting dinner on the table, she sat beside Marty on the couch, almost touching but not. She could feel the heat radiating from him, and his fragrance invaded her senses, making her a little dizzy.

"I'm trying to picture what Renee looks like. Do you have a picture of her?"

He seemed to blank for an instant. "Uh, I'm not sure." He pulled his phone from his back pocket and scrolled with his thumb. His other hand balanced a bottle of beer he'd been nursing since they'd arrived. "Maybe one in here," he muttered. "Hmm. Oh. Here's one." He handed Claudia his phone.

The picture was a selfie of the two of them at—what else?—a hockey rink. Marty frowned, as if he was concentrating on taking the picture, while beside him, the pretty blond woman laid her head and hand against his chest and sported a wide white smile. Such an intimate picture, and Claudia felt the contents of her stomach churn.

"What have we got?" Alice startled her when she breezed in, a wooden salad bowl filled with leafy greens in hand, and peered over their shoulders.

"That's Marty's girlfriend, Renee," Claudia blurted.

He held up the phone so Alice could get a better look. She tipped her head. "She's really pretty, Marty." To Claudia, she said, "She reminds me of you." As she headed for the table, she called over her shoulder, "Kind of like all Marty's past girlfriends."

Marty shot Claudia a sheepish look and slid the phone back into his pocket.

While her mind turned over his past girlfriends and the coincidence of their looks, Alice's words about them making a good couple bounced through her mind.

They spent dinner laughing and talking over old times, with everyone sidestepping the subject of Zach Pruitt. Rex got close when he asked what had become of Zach's old teammate Steele.

Marty twirled his now empty beer bottle. "He was sent down to the minors for a rehab stint, and to my knowledge he never made it back to the big league again. I also heard he got married."

Rex sat back. "Whoa! I wonder who the poor girl is."

"She's a stripper, and her name is Honey or Sugar or—" Alice's eyes widened and landed on Claudia.

"Or Brenda or Trixie?" Claudia finished for her with a smirk. *Ouch! Why does that still hurt?* Because while she conjured the devastating scene from so many years ago with less frequency, it was no less vivid. She could feel Marty's eyes on her even as his big, warm hand gave her knee a brief squeeze under the table. The touch infused her with confidence so that when Alice stumbled over her apologies, Claudia was able to pat her arm and reassure her it was okay—and actually mean it.

At the end of the evening, Marty pulled behind her car in the driveway and hopped out, insisting on walking her to her door. They faced one another on her front stoop, the porch light casting shadows over his chiseled jaw. The air hovered below freezing, and as she spoke, her breath hung in a cloud of steam between them. "Do you want to come in? I'm sure Popcorn would love another crack at you, and Eggroll hasn't met you yet."

He raised his eyes and looked around, as if calculating, before dropping his gaze back to hers. "I better not." Sadness, wistfulness, something she couldn't quite identify played in his brown depths. Then his mouth twitched with a smile. "Tell the cats some other time."

Drawing in a sharp breath, she decided to fling herself into an abyss. "Will there be another time?" she asked softly. He stared at her, his eyes moving between hers and the bottom lip she tugged between her teeth. *Guess that's my answer.* Her stomach roiled as she rushed into the silence with a string of babble. "I'm sorry. I didn't mean to put you on the spot like that. From my own selfish perspective, I hope we can still jog together once in a while or grab a coffee; I didn't realize until I saw you at the hospital how much I've missed our friendship. But I get it. Maintaining a friendship with a woman from your past might cause problems in your current relationship, and I don't want to rock the boat. Especially now that you've found someone you're serious about."

Planting his forearm on the wall alongside the doorway where they stood, he leaned in, his scent wreathing her head. "When you asked me two weeks ago if things with Renee were serious, I knew the answer, and it was yes. It was so simple then. Now I'm not so sure—I'm not sure about anything—and I don't know what to do with that." He planted a soft kiss on her cheek, his warm breath caressing her skin, then pulled away before she could fist his lapels and yank him closer like her instincts demanded she do. Taking a few steps down the stoop, he looked at her with emotion brimming in his eyes. A sad smile curved his mouth. "Good night, CC." He turned and walked away.

Claudia's mouth hinged open, but no words came out.

Good-bye, Marty.

Chapter 27

Pretzel Logic

"What's going on, Marty?" Renee stood in his kitchen, hands parked on her hips, her expression a cross between frustration and bewilderment. All the way home from the airport, he'd been quiet, prompting her with questions and not tuning in when she talked. His brain had been busy lurching through thoughts of Claudia instead and how he had almost given in to the urge to kiss her mouth. Thank God a shred of sanity had made him change direction at the last second and land the kiss on her cheek. Then he'd fled, needing to get away, to go somewhere, anywhere, where he couldn't get lost in those big brown eyes or fantasize about that ripe-strawberry mouth or have her fragrance waft up his nose and intoxicate him.

With all these visions bombarding his brain, he had yet to find his balance. He'd struggled to pick his way safely through the minefield of conversation with Renee, and consequently he'd said little to her.

Though he hadn't contacted Claudia since dinner at Rex and Alice's five nights ago, it hadn't stopped a deluge of images of her from flooding his mind. His conscience had been at war, "the right thing" raging against wishes and desires. If wishes and desires were a hockey team, they would have been up by ten goals with less than a minute left in the game.

He turned his focus on Renee. “I’m sorry. With Mom and Lexi coming into town for Thanksgiving and our last loss, I’m just distracted.” *Wow, that was lame.*

The furrows creasing her forehead told him she agreed on his lameness. “What happened to ‘put it behind you and focus on the next game’? You’ve never let it get to you like this before.”

His phone rang. *Saved by the bell.* “Hey, Dani. What’s going on?”

“I just wanted to check and be sure you’re still bringing the wine and pumpkin pies tomorrow.” They would be spending Thanksgiving at Danielle’s, where his mom and Alexis were currently staying. Lexi’s little boy was with his dad for the holiday, which might limit some of the kid chaos, though Marty didn’t mind it.

“I’ll get the wine today, Dani.” He raised his eyes to Renee. “Dani wants to know about the pies.”

Renee blew out a loud breath. “What about the pies?”

“Maybe I should let you two talk.”

Before he could pull the phone from his ear, Dani’s voice hissed, “Don’t pull a Mom, Marty! I’m having this conversation with *you.* Don’t pass me off to Renee.” Okay. So Dani wasn’t crazy about Renee, but did she have to be so pissy about it? Then again, she had a house full and, knowing Dani, was super stressed about the big meal tomorrow.

“We’ll bring the pies, Dani.” He would figure out if they were store-bought or fresh later.

“And whipped cream,” Dani added.

“Yeah, that too. I’ll ... *we’ll* see you tomorrow.” *Shit! Brain fart.*

He hung up, and Renee’s eyebrow dipped a little lower. “I don’t buy that you’re being distant because you’re distracted. I think something else is going on.”

Oh boy. No getting around this conversation now. “I didn’t realize I was being distant.” *I’m definitely distracted, but for an entirely different reason.*

“Well, you are. I’ve never seen you let coaching spill over into your personal life like this before. And then there’s the other issue.”

He braced himself. “Other issue?”

"Yes. You barely kissed me when you picked me up. In fact, you haven't touched me in weeks! Did something happen recently?"

Claudia walked back into my life. He stared at Renee while his mind ping-ponged through various scenarios. But what was there to tell her? He barely knew himself.

When he didn't answer, she went on, and the tremor in her voice racked him with guilt. "Have I done something wrong?"

"No, you didn't do anything wrong. I *have* been distracted. Now that our season is taking shape, I've become consumed with it. I'm also tired because I haven't been sleeping well. I've had a lot on my mind." *Like you and me and our future. Whether I want you to give up your place and officially move in.* Could he say it out loud? He had only come to the realization a short while ago himself. The truth might crush her, but keeping her in the dark wasn't fair either. He had already learned that painful lesson once. But even if he did lay it out there, he wasn't sure what to tell Renee.

I thought I loved you, but now I don't know.

I might want to break up, but I'm not sure.

I'm distracted because I'm obsessing over my old best friend.

I thought I didn't want her anymore, but I could be wrong.

The last insight startled him. What he once believed was a long-dead blaze of desire had sparked to life again, stoked by the woman herself.

What was he going to do about that? What *could* he do? Was his desire for Claudia a mere manifestation of her being unattainable for so long? The old you-want-what-you-can't-have principle at play? Even if she wanted *him* and they wound up together, was his crazy love for her real, or was it propped up by fantasies?

Over the years, he had caught a faint glimpse of love, but it had never blossomed. Was that because he was a guy who always kept his heart on the outer edge of a relationship, never diving too deep? Was he capable of more? Or did he lack a certain breadth of passion? Maybe that's why he couldn't crack the NHL. Maybe that's why he hadn't won Claudia in the first place.

What would have happened if he'd told her how he felt about her all those years ago?

These questions twisted in his gut as he crawled between the sheets that night. When Renee reached for him, he could only hold her, nothing more. As she eased against him and drifted off to sleep, he lay awake, staring into the void, wondering at how quickly his sedate world had turned upside down.

"What's eating you, bro?" Dani wrestled a platter from a cabinet. They stood in her kitchen alone for the first time that day, while the rest of the family burbled in a different part of the house.

"What do you mean?" He crunched down on a humus-laden celery stick.

"You're a million miles away, on some other planet."

"Huh. Renee says the same thing."

Dani straightened and wiped her hands on a kitchen towel with turkeys printed on it. "Then something *must* be going on with you because she and I never agree on anything."

He pointed his celery stick at her. "Why is that? Why don't you like her?"

She slid him a sidelong glance. "I'm not sure I can put a finger on it. It's more about how you two fit together—or don't fit together. You live and breathe hockey, and she lives and breathes ... nothing. She's a bit of a chameleon who's hard to pin down. Trying to talk to her can be painful because she doesn't engage. I can't get a bead on what makes her tick ... besides you, that is."

He grinned. "So my magnetic personality leaves her in a daze. What's wrong with that?"

Dani rolled her eyes. "Nothing, if you want to be with someone whose identity leeches off of yours."

"Wow. That's kinda harsh."

"Maybe, but think about it. Does she ever say, 'See ya, Marty. I'm playing tennis with my girlfriends,' or, 'I'm off for a weekend quilting retreat'? No. Because she has no hobbies, no interests outside of you."

He narrowed his eyes. "What's a quilting retreat?"

"Never mind. My point is her world revolves around what *you* do. She spends all her spare time with you. If you weren't around to hold her up, she'd fall over because there's nothing to her." He didn't disagree, sharpening his attention as Dani went on. "I can see why you hang out with her. She's pleasant, and she's attractive. But I see you with someone who's confident, who gives you a little sass, who keeps you on your toes."

"Claudia Campbell lives in Loveland," he blurted.

Dani's eyes popped wide. *"Your* Claudia? From BC?"

"She's not *my* anything. And yes, that Claudia. I bumped into her a few weeks ago at UCHealth. She's a nurse, and she's been living here for the past six years."

Dani covered her mouth to—apparently—hold back a shriek, and she began dancing in place.

He leaned against the counter and crossed his arms, waiting for her to settle down. "It was nice to see her, but I don't know that it merits a happy dance," he said dryly.

Leaning her palms on the counter beside him, she grinned up at him. "How does she look?"

Smoking hot. "About the same as she did ten years ago."

"In other words, stunningly beautiful?" She poked her pointy elbow into his ribs, and he faked doubling over. "Did she remarry?"

"No, she's single." *Like me. Wait. I'm not single. Just unmarried.*

"I'd love to see her. I always liked her." She swatted his arm with a dish towel. "Now *she's* someone who would keep you on your toes, big bro. Have you seen her since?"

"A couple of times. You remember Rex and Alice? We went to dinner at their place last week."

"Who are Rex and Alice, and who's the 'we' who went to dinner there last week?" Renee's voice startled them both and had them spinning in unison to face her as she stood in the doorway between the kitchen and mud room. *How did she get there?* She had a plastic smile plastered on her face that made Marty flinch.

Dani shot him a quick look. "Renee, perfect timing. I could use your help."

Marty mouthed a thank you just as his niece came squealing around the corner and launched herself at him. "Uncle Martyyyyyyy!" Behind her came his mother, an expression on her face he clearly understood from having seen it throughout his childhood. It was part indulgence, part exasperation, and it warmed him all over.

He scooped up his niece. "How much sugar have you had, princess?"

"No sugar. Flip me," she demanded.

"Yes, Your Highness." He tossed her in the air, and she exploded in a fit of giggles. Then she exploded ... all over his dress shirt.

Renee side-eyed him hours later as he drove home, his brother-in-law's too-tight long-sleeved T-shirt chafing at his neck and armpits. "Nice Hulk look you've got going on there."

"Gee, thanks? I'm taking a shower as soon as we get home." He'd rinsed what he could off his torso and hair at his sister's, but he had caught a whiff of vomit every time he'd turned his head. The odor had put a damper on dinner and soured his mood.

"I could take one with you." Renee's eyebrows bounced when he swiveled his head toward her. Why was the thought so unappealing? Not so long ago, he would have been totally down for that kind of action.

The question must have shown on his face because her next words cut like flint. "Or not."

"It's just ... I stink, Ren."

She crossed her arms, locking them down tight over her chest. "You never answered my question."

"What question?"

"I overheard you telling Danielle that 'we' went to your friends' house for dinner. Who are the friends, and who besides you went?"

He pushed a silent breath through his lungs. "Alice and Rex are old friends from college. I haven't seen them in ten years."

"Friends of yours and Claudia's, I take it?"

"Yeah. There was a small group of us who did everything together. They were in that group. I didn't realize they were here in Loveland until I ran into Claudia."

"So you and she went to dinner there together, I take it?"

"Uh-huh. We rode together because it was more convenient; she lives right on the way. It was a last-minute thing. You were invited too, but you were out of town. You probably would have been bored anyway because all we talked about was college." He attempted a lighthearted laugh that fell short before it could get any lift.

Endless moments of silence charged the air.

"When were you planning to tell me about this intimate little dinner between old friends, or had you just 'forgotten about it' because it was so, oh, I don't know, unremarkable?" The bite in her voice was unmistakable.

"I'm sorry I didn't tell you sooner. I would have told you this weekend." Would he have, though? He was too exhausted to debate it with himself.

"You know, it seems as though your 'distractions' began about the time you bumped into your 'old friend.' You sure you're just friends, or is there something else there you care to tell me about?"

Traffic was light—most people were probably indulging in turkey sandwiches by now—and he turned his head toward her. *Tell her! Tell her now!* Except it was Thanksgiving, and he was exhausted.

"There's nothing going on between Claudia and me. In fact, I'd like for you two to meet sometime. Then you'll be able to see for yourself." He reined in his irritation; he was clueless as to where the irritation sprang from in the first place.

"You're on the road again next week, aren't you?" In his peripheral vision, she stared out the window.

It wasn't a real question; she knew his schedule. He cut to the chase. "And that bothers you."

"What, the fact that you're sneaking around with your old girlfriend?" she groused.

"She's not my old girlfriend, and I'm not sneaking around." *Even though I'm acting like I am.* "What I meant was, it bothers you that I travel. Have you ever thought about maybe going back to school? Exploring mountain biking trails with friends? Something to keep you busy while I'm away?"

"Nice try, but none of that would keep me from wondering about what you're up to when you're away."

Anger began a slow boil inside him. "What does *that* mean?"

"Figure it out, Marty. Lots of bars, lots of spare time, lots of opportunity."

He gripped the steering wheel a little tighter. "Tell me you're kidding." Her sullen silence had him barreling ahead. "I've never been unfaithful. Not once. In fact, since the day I met you, you're the only woman I've been with."

"Which is *exactly* why I don't believe you when you say you're not sleeping with Claudia!"

He gave his head a quick shake to dislodge the mental whiplash. "That doesn't make sense."

"You don't sleep around, Marty. And if you're sleeping with *her*, that means you won't sleep with anyone else. And guess what? You're not sleeping with me! Therefore, you're sleeping with her."

Closing his eyes briefly, he exhaled in defeat. What was the use in arguing against her twisted-pretzel logic? "I'm not sleeping with her," he repeated, his tone soft. "Can we not do this right now? It's Thanksgiving."

He turned his head to look at her once more. The granite set to her chin told him his appeal was a lost cause. She didn't believe him. When they returned home, she gathered up a few personal items before leaving for her own place. "I haven't been home in a while, and I need to go check stuff."

He wasn't the only one conjuring lame excuses, but he welcomed the solitude.

As he lay in bed watching TV, his phone chimed with a text from Claudia saying she hoped he'd had a happy Thanksgiving. He had tried to banish all thought of her for days—the operative word being "tried"—yet she had thought of him. That message led to a short exchange—the lone bright spot in his evening—that brought a smile to his face.

Marty: *I've had better Thanksgivings.*

Claudia: *You didn't spend it alone, did you?*

Marty: *No. I was at Dani's, and my niece threw up on me.*

Claudia: *ROTFLMAO. Sorry. Laughing at your expense. Did she catch a bug?*

Marty: *No, her Uncle Marty tossed her in the air one too many times. Dani says I got what I deserved. What did you do?*

Claudia: *Took a few days off to spend the holiday in MA with Mom and Bev. I fly home tmw.*

Why this startled him, he had no idea. Of course Claudia had a life outside of work and ... him. There was so much he didn't know, and he found himself wanting to pull the curtain aside and glimpse her life behind it. Did it include lovers? Maybe he didn't want a glimpse after all.

Marty: *What are you doing this Saturday night?*

Claudia: *Washing my hair? Pruning my plants? Watching a rom-com with my cats? God, I sound like an old woman!*

He laughed out loud before tapping, *Then maybe you should get out more often. How about coming to the Hawks game?*

Claudia: *Can I bring a date?*

Marty's first instinct was, "Hell no!" Instead, he typed, *Sure. Renee might be there. Maybe the 4 of us can go out after. Anyone I know?*

Claudia: *Rex. He's dying to go to a game. He's also dying to get away from his in-laws, who are here for the holiday, lol.*

Marty's shoulders unclenched. *Looking forward to it.*

A grin stretched from ear to ear as he put his phone aside, and he admonished himself for getting carried away.

Maybe Renee's convoluted logic had some merit: he wasn't sleeping with Claudia—physically—but in the fantasy world where he'd been spending a lot of time lately, he'd definitely crossed that line.

During the next two days, Marty seesawed between breaking up with Renee now and holding off until after the holidays. How shitty would it be to end a relationship at this time of year? Then again, a whole other part of him hoped Cupid would unleash a heated dart that could ignite his tepid heart, driving him to ask Renee to move in with him permanently. Though he hadn't seen her for two days, a slow thaw had begun between them. When she couldn't come to the Hawks game that Saturday night, he told her Claudia and Rex would be there.

"It's their first Hawks game," he explained. "Why don't you join us afterward? You can meet them both, and we can all go grab a beer."

"Can't. I'm heading up to Breckenridge to ski with some girlfriends from work. It was a last-minute invite. I hope that's okay."

"Of course it's okay." A small cheer rose up inside him. She was flexing an independent muscle, even if she was quasi asking for his permission. "We'll all get together another time."

He had told Rex and Claudia to meet him in the family and friends area, and when he strolled in, his eyes found Claudia and latched on. Maybe because the place had thinned out, but even if it had been packed to the gills, she would have stood out as the brightest light in the room, and his heart lifted despite his team's loss.

"There she is," he said aloud and strode to her, utterly unaware of Rex or anyone else in proximity. He leaned down and hugged her, inhaling her fragrance, then set her apart and shook Rex's hand. "Glad you could make it."

While Rex expounded on the game, Marty's eyes traveled swiftly up and down Claudia's body, taking inventory. Tonight she was dressed in black skinny jeans tucked into tan-colored ankle-high, fleece-lined snow boots, topped by a blue Hawks jersey that hung on her petite shoulders, its hem hitting her mid-thigh. A pleasant picture of her in nothing but that jersey soared into his consciousness, and he nearly choked.

She patted his chest. "Nice suit."

"Yeah, I have two now." He grinned. It was so easy to smile around her. The notion that it always had been came rushing back as the past compressed and he was twenty-three again.

He found himself grateful for Renee's sudden ski trip.

Claudia was pretty sure she wore a goofy smile as she looked up at Marty, but she didn't care. Nor did she care about the people watching them with intense curiosity. She would feast her eyes on his ruggedly handsome face and his frame that fit his suit so well. His hair was neatly combed back, his face was clean-shaven, and his crisp white button-down was fitted around the contours of his muscles. So she was drooling over him. So what? At least she was being discreet about it.

She and Rex had driven together, so there was no danger of her trying to climb Marty later tonight. Thank God because he would probably be horrified and there would go their friendship again. Part of her was disappointed his girlfriend wasn't around because Claudia burned with curiosity. Another part of her, though, was thankful to have him somewhat to herself.

"Coach?" A man's head appeared in the doorway. "Can you spare a minute for the press?"

Marty buttoned his jacket. "Yeah, sure. Be right there."

"Can we watch?" Claudia blurted.

"If you want." Marty pivoted, and she and Rex fell into place. They were ushered into a cramped room filled with mostly men. Marty stepped up to a podium, and as he fielded the reporters' questions, Claudia was overcome with awe at his poise. This was not the same man she had known in her early twenties. He had always lived inside Marty, but he had burst from his shell and taken over. He might not be the head coach he aspired to be—yet—but he clearly carried himself as though he was, and the journalists' respect was palpable. Confidence oozed from him.

As he spoke about broken plays and defensive miscues, she zoned out and imagined him at a similar podium, a backdrop behind him that sported the NHL logo. He would be at the pinnacle one day. Unexpected sadness pricked at her that another woman would be at his side as he made that final ascent. *She* would be the one to celebrate with him when he crested the peak.

Lucky Renee.

Around midnight, Claudia was curled up on her couch watching *Sleepless in Seattle*—again—when her phone buzzed. Muting the TV, she picked up the call. "Why are you up so late?"

"I could ask you the same thing," Meg said dryly.

"I'm still trying to wind down after the Hawks game tonight." Claudia had caught Megan up on their old friend the night after she had seen him at the hospital.

"Yeah? And how was it? Did Smarty Marty coach the hell out of the game?"

Claudia stood to refill her wineglass, despite the hour. *It's Saturday night, damn it, and I'm not old!* "You would have been proud, Meg, especially afterward, when he gave an interview. He was Mr. Cool-Calm-and-Collected. He was magnificent!"

"Whoa! Magnificent? Don't think I've ever heard you use that word in the same sentence as a man's name before. Only Baked Alaska, and deservedly so, in my opinion. Sounds like you might be falling for him, CC."

"Nah. Just happy for an old friend. Besides, he's got a serious girlfriend, remember?"

"Eh, knowing Marty, it's casual. Have you met her yet?"

Phone cradled between her ear and shoulder, Claudia fetched a fresh bottle from her wine rack. A flash through the window caught her eye, and she peered down at a dark SUV idling in the alleyway between her driveway and the neighbor's across the way.

"Not yet. Meg, there's someone parked down below and—oh! She just looked up here and ducked her head. How weird."

"She? How can you tell?"

Claudia tracked the SUV as it surged to the end of the alleyway, executed a three-point turn, and raced back to the same spot, but facing the road now. "What the hell? As soon as she saw me, she flipped a U-ey."

"Maybe it's Marty's girlfriend! Should you call the cops?"

"No, she just turned onto the road and sped away." Claudia paused to get her hammering heart under control. "It was probably someone who was lost and got spooked when she saw me looking out."

"You should write down the details. Did you get the license plate?"

"Only a number or two, but it was from Colorado." Claudia grabbed a pen and paper and wrote *dark blue RAV4*, the few numbers she recalled, and the time.

"What did the woman look like?"

"Long blond hair, pale face. It all happened so fast, and I only caught a glimpse of her."

By the time she climbed into bed, Claudia had convinced herself it was no big deal, but then the woman's face and hair flashed through her mind. *You're just being paranoid.* Or was she?

Chapter 28

I See You

Marty was roused by a pleasant aroma drifting through his house. A glance at the clock told him it was past noon. No surprise there, considering he hadn't climbed into bed until nearly 5:00 a.m. after a delayed flight from Ontario. He yanked a T-shirt over his head, skinned on a pair of sweats, and padded to the kitchen, surprised by what he found. Renee, bent at the waist, peered through the oven window. He had been gone a handful of days on the team's road trip, where he'd been completely immersed in hockey, and he'd been so preoccupied that he'd only exchanged a few texts with her. He'd gone dark on Claudia again—not that she had expected anything from him—because he wasn't sure what to make of the confusing emotions that mushroomed inside him every time he came into contact with her.

"What's this?" He offered Renee a tentative smile as she straightened and whirled toward him.

"I didn't hear you walk in. You scared the pants off of me."

His eyes dipped. "Apparently not because you're still wearing them."

She appeared flustered and moved with herky-jerky abruptness as she gathered up this or put away that, her back to him. "Well, maybe we can change that later."

Sirens sounded in his head. He leaned against the counter and crossed his arms. "What's happening later?" He was being purposely obtuse, but he wanted to be extra clear about her expectations.

"Well, after a nice meal where we finally have that talk, I'm hoping you'll want to get me naked."

The sirens grew louder. "What talk is that?"

"The one about me moving in?" She glanced at him over her shoulder. "You know, the one you keep putting off? I want to tell my landlord I'm not renewing."

"But your lease isn't up until the spring, so why are we dealing with this now?"

She paused, jutted out her hip, and parked a fist on it. "Because if I don't push the subject now, you'll continue putting it off."

She was right, but he didn't have to like it. "I've been—"

"Busy. Yes, I know." She turned back to whatever held her attention on the counter, leaving him feeling like a scolded child ... which he probably deserved.

Still at an impasse with himself as to what to do, he gave her a nod. Cupid's dart with her name carved on it hadn't found him, but he was having a hard time picturing breaking it off—especially with Christmas only three weeks away. And what about Claudia? *She has nothing to do with whatever is happening—or not happening—between Renee and me.*

"That smells really good. What are you cooking?" *Please tell me there's some kind of meat.* While he was grateful for any meal she prepared, they had always disagreed about including meat, or some kind of protein, in their meals. Why was he suddenly noticing these little details in their relationship? Because he was grumpy. That had to be it.

She pivoted and grinned at him. "Wild rice casserole. Your favorite."

Not my favorite, but I'm okay with it as long as it has meat. "Is it a side dish for something else?" he asked hopefully.

"No, it's the main meal." She rolled her eyes. "I promise it'll fill you up."

He stuck his head in the fridge. "Do we have any cooked chicken to throw in there?"

"You don't need it."

Lifting his head, he gawked at her and realized she was serious. "I'm an athlete. Athletes need protein." He tried to keep the annoyance from his voice as he closed the fridge door. He needed to keep himself in check.

"You're not an athlete. You're a coach. And either way, you need to eat healthy." She blinked her hazels at him.

Just don't go there right now. You're tired. She means well. Hell, she's making you a meal, dickwad. With a resigned sigh, he pulled out a bottle of milk and poured its contents into a glass. It only filled the glass halfway. "Is there any more milk?"

"Oh, sorry. I finished it when I got here this morning."

"How long have you been here?"

She shrugged. "A couple of hours now."

Why did he find that so disconcerting? "Don't you have work today?"

"I took the day off because I knew you'd have today off too. We have some important issues to work through about our future—like your cold feet. Setting time aside now seemed like a good idea."

Cold feet. He hadn't looked at it that way before, but from her perspective it made sense. At one time, he had suspected he had cold feet too, but now he knew better. The truth had been marinating over a period of time, and suddenly it crystallized. His feet weren't just cold; they were buried under a glacier. She wasn't the one for him, nor was he the one for her. Though he wasn't crazy about her tactics right now, deep down he knew it was time.

"I've been thinking about you moving in a lot lately, Ren." A hopeful look came into her eyes, and he pulled in a silent breath of courage. "I'm not ready for that step. I'm not sure I'll *ever* be ready."

The hope in her eyes transformed into hurt, and her lower lip wobbled. "Why?"

I'm not in love with you. His eyes snagged on the dark, bare branches of a catalpa just outside the kitchen window before landing back on her. *Make this as painless as possible.* He used the softest tone he had. "All my life I've wanted to be in the NHL. I got my chance once, and it lasted a minute before I was injured. Then I was done. I want to help these young guys get to where I couldn't go, and to do that, I have to give them—the team—a hundred percent of myself. That doesn't leave much energy for a relationship, and I don't want to keep you dangling on a string. It's not fair. You deserve someone who's willing and able to focus all his attention on you. That guy's not me."

She narrowed her eyes. "This is about Claudia, isn't it? We were fine until she came into the picture."

He flattened his palm against his chest. "Honestly, this has nothing to do with Claudia. Whether I bumped into her or not, you and I would have ended up at this same place." And there it was: the truth that had become crystal clear.

Renee's eyes filled with tears. "I shouldn't have pushed you."

It wouldn't have mattered. He reached out and ran his hands up and down her arms. "You pushing didn't bring us to this point. You need something more from me that I'm incapable of giving you, and you shouldn't be content to settle for my half-assed attempts at making things work. You're too good for that."

Her brows drew together in a fierce knot. "The old tried and true 'it's not you, it's me speech.' I *do* deserve better, Marty." She threw down a dish towel and gathered her purse from a counter stool. "Well, good luck to you and Claudia. You know she's seeing other guys, right?"

He gave himself an inner headshake. "Again, this isn't about Claudia. But how would you know she's seeing other guys?" *How do you even know what she looks like?*

Renee took angry swipes at her wet cheeks. "I saw her the other night with a guy with dark hair and glasses. They drove up in his car and got out and walked into her place."

"What night was this?"

"Last Saturday."

He dipped an eyebrow. "Weren't you out of town that night?"

Horror overtook her features and quickly gave way to posturing. "My plans fell apart so I ... I ..."

"So you stalked Claudia?" Steam rose, threatening to pop a gasket in Marty's head. "Who does that?"

"I just happened by."

"How did you know where she lives?"

"You probably told me."

"No, I didn't."

"It doesn't matter how I found out. The truth is, she's seeing other guys."

"Which she's perfectly entitled to do. By the way, this 'other guy' you're describing sounds exactly like Rex, which makes sense since they came to the game together. A game *you* said you couldn't attend because you were skiing with girlfriends. What the fuck, Renee?"

"What the fuck yourself, Marty!" She pulled his key from her purse and slapped it on the counter before marching out his front door.

"Well, that went well," he muttered to himself as he bolted the front door. Breaking up sucked! Even if it *was* the right thing to do.

He dropped into an armchair and scrubbed his hands over his jaw. Why did he let himself drift into relationships he had no intention of taking to the next level? *Because you're always hopeful that woman will inspire you to go to the next level,* the little voice responded.

His phone rang from across the room, and he hesitated. What if it was Renee calling to give him another earful? Or worse, a tearful apology and a plea to get back together? He stood and sauntered over to the device, relieved when it displayed Dani's number.

"Hi, sis. What's up?"

"How was your trip?"

"It was okay. We won one, and we lost one. I'll take a split on the road anytime."

"You don't sound so good."

"We got in really late. I'm just tired."

"Well, I won't keep you. I just wanted to talk about Christmas. We've decided to host it here, so I'm hoping you and Renee can join us. What does your schedule look like?"

"I'm off for three days, so I'm available. But Renee won't be coming."

"Is she visiting family?"

He glanced back out the window at the same forlorn tree. "I have no idea what she's doing. We just broke up."

She sucked in a breath. "I'm so sorry. Her idea or yours?"

"Mine, and I feel like a total asshole for doing it."

"Want to talk about it?"

"No, I don't." After a few moments of silence, he said, "You don't seem surprised."

She exhaled. "I'm not. Honestly, I thought it would happen sooner. I know you feel like crap right now, but I think you'll look back on this and say it was for the best."

"It really bites to do this during the holidays."

"Why didn't you wait and break up after?"

"I should have done it sooner. To tell the truth, I hadn't decided, and she sort of pushed the issue, but it was the right time. I couldn't keep stringing her along." He let out a mirthless laugh. "I was thinking how much it sucks for her that we broke up now, but as I think about it, it leaves me without a date for the team dinner."

"Can I offer you three little words of advice?"

"Sure."

"Get a locksmith."

He chuckled, but there was no humor in it.

"I'm serious, Marty. You don't want to end up like the rabbit in *Fatal Attraction*."

"I doubt Renee would try to boil me in a pot or take a stab at me. And if she did, I'm pretty sure I have the upper hand physically."

"Well, do it anyway. For me. In the meantime, hang in there and let me know if you need anything."

Stumbling around his house, he unpacked, took a shower, and went through the motions in a fog until an acrid smell reminded him the casserole was still baking. Smoke rolled out of the oven door when he opened it, setting off an ear-piercing smoke alarm. He threw open a window and frantically fanned a kitchen towel under the damn thing until it stopped screeching, at which point he tossed the entire casserole—dish and all—into the trash. "Well, I needed to go to the grocery store anyway."

Hours later, he found himself in a King Soopers parking lot on a different side of town. Night had fallen, and he couldn't muster enough energy to get out of the Suburban to shop in the unfamiliar store. Instead, he started up the engine and cruised to Claudia's neighborhood, which happened to be a few blocks away.

He held his breath as he approached her unit. Her car was in the driveway, with no other vehicles parked nearby. He brought the

Suburban alongside the street curb and threw it into park, unsure what to do next. But that's how it was with Claudia. His emotions were always jumbled, and he struggled to make heads or tails out of them.

His phone chimed with a text, startling him. He looked at the screen and smiled.

Claudia: *Are you parked outside my place?*

Marty: *Caught me.*

Claudia: *Are we supposed to go somewhere and I forgot?*

Marty: *Nope. Just happened to be in the neighborhood.*

Claudia: *Come on up, if you want. I'm making spaghetti, and I just opened a bottle of wine.*

God, that sounded like heaven.

Marty: *I can only stay a few mins.*

The front door opened, and there she stood, smiling as she held her phone. She beckoned him with a wave of her hand, and energy surged through him. He had no problem piling out of his Suburban and following her up her stairs.

The sound of soft jazz and the smell of spaghetti sauce hung in the air, and his stomach rumbled. When was the last time he'd eaten?

"Can you stay long enough for a glass of wine?"

He nodded, and she reached up into a cabinet and pulled down a wineglass. "For a sec, I thought you might be my peeping Jane." She poured wine from an open bottle.

"What's a peeping Jane?"

She passed him the balloon glass filled with dark ruby wine. "Last weekend, there was this dark RAV4 being driven by a blond woman that parked behind my driveway. It was kinda shady. When she saw me watching her, she flew out of here like a bat out of hell. I wrote down what little I could see of the license plate."

He had just taken a sip of wine, and he fought not to choke on it. "Uh, have you seen her since then?"

"No. If she's been down there, I've missed it. I know. Paranoid, right? She was probably looking for someone at the wrong address."

"Can I see what you wrote down?"

She rifled through a kitchen drawer and pulled out a pad. He looked at the two numbers. While it wasn't complete, what Claudia had recorded matched Renee's license plate. *Son of a bitch.*

"Renee drives a navy-blue RAV4, and her license plate has those same numbers. We just broke up," he blurted.

Claudia's eyes widened. "Do you think ..."

He nodded. "Yeah, I *do* think because she told me she saw a dark-haired guy with glasses walking into your place with you. How else would she know that? I'm still puzzling out how she knew what you look like and where you live."

"Last Saturday ... That was Rex! Wait. Wasn't she out of town skiing or something? It couldn't have been her."

"It was her." The whole thing was creeping him out.

"Is she the stalking type?"

"Not that I'm aware of. Then again, she wasn't too happy about you resurfacing in my life. I tried to tell her we were just friends."

"I'm so sorry, Marty. Is that what brought you over here tonight?"

He sipped his wine. "I could say no, but I think I needed to talk this through with my best friend because I'm worried I was too big a dickhead. I just kind of wound up outside your door."

"Well, I'm glad you did." Her forehead wrinkled with concern, and she gave him a half-smile. "I can't imagine you being a dickhead, let alone a big one."

He spent a few moments describing what had happened.

"Like I said earlier, you're no dickhead. Breakups are just ... hard. Unless it's mutual, someone loses, like in sports. Not everyone gets a trophy. Someone gets hurt regardless. Wait. Are you grinning?"

He nodded. "I can't believe you just turned a breakup into a sports analogy."

"Ha! I figured it was something you could relate to." She lifted the lid on a pot and stirred its contents with a tomato-stained wooden spoon. "I hope you're hungry because I've got a lot of spaghetti here."

"Famished." His heart stuttered a step. "Were you cooking for someone else?"

"No. I usually fix a big batch of something on the weekends and eat it throughout the week so I don't have to cook for myself. Tonight it's spaghetti Bolognese."

"That has meat in it, right?"

"Oh yeah. And lots of wine. I don't know if that's traditional, but that's how I fix it."

"Sounds fantastic."

"Good! Then you'll stay for dinner and save me from eating alone?"

"Yeah. I'll stay for dinner."

She lifted the spoon and cupped her hand under it as she presented it to him. "What do you think? Does it need anything?"

He slurped the bite she offered. Taste exploded on his tongue. "No, it's perfect. Can't wait to dig in."

With a satisfied smile, she placed the lid back on the saucepan. "I'll get the noodles going. It won't be long." She fired up a burner beneath a pot filled with water. Without looking at him, she said, "What are the chances Renee followed you over here tonight?"

"Shit, I hadn't thought about that." He craned his head out the window but saw no one. "Wait. It doesn't matter because she and I are done."

Claudia side-eyed him. "Are you sure about that? I mean, you only broke up a few hours ago, and this one was serious. Or was it?"

He huffed out a breath. "Are you asking me if it was just another casual thing?"

She nodded.

"I didn't think so. We dated for two years. We were practically living together, and I *thought* I was ready for the next step, but ... let's just say doubts were holding me back for a reason."

"Was the next step her idea or yours?"

"Hers. She pushed for more, and I backed away. But I guess that's what I do. Can I tell you something without you thinking I'm a total douche?"

"Yeah, of course." She opened a package of spaghetti and checked her water.

"For me, the relationship was over a while ago. I've been going through the motions because I didn't want to hurt her, but I was wrong to string her along. Funny, but I didn't realize any of it until I saw you." Her eyes snapped to his. So many questions streamed in those chocolate depths, but the water began boiling, and she turned her attention to the meal.

By the time dinner was over, he had pushed Renee and the way their relationship had ended to the back of his mind. After taking him on what Claudia called the "dime tour" of her two-bedroom condo, she sat with her legs curled beneath her at one end of her beige living room couch. He sat at the other end, a cat purring in his lap. Fire danced in her hearth, and candles flickered on the mantel. Other than the soft light from one standing lamp in a back corner, the room was lit entirely by mellow flames. His limbs were loose, his mind floating in a warm cloud.

The cat began kneading his crotch, and Marty looked down at it. "Uh, his claws can't go through jeans, right?"

Claudia leaned over and plucked the furball from his lap, plopping it between them, all while holding her wine. "Let's play it safe." She laughed before taking a sip, and he was mesmerized by the musical lilt and her graceful movements. He stared at her profile as she talked about some of the emergency room cases she had dealt with the past week, but he listened with half a brain because the other half was busy cataloging her upturned nose, the becoming pink blush on her cheekbones, and her full mouth. Her hair skimmed her shoulders, strands of gold he wanted to weave his fingers through.

She wore a pair of gray-and-white-striped flowing pants that tied at the waist and an off-the-shoulder light gray sweater that revealed a thin black strap. Bra? Cami? He wasn't sure, but the strap was tantalizing. The uncovered swath of skin was smooth and creamy, inviting his eyes to do what his hands couldn't: stray there and stay there.

When she paused, he leaned forward and set his empty wineglass on her coffee table. "I should get going. It's late, and I only planned to stay a few minutes."

She glanced at a clock. "That was a few hours' worth of minutes."

"I know. That seems to happen whenever I'm around you." *I enter a different zone where I lose all sense of ... everything*. "Time flies." They had covered subjects serious and light, from BC days to his breakup today to life after Zach to the latest episode of *Parks and Rec*. Conversation was easy, natural, flowing like a river to a lake.

Sparkling brown eyes the color of roasted coffee held his. "For me too. This has been nice. I'm glad you were in the neighborhood."

He stood and stretched his arms over his head while she put down her wineglass and hoisted herself to her bare feet.

"When did you get to be so short?" he teased.

"Probably about the same time you got to be so tall," she tossed back. "I'll walk you out. Your coat's hanging downstairs by the front door."

He pulled his keys from his pants pocket. "We should do this again sometime."

"Have me cook you dinner, you mean?" She gave him a smirk.

He grinned. "No, just us hanging out together. Being with you turned a shitty day into a nice evening. In fact, I'd like to do more of it and, uh, maybe even go out." *As more than good friends.*

Her hair had caught on her strap, and he reached to free it. His fingers lingered a moment too long. *I need to get out of here.* Her eyes caught his and held for a breathless instant. Instinct took hold, and he lowered his head to hers, his hand resting lightly on her shoulder. She rose on tiptoe to meet him, her hooded eyes on his mouth, her lips parted. He hesitated. Could she really want this ... with *him*? Her signals were clear, yet his mind was unable to process that Claudia Campbell could want Marty LeBrun. Should he keep going or pull back?

She did the processing for him when she fisted his Henley in both hands and pulled his mouth to hers. "I gave up dating hockey players ten years ago."

"Good thing I'm a hockey coach." With her so close, with her fragrance filling his head, he was amazed his mouth and brain connected long enough for him to get out a coherent sentence.

"So you are. Well, then," she whispered, "kiss me." Her eyes fluttered closed.

His lips landed on hers, tentatively at first. Internal debates—and most everything else—were ejected from his head. Her mouth fit his perfectly, and he marveled at how warm, soft, and inviting it was. He dropped his keys and wrapped her up in his arms, slanting his mouth over hers, his tongue nudging its way in. In a heartbeat, the kiss flipped from tame to ten on the Richter scale. This was a moment he had longed for, had dreamed of for untold years, and he claimed her mouth with a fierceness that caught him off guard. His tongue explored hers, and he relished the taste of her, all wine and sweetness he could drown himself in. She met him stroke for stroke, spurring him on. His chest heaved in time with hers. On the verge of giving himself over to caged desire, he suddenly broke the kiss to read her expression. The lone sliver of logic in his grasp struggled to reconcile that she wanted this as badly as he did.

"Why did you stop?" she panted.

"I wanted to be sure it was okay," he blurted like the stupid thirteen-year-old currently occupying his body.

Her hands glided across his lower back, and she stared at his mouth through hunger-glazed eyes. "More than okay. You make my toes curl."

He reared his head back. "Is that a good thing? It sounds like I give you toe cramps."

A small laugh escaped her, then desire glimmered in her eyes once more. Sliding one hand up his chest, she took his chin in her grasp. "It's *very* good, so stop overthinking and kiss me again."

Lips twitching with a smile, he took her head in his hands and caressed her brows with his thumbs before pushing his fingers through her hair. "You're kinda demanding, aren't you?" *And I love it.* "Why doesn't that surprise me?"

"And you talk too much."

Tightening his grip in her tresses, he angled her head just the way he wanted and crashed his mouth back to hers, deepening the kiss, taking what he wanted, giving everything she asked for with her body and her throaty moans. She molded herself to him, and he curled himself around her, bending her backward. His hands were everywhere, running over her shoulder blades to the backs of her thighs. He cupped her sweet ass and yanked her closer still. She hooked a leg on his hip, her fingers clawing at his shoulders, and she ground against his rock-hard length. Fire flooded his veins, and his cock surged, straining against his fly with a will of its own. Its sole purpose in that moment was to get to her, to bury itself deep inside her.

Frenzied moments later, she pulled back, and every part of him stopped moving. Her eyes delved into his. "If this is going where I think it's going, then we're crossing a huge line here. Are we gonna be okay?"

His breathing was ragged and choppy, his thoughts tattered. He cradled her head in his hands once more and gulped in air to get his bearings. "This is not a rebound, if that's what you're worried about. I want you, Claudia. I've wanted you for a long time. But we can stop right here; just say the word. If we do cross that line, I can't make you any promises about how it'll be on the other side, and you'll need to understand one other thing."

Her hold on him eased. "This is strictly casual?"

He shook his head. "No way. Exactly the opposite. Nothing about you is casual. That's what you need to understand." *You're my forever girl.* His eyes drilled hers with every word and every desire coursing through him so she would see what was written in his heart. "Are you okay with that?"

Confusion briefly danced in her luminous brown eyes, chased by a slow, knowing smile. She scanned his face. "Yeah, I'm okay with that." As her lips sought his, she murmured, "Because I don't want casual either. Take me to bed, Marty."

He scooped her up, hands beneath her ass, and crushed her to him, eliciting a gasp. Her fingers plowed through his hair, and her legs wrapped around his waist in a boa constrictor hold. He charged down the hallway to her bedroom.

Chapter 29

OH YES

Claudia's weight in his arms reminded Marty of a doll's as he made his way to her bedroom. Maybe he had acquired superhuman strength in the last minute. Maybe he was being propelled along a cloud in another dimension. Or maybe he was so consumed by the woman he carried that he could process little else. Her moist lips pressed to his neck unleashed a cascade of chills down his spine and along his limbs, and he repeatedly asked himself if this was actually happening. If it was only a dream, it was the best fucking dream of his life and he prayed it wouldn't end.

Her words whirled in his head: *I don't want casual either. Take me to bed, Marty.* He wasn't sure where this train would wind up, whether it would destroy their renewed friendship or turn it into something far richer, but there was no stopping until it reached its destination. In this moment, that was a chance he was willing to take.

The bedroom was dark but for the dim glow of a bathroom night-light, and it took a moment for his eyesight to adjust after he deposited her gently on the bed. He sat beside her and trailed his fingers along the side of her face, down her throat to her collarbone, marveling at the satiny feel of her skin ... and the fact that after all this time, he could actually touch it.

"So soft," he murmured. "Like velvet." *And like nothing I've ever felt before.* Eager to explore what he'd fantasized about for so many years, he bent his head, landing his lips on her jaw, following the path his fingers had blazed.

When he reached her collarbone, he flicked out his tongue and traced its delicate outline, traced the hollow, before moving to the other side. A profound yearning to know every inch of her surged inside him.

Planting her hands behind her, she leaned her weight back and dropped her head, raising her chest to him. He struggled to leash his overwhelming need but resisted what she offered.

Not yet. Twelve years is a long time, and I want to take my time and savor every second.

Threading his fingers through her hair, he brought her head up and mined her eyes, silently telegraphing the depth of his desire for her. The flames reflected in her chocolate orbs told him she wanted this as much as he did. His mouth found hers, delving into its succulent depths with the same slow, probing pace he had used on the base of her neck, and he feasted. As he made love to her mouth, their tongues danced back and forth, a sensual push-pull rhythm that mimicked the way his body craved moving in and out of hers. The soft moans rising and falling in her throat shot him through with fresh jolts of desire, raising the fine hairs on his entire body, spurring him on.

He'd never known it could feel like this, and he had barely started.

Breathless, dazed, he broke the kiss and explored the column of her neck. He pulled back once more and, holding her smoky gaze, slid her sweater up her torso and over her head. A soft plop sounded when he let it go, but he barely registered it for the tiny gasp that escaped her. It was a beautiful sound.

Only her cami covered her. As his eyes traveled over her perfect curves, a longing to feel her skin against his swelled, and he wasted no time ridding her of the cami, baring her from the waist up. His hammering heart stuttered in his chest, and he sucked in a breath at the sight of her perfect pale globes and rosy pebbled nipples. She didn't shrink from his blatant, wonderstruck perusal, seemingly pleased as she boldly watched him take her in.

A beat or three later, she tugged up the hem of his long-sleeved T-shirt. He yanked it off in one motion and was rewarded by her eyes and fingers gliding over his skin. Though her touch was featherlight, it raised a pucker everywhere it landed.

He mimicked her movements, tracing, touching, until he palmed her breasts. God, they felt amazing! As if they'd been sculpted of soft clay for him alone. Closing his eyes, he released a silent sigh, loving the weight of those breasts in his hands, the way they filled his palms. He cupped and caressed them, rolling her nipples between his thumbs and fingers until they tightened into pearly buds. Laying her on her back, he lowered his head to one nipple, his mouth drawing in her flesh. Her fingers plowed through his hair, tugging him closer as she pushed her breast into his mouth.

I'm dead, and I'm in heaven. And I'm more than okay with that.

He mapped her contours with his hands and tongue, relishing her soft sighs and her sensually bucking body beneath him. Closing his mouth over a nipple, he sucked softly at first, increasing pressure while he gave her nipple a hard flick with the point of his tongue. Her back bowed off the bed, pulling a groan from him, and her hands gripped his head tighter. Following her body's cues, he doubled down, alternating between sucking softly and forcefully, all the while flicking and twirling his tongue over her bead.

As he moved between her breasts, his hands took great care with the one not being worshipped by his mouth. She bucked, moaned, hummed, and yanked on his hair, making his cock swell to a granite hardness that ached. But he took his time, delighting in every sensation until another urge swamped him.

While he lavished her breasts, he loosened the tie on her pants and pushed them and her panties down her silky legs. She helped him out by kicking them off her ankles. Unable to help himself, he pulled back and propped himself up beside her, cocking an elbow and resting his head in his palm as his eyes roved over her. She was the most perfect woman he had ever seen. He wanted to bow to her, to worship her for the goddess she was.

She smiled at him in a way she'd never smiled before, as if acknowledging the boundless and otherworldly intimacy they shared. The intensity of the moment nearly did him in, and he forced his eyes from hers, giving in to the need to touch her instead.

Starting at her neck, he stroked the smooth skin along her shoulder, down her arm, across her abdomen, down one thigh and back up the other, loving how goose bumps erupted along the way. It was wonderful to know he could give her chills like the ones she gave him, and his confidence soared.

Massaging her breast, he gently pinched her nipple between his index and middle fingers, bending to lick and nip and tease. She gasped and squirmed. After giving the other breast the same treatment, he trailed open-mouthed kisses down her torso, pausing to let his tongue discover and lave sensitive patches of skin.

He loved how her skin tasted, and the need to taste all of her seized him. He moved down her flat stomach to her belly button, where he dipped his tongue. Then he angled his head downward and clamped her soft inner thighs in his hands and spread them.

Her body tensed, and she peered down at him, her chest rising and falling rapidly.

"I'm dying to taste you," he murmured. "Is that okay?"

She crinkled her nose, rasping, "This morning was a long time ago, and that was the last time I showered. I probably smell like a fish market."

Not even close. She smelled like sweetness and nectar and earth, but he wanted her to enjoy every bit of what they were doing, so he released her and pulled himself up until his head was once more level with her stomach. Her body seemed to melt into the mattress.

One corner of his mouth quirked. "I disagree, but if you'd be more comfortable, let's take a shower." Keeping his eyes fastened on hers, he licked a path to her belly button and lashed it with his tongue. Meanwhile, he slid his hands up her ribcage to palm her breasts.

"Shower?" he repeated. "If you don't want me to look, I won't look, but I promise you'll be squeaky clean when we're done." He gave her his most devilish smile. She seesawed her bottom lip between her teeth like she did whenever she pondered. He took the opportunity to up his sales pitch. "I really want my mouth on you, but only if you want that too. I want you to tell me everything you like and don't like, Claudia." His words surprised him when they came out. He had always been about equal opportunity pleasure in the bedroom, but he couldn't remember being entirely focused on what *she* wanted above what he wanted. In that moment, his sole desire became serving hers.

She hoisted herself onto her elbows and grinned. “Okay, but you have to move so I can get up.”

“Done.” He was seated upright in a nanosecond, feet planted on the floor, and she laughed as she scooted off the bed.

His eyes trailed her gorgeous ass, the sweep of her waist, and her round hips as she sashayed from the bed to a glass-walled shower. He checked his chin to be sure his mouth wasn’t hanging open and thanked God his pants were coming off because his throbbing cock was on the verge of splitting his zipper.

As she cranked on the water, she slid him a coy look over her shoulder. He hadn’t moved from the edge of the mattress, but that changed when she pointed a finger at his jeans. “Those need to come off.”

He shot to his feet and unfastened his belt. Hooking his thumbs in his waistband, he arched an eyebrow at her. “Am I taking them off, or are you?”

Fuck, what would it be like to have her in front of me, her breath warm on my cock as she worked my pants down?

She turned and faced him, her hands on her hips, giving him a full frontal that had him swallowing to coat his parched throat. He wasn’t sure who was winning the battle for biggest turn-on, but the game was titillating as hell.

“I think you’d better handle it, or we might not make it into the shower,” she purred. *We might not make it anyway.* “I’ll light some candles.”

He unzipped his fly and yanked off his pants and boxers. He stood frozen to the floor, watching her body’s sensual sway as she plucked a pack of matches from a drawer and lit three pillar candles on the shelf of a soaking tub abutting the shower.

When she turned around, her eyes zipped over him and widened with appreciation. The hours spent sweating in the weight room were totally worth it for the expression on her face. She bit her bottom lip, and he contemplated dragging it from her teeth to nibble on it.

Steam billowing in the shower caught his eye. “Might want to dial things down a bit. That’s a lot of steam.” He pointed toward the cloud in her shower.

Her eyes slid in that direction. "Oh, *that* steam." Fanning herself with her hand, she gave him a lusty smile.

He couldn't contain the cocky grin that spread over his face.

Stepping into the shower, she fiddled with the knobs, and he followed her in with a soft click of the door. The stall wasn't big enough for two, and his hard shaft nudged her hip—not that he was complaining. If he had his way, the two of them would shortly be one writhing mass.

Like prey backing away from a predator, she moved under the stream. *Yeah, I'm after you, sweetheart.* Eyes locked on hers, he casually picked up a bar of soap and began lathering his hands, itching to slide them over all that beautiful skin.

Shyness crept into her features, strumming every one of his heartstrings. She licked her lips. "Um, I hope it's okay if that's Dove for sensitive skin."

He kept lathering, slow and steady. "Doesn't matter to me. Do you want a shampoo with that?" His eyes traveled languidly, blatantly down her body and back up again. He stopped to waggle his eyebrows.

Her eyes darted from his face to his hands. "Think I'm good on shampoo."

He returned the soap to its holder and twirled his finger. "Turn around." She obeyed, and his knees buckled.

Fuck, when the Greek gods created woman, this girl was their model. Wait. Did Greek gods create woman? Fuck. I can't think straight. Can't think at all.

"Might be easier if you put your hands on the wall." His voice came out husky, croaky.

She burst out with a laugh. "Are you going to frisk me?"

Fuck yeah.

She wiggled her ass at him, and he wanted to drop to his knees and sink his teeth in. Resisting *that* impulse, he moved swiftly behind her, dropping his mouth to her ear, low and growly. "Not yet. Frisking comes later. For now, I'm enjoying the view."

For long moments, she probably thought he was eye-fucking her, which he was, but in truth, he was also trying to get himself under control so he didn't come right then and there. The sexual fireworks were mounting and on the verge of exploding. Christ, he'd never been to a fireworks show like this one before.

After running through a few hockey plays in his mind, his libido was caged enough that he dared press himself to her back, his angry, engorged cock snug against her ass. He could have sworn he heard it sigh. Having her naked against him was a dream come true, and he could have stayed just like this for hours. Instead, he slid his thigh between her legs, forcing them apart. She let out a squeaky little "Oooh!"

Fuck, he wasn't sure how much of this he could stand before he erupted. He couldn't recall ever being consumed like this, his sanity and control suspended from one flimsy thread.

He pulled in a steadying breath and dropped his hands to her waist, and his soapy hands went to work. Slowly, he moved them up, skimming over every silky inch of her abdomen and ribs. When his fingers finally glided over her breasts, she mewled and rocked against his quads. He was right there with her.

While he kneaded and massaged her slick skin, his touch swinging from light to firm, he dropped wet kisses on her neck, her ear, the freckles on her shoulder, and she tilted her head to give him better access, whispering, "Oh my God, that feels so good."

Warm water cascaded over their bodies, and the suds were long gone when she mumbled, "I think my girls are clean."

"Wanted to be extra sure," he chuckled. "Don't move. I need to reload." Their bodies remained nestled tight as he picked up the soap and re-lathered his hands. "You'll tell me if anything doesn't feel good, right?" Though he was pretty sure he would know because, like their jogging cadence, he felt completely synced to her right now.

She gave him a vague nod, and he soaped up her back, lingering on her shoulders, the small of her back, her ass, and parts between, loving how her body responded to his touch. She was a violin, her strings taut and supple, and he ached to coax sweet music from her. He backed out his thigh and widened her stance, holding her to him as he slid the bar lightly along her seam, up and down, back and forth. She bucked and whimpered, and soon he replaced the bar with his hand, repeating the motion.

Her hands wilted and slid from the tile wall, and she rested her weight against him. He slid a finger inside her and began a slow pump. Her hips started moving in time. Gliding his free hand to her breast, he cupped and kneaded her soft flesh, tweaking and pinching her sensitive nipple.

"I've got you," he whispered, and she wrapped her hands around his nape, pulling his head down. He watched his hands work her, hypnotized by the erotic visual of her body undulating to his strokes. She arched into his hold, and he added a second finger, increasing the tempo and friction. Her mewls bounced off the glass walls, and she bucked against his hand and rocked against his cock nestled between her ass cheeks. All of him wanted to make her come. He added his thumb, brushing, circling, softly pressing. One, two more pumps of his fingers, and she cried out as a shudder rippled through her.

Sliding his fingers from her, he held her limp body tight to his as she descended through the steam. He laid kisses along her neck, whispering, "You're amazing." She sighed in response. With a smile, he added, "I think you're clean now."

She turned in his arms and let out a weak laugh. He grasped her head and pulled it to his, unleashing a tidal wave of pent-up passion as he took her mouth with hungry strokes of his tongue. His mind was lost to the primal need behind the kiss, and he wanted to climb inside her. Mark her. Possess her.

She broke the kiss, and before he could act, she sank to her knees and took him in her mouth, letting out a strangled noise when his crown hit the back of her throat.

The sensation of her hot mouth wrapped around his cock sent a jolt of pleasure through the length of his body, and he nearly dropped to his knees beside her. He groaned out a string of words even *he* couldn't understand and threw his head back, his fingers diving into her hair. She seemed eager to explore his length with her tongue, just as he had done to her, and she sucked and licked and teased, her hand pumping him as she did.

On the verge of exploding for what seemed hours now, he couldn't take any more. He smacked at the controls until the water shut off. She looked up, and water droplets slid from her hair. His eyes drilled into hers, lust and love and God knew what else pulsing inside of him. The look she returned was brimming with raw desire, yet behind it was something akin to love—for *him*.

He hauled her up and out of the shower. She snatched a towel and began patting him dry, but he shook it from her grasp and wordlessly carried her to the bed, where he laid her down.

Claudia had stirred a beast Marty didn't know lived inside him and dragged him out. And that beast was in charge, climbing up her wet body, carrying his weight on his forearms as he caged her in. She pulled him down flush to her, and where his skin touched hers, fire burned. He worked her mouth long and deep, his tongue battling hers, their lips colliding and crashing over and over as they devoured one another.

A thought managed to break through his fog of desire, and he froze. Drawing back, he peered down at her. They were both gasping for air. "I don't have a condom."

She blinked. "I'm on the pill."

God help him, it didn't matter if she was on the pill or not. No, he had stopped for her sake, in case *she* wanted protection. He was ready to blaze ahead, and damn the consequences because they were consequences he could handle—*wanted* to handle—as long as they involved her.

"Nothing welds a woman to you like having your kid."

Get the fuck out of my head, Zach Pruitt!

Marty nuzzled Claudia's neck, kissing her jaw and her cheek as he went, slowing their torrid pace so he could think straight. "I haven't been tested, but I've only been with one person the last two years, and not with anyone since I first saw you at the hospital."

"That was a month ago. You mean you haven't slept with Renee this entire time?" Claudia's words held befuddlement.

He raised his head and shook it. "No. I couldn't. Not after seeing you." And that was the pathetic truth.

Apparently, Claudia didn't find it pathetic because she caressed his jaw with the back of her hand, and her eyes grew misty and overflowed with tenderness. "I can't believe I never saw what was in front of me, Marty LeBrun. I've wasted so much time."

He captured her hand against his face and turned, kissing each of her fingers. "That was then, Claudia Campbell. We can only control now."

She smiled. "You're *Smarty Marty* for a reason."

Marty returned the smile and dropped his mouth back to hers, pouring his soul into the kiss. Kissing her whipped up so many emotions inside him. It was intoxicating. Addictive. If he kissed her every minute of every day for the rest of his life, he would never get enough.

"I am clean, by the way," she whispered when they pulled apart.

"I know. I trust you." Weaving his fingers with hers, he pulled her arms loosely above her head, fitting them like a crown, and trailed more open-mouthed kisses down her throat, her chest, latching on to a nipple. He sucked vigorously and flicked her nipple with the hard point of his tongue, and soon she was writhing and moaning for more beneath him. He alternated between that treatment and soft, thorough suckling, punctuated with playful nips, while he flexed his hips against her leg. When he released one breast to attend the neglected one, she wrapped her legs around his waist, beckoning him to enter.

"I want you inside me, Marty," she breathed.

Fuck yeah! Marshaling restraint, he nudged his shaft against her entrance but didn't breach it until he was done lavishing her breast. Inch by torturous inch, he fed her his full length, and she was so damn wet that her body took him in, wrapping him up in its heat.

He began to move, gliding in and out of her, in and out, over and over, until starbursts pulsed on the black backdrop of his mind, and he thought he might fall over a carnal edge. But he wasn't ready to take that plunge yet. Not until he had made her fly off that edge first.

She grasped his shoulders, urging him deeper by digging her heels into his butt. He didn't relent, thrusting in and out of her at the same deliberate pace, smiling to himself when she growled in frustration. He released the arms he'd pinned above her head and pulled out completely.

"Wh-what are you doing?" she panted, her fingers clutching his biceps.

He panted in time with her. "There was a reason we took that shower."

She blinked in apparent confusion. He slid down her body, tossed her legs over his shoulders, and laved her seam with the flat of his tongue.

"Oh!" she gasped.

One taste was all it took, and he let himself go, caressing and tormenting her with his mouth. All the while, he was surrounded by her growing pants and cries. He felt her body shudder and shake because of what *he* was doing to her. She bucked and writhed, but he immobilized her hips with his hands and feasted on her like a starving man. Never had he lost himself in a woman's body like he did hers. She was a first for him in so many ways.

Though his cock begged him for release, he maintained control, drunk on the power he held over her body as he strummed it relentlessly. All she could do was clench the covers, moan and mewl, and toss her head from side to side as she rode one orgasm after another.

When she finally begged him to stop, he climbed back up her body and cradled her face in his hands. "Tasting you makes me even hungrier for you, and here's why." He took her mouth, sweeping it thoroughly with his tongue. A moan rose in her throat. He broke the kiss and pecked her bruised lips. "Still think you taste like a fish market?"

She shook her head.

"That's nectar, CC, and it makes me drunk on you."

"Oh, Marty." Her voice was all breathiness. She wrapped her arms and legs around him, and he plunged back inside her welcoming center, unable to hold himself back any longer.

Heat and madness overtook him, driven by a decade of pent-up feelings and the storm they unleashed inside him, and he lost himself inside her, giving all of himself to her without restraint. When her body juddered and clenched, liquid heat pooled at the base of his spine and exploded, racing to every nerve ending. For one insane second, he thought the sensation overload might kill him ... and he was okay with that. He let himself skyrocket to the stratosphere, where he exploded with a roar.

Bits of his consciousness floated back down like so many particles of confetti. As he drifted off, tangled in her embrace, it occurred to him that what he had just experienced was nothing like sex he had had before ... maybe because it *wasn't* sex. It was love, adoration, worship. All rolled into one. Emotions he had never felt before tonight. Anything that had come before not only paled in comparison, it couldn't even *be* compared because it was on a different plane.

And sensual showers were his new favorite thing.

Chapter 30

MY FOREVER GIRL

Claudia stirred in the dark to a dizzying blend of cedar, musk, and man, fully aware of who lay beside her. Rolling onto her side, she placed her hands under her head and smiled to herself as she watched breath move in and out of Marty's sculpted chest. He was on his back, covers around his hips, his face turned toward her. Her eyes flitted over his handsome face, his bare shoulders, his pecs, lowering to his abs. Reaching out a hand, she skimmed her fingers over him, relishing the feel of smooth, taut skin over solid muscle before snatching her hand back.

He was magnificent. Everywhere.

The attraction had always been there, but she hadn't seen it until the film of their friendship had been peeled away. He was no longer simply her good buddy and Zach's sidekick; he had shifted into a spotlight of his own. Quietly powerful, his energy all masculine, his movements measured and fluid. And so damn sexy.

She'd never been kissed the way he kissed her, as if she were his last meal. The way he had touched her, the way he had taken control of their lovemaking—the memory left her knees rubbery, even though she was lying down. His uninhibited exploration of her had been unexpected, worshipful, yet more erotic than anything she had ever experienced. A banked fire she hadn't realized lived inside her had been stoked.

Her gaze dropped to his big, strong, callused hands with their long, thick, tapered fingers, and a delicious shiver ran through her. His touch was fire and ice, heating her up while shooting arctic shards through her body.

Every time his eyes had roved over her, her heart rate had soared. No man had ever looked at her the way he did, with a mixture of aching tenderness and unbridled hunger. And, holy hell, the exquisite torment his wicked mouth had unleashed that had had her squirming with need! That mouth had done things to her she hadn't known mouths could do, like bring her to orgasm over and over as though she traversed a series of mountain peaks on an astral plane.

And when he had been inside her? She had no words for the sensation. It had felt as though they'd been made of opposite molds because the fit was so perfect. Being with him was so right, so natural. So safe. When had she felt like this? Maybe early on with Zach, but nothing since compared.

It was quite possible she was in love with Marty LeBrun.

The sound of a car engine pulled her attention toward the window, and she slid from the sheets and padded over. The moon was full, outlining the world in a silver glow as she peeked through the upper part of the window not covered by the shade. Below, on the street behind Marty's Suburban, the dark RAV4 idled, and her heart leapt to her throat. Before she could think what to do, the vehicle sped away. She kept her eyes glued to the road for long minutes, but the RAV4 didn't reappear, and she was able to slow her racing heart.

Heat washed over her back, and strong arms encircled her. "Hey. Is everything all right?" Marty rumbled, his voice rich and warm and decadent.

Leaning into him, she hummed a yes, relishing the heat of his warm skin sliding against hers. Nothing could be wrong in the world right now. Behind her, his glorious cock hardened and pushed against her.

He dropped a kiss on her head. "Any SUVs lurking down there?"

"Mmm, a dark RAV4, but it took off."

His entire body tensed.

She tugged his hands from her belly to her breasts and covered them with her own, loving the feel of his powerful, rough hands on her soft skin. "It's okay. She's gone."

"I'll talk to her."

"Don't worry about it." Her head lolled on his shoulder, and she felt him ease. "I was admiring the moon. When it's full, I have a hard time sleeping."

He rested his chin on her head. "I didn't know that."

"Now you do." *We know so much about each other, yet there's so much more to discover.*

While his hands fondled and toyed with her breasts, he kissed her neck. "I love how you feel in my hands."

A moan escaped her throat, and she pressed her ass against his raging hard-on and wiggled. *Two can play at this game.* Of course, the last time they'd played, she'd turned into a boneless heap in his arms. *Advantage, Marty.*

With a grunt and a groan, he pushed back. "You're playing with fire."

"I like fire. It keeps me warm," she murmured.

He lowered his mouth to her neck and licked a trail to her ear. "Come back to bed with me. I'll show you some fire you can play with."

She turned in his hold and tunneled her fingers in his hair, toying with the silky ends.

His eyes were dark with lust, and they locked on hers. "I want to crawl back inside you."

Chills chattered up and down her spinal column. The anticipation of fitting her soft curves to his hard, chiseled planes again, of his hot, heavy body smothering hers had her core aching with need. She'd had a taste of Marty LeBrun, and she craved more.

She squashed her breasts against his sculpted chest. His dick nestled against her mound, its head grazing her stomach, and she dropped her fingers to his crown and played them over his sensitive skin.

His cock jumped, and he sucked in a breath. "You keep doing that, and I'll have your back pressed to that window."

"Oh, we don't want the neighbors to see *that*," she giggled. With one hand still buried in his hair, she wrapped the other around his girth and tugged gently. “Come with me.” Her voice came a little breathier than she’d meant.

“Pretty sure you could lead me straight into a stump grinder right now,” he rasped, making her soar inside as he followed.

She led him to the edge of the bed and pushed him on his back. She climbed aboard, settling her ass so his cock jutted in front of her. Her fingers danced up and down his silky shaft. He laced his hands behind his head and broke out in a cocky grin. His eyes did that slow, sensual sweep up and down her body, emboldening her. She took good care of her body, and she didn’t shy away from his appraisal, especially with the appreciation that shone in his eyes. He made her feel beautiful, like a goddess he worshipped with his eyes, his hands, his mouth. *Ogle away.*

Leaning over him, she teased him by brushing her nipples along his chest—though she likely merely teased herself, as more tingles cascaded through her. Her nipples tightened to pebbled points, and she swallowed the knot of need in her throat before she could burst out with an inane comment—or openly drool and pant over his magnificent frame. *He’s not the only ogler here.*

She dropped a soft kiss on his neck, then brought herself upright and slowly ran her hands over his chest and abs while his muscles bunched and smoothed beneath her fingertips.

His grin broadened. “What’s going on in that beautiful brain of yours?”

“I like looking at your smooth skin.”

“I like looking at your smooth skin too. A lot.” His finger traced a path from her collarbone down her sternum to the fold below her belly button, leaving goose bumps in its wake.

She gave him a teasing smile. “I asked Megan once why nothing caught hold between you two, and do you know what she said?”

“I can only imagine,” he said dryly.

“She told me she thought you were in love with me.” She tilted her head. *Is it true?*

In the moonlight, the flush in his cheeks was noticeable. Had she gone too far?

“You, of all people, know what a rabble-rouser Megan is. She loves to stir things up, and if she has to invent something to get a pot going, she will.”

A tendril of disappointment snaked through her. "You're not answering my question."

"You didn't ask one."

"Okay. So that's how we're going to play this, huh?" She feigned amusement.

"Yep." He unlaced his hands and reached for her, pulling her to him so she hovered over his chest. Her breasts swayed, pulling his eyes to them. His cock, heavy and thick, seemed to surge, and the sensation blasted any disappointment she harbored from the bed and replaced it with fire and desire.

One hand still holding her arm in place, he sifted her hair through his fingers. "Can we kick out the people from our past and get back to just you and me?"

"I think we can do that." Lifting her bottom, she grasped his cock. As she lowered herself, every nerve ending fired off, and she sank down with a sighing moan. "Just you and me," she repeated with a sharp intake of air.

Shock—or was that pain? Transformed his features, and panic welled inside her. "Oh no! I hurt you. Are you okay?"

As she lifted her hips, he gripped them and drove into her with one powerful move, stealing her breath as he grunted, "That's pure pleasure you see, not pain."

Rational thought fled, and she let the sensations take her. She threw her head back and felt her body undulate to his rhythmic thrusts. She mewled his name, and something wild seemed to possess him. He surged upward, tossed her on her back, and buried himself deep inside her. Waves of pleasure rolled through her as he picked up the pace and gave it to her deeper, faster, harder, just the way she wanted it. The power behind his movements was electrifying, and she quivered with anticipation of the orgasm that was building deep inside her core.

He slammed into her over and over and over, and she rode on a wave of insanity until it shot her over the edge like a cannon out of a barrel. Soon after, he followed her, his body seizing and juddering as he emptied himself inside her. He collapsed on top of her, whispering, "My forever girl."

Her heart could have burst in that bed from all the joy filling it up.

Several short hours later, the sky was lightening and Marty was roused by Claudia's soft, warm body snuggled against his. The sighs she emitted in her sleep had his cock straining, reaching for her. Hell, she could have been dead silent, and his dick would have driven him to sheath itself inside her. Being joined with her was pure heaven, and the only place he wanted to be. So he stroked her hair and caressed her arm, sneaking peeks at her beautiful bare body like a prepubescent boy until she shifted and mewled. Fuck, he loved that sound—especially when it included his name.

One brown eye peeped at him, and she gave him a sleepy smile. "You look like a man with a mission on his mind."

"Definitely have something in mind." He rolled her on her back, covering her with his body, and began a slow assault with his mouth on her lips, her throat, her ears. He was powerless to check the desire that captivated him. She could have maneuvered him on strings she made twitch and dance, and he wouldn't be able to stop her. The feeling of helplessness was new for him, but he was prepared to turn himself over to her and let her drive his emotional bus wherever she wanted to take them.

With that thought hovering in his consciousness, he was soon making love to her again, once more blasting into space, emptying himself inside her slick, hot core.

As he panted against the crook of her neck, she let out a soft giggle that had him asking, "What?"

She craned her head and peered at him, her eyes twinkling with mischief. "I didn't know you had that in you, Marty LeBrun."

"What? A third time? I seem to have plenty of juice around you, CC."

She grinned, then her eyes fastened on something above his head and widened. "Oh shit! I'm gonna be late!"

He rolled his head toward a digital clock. "Crap! So am I!" He hauled her to him and pecked her lips. "Totally worth it, though."

They both scrambled out of bed. "Want my help in the shower again?" He flashed her a wicked smile.

"Not unless we both plan on skipping work today," she shot back.

Moments later, he was poised to exit her front door for his walk of shame—*nothing shameful about it*—when she asked, "Where do we go from here?" The question stunned him. In all fairness, he was floating on a sated cloud. He was also already locked and loaded on their future together, taking it as a given without considering she might have a different opinion.

"Where do you *want* to go from here?" He held his breath.

She chewed on her bottom lip, and he plowed ahead, afraid of an answer he didn't want to hear. "I hope you want what we started to go the same place I do, which is as far into the future as it'll take us."

His gut uncoiled the moment she beamed him a smile ... only to rewind itself with her next remark. "Is that what you say to all your hookups?"

He dropped his jacket and keys right by the front door to cradle her face and delve into her eyes. "You are *not* a hookup, and I've never said anything like that before in my life. Are you looking at *me* as a hookup?"

Her eyes went saucer-wide—whether from his question or his dramatic shedding of stuff, he wasn't sure and he didn't care. "No, of course not. I guess I'm not handling the awkward morning-after thing well."

He stroked the corner of her mouth with his thumb. "It's only awkward if you want it to be." Then he kissed her, his heart soaring when she returned the kiss with equal fervor. When he pulled away, he fought for air. "I want to see you tonight. Can I take you to dinner?"

She nodded and dazzled him with another smile, and that was all the encouragement he needed as he scooped up his items and flew out her door.

"LeBrun!" Coach Graham barked. Marty lurched forward so hard he nearly piledrove his abdomen into the edge of Graham's round conference table. Dazed, he swept his gaze over five pairs of eyes trained on him. Expressions on the other coaches' faces varied from bland to baffled to amused.

Graham leaned forward on his elbows. "Did you hear what I just said about Seth Hughes not being cleared to play? He's on the IR at least two more weeks."

Marty coughed. "Sorry. I didn't get a lot of sleep last night—" He ignored the goalie coach's snort and went on. "Sometimes I can't sleep when it's a full moon." *And I'm being straddled by the world's most beautiful woman.* "I, uh, I focused on issues around our play instead. Last night my mind was stuck on ways to improve our transition game."

Graham's steely gray gaze drilled into him. "Care to elaborate on these insights?"

Fortunately, Marty *had* been churning through these thoughts several nights prior, and he was able to list them without making himself sound like a total idiot. "I think we need to work harder with the D to look for the smart outlet passes, not just throw the puck up the boards. We need to work on their on-ice vision so they *know* where the forwards are without having to look up and think, 'Where's my guy?' That's what's happening now, and they're too slow."

A discussion followed, and Marty struggled to stay engaged. Normally, this wasn't a challenge for him, but today his mind was constantly tugged into a warm, cozy bed that smelled like Claudia and sex. Both body and mind wanted back in that bed.

He had texted her as soon as he'd gotten to work. In fact, he hadn't really stopped. Most of the messages were silly, but he indulged himself because it felt so damn good and she hadn't told him to knock it off ... which gave him hope she enjoyed it as much as he did.

When the meeting ended, he ambled from Graham's office, checking said phone as he went. His counterpart on the coaching staff, Greg, fell in beside him. "Think Graham's going to institute any of your suggestions?"

Marty slid his phone back into his pocket, itchy to read a text Claudia had sent him. "I don't know. Time will tell."

"So Kelly wanted me to ask if you and Renee want to drop by for cocktails before the Christmas dinner. Then we can all ride together."

Marty stopped in his tracks. The team holiday dinner was only nine days away. "Uh, Renee and I broke up, so tell Kelly thanks, but I'll skip cocktails this time."

Greg's mouth swung open. "Oh shit, dude! I'm so sorry. I can't believe Kelly didn't tell me."

Renee and Kelly had become good friends after attending the myriad team social functions. Marty's mind darted to how Kelly would react to Claudia. "She might not know yet. It just happened yesterday." *Seems like a lifetime ago.* "It'd been coming for a while."

"God, that blows. I thought you two were solid." Greg puffed out a breath. "Kelly's going to ask *me*, so I have to ask *you*. What happened? And you don't have to answer."

Marty began walking again to move the conversation from the hallway. "Difference of opinion." *She wanted a ring, and I want to put it on someone else's finger.*

"Huh. Well, do you want me to see if Kelly's sister is interested in going so you're not alone?"

Marty shook his head, stifling the goofy grin that wanted to erupt from thinking of bringing Claudia. "No, I'm good, but thanks."

In his office, Marty read Claudia's text about Ms. Nosy Norris patrolling the nurses' station, and he nearly laughed out loud. Then he fired off a text of his own: *Want to come to the team dinner with me on the 10th?*

Claudia: *Isn't it too soon?*

Marty: *For what?*

Claudia: *You and Renee just broke up.*

Marty: *There's no social mourning period, CC.*

Claudia: *There are probably a few Renee fans who will be Claudia haters.*

Marty: *Don't care. They'll become Claudia fans the second they meet you. What time am I picking you up tonight?*

Claudia: *How about you just bring your sexy ass over here and I order pizza? We can snuggle and watch a movie. Popcorn wants to sit in your lap.*

Popcorn had apparently developed a thing for Marty as his personal kneading pillow, and Claudia had had to lock both cats out of her bedroom.

Marty: *No offense to Mr. P, but I'd rather YOUR sexy ass sat in my lap. FYI, no clothing required.*

Claudia: *I'm sure that can be arranged.*

God, his dick was at half-mast and headed to full wood just thinking about her bite-worthy ass wiggling in his lap. He had it bad.

Coach Graham burst into his office and pulled up short. "LeBrun, what is with you and the stupid look on your face? It's been pasted there all morning."

"Sorry, chief. Just got some good news." Marty slid his phone into a drawer and pulled in a breath. Sexy time was over. *Back to work.*

"Well, you're about to get some more. I just found out I need hernia surgery. It's scheduled after the first of the year, and I'm going to miss a few days. I'm putting you in charge with Greg as your assistant, if you think you can stay focused and handle the job."

Hell yes! "You can count on me."

The day of the dinner had arrived, and Marty wasn't so sure about his bold declaration to Coach Graham. Thoughts of Claudia continually crowded out everything else. When he wasn't doing inner backflips over the somewhat incredulous notion she wanted to be with him, he was fevered, fixated, and no amount of being with her seemed to cure him of his obsession.

When he wasn't with her during the day, his frenzied mind continually traveled to being with her again. Sometimes it was late, after a game, at his house or hers. His favorite times were when he didn't have a game and his evening was free to be with her to go out or hang at home. The worst was the one Texas road trip where he'd been away for three days, and his craving for her had messed with his synapses. His only consolation had come from their frequent conversations and being able to let himself into her place at 2:00 a.m. after a long flight home. She had left her front door unlocked, and he hadn't hesitated to take advantage and let himself in. Within five minutes, he had been naked and under the covers, wrapping himself around her and burying his nose in her hair.

Exhausted as he had been on the drive from the airport, it had only taken one brush of her silky skin, one sleepy sigh as she'd shifted in the bed, and he'd been fully aroused and ready to go. And she had welcomed him into her warm body, rocking him into oblivion.

Tonight was one of those rare times he was alone at his place; they had decided he should dress here to keep Popcorn hair off the dark suit he would wear to the dinner. He checked his watch. Soon he would introduce Claudia and show her off to his team—their official coming-out as a couple. He couldn't wait; she was tentative.

As he went through the motions of knotting his tie in the mirror, his thoughts strayed to the change in his psyche over the past few weeks. It had been nothing short of remarkable. He was like a man whose senses had been dead and were now suddenly alive. The world around him buzzed with surround-sound and sparkled with vivid color. When he was with Claudia, sparks flowed in his veins and he had a sense of being right where the universe meant for him to be. How long could this dream last?

He wanted to shower her with flowers and gifts, but he was mindful she had had all that once—the jewelry, the clothes, the cars. No way could he compete with that level of luxury, no matter how much he wanted to. But he could lavish her with love. He could be the guy who laid his coat across a puddle so she wouldn't have to dip her foot in the water. Hell, he would *be* the coat across the puddle.

Yeah, he was a mad man, and he had no idea how to corral the madness.

He patted his tie, and the excitement that constantly thrummed in his veins vibrated, growing raucous, as he thought of being with her tonight.

Corral the madness he eventually would—he would *have* to—but not tonight.

Chapter 31

Returns of the Season

Claudia's stomach currently housed a colony of excitable frogs, and she checked herself in the mirror one last time. The reflection looking back at her wasn't the problem. No, she looked pretty damn good, if she did say so herself. She had kept little from her marriage, but in this moment, she was pleased she had held back the sleeveless red sheath dress with the lace decolletage. Striking but chic. Sexy but classy, like the black hose she had donned. And it paired beautifully with another holdout, ankle-strap red pointy-toed stilettos.

She had swept her hair up in a classic French twist, with a few tendrils framing her face. Makeup smoky-eyed but soft. Simple crystal-drop earrings and a red clutch.

The entire look was her armor against whatever might come her way tonight. Hopefully, it wouldn't be necessary, but she had attended enough team to-dos to observe how significant others treated the new girl on the block. The gamut ran from curiosity to suspicion to out-and-out cat spats. The fact that this was an AHL team party, not one populated with NHL-sized egos, might be the difference between curiosity and cat fight. She would soon find out.

Added to the leaping amphibians was the email she had received from Zach today. She hadn't talked to Zach—had barely heard from or about him—during the past five years, but somehow he had found her and wanted to see her. He had to talk to her. He was coming to Denver in January. How could she deny him, given their history? His words, not hers. *Given our history, I don't want to see you again, Zach Pruitt.*

She didn't plan to tell Marty about the email tonight. This was *his* celebration with his tribe, and she didn't want to spoil it. Her nerves alone had the potential to do that.

She flipped off the bathroom light and was headed into the hallway when she heard a knock, followed by Marty calling her name. Anticipating his arrival, she had left the front door unlocked. She loved that he felt comfortable enough to walk in. Her Christmas budget was small, but she'd been toying with gift-wrapping a key for him. The thought brought a smile to her face.

"Coming," she called back.

As she emerged into the open living space, he reached the top of her stairs and froze. "Jesus Christ!"

Her heart sank, and her hand flew to smooth her hair. "I can change if this is too much."

His voice cracked. "Holy hell, don't you dare." He took a few hesitant steps toward her, as if he was afraid to get too close. His brown eyes were filled with awe. "You've really upped your game, CC. I mean, you're always stunning, but this ... Can you see drool dribbling on my chin?" He patted his chin dramatically, and she burst out with a relieved laugh.

He held up a finger. "Don't move. Not yet. I'd like to look for a while." She stood still while his eyes swept her slowly from her shoes to her French twist. She could feel rising redness blazing her cheekbones. He tugged on the collar of his dress shirt with his forefinger. "My biggest challenge tonight—besides fighting off other dudes—will be hiding the bulge in my pants and not dragging you off somewhere private so I can ... muss your hair."

She shot him a sly smile. "You can muss my hair when we get home."

"Promise?" He gave her a lopsided grin. God, he was adorable! How had she missed it before?

"I promise." She strutted toward him. When she reached him, she straightened his tie, which needed no straightening, and lifted her eyes to his. "You say the nicest things to a girl."

He cupped her shoulders lightly. "I've always thought *things* like that about this particular girl, but I couldn't say them before. I'm glad I can now." He leaned down, and she held her breath in anticipation of the warm touch of his soft lips, but instead of kissing her, he rubbed her nose with his. "Can't wait to muss you," he whispered, then pulled back with his grin back in place.

She rested her hands against his broad chest. "I'll give you one better. Not only can you muss me, but you can undress me too. And FYI, I'm not wearing a whole lot under this dress."

He dropped his head back. "Christ, woman! You're killing me."

She lowered her hand to his crotch and rubbed his erection through his pants, delighted when he sucked in a breath and snapped his eyes to hers. She relished the power she had over him and the way the man in him drew out the woman in her. Never had she felt as desired as she did with him. "Ooh, I am making life *hard* for you, aren't I?" she cooed.

"You're going to end up on Santa's naughty list, you little tease. And if you keep it up, we're skipping the party."

She applied a little more friction. "I *am* keeping it up."

"Two can play this game, sweetheart." He yanked her to him and snaked his hands under her dress, making her gasp when he squeezed her bare ass cheeks. His eyes went round. "What are you wearing? Or not wearing?" His strong fingers dug in and began kneading her flesh, and she rocked against him, stifling the urge to close her eyes and moan. The feel of his warm, rough hands made those frogs hop as though they'd been dropped into a hot pot.

"Shit. I don't want to know," he hissed. "Don't tell me."

She told him anyway, purring, "I'm wearing lace-top thigh highs and a new crotchless lace thong I bought just for you. You'll have to guess the color of the thong ... or wait and discover for yourself later. Although I might just take it off. It's soaking wet."

He groaned. "Fuck. Me."

"After the party, handsome. As much as you can take."

He gave her a hard pinch, slid his hands out, and straightened her dress. *Damn!*

"I'm losing this battle," he rasped and moved her hand away from his fly. "We better go."

She was grateful for the ego boost their foreplay had given her when, an hour later, she stood at the party trying to act like she belonged. The scene reminded her of walking into a classroom for the first time halfway through the semester, where you knew no one and the students had obviously bonded. Oh. And being naked when you did it. Marty had been wonderful about sticking close, but the head coach had just pulled him away, and Claudia took up space beside a potted plant, holding her wine and plate of food in front her like a shield. Maybe she could disappear behind the leaves.

"Hi, I'm Kelly." A pretty brunette with olive skin approached, her hand extended for a shake.

Oh thank God! Except Kelly wasn't smiling.

Claudia set the mostly full plate on a nearby table. "Nice to meet you. I'm Claudia."

"So I heard. You're the new Renee." Kelly's features remained placid.

Claudia's back prickled, and she drew herself up a little taller. The heels helped. "Hmm. I don't know Renee, but I'm the *old* Claudia."

Kelly's face scrunched up, looking as though she had sucked on a lemon, but she quickly recovered her bland expression. "I should warn you, Renee and I are best friends."

"I should warn you, Marty and I are best friends. We have been since college." Claudia gave Kelly her shiniest smile. *Take* that *to your best friend.*

Marty's deep voice rumbled beside Claudia. "Hey, sorry I had to leave." He draped an arm around her shoulders and dropped a kiss against her temple, the move a statement that they were together rather than a caveman claim. He flicked a glance in Kelly's direction. "Oh hey, Kelly. Have you met Claudia?"

Kelly's smile was as saccharine as Claudia's had been. "We were just getting acquainted. How did you two hook—I mean, meet up after all these years?"

"She's a nurse at UCHealth and was on duty when Seth was cut."

"Color me surprised that you moved on so quickly, Marty, especially after *two* years." She held up two fingers as if to emphasize the number.

"Life is full of surprises, isn't it?" he rejoined. "Oh, by the way, Greg was looking for you." When she excused herself, he looked down at Claudia, his brows furrowed. "That was ... interesting. What else did she say to you?"

"Nothing much. She just introduced herself as Renee's best friend."

He rolled his eyes and blew out a breath.

She closed her hand over his resting on her shoulder. "It's okay. She's just sticking up for her friend."

Marty's eyes drifted in the direction Kelly had gone. "Well, she's going to have to get used to the idea of us being together." Claudia felt as though her heart had taken an elevator ride up a half dozen floors. He turned his head back to her, and something unreadable passed behind his mocha eyes. "We are together, right?" His jaw muscle jumped. Her heart climbed a few more floors.

She bumped her hip against him. "Well, seeing as how we've spent the last ten days together, we're standing here clutching each other, *and* you're taking me home tonight, then yeah. I'd say we're together."

The tension in his jaw visibly eased, and he picked up her hand and kissed it. "What do you say we make the obligatory rounds and sneak out of here to have our own celebration?"

"Thought you'd never ask."

When they returned to her place, she shed her coat and led him through her darkened condo to the bedroom, where she closed the door. One bedside lamp brushstroked the shadows with its golden glow. Enough to see but not enough to sharpen. Holding his gaze, she pushed his jacket from his shoulders and carefully laid it on an armchair. Then she bent before him and slipped off his socks and shoes, hovering her head torturously close to his crotch.

Rising to her feet, she presented him her back. "Unzip me?"

His breath seemed to stutter in his chest as he drew the zipper down oh-so-slowly to where it stopped at the small of her back. He peeled the dress from her shoulders, and it caught on her hips. Walking her backward, he dropped on the edge of the mattress and pressed wet kisses to her bare back. "I love these," he whispered as he flicked out his tongue and tasted her twin dimples, leaving goose bumps in his wake.

Soon he slid the dress off her body, and she stepped out of it while his fingers played across the top of her ass, tracing the lace scallops of her thong. His touch sent chills racing up her spine.

"Red," he murmured. "I love red." She held her breath while he fondled a few moments longer, relishing his touch against her sensitive skin before she took a high-heeled step and pivoted, facing him. Her hands went to her French twist, and she wordlessly removed the pins and shook out her hair, eating up the way his eyes prowled her body.

"You are the most beautiful fucking thing I've ever seen." His voice was thick with awe.

Emboldened, she unclasped her red lace demi-cup bra and tossed it on top of his jacket.

He drew in a sharp breath, and his eyes darkened and gleamed. "I know it's not polite to stare, but can I have a moment here?"

Shyness suddenly overtook her, but she managed a sultry, "Take all the moments you need," as she dangled her hands at her sides, unsure where else to put them. *Where are Marilyn Monroe's tips on sex-kitten poses when you need them?*

He shifted on the mattress and began a languid perusal that ended with a strangled, "Come here."

She took slow steps. When she reached him, she threw a lazy leg over his solid thighs, straddling his lap, and loosened his tie. Unbuttoned his cuffs and switched to his shirt buttons, one at a time. Fire flared in his eyes as she continued her methodical ministrations, and she pressed herself against the rock-hard rod behind his fly. *She* had done that to him.

"You're so damn sexy," he croaked. "You're also a tease."

She pushed his shirt off his sculpted shoulders, down his muscular arms, running her hands over his hot, smooth skin as she went. "Mm-hmm. Do you want me to stop?"

"Oh hell no." He let her pull off his shirt the rest of the way and cocked an eyebrow. "You taking off the tie or leaving that up to me?"

She fisted the tie and pulled his head close. "Neither."

One corner of his mouth quirked. He raised his hands and cupped her breasts, his thumbs rough as they brushed her nipples, pulling a gasp of pleasure from her. "If the tie stays, then so do the stockings and heels." Then his mouth was on hers, hot, demanding, matching his hands moving down her body to her ass. He yanked her tight against him. "Two can play this game."

"So I've heard," she breathed and unbuckled his belt.

In one swift move, he discarded his pants and underwear and had her pinned beneath him, flat on her back. Her pulse rate kicked up, and her eyes widened.

He caged her body with his forearms and didn't take his eyes off hers. "Did you say 'crotchless thong' earlier?"

She nodded, mesmerized by the raw power vibrating through him.

"I need a closer look." He moved down her body, parted her legs, and tilted his head as he stared. "I see how this works." With a growl, his tongue was on her, in her, and it strummed her like a finely tuned instrument, making her body sing.

She was fighting for air two orgasms later when his mouth finally released her. He slid the thong down her legs and off her ankles and slithered back up until his head was level with hers. "Interesting little piece of clothing, but I don't want *anything* getting between us when I come inside you."

And his mouth was back on hers, possessing it, staking its claim.

Oh. My. God!

Interlacing their fingers, he raised her hands above her head and lowered his body flush against hers, heat and electricity pulsing between them everywhere their skin came into contact. On the brink from his mere touch, she flung her legs wide and grasped him in her hand, guiding him inside her body.

She cried out, and he grunted an incoherent curse when he entered her. He began moving, picking up speed, pounding into her harder and harder until he'd driven their interwoven hands against the headboard.

Yes!

Two more powerful thrusts, and she went sailing over the precipice into blissful oblivion. In the hazy distance, she heard him shout out his climax and follow her over.

He flopped on top of her, their chests moving together in time, their ragged breaths mingling. She slid her hands from his, pressing them into his back to pull him closer. She loved his weight on top of her. Loved being in his arms. He took her to a place of joy and warmth and love she hadn't experienced before.

As she lay looking at the ceiling, she allowed her mind to wander through its memories. She had been with other men since the chaos that had been her marriage to Zach, but no one had touched her emotionally. Maybe those failed relationships had been attempts to reaffirm her own attractiveness. While they had left her with no doubt she was physically desirable, her appeal as a long-term partner lived in a shadow of doubt. Then again, none of the affairs had tempted her to jump back into serious-relationship waters, so the fault quite possibly lay with her. Zach had been her first on so many levels, and she had been young and naïve. Trusting. With neither time nor experience to build up calluses over her heart, the full impact of his betrayal had slammed into her head-on. Besides how she had continually second-guessed her culpability in the breakup, she had questioned whether her relationship with Zach had damaged her ability to reconnect with anyone on a deep level.

Until now. Was it possible she had been trying to connect with the wrong men when the right one had been there the whole time, like he had always been? She had a connection of the *heart* with Marty. The thought both warmed and terrified her. She could picture herself letting him in all the way—deeper than Zach had ever gone—but he could also slay her more thoroughly than Zach ever had.

But this was Marty, and she had always trusted him ... until she hadn't. *With time, you finally recognized the truth, and you loved him even more for it. The wounds are healed. You forgave him, and he forgave you.*

Maybe it was time to let go of the past and move on to something quite ... wonderful.

Chapter 32

THE HEART CONNECTION

At work five days later, Claudia's phone chimed with a text as she sat at the nurses' station.

BFF: *Sending out an SOS to Loveland, CO! Anyone seen Claudia C lately?*

Shit! Claudia hadn't talked to Meg since she and Marty had taken things to the "next level." Then again, Meg hadn't contacted her either. The holidays were hectic for everyone.

Claudia: *There was a sighting. Same question for Meg in Chicago.*

BFF: *I've been busy.*

Claudia: *So have I. What's keeping you busy?*

BFF: *Christmas and my crazy mother-in-law. You?*

Claudia pulled in a breath and tapped her answer. *Marty LB.*

BFF: *WTF? Busy as in me and my BF are doing stuff, or me and BF are doing STUFF?*

Claudia: *I'll call you after work and fill you in.*

Marty was back on the road, and Claudia had returned to her predictable schedule filled with work and her cats, with an extra serving of Christmas season frenzy. Still, she should have called her BFF and told her about the ... developments.

The swish of Ms. Norris's scrubs warned Claudia to stow her phone, but she couldn't resist one last peek to see if Marty had texted her. She was reeling from how much she missed him. In fact, she had caught herself daydreaming about him multiple times while staring at her computer screen. Like right now.

Ms. Norris gave her an approving nod, and Claudia released a relieved breath. She liked working the day shift, and she *needed* this job, so she had to start concentrating on work and not let herself trip off to her fantasy world featuring one hot hockey coach in the starring role.

Back at home, she poured herself a glass of wine and settled into her couch. She had exchanged a series of flirty texts with Marty, and now he was in the midst of a game. They had to be starting their second period, which gave her a block of spare time before she heard from him again.

She dialed Megan's number. "Is this a good time?" she asked when Megan picked up.

"Oh yeah. I cleared the decks so I can hear all about hottie Marty. But first, what's up with the girlfriend? Is she your stalker?"

"Yes, she is. Or was. They broke up a few weeks ago, but I've only seen her car once since that first time, and it's been a while." Claudia harbored guilt over the breakup, as though she had caused it. But she hadn't. Then again, she hadn't hesitated to jump him as soon as she'd learned he was free.

"Hmm. Did you have something to do with it?"

"I-I don't know. I didn't think so, but ..."

"He's always been in love with you, CC. Even I saw that while I was crushing on him and you were with Zach. I think that's why he wouldn't get romantically involved with me. He, uh, spent your wedding night with me in my hotel room. Before you jump to the conclusions any normal human would, you need to know nothing happened. I have no biblical knowledge of Marty LeBrun. But one thing I do know is his heart was broken that day."

Claudia had just taken a big sip of wine and nearly choked on it. "You never told me that!"

"Didn't see any reason to. You were happy with Zach, and I thought it would be weird if you knew, seeing as how you and Marty were so close. Looks like you have a shot at him now, though, assuming you want to take it."

"Meg, I do. I did."

Meg let out a raucous laugh. "Are you shitting me? That is *awesome!* Does this mean you guys are more than friends now?"

"We are." *Much more.* "Is that weird after our history? I mean, he was Zach's best friend."

"It's not weird at all." A note of awe carried through in Megan's voice. "In fact, it's perfect. It's as though the universe finally succeeded in getting you two together. What are the chances you'd end up in the same town, at the *same* hospital, on the same day? You guys were always meant to be, and if things had gone a little differently that first night at the Pint Pot ... Well, let's just say it took you a while to get together, but now you're right where you're supposed to be."

Joy burst and spread through Claudia's chest. "God, Meg, I'm so happy to hear you say that! I think I'm in love with him."

"Maybe you always have been."

When Marty called hours later, Claudia still floated on cloud nine. "How did your game go?"

"Like shit," he groused. "We lost, and it's my fault. I don't know what's wrong with me. I'm not seeing the plays, not able to make adjustments to our game, and the players are tuning me out. And who can blame them? Thank fuck they're listening to Coach Graham and Greg because my coaching sucks. Maybe the AHL is too big for me and I don't have a future in this league after all."

"Whoa there, Coach. Being a little hard on yourself, aren't you?"

"Just calling it like I see it. A fuck-up's a fuck-up." His frustration was clear in his voice.

"So what's different now than say, last week?"

"I was fucking up then too, but it wasn't showing up in the standings."

Eggroll was curled up in her lap. She gave the cat a scratch on her head and was rewarded with a loud purr. "I doubt Coach Graham would keep you around if you were that bad. Can you pinpoint when you started fucking up?"

Pretty sure he'd have to puzzle it out, she was surprised by his quick answer. "Yes. Two weeks ago."

"What changed two—you mean, when *we* got together?" Though he couldn't see her, her mouth swung open. "Is this because of me?"

"Don't take this the wrong way, but I think it might be." A warm chuckle rumbled through the phone, and he followed it up with a sigh. "You're all I think about, day and night. When I'm awake, I wonder what you're doing, where you are, what you're thinking, when I'll see you again. And I don't get away from these thoughts while I'm sleeping because you fill my dreams. I can't eat. I can't focus. You're like a drug, and I can't get enough."

Oh. Happy bubbles popped in her belly, and warmth filled her bloodstream. "You never do things halfway, do you?"

"Don't know how. Not where you're concerned."

She barked a laugh. "Well, if it makes you feel any better, I'm having the same problem. And I need to focus because I've got patients depending on me and a job I want to keep."

"Huh. So we're both kinda screwed. What's the cure, do you think?"

"To being screwed? I can think of a few things," she teased.

He let out a playful growl of frustration. "I need my fix. I'm home in two days, in the wee hours on Thursday. Can I wake you up and show you what I've been thinking about while I've been missing you?"

"I agreed to help out a co-worker, so I'm taking his night shift. I won't be home." *Damn!*

"So what are you doing Thursday night?"

Playing horizontal hopscotch with the coach. "Cooking you dinner? I've been practicing pie-making lately. How does apple sound?"

"Wonderful. And after that? Do I get to play doctor and nurse with you the rest of the night?"

God, yes! She marshaled restraint. "Once the dinner dishes are cleaned up, I'm all yours."

"*All* mine? I can't fucking wait." His tone turned solemn. "Claudia, I ..."

A frisson of worry snaked through her. "Yeah?"

"Never mind. It'll keep. I'll see you in two days."

And seven hours, thirteen minutes, and forty-five seconds.

They exchanged good nights and hung up. What had he been about to say that would keep? She put the question aside and let her heart execute a few flips. When had she been this giddy about seeing someone before? The stunning answer struck her: never, not even when she'd been with Zach.

Another question presented itself: How on earth would she get anything done over the next two days?

Butterflies danced and fluttered in her tummy when she spied Marty through her peephole parking his Suburban in her driveway. Tall, Dark, and Handsome emerged from his vehicle and started toward her front door, a mouthwatering man vision in gray button-down, dark slacks, and matching jacket. Shivers cascaded down her spine at the sight of him, and she stared a beat or two longer. He looked every bit the stylish *GQ* gentleman. Come to think of it, he always behaved like a gentleman—except in the bedroom, where he transformed into a beast who loved giving pleasure as much as he enjoyed taking it. In other words, he was the *perfect* man. She was looking at her old friend through a new lens, and it sparked a familiar question: How had she not seen this Marty before?

When he reached her door, she threw it open and crashed into his arms.

He laughed and cinched her tight. "Were you standing at the door this entire time?"

Pulling in his dizzying man scent, she wrapped her arms around his trim waist and squeezed with all she had. "Yep, I was watching your hips swing as you walked up my steps."

"You're stealing *my* line."

Closing the door, she led him up her stairs. "I took a long nap today. Did you get any sleep after you got in early this morning?"

He shrugged out of his jacket and draped it over a dining chair. "I managed a few hours between catching up on mail, laundry, groceries. The usual stuff." His gorgeous mouth curved into a devilish smile, and he cocked an eyebrow at her. "Why? Worried I'll face-plant the minute we walk into your bedroom?"

She returned a sly smile of her own. "Who says you're getting into my bedroom?"

He threw his head back and groaned. "What am I doing wrong?"

A giggle escaped her. "Actually, I have something for you that will give you access everywhere." She reached into her purse, pulled out a tiny paper envelope, and handed it to him.

His brows knotted together. "What's this?"

"An early Christmas present. Open it."

He lifted the flap, and a shiny silver key slid into his palm.

She pointed at it. "That's a key for here."

He sucked in air and looked at her with wide eyes. "I get my own key?"

No lovers had ever possessed a way into her home before. Then again, even if Marty *wasn't* her lover, she wouldn't hesitate to give him a key. "This way, when it's 3:00 a.m. and you're just getting home from the road, you can come straight here—if you want to—and I don't have to remember to leave the door unlocked or figure out where to hide a key if I'm at work."

He turned the object over in his hand, seemingly stunned. "Are you sure you want to do this?"

Had she jumped the gun? What if she'd misunderstood the nature of their relationship? *Casual Marty.* "I know fourteen days does not a relationship make," she stammered, "but I feel closer to you than I've ever felt to anyone. So yeah, I'm sure."

He raised his eyes to hers. "It's been more like twelve years, but thank you. I'm ... speechless. And honored." He gave her a broad grin. "And now I don't have to wake you up."

Relief eased her shoulders. "Oh yes you do because that key carries one condition: you *have* to wake me up if I'm asleep."

The grin faded, and a lusty gleam made an appearance in his eyes. "Any particular way you'd like to be awakened?" His voice was husky, and the deep timbre rolled through her, making her tingle all over.

"I'll leave that up to you and your imagination."

He dropped the key back into its envelope and slid it into his pants pocket. "Now I *really* won't be able to focus on work. Especially when I'm on the road and thinking about coming home to you." He closed the short distance between them and wrapped his arms around her. His big hands stroked her back. "I'll be the guy standing at the foot of your bed with blue balls."

She giggled like a schoolgirl. "You'll be the *only* guy standing at the foot of my bed."

"Oh, I like hearing that. Speaking of bed, I'd like to take you there right now."

"Aren't you hungry?"

"Hungry for you only. Food can wait."

Her heart flipped. How was it two short sentences could do that to her? "It's been a long day. I think I need a shower first." She ran a teasing finger along his jawline, down his neck, to the top button of his shirt. She gave it a flick.

His eyebrows bounced. "Need someone to scrub your back?"

"Mm-hmm. Know anyone who'd be willing?"

This time she let him lead her down the hallway.

After a shower that used up every drop of hot water, she stood perpendicular to the mirror, a pale blue towel wrapped around her torso. Marty had just wrapped another blue towel around his waist, and currently his chiseled body was occupying her vision. She moved from his well-defined obliques to his six-pack, up to his carved pecs and his broad shoulders, darting to his sculpted biceps and—*oh God!*— those forearms. Apparently, she had a thing for forearms, and his were the gold standard by which she would measure all other masculine forearms. Not that she planned on examining any other forearms in such detail anytime soon. Maybe never.

"Are you checking me out?" His words—and his cocky grin—pulled her from her wayward thoughts.

"No! What gives you that idea?" Heat rushed to her cheeks.

"The way you were checking me out. I thought you got an eyeful in the shower."

She raised her chin, going for haughty. "You wouldn't let me. You were too busy turning me around and ogling *me* from the rear." Reaching for a brush, she presented him with her back.

"Damn straight. Thanks for reminding me it's time to ogle you from the front." He gave her towel a tug and tossed it to the side.

She dropped her brush with a squeak. Before she could protest, his hot body was flush with hers, his back to her front. He wove his fingers with hers and wrapped his arms around her middle, turning her so they faced the mirror. Resting his chin on her head, he smiled at her reflection. "Look how perfect you are," he said in a hushed, reverent tone.

Self-consciousness had her turning her gaze up to him and away from the view. She stole a quick look and decided she liked the look of herself in his arms, pale skin against tan.

His gaze remained locked on their reflection. "I've never seen anything so beautiful. You're a true work of art, Claudia."

Closing her eyes, she leaned back into him. Now he could look all he wanted, and she wouldn't be embarrassed. He released her hands and ran his up and down her arms, across her belly and chest, making her skin raise with goose bumps. Wrapping a hand around her throat, he turned her head to his and kissed her, a languid toe-curling affair, his tongue sweeping into her mouth and claiming it while his other hand slid between her legs. Never breaking the kiss, he traced her seam with a light touch, over and over, top to bottom. By the time he slipped his finger inside, she was drenched, and soon he drove in a second finger. His fingers were long and thick, and she whimpered into his mouth as he pumped in and out of her. She rocked against his hand, unable to stop herself. All the while, their tongues dueled and rolled over one another. He increased the tempo, and she couldn't catch her breath. How was it he could stay in control when she was losing her mind?

He did something with his thumb—or was that a different finger?—and the motion fired off an exquisite rush of sensation that racked her body. He released her mouth and banded his arm around her body just as she shattered into a million shards of pleasure.

When she opened her eyes, he was staring at her in the mirror, his eyes dark and feral. His fingers remained buried deep inside her, and he cupped her, making her feel as though he cradled her and would never let go. Her chest was stained pink and moved in and out with her breathing. "Wow."

"Yeah. Wow."

An hour later, they lay in a tangle of limbs and sheets, facing each other. He caressed her bare arm as she ran her fingers down the long channel of his spine.

"I don't think I ever told you, but I loved watching you with Seth the day I brought him in," he said softly. "You have a really nice way with your patients."

"I thought you were going to say you loved watching me come in the bathroom mirror."

"That too, but that affected a very different part of my psyche." He waggled his eyebrows.

She chuckled. "Helping patients charges my batteries when they're low, especially when those patients are children. They're so innocent and trusting. Kids restore my faith in humanity."

"I get that, and it shows on your face when you're with them. Do you still want children of your own someday?"

She flattened her palm against his chest. "Assuming the right man's in my life, yes. By the way, Meg has given us her blessing."

"I didn't know we needed her blessing." He covered her hand with his. "I need to ask you something, and I want an honest answer. Does dating a lowly assistant coach who makes squat bother you? I mean, you lived the penthouse life once and—"

Shaking her head, she raised her hand to his jaw and brushed her thumb over his lips. "Stop. First of all, my needs are simple, and trying to fit into that world was uncomfortable. Besides, the penthouse life came with a price tag that was too steep. You of all people should know that after watching it disintegrate. Second of all, I'm not dating a lowly assistant coach. I'm dating my very hot best friend, who happens to be working a job he loves."

"I do love it, most of the time, but I'm not content to stay there. It's the path to my dream job, and it's going to take a lot of time and hard work to reach my destination. If and when I get there, the spotlights are going to shine brighter and hotter, the pressure will be ten times what it is now, but my paycheck will have a few more zeroes before the decimal. It won't be easy catching that train with me."

Emotion welled inside her for reasons she couldn't fathom. She cupped the side of his face. "You may be on the mezzanine for now, but you won't stay there. I know you'll get to the top, and you'll kill it when you do." *And I want to catch that train with you. I want to be there for every glorious minute.* "In the meantime, I like hanging here with you. That's a world I can fit into, and I *want* to fit into it."

Unshed tears rimmed her lower lashes, and he smiled at her with such tenderness that one of those tears slipped out and clung. "You absolutely slay me, Claudia Campbell. The only times I've ever been speechless in my life are when I'm with you. You've always owned my heart. I think that's why I've never been able to give it to anyone else." He kissed her softly. "As for fitting into my world, you fit like a glove. Don't ever doubt that. But it goes both ways. I want a place in yours too."

"You have it." The tears she had penned up spilled over.

He kissed her forehead. "You gotta know by now how much I love you, and as more than my best friend."

"I know," she whispered. "And I love you too ... as more than my best friend." She settled into his strong embrace, warm and safe.

Chapter 33

THE RUBBERBAND MAN

"Let's go, boys! You've got this! Just keep it simple," Marty barked to his players hopping over the boards. He was struggling to maintain a cool composure, but they were six minutes into the third period and down three-to-one against the visiting Tucson Roadrunners. His frustration grew with each shift. The boys didn't seem to have their legs tonight, and he wasn't sure if their uninspired play was due to a holiday hangover—New Year's had come and gone a week ago—or if it was because he was filling in during Coach Graham's absence. It didn't help that Greg seemed to misunderstand Marty's on-the-fly adjustments to the other team's moves and continually communicated the wrong instructions to their club. Consequently, their players weren't only sluggish, they were confused.

A lot was riding on today's home matinee game. Not winning meant a three-game losing streak on Marty's watch, which would no doubt result in a squandered opportunity. He would never be put in charge of the team again.

Keeping his eyes on the play unfolding on the ice, he leaned down to a defenseman who had just returned to the bench. "Jonesy, next time it comes to you, just chip it out. No need to get fancy. Make 'em work for every inch of ice." He gave the kid an encouraging pat.

As Marty straightened, his eyes tracked Seth Hughes heading full steam for a Roadrunner who had the puck in the offensive zone. Marty clenched his fists. "That's it, Hughes! Forecheck! Forecheck!" At the last minute, Seth pulled up. "Come on, Seth! Take the body!" Marty growled. The other player made an outlet pass to one of his forwards, and Seth was caught flat-footed. *Goddamn it!* He had to turn and chase as the play moved up ice into his own defensive zone. The Arizona forward got a shot off, and by some miracle, the puck pinged off the post. But the Roadrunners kept his Hawks pinned deep in their own zone, eating time off the clock and protecting their lead.

Marty dragged a hand over his jaw. When the puck went out of play and the ref blew his whistle, Marty called a timeout. As his players huddled around the bench, he took the entire minute to explain—again—the execution he wanted from his team, with the added instruction that they would look to *him*, and only him, for their signals. Maybe that would cut down on some of the confusion.

The talk almost worked. Seth drew a penalty and potted a goal on the power play, bringing them within one of tying the game. But despite pulling their goalie in the last minute, the Hawks couldn't convert. The game ended in another loss under Coach LeBrun.

After addressing his dispirited group in the dressing room, Marty retreated to his office for a follow-up debrief with the other coaches. Coach Graham would be back in another ten days, but that didn't mean he wasn't involved; a painful phone call from the head coach awaited Marty. His one bright side to this dismal day was that it would end at Claudia's.

As he rounded the corner, he was caught off guard by a woman and a man who stood arguing in his office doorway. His brain stuttered a moment as it processed one of the trainers and Renee.

The trainer turned his frown on Marty. "Coach, I tried to tell her—"

"Marty, I need to speak to you." Renee slid the trainer a harsh side-eye. "In private."

Marty held up his hand. "It's okay, Steve." When the trainer spun on his heel, Marty ushered Renee into his office and shut the door.

She looked like shit. He bent to give her a quick hug, and she clung to him, making the separation awkward. Resisting the urge to place the desk between them, he perched on its corner while she settled into one of two visitors' chairs. "Are you okay?"

Her voice quavered. "No, I'm not okay. In fact, my whole life is shit." Those eyes glossed over, which was when he noticed they were rimmed in red.

His heart clenched. "What's wrong?"

Tears spilled down her cheeks. "I miss you. I was hoping you missed me too, and we could ... we could go somewhere and talk about it."

Oh fuck! Her distress made his heart lurch in his chest. He pulled in a steadying breath, his mind spinning with what to say and how to say it. "I think we said all there is to say, Ren."

She stared at him with watery eyes. "So that's it? Two years, and you're done? Is this because you're with *her* now?"

"Renee, this is not about someone else. The fault's with me. You're a wonderful person with so much to give, but I'm not the guy. I can't give it back. You should be with someone who not only appreciates you, but who will return that love tenfold because you deserve that every day of your life."

God, how feeble did that sound? She can see right through me. And she did.

Her hazel gaze swung back to his and hardened. "Stop patronizing me. You lied to me then, and you're lying to me now, so don't tell me it's not about her. You went over there the night you broke up with me, didn't you?"

He hung his head. "Ren, don't do this." *You're only hurting yourself.*

She turned up the volume. "Admit it, Marty. I saw your Suburban parked by her place all night. Did you also lie about not sleeping with her when we were together?"

He raised his eyes to hers and narrowed them. "No, I didn't. And why were you watching her place all night?"

"Because I knew you were lying! You were there, weren't you?" she repeated, her voice shrill.

"I didn't lie about sleeping with her when you and I were together. Yes, I was there that night." He bit back the long-winded explanation forming in his mind about how he hadn't *meant* to go over there, hadn't *meant* to eat dinner there, hadn't *meant* to stay over. Though he had nothing to defend himself against, the more he argued, the guiltier he sounded. Instead, he said, "You know you can't be stalking people, right?"

Her face crumbled, and she began to sob softly, covering her face with her hands. "I know, and I haven't done it since. It hurts too much."

He reached out and rested his hand on her shoulder, at a loss as to what to do or say. "Don't cry, Ren. Please."

Several long beats later, she peered up at him. "Are you going to marry her?"

Yes! The answer reverberated so loudly in his head he fumbled for words. "I don't know. It's not something we've talked about."

Sadness transformed into incredulity. "Which means you're considering it."

"I didn't say that."

Her eyes sparked, and her mouth firmed into a hard line. "What if I'm pregnant?"

He reared back as though he'd taken a slapshot to the jaw. Disbelief flooded him, along with adrenaline and a wad of emotions. "*Are* you pregnant?"

Her chin inched up. "I could be. I missed my last period."

"But you're on the pill," he spluttered. *So she can't be pregnant. Can she?*

Casting her eyes down, she looked away. "I was having some unpleasant side effects—headaches, bloating—so my gyno told me to stop for a while. I did stop, a few weeks before the last time you and I slept together."

He threw out an arm. "You never told me any of this! You're totally blindsiding me here!" *Shit! She* can *be pregnant.*

"I know, and I'm sorry." The expression on her face was more triumphant than sorry.

"Have you taken a test? Seen a doctor?"

She shook her head.

"Then you have to do that, Ren. I'm no expert, but I'm pretty sure a pregnancy test from the drug store will give you an answer right away. We can go buy one right now and find out."

She stood up. "I have a busy schedule. I'll see when I can fit it in."

Corralling his anger, he rose to his feet. "Well, *fit it in* soon."

Her smug look faded, returning to one of sheer misery. His heart would have hurt for her, but it was too busy hurting for himself. As she left his office, panic he had held at bay began a steady bloom inside him that seeped into his soul and smothered joy. What if Renee *was* pregnant? What about Claudia? What about ... his entire life?

As the possibility took root, his knees buckled from the gut-punch.

Good-bye future with Claudia. Good-bye NHL coaching dreams. Hello lifetime tied to a woman I don't love.

Marty faked his way through his coaches' meeting; their curious glances told him he hadn't done a convincing job. He fled the arena, driving blindly, unsure where he was going, until he found himself atop Horsetooth Mountain, staring out his windshield at Horsetooth Reservoir and Fort Collins sprawled beneath him.

He had texted Claudia to let her know he'd be late, but how much longer could he hide up here before he had to face her? For a fleeting moment, he had considered hiding Renee's bombshell from her—at least until he knew the test results. Once Claudia found out, their relationship was over. But hiding the truth from her had backfired on him once before, and he couldn't escape what he needed to do. He had to tell her—now—and hope for the best. With any luck, he might salvage their friendship. *Small consolation.* He would rather lose an eye than give up what he'd found with her.

As he struggled to wrap his brain around the possibility of being a father, of having a child with Renee, his mind darted to financial support. How the hell would he take care of her and the baby while he was struggling to support himself and pay off his mom's mistake?

He lingered a few minutes longer, scanning the vista, pushing aside the bleak questions clogging his synapses. Up here he was in a world where Claudia didn't know, where she lived in the bliss he'd occupied with her when he'd woken up beside her this morning. Not only might his world be crushed, but hers would be as well. *Their* world.

With a sigh, he tapped her a message that he was on his way and turned on the ignition.

Forty-five minutes later, Marty parked in Claudia's driveway beside her Honda and heaved himself and his heavy heart out of the driver's seat. He unlocked the front door and called out her name as he slid off his coat and hung it on one of the nearby hooks. If Renee *was* pregnant, this would be one of the last times he did this. Claudia wouldn't want anything to do with raising his kid by another woman—which meant she wouldn't want anything to do with *him*—and he wouldn't blame her.

She appeared at the top of the stairs wearing a Hawks sweatshirt, stretchy black pants, and that dazzling smile he loved so much. Prancing at her feet was Popcorn, who seemed as eager to see him as Claudia did.

Suddenly, Claudia flew down the stairs and flung her arms around his neck. She pulled his head down for a hungry kiss. When she pulled away, she was breathless. A shy smile curved her beautiful mouth. "I missed you."

I don't want to lose this! He mustered a small smile. "I like you missing me, especially if it means a greeting like that."

With a light laugh, she led him up the familiar flight of steps, her round hips swaying in that sensual way they did. As he stepped into her comfy living space, he looked around, taking it all in. It was imbued with her essence, from the thriving plants to the framed pictures on the mantel to the smell that stirred visions of home and hearth and cozying up on her couch, his head in her lap while she toyed with his hair.

She headed for her kitchen island. "You must be hungry. I made an Italian sausage stew."

He shook his head.

"Maybe later, then." She tilted her head, her brows furrowed with concern. "That was a tough loss today. I wish I could take away the pain. Something to drink instead?"

"Whiskey, if you have it."

Of course she had it. She was no whiskey drinker, but she kept Jameson Black stocked just for him, and she pulled a full bottle from her tiny liquor cabinet. This was one of a million reasons why he loved her so much.

After fetching a tumbler, she opened the bottle. “No offense, but you look like you could use a double.”

“Better make it a single.” *I won’t be staying long ... not after you hear what I have to say.*

She poured the Jameson, handed it to him, and picked up a glass of red wine from the counter, which she held up to him in a silent salute. Eyes trained on his, she took a sip.

“Want to sit?” She motioned toward the couch.

“Yeah.”

Low flames danced in her fireplace, and he lowered himself onto her couch and stared into their yellow-and-orange depths. Maybe he could jump into them and lose himself. Or become one with them and use the mesmerizing motion to convince Claudia not to dump his sorry ass.

They sat side by side, and he couldn’t keep from seeking her warmth, so he pressed his leg to hers, relishing the contact. Sipping quietly, they remained that way for long minutes, until he sucked in a breath of courage and angled himself to face her. “I have something I need to tell you.”

She turned toward him, tucked a leg under her butt, and offered him an encouraging half-smile.

He wiped his sweaty palms along his thighs. “Renee came to see me after the game. She thinks she might be pregnant.”

A multitude of reactions occurred in the blink of an eye. Claudia recoiled and whipped her hand back. Her eyes widened, and her mouth went slack. She yelped, *“What?”*

All of him deflated. “She doesn’t know for sure. She hasn’t tested yet.”

“But I thought you said ... you said you hadn’t slept with her after we ran into each other.” The pain in her voice laid him open.

“I didn’t. But she missed a period, and the timing would put conception right before I, uh, stopped sleeping with her.”

Those brown eyes narrowed. “Why hasn’t she taken a test?”

“I don’t know, but she says she will.” *When she can fit it in.* Anger surged inside him once more.

Claudia blinked rapid-fire, thoughts streaming behind her eyes, but she didn't seem mad, as he had expected. "Well, then, I guess there's not much to do until you find out. Can you trust her to tell you the truth?"

He puffed out a breath. "Honestly? I don't know. I didn't realize how much I had hurt her until I saw her today. Shit, I caused that." The memory of Renee's dejected expression dissolved his irritation. He scrubbed his hand over his face. "My whole life, I've drifted in and out of relationships without getting too deep, but this time, I led her to believe ..."

Eyes trained on his, Claudia set down her wineglass and leaned forward. "Because you also believed, Marty. You didn't lie to her. You thought you were going to build something permanent with her."

He nodded. "Maybe. But now I wonder how many other people I've hurt. I never should have gotten involved with anyone."

"I think you're being a little hard on yourself. We all need companionship, so we look and look, always hopeful we'll find it. We can't know if it's a good fit unless we spend time with that person, and let's face it, some people fall faster than others."

He took her hand and wove his fingers with hers. "Yeah, but none of them was ever you, and I knew they never would be. I was a dick to have started anything. No one would have gotten hurt if I'd left well enough alone."

She squeezed his fingers. "Well, let me point out that any man who is thoughtful enough to give me plants *and* take me to Blossoms of Light at the Denver Botanic Gardens, followed by decadent desserts and Irish coffees at D Bar Denver simply can't be a dick. It's impossible." Her eyes strayed to the three polka-dot pots he'd filled with miniature succulents and given her for Christmas, even though they had agreed not to exchange material gifts.

"Nice of you to say, but I beg to differ." His eyes returned to the flames. "What am I going to do if the test is positive?"

"You mean, what are *we* going to do, don't you?"

He gaped at her. "Are you saying you'd stay with me under the circumstances?"

"That depends. Would you go back to Renee?"

He was caught off guard by her question and by the fact that she wasn't dumping him outright, and he stumbled over his answer. "Not in terms of a romantic relationship, b-but we'd definitely be in each other's lives." *All the fucking time.*

Claudia gave him a wistful smile. "I grant you the situation wouldn't be ideal, but I can't imagine leaving you to tough it out on your own. It won't change what we have together. But why don't we save our worrying until we know for sure?"

The way she said "we" lightened his despondency. As he stared at her in wonder, his mind tried to lock out a future where he was a father at the end of the year and Renee was the mother. Instead, he compelled his thoughts back to the pleasant holiday break he had just spent with Claudia. A string of days where they had lazily lolled together—both in *and* out of bed—and where Christmas had been spent at Danielle's, surrounded by family. Dani's kids had abandoned Uncle Marty in favor of Claudia, and he had sat back and watched, warmed by visions of her as a mom sometime in the future—*their* future.

He let those same images fill his head now, along with the thought that *this* was what it was supposed to feel like. You had a horrible day, and you came home to someone who cared about you and shared your troubles and who had your back, no matter what. Someone who could ease your aches and pains by merely looking at them.

Her hand felt good laced with his, and he grinned for the first time that night. "I guess I did okay on the Christmas stuff, huh?"

She rolled her eyes. "More than good, but don't let it go to your head, Coach."

His heart lifted a few inches. Overcome by the pictures playing in his head, he released her hand, set his drink on her coffee table, and leaned toward her. "Come here."

She sprouted a little smirk. "Why?"

Cupping her face in one hand, he searched her eyes. "So I can tell you how much I love you. In fact, you've become my whole world. To the exclusion of pretty much everything else. Even coaching."

Confusion clouded her beautiful chocolate eyes but quickly cleared.

"The thing is," he ran on, "I've dreamed about building a life with you. Forever. Buying a little house together, having kids, cats, dogs, fish. But ..."

She laid a hand on his knee. “Are you sick?”

He threw himself backward with a laugh. “I’m obviously doing this all wrong if you think I’m sick.”

She squeaked an apology. “You started to say ‘but’ and stopped. What were you trying to tell me?”

He cradled her face in both hands this time. *I am going to marry you.* “I was going to say *but* I’m not sure you feel the same way.” And he wasn’t. Was she as consumed with him as he was with her? Was she offering to stick with him out of pity?

She kissed him. It was a soft kiss, filled with tenderness and longing that snatched the breath from his lungs. He had to suck in air when she pulled away. “Does that answer your question, Coach?”

Oh yeah. And so many more.

Another kiss, with more passion packed into it, and when she broke the kiss, *she* was gasping for air. “Does that take your mind off your troubles?”

“What mind?” He pulled her to him, ready to take her mouth—and every other part of her.

Yeah, this is how it’s supposed to be.

He welcomed the chance to lose himself with her, but a nagging little voice whispered doubts inside his head, holding him back. Sure, Claudia had said a baby wouldn't change anything between them, but how could it not? How was she going to feel when every time she looked at that baby, she was reminded his first child was with someone else? How was she going to feel when he shared what little extra time he had with Renee and the baby?

He prayed he would never have to find out.

Coach Graham stuck his head through Marty’s office doorway three days later. “LeBrun? My office in two.”

Marty looked up from his phone where he had been hoping for a message from Renee, who had been ghosting him, leaving him in a limbo where he had no clue what his future held. “Be right there, Coach.” *Ah, shit. Here it comes.* The disastrous losing streak might have been in Marty’s rearview mirror—he’d coached his players through one win in the three days since—but Coach was back and growling at everyone like a wounded bear.

Standing, Marty straightened his collar. His best hope was he wouldn't be canned until the end of the season so he could at least continue to draw a paycheck for the next few months, what there was of it.

He entered Coach's office, and his boss, without looking up, flicked a finger toward a chair and grunted at him. Marty sat ... and sat ... and sat while Coach poured over some papers on his desk. Jesus, the guy was really enjoying turning up the heat under Marty's barbecued ass, wasn't he?

Finally, Coach looked up and steepled his fingers. "Let's talk about the team's record while you were in charge." *Yep. Let's just get right down to it.* Marty mostly respected Coach Graham's bluntness, but occasionally—like now—it made him cringe. "How do *you* think you did?"

"Not well."

Graham pierced him with a hard stare. "Why do you think that is?"

"I didn't effectively communicate the game plan to our players. When I wanted to make adjustments, I was unable to get those adjustments across." Marty paused, but Coach's intense stare made him rush into the silence. He listed every one of his faults and errors, all of which he had become well acquainted with after spending these past days dissecting himself. Coach wrote notes as Marty spewed.

When he was done, Coach stopped writing and looked up. "What would you have done differently?"

This was another question Marty had posed to himself, ad nauseam, and he rattled off those answers too. Coach kept his gaze trained on him this time.

When Marty finished, Coach simply nodded. A riot of thoughts arranged and rearranged themselves in Marty's brain, and he held his breath in the weighted silence. How long did he have to sit here before Coach said those two dreaded words? Coach surprised him when, instead of saying, "You're fired," he said, "Nowhere in your comments did I hear you blame the assistants or your players."

Surprised, Marty blinked. "Because ultimately, the failure's mine."

"And the victory? Is that yours too?"

"Well," Marty stammered, "I don't think so. That belongs to the players. They're the ones who scrapped for it."

"I disagree. You scrapped too, *in spite* of your assistant throwing you under the bus." Coach chuckled. "Don't look so shocked. I know exactly what was going on behind that bench, and to your credit, you didn't stick it to Greg like he tried to stick it to you. You were trying to make the same kinds of adjustments I would have made, but I bark louder and people listen. You're going to need some of that swagger. And another piece of advice? If you're going to take responsibility for the losses, LeBrun, you'd better take it for the wins too, or you won't get very far in your coaching career. People are quick to lay the blame at your skates, but they can be slow on the uptake when it comes to plusses. Oh, I'm not saying break your hand patting yourself on the back or get on a megaphone, but be damn sure some of that credit attaches itself to you." He sat back and grasped his armrests. "Now get back to work."

"You mean ..."

Coach bent back to his papers. "No, the team's not firing you. Yet. But if you keep standing there gawking at me, all bets are off. Now get out of here."

"Yes, sir." Marty pivoted hard and nearly smacked into the door. Outside Coach's office, he broke into the first Hawks-related smile he'd felt come on in days.

He hurried back to his own office, where his phone glowed on his desktop with a missed call. He picked it up, his heart a jack rabbit in his chest. Renee had *finally* returned his calls from the last few days. As he listened to her voicemail telling him she had news to share, part of him wondered what had taken so long while a different part dreaded hearing the outcome. Would he be sinking into the depths of the Mariana Trench or skyrocketing to Antares? Closing his office door, he hit her number and held his breath.

She answered on the first ring. "Hi, Marty." The grimness in her voice left him little hope for optimism.

"Hey, Ren. I got your message."

"So you're calling to find out whether you're going to be a dad or not, I assume." She huffed out the remark, which confused him. Hadn't *she* called *him*?

"Um, yeah."

"Well, you'll be relieved to know you're not."

Flabbergasted, he dropped into his chair, blowing out the breath trapped in his lungs as though he'd just sprinted five miles. *Not. The most glorious word in the English language.* "I take it the results came back negative?" He refrained from punching the air and hollering, "Yes!"

"I never took a test."

"Oh. So that means—"

"My period started this morning."

"Wait. Why didn't you take the test a few days ago after we talked?" *Why did she drag this out?*

Her sigh vibrated through the phone. "I was afraid it would be negative."

What? He gave his head a shake. "Are you saying you *wanted* to be pregnant?" This made absolutely no sense.

"I didn't want to be pregnant, Marty, but I didn't want to lose you either, and I thought that if ... well, if you thought there was a kid on the way, maybe you'd come back and we could work things out between us."

Whoa! "Ren ..." Words escaped him.

"I'm sorry, Marty," came her small voice. "I guess it was a last-ditch effort to hang on. As long as I didn't know, there was the illusion we could still be together one way or another." She let out a bitter laugh. "Actually, I was relieved when I got my period. Not only did it *not* bring you back, but I realized how desperately I was behaving. I had become too dependent on you. Quite the eye-opener, and I didn't like what I saw."

He closed his eyes and heaved out a breath. "Ren, will you be okay?"

"Yeah, Marty. I'm going to be just fine."

The hint of lightness in her voice released a flood of joy inside him. When they hung up, he leaned back in his chair, a knot of tears wedged like a fist in his throat. He laughed out loud, giving his emotions an escape.

Outside, a blizzard cast a bleak pall, but Marty's world was lit by a blinding beam of sunshine. And he couldn't wait to share that ray with the one person who mattered most. Claudia was at work, and Marty began plotting the perfect way to celebrate.

Chapter 34

Life Through a Different Lens

Claudia blinked at the email glowing on her computer screen—the one that had startled her from a pleasant, routine early morning and caused her to call in sick for the first time in two years.

Scanning the message for the tenth time since she had opened it, Claudia absentmindedly scratched a purring Eggroll where she sat in Claudia's lap.

"I know I'm being a coward," Claudia sighed to the cat, "but I'm not ready to deal with Zach Pruitt yet, even if he's honestly looking for redemption."

This was his fourth message in as many weeks, starting with the one he had sent shortly after she and Marty had sprinted from the friend zone to lover's leap. In that time, his missives had grown more desperate, and she wasn't sure what to make of them. He had to see her. He had to apologize in person for his past transgressions. He wouldn't take no for an answer.

Well, for now, she would disappear and not give him a choice. But her guilty conscience was niggling at her. What harm could it do to let him apologize and move on? If she could marshal a battery of defenses, she might meet up with him in a day ... or two ... or ten.

She had only responded to him once, and she had done so curtly, saying she was busy and asking if he had reached out to Marty. *Speaking of those you've hurt.* "Didn't know he was coaching in Colorado, so not yet," he'd replied, but he'd promised he would, and would she please not mention the visit to his old buddy in the meantime. *Same old Zach, vomiting out promises.* And apparently, she was the same old Claudia because she had done Zach's bidding by not telling Marty about Zach's emails.

Then again, Marty had been struggling at work, and she saw no reason to dump more on him by bringing up the complicated and unpleasant past they shared. Better to find out first if she *was* dealing with the same old Zach before letting Marty in on his visit. And if she ended up not seeing Zach after all? Better that Zach reached out to Marty himself.

I'm clean and sober, his message read, *and have been ever since I woke up five years ago and realized my behavior had chased you away (again). I'm coming to Colorado so I can apologize in person. I've been through AA, DAA, and SA, and as I move through these recovery programs, I realize more and more how badly I need to tell everyone I've hurt that I'm sorry. You're the first—and most important—person on that list.*

DAA and SA, she had learned, stood for Drug Addicts Anonymous and Sexaholics Anonymous. Vaguely, she wondered if there were any addictions Zach *hadn't* familiarized himself with.

The part of the message that had spurred her to call in sick stated, *This is a crucial step for me, and I'll come to the hospital and find you there if I need to, but I will find you.*

Shouldn't a recovering addict understand that some people from their past didn't *want* to hear from them again and that being heavy-handed might backfire on them?

While he *might* be able to track her down at the hospital, he didn't know where she lived, so she was safe as long as she stayed away from work. Tomorrow would have been the start of her weekly four days off, so now she could lay low for five.

She minimized the email and placed Eggroll on the floor. "All right. Enough of Zach Pruitt."

Looking around, she pondered what she could lose herself in for a while to give her mind a Zach break. The blank wall reminded her the dresser in her garage—which she'd finished painting during the holidays—needed sanding for that just-right distressed look she was going for.

"Some rocking tunes, a little sandpaper, some muscle from Marty to get it up the stairs, and I'll be able to fill up this space again," she said aloud.

The day was dreary, blanketed by damp gray clouds that promised snow, so she pulled on a down jacket, turned on a classic rock station, and got to work scraping and buffing.

A dozen songs later, she stood back and inspected her work. "Ooh, I think I'm done!" She screwed the knobs back on the drawers and hauled a few upstairs. The dresser itself would have to wait until Marty came over.

As she passed by a side window, she realized the looming snowstorm had arrived with a vengeance. Fat falling flakes were coating the outside world, and her car would soon disappear under a thick carpet of white. Back in the garage, she eyed the dresser. If she could maneuver it out of the way, the Honda might fit in the garage now.

Pushing and pulling, she coaxed the heavy piece until it sat at an awkward angle. "Hopefully that's far enough," she muttered to herself and hit the garage door opener. She froze in her tracks.

"Hi," Zach greeted from the driveway.

Electric shocks jolted through her, and she gasped. "What are you doing here?"

"Can I come in?" he shouted, and she realized AC/DC was blaring "You Shook Me All Night Long." Alarms screeching in her head, she snapped off the radio and pivoted back to face him.

Looks like you're already in. He dusted off his hands as he stood in her garage.

"What the hell, Zach? How did you find me?" she squeaked.

He gave her a tentative smile. "I used a skip tracer. You weren't that hard to find."

She gaped at him. "Did you go to my work?"

"Nope. Thought I'd try here first." His eyes made a cursory sweep of her frame. "You look great, as always."

He looked healthier himself, his face fuller than the last time she had seen him, when he'd been pale and gaunt. Could have been in his color or the way he carried himself, she wasn't sure, but if he was indeed clean and sober, it agreed with him.

He flicked a finger toward her dresser. "Need help with that?"

"No!"

He put his hands up in surrender. "Okay. Just thought you'd like to get it out of the way so you can pull your car in. This storm is supposed to dump at least a foot of snow."

"That's what I was trying to do."

"Well, the car isn't going to fit with the dresser there."

"I need to get it upstairs," she blurted. *Wait. What am I saying?* So much for gathering her wits about her.

He grinned. "I can help with that."

She pulled in a steadying breath. "Zach, there's a reason I didn't email you back. I'm not sure I want you here."

The grin slid from his face, and he shoved his hands in his pockets. "I understand, I guess, but I really would like to talk to you face-to-face. Just for a few minutes. How about this? Let me help get your dresser upstairs, and by the time that's done and your car's stowed, if you decide I still need to go, I'll go. No pushback."

The sincere look on his face was an echo of Old Zach, and her defenses wavered. "Promise?"

He bobbed his head. "I haven't given you much reason to believe in my promises, but yeah, you have my word."

Zach did most of the heavy lifting as they hefted the dresser upstairs. While she pulled her car into the garage, he hustled the remaining drawers up to her office and slid them in.

She stuck her head through the office doorway and spied Zach using a rag she'd left on a bookshelf to buff the dresser. The shock of seeing him hadn't worn off yet, but he was obviously trying his best to make a good impression. She suppressed an eye-roll and headed into the kitchen, where she fired up the tea kettle.

Zach sauntered out from her office and looked around. "I like your place. It's homey. It reminds me of you."

When she didn't respond, he added, "Hey, can I have some of whatever you're making? As long as it doesn't have any alcohol, that is."

"I'm making tea." *I need something to settle my nerves, and coffee will just make them jumpier.* She didn't hate the idea of him being here, and she owed him *something* for helping her with the dresser. Plus, it would be rude to fix herself a cup and not offer him one, so she pulled a box of loose tea samples from a drawer. "What flavor do you want?"

"Doesn't matter. Whatever's easy."

She prepared two tea balls of hibiscus orange, placed them in Hawks mugs, and poured boiling water over them. "So tell me about needing to see me face-to-face." Leaning against the counter, she crossed her arms and waited while the tea steeped.

He pulled in a breath and held her gaze. "Like I said in my email, I've been living clean and sober for the last five years. I want to give back, I want to counsel other addicts, but I'm still working through some steps in my own program. I'm almost there, and one of the biggest is apologizing to people I've hurt, so here I am."

"And stalking me to get here."

He cleared his throat. "I might have overdone it, but in order to do this well, I needed to say some things to your face, not over the phone or in an email. I didn't think waiting for your permission was going to get me here."

"Hmm, tell me where I've seen this before. Charge ahead and ask for forgiveness later." *Some things don't change.*

He let out a mirthless laugh. "I didn't think about it that way, but you're right."

She removed the tea balls and motioned toward the couch. "I haven't kept up on hockey. Are you still playing?"

He raised his mug, and one corner of his mouth twitched. "Yet you have Hawks cups." Heat blazed her cheeks. If he noticed, he didn't let on. "I'm still playing in Tampa, but ice time is getting shorter, and the body is slower to heal. The organization has offered me a position in the front office, and I'm considering hanging up the skates and taking it."

"You're thirty-three. You've had a long, successful run." She took a steaming sip and nearly scalded the roof of her mouth.

"The career maybe, but not much else," he said quietly.

She braced herself. *Okay. I'm ready. I think.*

He leaned forward, balancing his elbows on his thighs, holding the cup between his legs, his head bent. "This is hard for me, not because I find it hard to say I'm sorry, but because I'm reminded of how selfish I was and how badly I hurt you."

"You did a lot of apologizing when we were married and when I filed for divorce." *All of it empty.* "How is this different?"

He turned his head toward her, which was when she noticed the harsh lines etched on his face. "This time I mean it. And for the record, I never wanted that divorce."

Anger she thought dead and buried reared up inside her. "You should have thought about that before—"

He raised a hand to stop her. "Let me finish. I didn't want the divorce, but I didn't blame you, CC. Not after what I did."

Why was it that her nickname on Zach's lips gave her prickly heat but when Marty said it, she wanted to melt like a Fudgsicle in the sun? She took her anger, balled it up, and threw it at him. "You had them in *our bedroom*, Zach!" *And I thought I was over this.*

His blue eyes shimmered with so much sadness that tears nearly welled in her own. "I know. What I did, the way I treated you, was fucking awful. I was a disgusting, egotistical prick and so many other adjectives I can't name them all. I'd like to sit here and tell you it was because of the alcohol and drugs, but I'd be lying, and I don't want to lie to you anymore, Claudia. I, Zach Pruitt, am to blame, nothing and nobody else."

He raised a tearful gaze back to hers. "It kills me when I think of all the terrible things I said and did to you. Sometimes that stuff wakes me up at night. It haunts me. And I didn't do it because I didn't love you. I *did* love you, and I still do. I was an immature asshole caught up in my own hype. Shit if I know why I thought I had the right to act that way, but I understand now how wrong I was." His eyes shifted to his untouched tea. "I made the classic mistake of believing my career would go on forever, even though I said otherwise. Deep down, I thought I was different. Bulletproof. And that bled over into my personal life. But if I could climb into a time machine and go back, I'd wipe out every single time I hurt you. Then

I'd go forward and let you know every damn day how important you are to me."

Sorrow and confusion tamped down her anger. "Obviously, you weren't ready to be in a committed relationship, and I've often wondered why you asked me to marry you in the first place."

A corner of his mouth tipped up. "I was nuts about you, and I thought that if I didn't marry you, you'd get away. I guess I didn't believe I could keep you long-term without putting a ring on your finger." His smile turned wistful. "I'll never forget how beautiful you looked the day we got married. I still pull out the pictures and stare at them. Marrying you was the *one* thing I got right in my mess of a life." A humorless laugh escaped him. "My biggest mistake was being too stupid and too wrapped up in myself to hang on to you."

They sat in stifling silence a few moments longer until he spoke again. "You know that eighties song by Air Supply called 'All Out of Love'? I used to think that song was so fucking stupid, but it came on the other day, and I listened to the words for the first time. That song says everything I'm feeling right now."

The lyrics drifted through her head, and tears sprang to her eyes.

He put down the tea and took her hand in his. "I said I came here to apologize, and that's true. But there's more. I want you back, Claudia." She held in a gasp. "I've never remarried. Never even came close because I found myself comparing every other woman to you. All these years later, I realize how amazing you are and how special what we had together was. I want that back. I want *you* back."

As she looked at the man beside her, she saw him through a polished lens. He was both familiar and unknown, and she realized she had hung on to the anger and hurt for too long. He would always occupy a corner of her heart, but that was all. She didn't want to return to the familiar, nor did she want to uncover the unknown with him. He had stepped off the pedestal she had put him on; he could have been her next-door neighbor or a patient checking into the hospital.

He tugged her hand and gently pulled her against him. The move so shocked her that she barely registered the soft thud of a door. She braced her hands against his chest to push herself off him.

Zach held her in the awkward embrace. "I've changed, Claudia. Things will be so much better between us now. I swear. And I don't care where we live. I don't even care about taking the job in Tampa if it means having you. Hell, I'll move in here with you and die a happy man."

She softened in his arms for a beat while she turned over his surprising words. Once upon a time, she wanted desperately to believe him. Oddly, she believed him now, but it didn't matter anymore, and knowing that made her feel free yet sad. She was taking part in a funeral for what they'd once had.

The plea in his eyes tugged on her heartstrings, and she took her time to temper the words so clearly etched in her soul—words that would crush his hopes. "The change was a long time coming, and I'm glad you finally got there. I can't tell you what a relief that is. I care about you, but—"

Before she could get out the rest of her speech, bootsteps stomped up her stairs. She looked up, stunned to see Marty on the landing, plastic grocery bags dangling from one hand while the other clenched a bouquet of stargazer lilies so hard she thought he might snap the stems.

"What in the fuck is going on here?"

Marty had left work early so he could pick up the ingredients for beef Stroganoff and get it cooked in time for the end of Claudia's shift. He had it all planned out. She would walk into her place, bone weary, and he would hand her a big-ass glass of zinfandel—which he'd purchased at the liquor store on his way over—and give her a neck and shoulder massage. After that, he'd feed her dinner and a gooey lemon dessert he'd selected. Claudia loved anything with lemons in it.

A last-minute grab had been a bright bouquet of pink-and-white flowers with little orange centers she loved. He had planned to have them nicely arranged and sitting on the table for her to enjoy while she drank her wine.

After parking in her driveway—leaving her plenty of room to park beside him—he had let himself in to work on his surprise ... and had gotten a shock when her voice had drifted down the stairs, followed by a man's familiar voice.

Zach.

Marty paused, gathering himself as he listened to Zach say how things would be better than before, how he would give up Tampa and live wherever Claudia wanted, that he was willing to move into her condo with her. How he would die a happy man.

Every show of success Zach had hurled at him, every slight Zach had committed against him, every time Zach had bested him and rubbed his nose in it, every insecurity Marty had felt whenever he compared himself to his ex-best friend welled up inside him and threatened to overflow their banks like one hot river of lava.

He stormed up the stairs, his knees almost giving way with the nightmare before him—a scene where Claudia was wrapped up in her ex-husband's embrace, looking deep into his eyes while she told him that she cared for him.

Thousands of thoughts burst in Marty's mind at once, like firecrackers igniting on the Fourth of July. He had never been good enough, would *never* be good enough to give Claudia what Zach could. Zach still had it all, including the girl. Marty's world disintegrated.

"What in the fuck is going on here?"

Claudia pushed Zach away like a teenager who'd been caught making out and vaulted from her seat. "Marty, what are you doing here?"

Marty pointed the flowers at Zach. "What am *I* doing here? What the fuck is *he* doing here? I thought you were at work! Where's your car?"

Eyes wide, she patted the air as though trying to calm a crazy patient. "I didn't go in today. Zach helped me with the dresser, and I was able to park my car in the garage. I was going to tell you about Zach, but—"

Zach lurched to his feet and hitched his jeans as he stared at the back of Claudia's head. "Wait. How did he get in? Don't tell me you and ... and *Marty?* You're with *him?*" He made a derisive sound. "I don't fucking believe this. You're really scraping the bottom of the barrel, CC."

Marty didn't recall dropping the flowers and groceries. Suddenly, his fists were full of Zach's sweater, and the pent-up past came roaring up.

"What don't you fucking believe, Pruitt? That anyone besides you could be at the *top* of the barrel? Don't kid yourself, motherfucker! You're the rotten apple at the bottom of it, corrupting everything and everyone around you."

Zach's head was craned backward, but he still managed a smirk. "I knew you were envious, LB, but isn't this carrying it a bit too far?"

Marty tightened his hold. "Envious of you? That's rich! That high opinion you have of yourself is what's gone too far. I might have wanted what you had once upon a time, but not since I woke up and realized what a user you are, how you like wiping your dirty boots on everyone like you're some fucking god who's above everyone else. You're not. In fact, you're wallowing in one of the biggest fucking mudholes in existence with other users, all of you feeding off each other, and I am so goddamn glad to not be in it with you. Watching you made me realize what I *don't* want to be. Ever!

"I may not make the money you do, or have the special privileges you love to flaunt, but you know what? I don't want 'em. I want to be able to sleep at night and know I did my damnedest that day for the people I care about. But you wouldn't know what that feels like, would you? Because you're too fucking self-centered to care about anyone but Zach Pruitt. He's always been your number one and always will be! You're thirty-three, and you're still so wrapped up in being the Zachinator that no one else is going to give a goddamn about you. You don't have a conscience or a thought for anyone besides yourself. I'm not perfect, but I'm a helluva lot closer than you'll ever be!"

Claudia wiggled her way between them. "Stop it, Marty!"

Between her yelling at him, the sharp pokes of her finger, and the fact that he had just disgorged twelve years of pent-up anger that left him spent, Marty came back to himself and released Zach's sweater. "I'm done. I'm not wasting another breath on this selfish piece of shit."

Claudia panted. "This isn't what you think, Marty! Let me explain."

Marty looked down at her. Hurt morphed into a new spike of fury that Marty turned on her. "And here you are, defending this asshole who fucked other women while he was with you! What the hell is wrong with you? How can you believe anything out of his mouth? All he's ever done is lie to you, and you come running back for more! Here you are, *again,* lapping up the shit he's feeding you."

Zach hadn't moved, and his bland expression torqued Marty's engine even tighter. He knocked Zach backward with his forearm, effectively planting his ass on the couch. "And *you*, you son of a bitch, you don't deserve her. You *never* did!"

Claudia shoved at Marty's arm, her face as red as a goal light. The tussle rocked her coffee table, spilling mugs and their contents onto the floor. "Marty! You're jumping to conclusions without the facts, so stop right now before you make an ass out of yourself!"

"Too late for that," Zach snorted.

Clenching his fists, Marty ignored him and kept his attention on Claudia. "Yeah? Well, I'm not the only one who's making an ass of himself because *you're* assuming this dickwad is telling you the truth. You don't fucking learn, do you, Claudia?" He spun on his heel and made for the stairs, firing off one last parting shot. "I'm out! Don't come running to me when he rips your heart out. I'm done being your shoulder to cry on."

As he flew down the stairs and out the door into the blizzard, Claudia's exasperated shout followed him the whole way. That goddamn little voice in his head prayed his anger would fill the hole left by her ripping out *his* heart.

Chapter 35

When Marty Met Claudia

Claudia strode to the top of the stairs, poised to chase the moronic man out the door and ... Where? Into the blizzard?

That would make me a moron, but it might also cool me off.

Instead, she narrowed her eyes at the other dumbass sitting on the couch where the first idiot had pushed him. Zach's expression was part confusion and part annoyance, mixed with a big dose of disbelief.

Disbelief, she assumed, that she could fall in love with Marty. The realization made her boiling temper release more steam.

Zach laughed, and it was a harsh sound. "You and him. Please tell me I read that wrong."

Yep. Nailed it.

She picked up the cups, then parked her fists on her hips to keep herself from slugging him. "Why?"

"Oh, please. You can do so much better than that loser. I doubt he's got more than twenty dollars to his name. And no wonder. He always was a hanger-on, never good enough to make it into the NHL. Hell, how long's he been slaving away in the minors and he can't do better than assistant coach?" Zach made an L out of his finger and thumb, stuck it to his forehead, and hung out his tongue.

Gritting her teeth, Claudia lassoed her rage. "I can do better how? By being with a cheating, lying, self-centered son of a bitch like you? I tried that, and I hated it. There's only one loser here, and I'm looking at him. Marty was right about so many things, including the fact that you *do* only care about satisfying your own whims." Zach seemed to flinch, but she ran on, undeterred.

She stabbed her finger toward the landing. "He was your *friend*, Zach! There was nothing he wouldn't do for you! Do you know how rare that is? Do you even know what that means? He was loyal and honorable and true to you, and you repaid him by shitting all over him!" She threw up her hands. "Hell, what am I even saying? You couldn't possibly know because you have no clue what it is to be a friend to someone, to care about their happiness more than your own! You could learn a lot about being a quality human from Marty. He gives and gives, and everyone who knows him loves him for it, including me!" *Even if I am pissed as hell at him right now.* "I don't give a flying fuck what's in your bank account or how many points you racked up last season. I *never* did. And you know why? Because they aren't the measure of a man." She pounded her fist against her chest. "What's in here ... that's what counts, and Marty LeBrun is far richer than you'll ever be."

She paused to take a breath and calm her racing heart. "Here's something else for your consideration: Marty is the best man I know. He's humble, he's unselfish, and his heart is pure gold. He's been there for me during the highs and lows, and he's never wavered. He's my rock and always has been, even when we weren't romantically involved."

"Well, your *rock* just skated out the door pissed as hell."

"Because he misunderstood. And while I disagree with his assumptions, I can't fault him for jumping to conclusions. Not with our past clouding his vision." As her remarks tumbled out of her mouth and sank into her mind, her anger drained away ... because every word she uttered was true.

Zach eyed her with curiosity. "Sure you're not kidding yourself?"

An inner calmness fueled by faith deep in Claudia's soul took charge. "I'm sure. And you know why? Because this is Marty we're talking about. He's not just my rock, he's an entire mountain. Being with him gives me balance. And given the chance, I'll do everything in my power to make sure he knows how I feel." *That I love him with all I am.*

Zach arched a skeptical eyebrow. "And if he doesn't give you that chance? Then what?"

She smiled and bent to pick up the discarded flowers. "Like I said, this is Marty. He's rational; he thinks the best of people. Once he calms down and has a chance to process, he'll look for answers. And I'll be there to give them to him." She hoped like hell she was right. Marty *would* process; this she knew with certainty. Where their relationship wound up after he processed was another matter. Yet, though her confidence wobbled, she dared believe he loved her too much to let what they had go.

How different this strange tranquility was. With Zach, she had been blinded. So many metaphorical shiny objects had kept her focus moving that what truly mattered had been blurred. Marty had the opposite effect on her. With him, the distractions were brushed away until all that remained in her line of vision was him. *Them.*

Zach swallowed, his Adam's apple visibly bobbing. "What about us, Claudia? It can't be too late."

She placed the flowers on the counter, eased herself beside him on the couch. "You say you've changed. Well, I've changed too. What I want now is worlds apart from what I wanted in college." *I didn't truly know* what *I wanted then.* "And let's face it, you and I aren't good for each other. We never were. I think deep down, you know it too, and the only reason you want me back is because it's the easy way out. It's less work than searching for someone better suited for you." *I wish her luck, whoever she is.*

"You're saying you've found that someone, and it's Marty?" Resignation and sadness crept into his eyes, ousting the smug incredulity from moments before.

"Yes." She peered at him and held her breath, praying he wouldn't ask her to say more that might hurt him.

Zach dragged a hand across his jaw. "He treats you right?"

"Better than right. He lets me know every single day that I'm the most important person in his life, whether it's with his words or his actions." She flicked a hand toward the grocery bags strewn on the floor. "Like surprising me with a homemade dinner. I know I'm always right here in his thoughts." She tapped her forehead with her index finger.

He nodded and stood, and she rose with him. Suddenly, he looked old and worn, his face a landscape of crags and crevices, the dimple she had once loved buried in one of those creases.

"I should go." His eyes scanned her face, and he let out an extended exhale.

She walked him down the stairs to the front door. With an achingly sad look, he hugged her one last time and said good-bye, whispering, "I'm sorry."

Whether he was sorry about what he'd done, sorry for his loss, or both, she couldn't be sure. She too felt a profound loss. "Be happy, Zach."

A flood of feelings washed over her when she closed the door. Part of her felt as though she had shed an anvil that had been crushing her for years. The other part wanted to climb under the covers and cry.

A feeling of lightness weighed down by melancholy. And looming in the background was the realization that when Marty returned, he might bring the impending birth of a child with him. His child with another woman.

Don't borrow trouble; wait for the results, she reminded herself. Hopefully Marty would be speaking to her by the time those results came in.

She dragged herself upstairs, turned on the radio, and gathered the abandoned groceries while Eggroll and Popcorn looked on with curiosity.

"I'm not giving up on him, kids. I'll be here whenever he's ready to talk and let me explain."

"Keep on Loving You" by REO Speedwagon came on. Unable to stop them, she let the tears come.

Lack of sleep coated Marty's eyes with grit while hurt and anger from the day before lay like a boulder in his chest. He sat in his office, squeezing a stress ball, waiting for someone to yell it was time to go. Another road trip. A chance to lose himself in hockey ... if he could stop losing himself in Claudia and Zach.

The all-star break would be here in two weeks. Maybe he should plan a trip to the beach, where he could soak in the sun and lots of liquor and chase Claudia Campbell from his mind. Before he could stray down the same old worn-out tangent about never being good enough, someone from the front office stuck her head through the gap in his door.

"Knock, knock, Coach. Someone who says he's an old friend is here to see you." She jabbed a finger to the side and in an excited hush said, "It's Zach Pruitt!"

Before Marty could answer, Zach nudged the woman out of the way and flashed her a blinding smile. "Thanks. I got it from here." She looked as though she might faint before returning a dazed version of the smile. He raised his gaze to Marty. "Got a minute?"

Marty sat forward and squeezed the ball with more vigor as thoughts swirled in his mind. *Beat his ass? Squeeze his head like this ball? Tell him to go fuck himself?* "Do I have a choice?" he groused.

"You always have a choice, but I think what I have to say is something you might want to hear."

Oh, this oughta be good. "We're leaving on a road trip any minute, so make it fast." Marty flicked a hand toward the chairs in front of his desk, and Zach pulled one out and sat down.

"Yeah? Where you headed?"

Marty was not in the mood for chit-chat, and he spat out the answer. "East Coast swing with a stop in Canada."

"Huh. Sounds like one of those eight-day slogs that sucks the life right outta you."

"So why are you here? I'm sure it's not to discuss the Hawks schedule."

Zach cleared his throat. "I'm here on the Zach Pruitt apology tour." He fidgeted in his seat. "I came here to say I'm sorry. For yesterday, for *everything* I did and said over the years. I'm also here to talk about Claudia."

Marty blinked. *Not what I was expecting.*

Zach let out a wry laugh. "I see I've left you speechless, not that I blame you. I'd be speechless too. Look, I've been doing a lot of soul-searching these last twenty-four hours, and I've come to some rather unsettling realizations, starting with the laundry list of shit I pulled on you that never should have happened. I've been wrong about a lot of shit, and I would like forgiveness for all of it. But there's one thing that's especially egregious and has been eating at me for a long time."

Marty's eyebrows hit his hairline. "And that would be?"

"Suggesting you were second best. Not recognizing or respecting you for who you were—are. You can't get to my level of assholery without stepping on a few heads along the way, and I stepped on yours more than anyone else's." He looked around the office at Marty's pictures and memorabilia from past teams. "Wow. You've won some hardware, my man. Kelly Cup in the ECHL, Clark Cup in the USHL, and it sounds like you're on the verge of snagging the Calder this year. Who does that? That's incredible."

"We need a few more months of wins before that happens," Marty deadpanned.

Zach shrugged. "You'll do it. Maybe not this season, but you'll get there. I have no doubt."

Marty frowned at him. Where the hell was Zach going with this?

As if he'd read Marty's thoughts, Zach continued. "I had an epiphany last night."

"About?"

"About you. I realized that while I can play, I can't coach. Never could. Wouldn't know where to begin. I also realized I should have spent more time planning for my future because my career's about over. I've had a longer run than many, but I'm at a point where I'm not sure what comes next. You, on the other hand, have your future set. You can coach forever because you're smart and you know how to *motivate* people. I can't motivate a moth to stop flapping around a light. Yet here you are, tearing it up in the AHL. You've won wherever you've gone, which is why teams are constantly poaching you, why head coaches want to add you to their staff. I know. I did some research. I will bet you a hundred bucks your coach here was hiring his replacement when he brought you on board. I mean, come on. Last year you were a video coach, and this year you're already an assistant? That's all you, LB. I'll also lay money down on you making it to NHL before you're forty. The trajectory you're on, the attention you're getting, it's inevitable. Anyway, I wanted to say that, for what it's worth, I noticed and I'm really happy for you. No one deserves it more."

Dumbstruck, Marty studied his friend, hunting for any clue he was having fun at Marty's expense. He only saw sincerity staring back at him.

Zach cast his eyes down. "And speaking of who deserves what ..." He swung his gaze up to Marty once more. "You once said that neither of us deserves Claudia. Do you remember that?"

Nodding, Marty pulled in a silent breath. "I remember."

"I agreed with you then, but not anymore. One of us deserves her, and it's you."

Marty spluttered, "But you ... What happened to you trying to get her back?"

Zach jabbed his forefinger at Marty. "She doesn't want me. She wants *you*." He went on to describe the rest of the conversation Marty *hadn't* overheard. "Don't blow this like I did, LB. If I hadn't had my head buried up my ass all those years ..." A look of pure dejection transformed his features.

Someone yelled in the hallway that it was time to go.

Zach blew out a breath and stood. Marty rose and held his gaze. Zach gave him a wry smile. "Do I get an invite to the wedding?"

Marty's brows cinched together a little tighter, not because he was mad, but because he was utterly flummoxed.

"Okay, so maybe not." Zach headed for the door, pivoted, and slapped his hand against the frame. "Wanna know something? The better man won when it counted most. Be good, bro."

Marty still stood gawping at an open doorway several beats later.

"Coach!" someone called. "Let's go!"

"On my way." *As soon as I pick up my jaw from the floor.*

Ten or so days after Zach's surprise visit, Claudia lounged at home, enjoying a much-needed night off. She had thrown herself into work, taking on extra shifts that padded her bank account, brought smiles to Ms. Norris's face, and put one stubborn, sulking dark-haired man on a back burner in her mind. Unfortunately, the peace and quiet surrounding her allowed said man to escape and take up space front and center.

After he'd stormed from her house, she had sent him a handful of texts. Okay, so only three, but she'd also called and left a voicemail. Why continue trying to contact someone who was obviously avoiding the contact?

"Ha!" she snorted aloud. "So much for Marty processing and searching for answers."

She had kept up with the Hawks, though, and knew they had returned a day ago after a long road trip, riding a five-game winning streak. How much had Marty's coaching had to do with their success?

The team had just started their all-star break, and her mind ziplined to what Marty was doing with his time off ... and why he wasn't doing it with *her*. Again, the question of Renee reared its ugly head.

What if she had guessed wrong and he didn't come back? Was it possible she had completely misjudged, and he had gone back to Renee? In her messages to him, she had left the burning question of Renee's status alone. He was the type of man she could see staying with a woman he'd gotten pregnant, whether he loved her or not. Damn, but there was a downside to the loyal type.

What if the greatest love affair of her life turned out to be merely a storm passing through? No. She wouldn't let herself go there. Instead, she snuggled into her safe place where she could stuff her cats and homely things around her like baffles.

If only she could forget how hurt he'd looked the last time she'd seen him. If only she could stop worrying about him. If only she didn't ache for him so much.

Seeking oblivion, she curled up on her couch under a quilt, where she sipped red wine and turned her attention to *When Harry Met Sally*.

She toasted the movie. When Popcorn stared at her as though she'd grown an extra head, she explained, "I love this movie because it's about two best friends who've known each other a long time, have seen each other at their worst and best, and their friendship grows into the forever thing with a happily-ever-after. It gives me hope. Or not, since I haven't heard from *my* best friend."

Her phone buzzed on the coffee table. She glanced at it, surprised to see Rex's number on the screen. She picked up right away. "Hey, what's up?"

"You sound stuffy."

"I have a cold." *Not really. I've been crying my eyes out over a dumb movie.*

"Well, I'm standing outside your front door with a hammered LB leaning on me. Do you want him, or should I take him home with me?"

She sat up, scattering her cats and nearly spilling her wine. "You mean, you're downstairs? Right now? And Marty's with you?" God, she sounded like an idiot!

"Yes, what I just said."

"Did he *ask* to come here?" She threw the quilt off her lap, stuffed her feet into pink rabbit slippers, and scrambled off the couch.

"Kinda. I had to translate his slurred speech, but I'm pretty sure that's what he wanted."

"You sound a little shit-faced yourself." She hiked up her flannel PJ pants, checked her reflection, and cringed.

"I am, which made it even harder to understand him."

"Should you be driving?" She raced down the stairs.

"Don't worry. Alice came and picked us up from the bar."

"You were together? Getting drunk?" She whipped open the door.

"Yes." Rex shoved his glasses up the bridge of his nose and grinned. One of Marty's arms was draped over his shoulders, and his head lolled close to Rex's, nearly knocking into it. "Where should I put him, ma'am?"

Despite the nurse in her who wanted to chastise them, she stifled a laugh at the two drunken idiots on her porch. Maybe it was because Marty was *here*, on her doorstep, and though he was a little worse for wear, seeing him caused her heart to vibrate with delirious beats. "You look like you're wearing a Marty coat." She leaned out and waved at Alice, who was peering through the passenger-side window.

Marty swung his head up, and his slitted eyes landed on Claudia. "Claudia?" Then he turned to Rex. "Is that Claudia?"

Her heart sank. Maybe Marty hadn't wanted to come to her place after all. But it soared the next second when he said, "I love Claudia. Since I first saw her. Did you know that?"

Rex patted his chest. "Yeah, dude. Everyone knows that. I'm going to leave you here with her, okay? We're going up the stairs now."

Grinning, Marty swayed like a palm tree in a hurricane, nearly taking Rex down. Claudia grabbed on to his arm and helped Rex drag him inside. Marty looked down at her. "Hey, pretty lady. What are you doing here?"

"I live here," she muttered. To Rex, she said, "I thought he knew where he was."

Rex puffed as they inched their way up the stairs. "He did when we got here. You sure you don't want us to take him home?"

"No!" Marty bellowed. "Wanna see the cat. He loves me." She and Rex exchanged question-mark looks.

Together they deposited Marty on her bed, and she walked Rex downstairs to the front door to be sure he didn't trip and break a body part. She called out, "Good luck!" to Alice, who yelled back, "You too!"

After shutting the front door, she raced back to the bedroom, where Marty sat on the edge of her bed. Crumpled on the floor was his pea coat. His belt and the top button of his jeans were undone, and he was struggling to pull a long-sleeved Hawks T-shirt over his head. One elbow was caught, and he grunted as she worked it off him. Then she went to work on his pants. Thoughts of drunk Zach assailed her, and her stomach clenched. But Marty turned out to be *nothing* like drunk Zach, which was good *and* bad because she craved a little Marty hotness, hussy that she was.

When she had him down to his boxers, she lifted the covers for him, and he flopped onto his back and drilled her with those soulful brown eyes of his. "Will you hold back my hair if I have to puke?"

She chuckled softly. How could such a drunk, disheveled man be so adorable? "Absolutely." Never mind that his hair was trimmed short, as always.

"I'm a fucking idiot, Claudia Campbell, and I can't blame you for, uh ... for ..." He closed his eyes and let out an alcohol-infused sigh. "Should have told you already, but I'm not gonna be a dad." Popcorn hopped on the bed and touched his nose to Marty's, and Marty flailed his hand at the cat.

I'm not gonna be a dad. The words jolted through Claudia. Champagne bubbles fizzed and popped in her bloodstream, and she swallowed a whoop that threatened to cut loose. She leaned down and caressed his sandpaper jaw with the back of her hand, then pushed his soft sable hair off his forehead and placed a lingering kiss there. "We'll talk about it later, Marty LeBrun."

"Mmm, Claudia LeBrun." He rolled over on his side, settling his big body right in the middle of her bed. Popcorn curled up on his pillow, and Claudia closed the door.

Chapter 36

PERFECT PRACTICE

Marty opened his eyes and looked around the darkened room, smiled, and sank back into the pillow that smelled like Claudia. He was having the best kind of dream, where she snuggled against his back, her delicate arm over his waist, small hand splayed over his abdomen, and her silky, bare leg draped over his.

If he rolled over, her plump strawberry lips would part and whisper his name, and he would take her mouth and pour himself into that kiss. But this was a dream.

A cat purred in his ear.

He lifted a gritty lid, and his thudding head reported to his brain that this was *not* a dream. *Good news, bad news.* Behind him, Claudia shifted and sighed. *That's the good news.* His heaving stomach was the bad news, but he made it to the bathroom in time. He scrubbed toothpaste over his teeth with his finger and rinsed, then glared at his reflection in the mirror. Shit! He looked like he'd been run over by a truck. His hair stuck out in all directions, he hadn't shaved in days, and the whites of his eyes could have been mistaken for pink-veined petunias. When he had perched on a stool in a seedy bar earlier this afternoon, he hadn't expected to wind up at Claudia's. Not that he didn't want to be here, but he would have cleaned himself up for the occasion.

He lifted his arm, stuck his nose in his armpit, and nearly retched again. In the reflection, he caught sight of the shower and couldn't help but smile as visions of sharing it with Claudia cavorted in his bruised brain. He loved that shower. But right now he would use it solo.

Lukewarm water coursed over him, and he soaked his head, found the Dove *for sensitive skin*—which made him smile wider because yeah, her skin was sensitive all right—and began scrubbing it over his body. God, it had been a hell of a few weeks. The last time he'd been here, he had walked in on Zach and Claudia talking about getting back together. Though his mind was mush tonight—or was it morning? Hell, he had no idea—a thin ribbon of logic reminded him of Zach's words. *"She doesn't want me. She wants* you.*"*

Marty's head throbbed with all the thoughts vying for attention inside it, so he shut off the water, dried himself off, pulled on his boxers, and quietly stepped into the bedroom, where the dim light from the bathroom cast inky shadows. Resisting the urge to climb back into bed, he paused to stare at Claudia curled up instead, her blond waves tangled behind her on the pillowcase, her mouth parted as she pulled in one soft breath after another. He wanted to cover her mouth with his and steal those breaths. One creamy shoulder peeked out, exposing a simple white strap he pictured himself toying with.

He tore himself away and padded to the kitchen, where he chugged a quart of Gatorade stashed in her fridge. The microwave clock told him it was 1:13 a.m. How long had he been here? How had he gotten here? Jesuuus! He hadn't been that drunk since ... Claudia's wedding. Why did being hammered into oblivion always revolve around her?

The goofy orange tabby appeared from nowhere and threw itself against his legs, meowing, and he picked the cat up. "What up, little guy? You couldn't sleep either, huh? Or did you miss your pillow?"

"I missed his pillow," came a sleepy feminine voice from the hallway.

Marty looked up, startled to see Claudia in flannel PJ bottoms leaning against the wall, arms crossed over a flimsy white tank top that hid little. His boxers hid little too, and seeing her all mussed and beautiful instigated serious tenting that was obvious to anyone who looked. He stepped behind the island to hide his growing problem.

"Where did you come from?" he blurted.

"The bedroom."

"I meant, why are you up? Did I wake you?"

She shook her head, and her hair swished around her bare shoulders, beckoning him to touch. "How are you feeling?"

"Like something your cat dragged in." He set Popcorn down on the floor. "I'm, uh, sorry."

"About what?"

"Blowing up and walking out on you. Showing up like this tonight."

"And not answering my texts or my phone call? Not telling me that you're not going to be a dad anytime soon?" Her lips quirked. "What took you so long?"

He raked his fingers through his damp hair. "Well, uh, time kinda got swallowed up in our road schedule and lots of coaching sessions."

"Sounds like excuses to me, Marty LeBrun."

He pushed out a breath. "I was mad and confused and hurt when I walked in on you and Zach. It sounded like you were getting back together."

"And now you know better?"

He nodded slowly. "I know better, but it took me a while to put everything in order."

She tilted her head. "Why didn't you just call me and let me help you do that? That's what best friends do. They also give each other the benefit of the doubt."

"You're right. I guess I wasn't ready to deal ..."

"Lots of old baggage there, I suppose."

"Yeah, but that's no excuse. I should have at least let you know about the pregnancy that wasn't." Wait. Why was he arguing against himself?

She nodded, apparently agreeing with him.

"Anyway, as time passed, I was ... I don't know, embarrassed, I guess, about how stupidly I behaved. I wasn't sure what to do or how to approach you so I didn't blow it again." He shot her a sheepish look. "Honestly? I was worried you might tell me to go fuck myself."

Her brows knotted in a cute little frown. "Did I ever give you the impression I would say something like that?"

"No, but if I'd been in your bunny slippers, *I* would have told me to go fuck myself." Amusement danced in her eyes, buoying him. A grin began to form on his face. "I was looking for a greeting card that said, 'I'm sorry I fucked up,' but they don't make cards like that. Then I ended up at the bar."

Her eyes darted to the ceiling and landed back on him. "We need to talk about your strategy when it comes to solving relationship problems. But not right now."

"I know. I need practice."

"You know, the part you heard about Zach wanting to get back together had a counterpart you didn't hear. I told him I wasn't interested. I also told him there was another man in my life I was crazy about, although I might have to reconsider." She tapped her chin with her index finger.

Marty rocked backward. "You're shitting me."

"Yes, Sherlock, I'm shitting you. I'm not actually reconsid—"

"No, not that part. Well, that part too. But mostly the part about you being crazy about someone else. Is that someone me?"

She gave him a much-deserved eye-roll. Christ, he needed to practice his delivery too. "Yes, Marty, I was talking about you. Now are you going to tell me why you got shit-faced with Rex tonight?"

"Because I didn't have anyone else to get shit-faced with? Dani was tied up with her family."

"Hmm. Let me reword this. Why did you feel the need to get shit-faced? Not that it's any of my business."

"No, it's a fair question. Our break just started, and I realized there wasn't enough going on to keep my mind off you. So I threw a pity party for one, which sucked, so I called Rex, and he joined me. He's great at commiserating, but he's a lightweight, so it didn't take much for him to get wasted. Did he drive me here?"

"No, Alice did. Where were their kids?"

"He said something about sleepovers? I don't know. Can we forget about them for now? I need to get a huge apology off my chest that's long overdue. I have some groveling to do."

She sauntered toward him, eyebrows arching. "You have all my attention."

Pulling her close, he broke out in an inner happy dance when she let him. He relished the way her contours filled his hollows. A perfect fit. Soon fire licked through his body, and he pulled away, resting his forehead against hers. He kept his arms looped around her body, loving the feel of her warm, delicate hands resting against his bare chest. "I am so, so sorry. I let my insecurities get in the way, and I behaved like a complete and utter ass. I should have trusted my best friend and listened before I went off, or at least circled back right away to hear what she was trying to tell me. I love you, Claudia. I always have. I want to be with you now and always. Do I even have a shot?"

Tears rimmed her lower lashes, and she nodded. "What kind of bestie would I be if I gave up on you so easily? I was waiting for you to wise up, and if you didn't do it soon, I was going to track you down and knock some sense into you." She balled one hand into a fist and took a fake swing at his jaw.

Heart swelling so large his chest could barely contain it, he dropped his head back and laughed despite its dull thudding. "If there's anyone on this planet capable of knocking sense into me, it's you." He lowered his head to hers. When he nudged her lips with his, she responded eagerly, and he delved in, savoring the sweetness he had missed more than the air he breathed. Soon he was falling into a vortex that would sweep him up in a tide of hunger and need and desire.

She broke the kiss. "That's some groveling, Coach." Her voice was breathy, sexy, and her eyes were bright with desire.

Pulse thrumming, he dropped his mouth to her neck and began a series of slow, sensual kisses that drew moans from her throat. "I'm not done yet. I need more practice," he breathed against her skin. "But I can grovel much better in the bedroom."

She pulled away, hooking a finger in the waistband of his boxers. She tugged and flashed him a coy smile. "We'd better get started, then."

He followed, his aching head forgotten. An idiotic grin was plastered on his face, and he floated on a cloud the entire way.

"Ms. Campbell? Coach says he needs to see you on the ice."

Claudia glanced up from her book at an earnest Seth Hughes and frowned. A pink scar resembling a lightning bolt decorated one side of his face. She loved that scar. If not for that injury, she and Marty might not have found each other three months ago.

"He does? Why?"

Seth looked stricken. "I don't know. He just said to come find you. It's never good to get on Coach's bad side."

She refrained from asking if he truly *had* a bad side. His players might think he did, but the only bad side she had witnessed was one Marty kept behind closed doors ... and was totally inappropriate to discuss with one of his players.

With the all-star break nearly over, Hawks practices had resumed, and today, her day off, Marty had asked her to come watch. Afterward, they'd have lunch and visit a Chevy dealer to look for a replacement SUV for him. They'd only patched things up a few days prior, and she couldn't get enough of him, so the decision to come had been a no-brainer. And watching him coach? *So* hot! Maybe she could talk him into bringing that whistle to bed and running naked drills, telling her what position—

"Ms. Campbell?" Seth looked downright panicky.

"Sorry, Seth." She sprang to her feet and followed him to the gate.

He grinned and sprinted away, wishing her a nice day or something similar that she didn't register because she was too busy ogling the coach on the rink in his dark track suit. He was gathering up pucks.

Wait. Why was *he* gathering them up? Shouldn't Seth and the other players be doing that?

Marty raised a gloved hand. "Hey! Help me out?"

"How? I'm in street shoes! Should I strap on skates?"

"Nah. You don't have to come out very far on the ice. I'm going to push these pucks to you, and you'll drop them in the bucket." He pointed his stick at a bucket that sat six feet from the boards.

Why couldn't he just shove the bucket toward her so she didn't have to slip and slide on the ice? And why didn't he have a scoopy thingie? *Hockey players*. They had their own strange way of doing things. With a shrug, she slipped-walked to the bucket. Flashing her a boyish grin, he slid a few pucks over to her, and she crouched and chucked them into the bucket.

"How's that, Coach?" She turned her head and grinned, surprised that he had glided toward her and was within reach, the pucks still scattered where he had left them.

His glove plopped beside her, and an odd metallic clink sounded. "Oops," he said. "Guess I dropped my glove. Would you mind handing it to me?"

Oh brother! She reached over and picked it up. A thin red ribbon dangled from one of the fingers—the one that matched a ring finger on a hand. She plucked the ribbon, intent on dropping it into the palm of the glove, when a sparkle caught her eye.

"What's this?" She cradled the glove in her hand and frowned.

"I don't know. Maybe you should take a closer look."

When she looked up at him, his grin broadened.

What is up with him?

She cast her gaze back to the glove, and an object with a little heft jerked the ribbon back out of the glove. It thudded against her thigh. She picked it up, taking a moment to register what it was: a diamond solitaire.

Thoughts cascaded in her head, and she raised her gaze back to his, only to have it yanked beyond him to the glass along the boards where a line of players stood. The first one raised a poster board that read "Claudia" in red marker. Another poster board went up with the word "Campbell." Like a stadium full of fans doing the wave, more signs went up that spelled out, "Will you be my best friend AND my wife?"

A woman stood at the end of the line, hopping up and down. Apparently, she had a sign too but struggled to maneuver it, folding it against the glass. When one of the players helped her out, the sign hung upside down, making Claudia laugh. She tilted her head and read "I love you forever" with big red hearts. The signs were in one uneven line that reminded her of a kids' art project.

The upside-down sign was righted, and Claudia's hand flew to her mouth. "Oh my God! Is that my mom?" She looked up at Marty again.

"Yeah. I asked for her permission. She said yes—on one condition. That she be here when I proposed."

Claudia sank to her heels, and tears sprang and leaked down her cheeks. Marty dropped beside her. "Is it too much? Should I not have ... Should I take the ring back? It's too small, and it's probably not the style you like and—"

She placed her fingertips on his mouth. "Stop. Just stop. It's beautiful. It's perfect. *You're* perfect. I'm just so overwhelmed; I don't know what to say."

"I do. Say yes." Soulful espresso eyes brimming with hope mined hers. "Marry me, CC."

"Of course the answer is yes!" She threw herself at him, and they both toppled to the ice. A cheer went up, but she barely noticed because she was too busy laughing and peppering his handsome face with kisses as she sprawled across him.

He pumped his fist in the air as he lay on the ice, and wild whooping on the other side of the glass went up. Players banged the glass and chanted, "Let's go, Coach! Let's go, Coach!" Claudia was positive her mother's squeals were in the mix.

Holding her to his chest, Marty craned his head and smiled at her. "You've been CC for so long, and I got to thinking how nice it would be if you were CL, though I'd never expect you to *change* to CL if you didn't want to. And if you don't like the ring or if it doesn't fit or it's too small, they said we could exchange it for something else. We can get a bigger diamond. The jewelry store is over at Centerra, and they've got a big selection, and there's a matching band, and there's even a man's version that would—"

"You're adorable when you're nervous! Do I get to try it on, or are you going to talk all night?"

He bobbed his head and wrangled them so they sat upright. Snatching the glove, he fiddled with the ribbon for a second or three before frustration had him ripping it off. She spread the fingers on her left hand, and he fumbled it on with shaky hands.

"I'm not so good at this," he grumbled. "Haven't had enough practice."

She giggled at the same time she cried. "For the record, you're wonderful at *this*, and I don't want you getting any more practice."

His mouth kicked up in a smile. "This is definitely the *only* time I propose."

Together they slid the ring on. An elegant square-cut diamond in an unadorned band of white gold, its simplicity and proportion fitting her hand as though it had been made just for her, and she gasped.

"It's absolutely perfect," she whispered. "You know me so well. I will never take this off." She swiped aside a few tears trailing down her cheeks. Tears shimmered in his eyes too, and he bent his head to hers, landing a soft kiss on her lips.

Another round of cheers had her grinning through the kiss. "Is there a reason in particular why you had your team in on this proposal?"

"Two, actually." He glanced toward the crowd, whose signs were a bit more askew, radiating a smile that reflected utter joy. "I figured I needed all the help I could get, and teamwork always wins. I also figured it would be harder for you to say no with an audience. Any other questions?"

Adoration swelled her heart, and it nearly catapulted from her chest. "Yes. Tell me why I love you so much. I never knew I could feel this way."

"I have no idea, but I do know I'm the luckiest son of a bitch on the planet. I may not deserve it, but please don't ever stop." He stroked her hair and looked at her with so much awe a fresh wave of tears spilled. "I love you too—so damn much," he whispered. "I *always* have, and I'll never stop."

She tilted her head. "Do you have a time in mind when I become Claudia LeBrun?"

He gaped at her. "You're taking my last name?"

Her brows pulled together. "Is that okay?"

"God, yes! Let's make it official today. Wanna fly to Vegas?" His eyebrows bounced.

She blinked, then burst out with a laugh. "You're kidding, right? Isn't that a little soon?"

He kissed the end of her nose. "I've waited over ten years, so no, it's not too soon. But I'll compromise for the day the season's over in June. That's still five months away, which will seem like forever, but I can do it." He feigned a grim face.

She let out a laugh. "June. I like that. It'll give me time to pull a wedding together. Something simple with family and friends. Is that okay with you?"

"Absolutely. I'd rather focus on the honeymoon."

She glided her hands up his chest and lowered her eyes to his mouth. "Speaking of honeymoons and practice ..."

"Yeah, I *definitely* need practice to make that perfect."

"Let's start right now, if you think you're *up* for it."

"When I'm around you, I'm nothing but *up* for it. But we do have an audience to think of."

"Oh shit, I totally forgot!" *I was completely lost in those gorgeous eyes and that amazing mouth.* She glimpsed the crowd—and her mom—still pressed against the glass, and she waved.

Marty barked to his players. "Boys! Let's get these pucks cleaned up!"

"Ooh, Coach! I love how you take charge," Claudia purred. She couldn't wait for sexy time, except ... "Where's my mom staying tonight?"

"I got her a hotel room." He gave her another eyebrow waggle. "But she's having dinner with us."

"Mmm, she eats early, and she's on East Coast time. Dinner at three isn't too early, is it?"

"Not when we have a honeymoon to practice for."

Epilogue

Seven years later

"There you are!" Claudia felt a rush of relief at the sight of Marty sauntering through their front door ... and the usual pulsing heat in her veins. Would she ever stop wanting to jump her hunky husband?

His eyebrows touched his dark hairline, now kissed with flecks of gray. The salt in his pepper hair gave him a distinguished look and made him that much sexier. "I got tied up with a few calls. Where are the kids?"

The serious expression on his face gave her pause. "I just dropped them off with your sister."

"Good. We need to talk."

Oh shit, oh shit, oh shit! She had left the kids with Dani because they'd been bouncing off the walls with excitement over the last family hurrah of the summer, a camping trip to Yellowstone. She still had final details to nail down. The park reservations had been made a year ago, she had arranged time off from the hospital, and the rental RV was ready. The adventure was set to begin tomorrow, and she had been waiting for him to get home from an impromptu team meeting so they could pick it up.

"What about getting the RV? The place closes soon."

He wrapped an arm around her waist and propelled her toward the kitchen. "We might need to delay. Let's go to the kitchen."

Oh no! The kitchen table hosted their most serious talks—like the one they'd had when he'd been promoted to head coach of the Hawks, and when he had agonized over his mother's care after a fall that had broken her hip, and when Claudia had delivered the happy news that she was pregnant with their first child. *Those* kinds of talks.

Then again, the little house they'd bought before their daughter's arrival three years ago was too cramped to offer a better meeting place, so to the kitchen table they went.

Marty pulled out a chair for her and motioned for her to sit. Holding his tie to keep it from brushing the tabletop, he parked his butt and took her hands in his.

She let out a nervous laugh. "This *must* be serious. You wore a tie to work when you weren't even supposed to go in, and you're holding both my hands. Afraid I'll throw something at you?"

He gave her a shake of his head. "I wore a tie because the brass decided to meet with the coaching staff. I'm holding your hands to keep mine from shaking."

Panic welled inside her.

He cleared his throat. "It seems the Blizzard's head coach just quit, even though training camp's only a little over a month away. Apparently, he decided at the last minute he didn't have it in him this year. He just told management yesterday, which leaves them high and dry."

A coaching change at this time of year would be devastating. She blinked as puzzle pieces began clicking into place. "So they drove up to meet with you specifically."

"Yeah. They need to fill the position ASAP. There are systems to be put into place, assistants to hire, roster spots to be evaluated. It's a mess." A tentative smile curved his mouth.

She gasped. "They want you to be head coach!"

Squeezing her hands, he nodded. "The job's mine if I want it."

She slid her hands from his and grasped his forearms. "That would make you the youngest head coach in the NHL! You want it, don't you?"

"I do, but I hadn't planned on the opportunity coming so soon. And the circumstances aren't ideal."

She reared back. "I admit this isn't the best situation to walk into, especially when you haven't coached at that level yet, but sweetheart, this is what you've wanted your whole life. It's your dream job."

"But if I screw it up, I won't get another crack at the NHL."

"If you don't take it, you might not get another crack either." She delved into those soft brown eyes she loved so much. "Besides, why would you screw it up? You've been successful at every level. You've won cups—two Calders since you took over the Hawks head coaching position—and other AHL teams are always trying to lure you away."

"It's gonna take a lot of time and energy." He sighed, but he couldn't fool her. He was buzzing like a livewire; she could practically grasp his excitement in her hand.

"So no more golfing with the boys?" she quipped.

"What? I don't golf with the boys *now*. Well, unless it's a charity thing. Whenever I get the chance to golf for my own enjoyment, it's either with you or Todd when he and Megan come to visit. And I wouldn't have it any other way. You know I prefer hanging out with you more than anyone else."

She did, and she leaned over and pecked his cheek. "You should take the job."

He raised an eyebrow. "It would be a huge change for you and the kids. It means moving to Denver, leaving friends behind. Nathan's about to start kindergarten."

She stroked his jaw. "They're young. They'll adjust. And Denver's not so far that we won't see Rex and Alice and Danielle."

"It means shortening our vacation."

"We'll survive."

"It also means switching jobs, CC, unless you want to commute between Denver and Loveland." He tapped the end of her nose.

"How much are they offering you?"

"Two million to start. They're including some incentives and a little extra on the front end to sweeten the pot. Like I said, they're desperate."

Her mouth dropped open, and she leapt to her feet. "Two million? Dollars?"

Lips twitching, he nodded as he fought a smile. "US currency, not pesos or yen."

She shrieked and launched herself into his lap, straddling him and burying her face in his neck.

A laugh reverberated through his chest. "I take it you're okay with me accepting?"

She pulled back and gaped at him. "More than okay! Oh my God, Marty! This is everything you've ever dreamed about." Tears sprang into her eyes. Her voice came out as a croak, strangled with emotion. "You're finally getting rewarded for the years you put in, for all your hard work and dedication. I'm so happy for you." Hot, salty tears flowed down her cheeks, and she didn't give a damn that she was ugly crying. "I'm more than happy. I'm so proud of you. I love you so much."

Tears shimmering in his eyes, he rasped, "This is as much yours as it is mine. I couldn't have done it without you." He pulled her to him in a fierce hug. They remained wrapped up that way for long moments until he cradled her head and raised it so their eyes were level. "You do realize you don't have to work if you don't want to, right?"

She laughed amid her tears. "And become a woman of leisure? Hell yes! Wait. We have a five-year-old and a three-year-old. I think being a woman of leisure isn't feasible. But I would get to stay home full-time with them."

"Or you could go back to school and get that teaching degree if you still want to."

She tapped his nose as he'd done hers. "I think I'd rather push out another little LeBrun before I hit the big four-oh."

A beatific smile spread over his handsome face.

"The idea of having another one doesn't send you running for the hills?" she teased.

"Nope. I'm fine with it, especially since we're going to need a lot of *practice*." He waggled his eyebrows. "You know how important practice is to a coach." His expression shifted, taking on a solemn quality. "Have I told you lately how much I love you?"

"You might have mentioned it while you were, ahem, in the throes this morning."

Another chuckle rumbled through him, warm and rich. "No, seriously. I don't think I say it enough. All these years, you've been so supportive, and it blows me away. Not that I didn't expect it, but still ... I wouldn't be where I am today without you, and I love you for it. But it's more than that. I ..." His voice cracked and a fresh sheen glossed his eyes, making her heart hitch. "I, uh, I finally have it all, Claudia. Everything I ever dreamed of. You, the kids, and now the job. Sometimes I think I'm dreaming and I'll wake up and find out it's not real."

Tilting her head, she leaned in and kissed him softly. "And I'll be right there to pinch you and let you know it *is* real. It goes both ways, you know. I'm living my dream too. With my best friend."

"Yeah?" His expression shifted to one filled with wonder, and he feathered his thumb over her cheek.

"Absolutely." Staring into his liquid brown eyes, she was overcome with emotion for this man she adored. "I love you, Marty LeBrun."

"And I love you more, Claudia LeBrun."

Two years later ...

Claudia waited anxiously for Marty to return from another coaches' meeting. His first year had been a little rocky, what with the upheaval from the previous coach's departure, but he and the entire coaching staff had righted the ship and were preparing for the team to break out this season.

But right now they had more important things to take care of, like the purchase of their next house.

Marty had flown out her mother, Aunt Bev, and his mother to help with the kids while Claudia prepared their current Denver house for sale and juggled the millions of other details that accompanied a household with two elementary kids and a one-year-old. While her mom and Bev entertained the older ones with a water park visit, Marty's mom was currently watching over their little guy who was napping.

Marty waltzed in from the garage way too casually and gave Claudia a cockeyed grin. "I'm not late, am I?"

The tease. She gave him an eye-roll. He *had* to know how anxious she was to meet the Realtor.

"No, but we need to be there in a half hour, and traffic is god-awful. Besides, if the baby wakes up and knows Mom and Dad are home, we'll never escape."

"You didn't tell the older kids what we're doing, did you?"

"No, of course not. I didn't want to get their hopes up."

"Like yours are." He dropped a kiss on her head. "What did you say the broker's name is again?"

She parked her fists on her hips. "Is that all the kiss I get?" Between his crazy work schedule, the extra adults, and the children tearing around the house, they were in the middle of a three-day dry spell, and she couldn't wait to end it.

He hauled her to him and squeezed her ass, and she let out a squeak. Fire, and a whole lot of hunger, flared in his espresso eyes. "Don't worry. I'll give you all the kissing you can handle later."

Heat rushed to her cheekbones. "Can't wait, Coach. But we better go."

"Damn."

After letting Marty's mom know they were off, Claudia clambered into the passenger seat of his Land Rover and strapped herself in. "The broker's name is Paige Anderson ... or Paulson. I'm not sure which because the company is Anderson Homes, and this house is her rehab project. She—Paige—says she's had a lot of interest, and I don't want to miss out on this house. It would be so perfect for us! The arena's close by, the kids would be in the Cherry Creek School District, and it's big enough for our brood. There's even a detached mother-in-law unit."

"All Realtors say they have a lot of interest, especially when it's a house *they're* flipping. It's part of the sales shtick."

She shook her head. "I think she's being genuine."

A few silent beats passed, and she asked how preparations for the upcoming season were going.

"There are still some holes in the roster to fill. I've got a line on a veteran for the blueline, but he makes me really, really nervous."

She turned in her seat to face him. "Why's that?"

"The guy's bit of a loose cannon. He reminds me a little of Zach back in his wilder days, but he's cheap and he's really, really good. An awesome D-man with great hockey IQ who can mentor the younger guys, and he still has a lot of jump in his skates."

"How do you know all this?"

"I coached him a long time ago, when he was a punky-ass teenager, before he broke into the league. He was always cocky, but he could back it up. He's won all kinds of awards."

She lowered the sunglasses down the bridge of her nose. "Why's he so cheap, then?"

"Like I said, he reminds me of Zach. His salary isn't a reflection of his play; it's a reflection of the head case he turned into. Just Google him, and you'll see what I'm talking about."

She frowned. "I don't get it. Why would you want him on the team?"

"For the reasons I laid out. Plus, I hear he's cleaning up his act. If that's true, he might not be that big a risk."

"What's his name?"

Marty flipped on his blinker and turned onto a tree-canopied street. "Beckett Miller."

"Hmm ... that doesn't ring any bells. Speaking of Zach, though, did you know he and his wife just had their second child?"

"No, I missed that. How'd you find out?" He side-eyed her.

Though they rarely talked about him, Zach's name could still trigger a little spike of jealousy in Marty. Then again, anybody he caught admiring her too much could cause the same reaction and wake up the possessive caveman inside him. And she loved it.

"Alice saw it on social."

Claudia studied his strong profile and nearly pinched herself. But for a random second-chance meeting in a hospital room, she might have missed out on sharing this life with her best friend and the love of her life. How had she lucked out? He would argue *he* was the lucky one, and he didn't hesitate letting her know. She never had to question that she was adored by this man.

"There it is!" Claudia pointed out the windshield and craned her neck as Marty pulled up to the curb, where a petite auburn-haired woman awaited them with a dazzling smile.

Marty killed the engine. He gawked at the house through the windshield and let out a soft whistle. "Okay. I get it now." Then he leaned over, grasped the back of Claudia's head, and laid a toe-curling kiss on her mouth.

When he broke the kiss, she was breathless and ready to climb him right there in the front seat for Paige and everyone else to see. "What was *that* for?"

He winked. "Just practicing. Wanted to see if I need to knock off some rust. After all, it's been three whole days."

Claudia fanned herself. "No rust here, Coach. And I'll prove it to you later in bed."

"Think she'll let us try out the bedroom before we sign on the dotted line?" His eyebrows bounced.

"Doubtful, but we can ask."

He gave her a playful growl. "Let's hurry up and buy this house so we can get home. Although I might need a minute before I can get out of the car."

She giggled. "Why don't I hop out and chat with Paige while you get yourself under control?"

He leaned in and stole another kiss. "Told you a long time ago that that's impossible whenever I'm around you."

Her heart turned gooey. He was good at doing that to her. "I love you, Marty LeBrun."

"And I will always love you more, Claudia LeBrun."

THE END

BECKETT MILLER HAS FALLEN FROM GRACE. Paige Anderson is a rising star. When their lives collide, will love score the winning goal? In case you missed the beginning of the series, here's an excerpt from *Taming Beckett*, Book 1:

> The guy had won the looks sweepstakes, and Paige worked at not gawking like every other female there—and a few of the males.

Added to his striking appearance was his presence, which electrified the room just by being in it. Despite the space between them, the voltage coming off him sizzled along her spine.

As if he felt it too, he looked over and winked. In spite of herself, Paige's pulse skyrocketed, and she tried to hide behind her hair—an anemic tactic that proved fruitless.

Reading her thoughts, Gwenn elbowed her. "It's hard not to get all moony-eyed over Beckett Miller. He's a god," she said. "Adonis, specifically."

Adonis sauntered over, and Paige's mouth went dry as Zack introduced them. How she'd managed to untangle her tongue and croak a "Hi" was still a mystery to this day.

Talk about the game followed, Zack musing over Beckett hitting everyone in sight and how his mouth had never stopped running.

"What did you say to get number eleven so pissed off?" Zack asked.

Beckett grinned, showing off perfect white teeth. "Not a conversation for mixed company. Some things are better left on the ice."

Laughing, Zack turned to Gwenn and Paige. "Trust me when I say you wouldn't want him kissing you with that mouth if you knew half the shit he says out there."

But Paige wasn't so sure she *didn't* want Beckett Miller's mouth on hers. He was gorgeous.

Later they'd stood alone, and he offered to get her a beer. She looked around, sure Adonis was speaking to someone else. But then he tapped her shoulder, surprising her. "I meant you, Red."

She mustered attitude. "It's auburn, not red." Grabbing her cup, she waved it in front of him. "This is red, and it's full. I'm set, thanks."

He chuckled. "So are you a freshman?" Adonis paused for a sip. "Or still in high school?"

She bristled. "I'm a junior."

"Really? Could've fooled me. You must go ninety, a hundred tops. How tall are you anyway? Are you even five feet?"

"Five-two." She fumed. "And *you* must be, what, thirteen?"

"Funny." He grinned, the cocky jerk. "Twenty-one. I'm a senior." He looked around then, and a bevy of beauties waved at him and glared at her. "What's your name again?"

"Paige Anderson."

"Paige? What kind of name is that?"

"What kind of name is Beckett?" she retorted.

He took a long drink of his beer and casually said, "Old family name. My brother's a car. Cooper."

"And people call you Beckett?"

"Unless they're mad at me, and then it's all kinds of other names."

He asked her if she wanted to leave with him, and she gave him a flat "no." His full mouth curved into a lethal smile, and his eyes glinted like moonlight on a dark sea. "Why not?"

"You appear to have a pretty big fan club already."

He shrugged. "Girls like me. I like girls. We're charter members of a mutual admiration society."

"Wow. How do you fit your head through the door?"

"Big doors. So what do you say?"

She shook her head vigorously. "I'm guessing you need a lion tamer, not another conquest."

He raised an eyebrow and laughed. "You're feisty. Maybe it's the redhead thing. What the hell's your name again?"

She blew out an exasperated breath. "Paige."

"I'm sorry. I'm fucking awful with names," he said. "Anderson, right? I'll call you Andie. I can remember that."

Get your copy of *Taming Beckett* at Amazon and find out if the forgotten good girl from his past is this bad boy's only shot at winning forever.

SEVEN PLAYMAKERS COUPLES unite for a winter wedding getaway, but there's trouble in Paradise. Claim your free copy of *Puck the Halls* at www.gkbrady.com and see if they can find the spirit of Christmas—and each other—before it's too late.

Author's Note

Thank you so much for reading *Line Change*! Coach LeBrun has been in nearly every Playmakers book, and I've always had a bit of a crush on him, so it was fun to finally give him his own story.

If you enjoyed Marty and Claudia's story, I would love it if you would leave a review on Amazon, BookBub, or Goodreads to help readers like you find the story. And if you do leave a review, I would love to read it! Email me the link at gkbrady@griffin-brady.com.

Stay up to date on upcoming releases, cover reveals, giveaways, and discount deals by joining my newsletter. Simply go to: https://www.gkbrady.com.

Trouble is brewing. Disaster strikes. Can they conjure a mistletoe miracle? Claim your free copy of *Puck the Halls* (Book 7.5), a Playmakers novella, when you join. Download it at https://gkbrady.com/bonus-content/pth/ or scan this code:

Listen while you read! The playlist for *Line Change* can be found on Spotify.

Acknowledgments

To Kyle, old soul that you are, thank you for being a wonderful son and person. Thank you for choosing to be a healthcare worker and for sharing your kindness and compassion with the world.

To Detective Popcorn and Eggroll, for being chill and sweet, just like your mom.

To my Alpha—you know who you are. I love that you slap me around (figuratively speaking, that is) when my stories jump the track. You never hold back, yet you let me have it with such kindness that it never feels like a slap.

To Lynn, for taking time out of your busy schedule and for your honest feedback. I listened!

To Jenny Q., for your generosity and collaboration. You share your knowledge, time, and ideas so freely, and you always help me create a better story with better characters.

To Stephanie, how do you do it all? I'll never know, but you sure do make it look easy.

To Judith, for your unwavering attention to detail and your always pithy remarks that crack me up.

My husband, Tim, for sharing adventures, for always making me laugh, and for supplying me with great lines.

To my Colorado Avalanche for a thrilling season and for bringing the Cup back to Denver. Go, Avs, go!

Also by this Author

The Playmakers Series®

Book 1 - *Taming Beckett*
Book 2 - *Third Man In*
Book 3 - *Gauging the Player*
Book 4 - *The Winning Score*
Book 5 - *Defending the Reaper*
Book 6 - *No Touch Zone*
Book 7 - *Twisted Wrister*
Book 8 - *Besting the Blueliner*
Book 9 - *Guarding the Crease*
Fall Novella - *Love Rinkside*
Winter Novella (Book 7.5) - *Puck the Halls*
Spring Novella - *Deking at Love*
Summer Novella - *Slapshot Summer*

The Fall River Series

Book 1 - *The Keeper*
Book 2 - *The Fixer*
Book 3 - *The Rescuer*
Book 4 - *The Harborer*

The Love in Destiny Series

Sunsets, Stick Saves, and a Honeymoon

About the Author

Since childhood, all sorts of stories and characters have lived in G.K. Brady's imagination, elbowing one another for attention, so she's thrilled (as are they) to be giving them their voice on the written page.

An award-winning writer of contemporary romance, she loves telling tales of the less-than-perfect hero or heroine who transforms with each turn of a page.

G.K. is a wife and the proud mom of three grown sons. She also writes historical fiction under the pen name Griffin Brady. She currently resides in Colorado with her very patient husband.

Connect with her on any of these platforms:

 www.amazon.com/author/gkbrady

 www.twitter.com/GKBrady_Writes

 www.facebook.com/AuthorG.K.Brady/

www.bookbub.com/authors/g-k-brady

 www.goodreads.com/author/show/19488321.G_K_Brady

 www.instagram.com/authorg.k.brady

 www.pinterest.com/gkbrady0993/

www.ingramcontent.com/pod-product-compliance
Lightning Source LLC
LaVergne TN
LVHW010557100826
845148LV00014B/2750